SINS OF THE FATHER

CAROLINE FARDIG

SEVERN RIVER PUBLISHING

Severn River Publishing
www.SevernRiverBooks.com

This is a work of fiction. Names, characters, businesses, places, events and incidents are either the products of the author's imagination or used in a fictitious manner. Any resemblance to actual persons, living or dead, or actual events is purely coincidental.

ISBN: 978-1-64875-586-6 (Paperback)

ALSO BY CAROLINE FARDIG

Ellie Matthews Novels

Bitter Past

An Eye for an Eye

Dead Sprint

Parted by Death

Relative Harm

Sins of the Father

To find out more about Caroline Fardig and her books, visit
severnriverbooks.com

To my muses

PROLOGUE

The full moon illuminated the darkness of the late October night, the celestial orb framed perfectly in the Palladian window the woman was painstakingly cleaning. Fall had always been her favorite time of year and Halloween her favorite holiday. At least it had been until her son had gotten too old to trick-or-treat and carve pumpkins with her. She remembered nights like this from years ago: the crisp autumn air, the earthy smell of fallen leaves, the clear skies for stargazing. She'd be content to sit for hours in her backyard enjoying a crackling bonfire, which also provided her a clever way to make the hot dogs she often had to serve for the third or fourth time in a week seem like party food.

The final task on her list was vacuuming, which she loathed. Her shoulders were always sore—they probably needed some sort of surgery, or even replacement—from years of repetitive labor, and vacuuming hurt them the most. She plugged in the vacuum and sighed. Her entire home could fit inside the waiting room of the doctor's office she'd been assigned to clean tonight. Taking out her phone to play some music, she stopped a moment to admire the new leather case her boyfriend had given her last week for her birthday. She put in her earbuds, hoping immersing herself in her favorite heavy metal bands would transport her back to her youth and take her mind off the inevitable pain that would grow until she could barely lift her arms.

She managed to get into a zone and largely ignore the physical work, but her incessant anxiety wouldn't let her block out her worries. She needed to pick up some extra hours. Two different collection agencies were breathing down her neck, and she was hopelessly behind in payments on her son's staggering medical bills. He'd been a minor when most of them were incurred, so even if he had a job and could help her pay them down, it was still her ass on the hook for the balance. Her boyfriend would loan her the money she needed for this month, even if it strapped him. He'd do anything for her and her son, but it wasn't his responsibility.

She was working up to asking her son's dad for help, but it would take some finesse to convince him to step up and be an actual father. She'd have to make him *want* to do it. If she played her cards right, she might even be able to convince him that he wanted to be her husband again, too. She'd done it before, but she'd been younger and thinner and hadn't been sacrificing her own self-care to tend to her son's needs. A state of constant fatigue was her new normal, and it showed on her face. The little sleep she got was haunted by nightmares in which she ran and ran and ran, and every time they ended with her being caught and dragged down into oblivion by the darkness that loomed over her even while she was awake.

The vacuuming was finally finished. Her shoulders were screaming, so she turned her music up even louder, her new goal to blot out her whole world. She gathered her supplies, set the alarm, and locked the door behind her. A blast of that chilly October air she used to love so much hit her, blowing some sort of debris straight into her eyes.

She dropped the heavy vacuum and caddy of cleaning products she was carrying and turned her back to the wind. Her eyes streaming from the blinding irritation, she gingerly rubbed and wiped at them until the offending particles were gone. The loud music was beginning to make her ears ache, so she got out her phone to turn it down.

A sudden powerful force crashed into her from behind, rocketing her up onto an expanse of hard metal. Disoriented and unable to feel her legs, it took a moment for her to realize she was on the hood of a car. A split second later, she began sliding fast and out of control toward the ground.

As her body hit the concrete, it stayed in motion, skidding across the parking lot. Her clothing ripped and tore, leaving her body unprotected as the concrete surface scraped off the top layer of every inch of skin it touched.

As she lay there on the brink of unconsciousness, she saw the car retreating and wearily closed her eyes. She snapped awake to her arm being crushed under the weight of a tire. Her cries died on her lips as her lungs failed, the unbelievable pressure on her chest so overwhelming that the darkness of her nightmares began closing in on her faster than it ever had.

For the first time in her life, she didn't try to escape the darkness. She welcomed it.

1

"The final blood spatter pattern we're going to discuss today is the drip trail, which as the name suggests is a discernable path formed by blood dripping from an object or an injured person. It can show movement of a suspect or victim. You can determine the speed and direction the person was moving based on the distance between stains and the shape of the stains."

The rear door to my classroom opened. Detective Nick Baxter strolled in and leaned against the back wall, grinning at me. My heart fluttered at the sight of him with his gun belt strapped to his waist and his badge hanging around his neck. I hadn't expected him to show up today, considering it was his first day back on active duty. He'd been shot six months ago while saving his brother and me from a madman, but after a lot of recovery work he was good as new. He'd been bored to tears during his recovery period and the lengthy month he'd been forced to spend on desk duty, so he'd made a daily habit of meeting me for lunch. Today, he should have had enough to do that he wouldn't have time to see me.

I felt a brief rush of anxiety that he might have come here in an official capacity, which would have meant there was a crime scene for me to help investigate. But now that Baxter was cleared for field work, a case for us to work together wouldn't be the worst news. I'd turned down plenty of consulting jobs for the department since he'd been hurt, my priority being to spend time with him and help him heal. Now that all that was behind us, I felt ready to jump back into field investigation.

I smiled, deciding to wrap up a few minutes early since I was having trouble concentrating on what I was saying with my handsome boyfriend staring at me.

"You can read all about it in your textbook. That said, it's always more fun to show someone something than to tell them about it, which is why we'll devote our lab practicum this week to blood spatter. I have some lovely cow's blood we can throw around to study how it lands. It's—"

The moment I uttered "cow's blood," one student's hand shot in the air. When I didn't stop immediately to take her question, she interrupted me. "Professor Matthews?"

I knew what was coming and figured I'd go ahead and address it. "Yes?"

"I'm vegan."

When she didn't expound on her declaration, I said, "Um . . . good for you?"

That got a few snickers from her fellow students, but she didn't think it was funny. "You don't understand. I can't be around animal products."

I dealt with this every semester when the blood spatter lab rolled around. I gave my standard reply. "You *choose* not to be around animal products. And you're an adult, so you can also choose whether or not to attend the lab. Standard policy for missing a lab applies—a three-page paper over the subject for full credit, or take the zero. Your choice." As she huffed about the fairness of her having to do extra work, I went on. "It's unlikely you'll get something on your clothing, but wear something you don't care about in case there's an accident. A couple of years ago, a full container of blood got knocked off a table, and we had a whole Carrie situation going on. See you tomorrow in the lab."

My students filed out of the classroom, nearly all of them greeting Baxter as they walked past him. Since he'd had a lot of time on his hands at the beginning of the semester, he'd been a guest speaker in many of my classes. There was nothing my students loved better than hearing stories of our many adventures firsthand, and Baxter was a way better storyteller than I was.

As he approached my podium, I closed my notes and joked, "Slacking on your first day back, Detective? After you said, and I quote, 'I won't have time for you today,' I wasn't expecting the pleasure of your company."

Baxter gave me a mock frown. "I don't believe I've ever said those words to you, Ellie."

I shrugged, needling him a little more. "The sentiment was implied."

"Also untrue. You know there's a penalty for lying to an officer of the law, don't you?"

I held out my wrists and wiggled my eyebrows. "Does it involve handcuffs?"

He blushed. I'd thought he might be able to handle discussing anything remotely sex-related with me at some point, but that day had yet to come.

I dropped my hands. "Don't let my razor wit fool you. I'm thrilled to see you. What's up?"

His cheeks returning to their normal color, he said, "I was in the neighborhood."

"Ooh. Is that a bad thing?" I asked, a mix of apprehension and excitement coursing through me. Maybe he was in fact here to whisk me away to a crime scene.

"Nah, my first case back is boring as hell and not the least bit dangerous. Porch pirates struck a fancy subdivision a couple streets over and the residents are up in arms. They've all got doorbell cameras, so it shouldn't be hard to get a good image of the culprits."

I smiled. "The hard part is going to be having to listen to all the bitching and moaning from the Real Housewives of Hamilton County."

"Exactly. I needed to see a friendly face first."

"I'm glad you chose my face."

"Me, too." He leaned down and kissed me.

"Get a room, you two," a voice said.

I turned to face my closest friend, Dr. Samantha Jordan, who was grinning at us from the doorway. "We're in a room. You're the one who barged in unannounced."

Sam laughed. "Not the kind of room I meant."

My friend Sam could throw around innuendo with the best of them, so I rerouted the conversation before Baxter could get embarrassed. "Did you come in here to shame me or meet me for lunch?" Since I'd thought Baxter was going to be otherwise occupied, I'd made plans with Sam.

"Can't I do both?" she asked.

Baxter chuckled. "I guess that's my cue to leave."

I turned to him. "No time for lunch?"

"Not today. But we're still on for a late dinner tonight, though, right?"

"Absolutely."

"It's a date." He reached out and gave my hand a squeeze, then left my classroom.

Sam let out an overly dramatic sigh. "What I wouldn't give for a hunky cop boyfriend who'd take a bullet for me."

I frowned, the flash of a bad memory causing a chill to run through me. "It's not so great when it actually happens," I muttered.

The idea of Baxter being back in harm's way suddenly wasn't settling well with me. I'd been so busy being euphorically happy with him that I hadn't given his return to work any conscious thought. The two of us had finally become free of any obstacles preventing us from having a full-fledged public relationship. The trial we had anxiously awaited—with me having to take the stand as a witness and victim and him having to take the stand as the investigator who broke the case—was behind us. I'd never been this happy and blissful in my life, and to feel that starting to crumble was horrifying.

Suddenly contrite, Sam threw her arms around me. "Oh, I'm sorry, sweetie. I didn't mean it like that." She let me go and made a face. "You know I blurt stuff out."

I pasted on a smile. "It's fine. He's fine. Everything's fine."

"Everything *is* fine. Nick is one of the smartest people I've ever met, and I know a shit ton of nerds. He's great at his job, and you've actually complained to me on multiple occasions that he's *too* cautious. Don't worry about him. If anyone around here is going to get into trouble, it's going to be you."

Shaking my head, I said, "Oh, hell no. Not me. I've been a model citizen for six whole months, and I plan on keeping it that way. I'm done with trouble."

Sam laughed. "I'll believe that when I see it."

AT THE END of my third time through the lesson on blood spatter, I was more than a little tired of the subject. And I'd managed to make myself ill thinking about all that blood, which never happened to me. Normally, I could deal with bodily fluids and gore like it was nothing. I could and often did eat while perusing crime scene photos. Today was a different story.

Keeping my eyes firmly fixed on my notes as I gestured to the slide on the Promethean board to my right, I said, "The final blood spatter pattern for discussion today is the drip trail, which is called a drip trail because, as you can see in this slide, it is a notable path of blood that has dripped from an object or an injured person. The trail can tell us everything we need to know about the movements of a suspect or victim. We can determine the speed and direction a person was moving by looking at the shape of the stains and the distance between them."

I paused for what was probably the tenth time during this lesson. I was still in shock that it hadn't occurred to me until my conversation with Sam that I had been repressing my reservations about Baxter's return to active duty. And talking about blood all day hadn't helped my state of mind. My brain kept flashing back to me struggling to keep pressure on Baxter's gunshot wounds so he wouldn't bleed out, which was something I hadn't thought about for months.

I began gathering up my things, needing to go home and decompress. I cleared my throat and curtly wrapped up my lecture. "Please read the section in your textbooks about drip trails. We will do some hands-on work with blood spatter in our lab practicum this week with cow's blood. Wear clothes you don't particularly care about, just in case. Class dismissed."

As my students packed up and left the classroom, my teaching assistant, Talia Scott, approached me and said, "Professor Matthews, are you feeling okay? You look pale."

I nodded. "I'm a little more nervous than I realized about Baxter's first day back."

Her face fell. She knew Baxter well, having picked his brain multiple times this semester for term papers she'd had to write for her grad school criminal justice courses. "Oh, right. I don't blame you. But he's a pro. And kind of a badass, if I'm to believe all of the stories he's told me."

Smiling, I said, "They're all true. I—"

"Ellie?"

Upon hearing a familiar gravelly voice, I froze.

"Ellie, I know it's been a long time, but . . . I need your help. Someone's after me."

"*You*," was all I could manage to choke out as I turned and instinctively shrank away from the man standing in my classroom. Old feelings of pure terror flooded me and turned my insides to ice. I fought against them, struggling to lock down my emotions by focusing on replacing my fear with anger.

"I know we didn't leave things good . . ." Pausing for a moment to stare at me, he shook his head. "Damn, you look like your mama."

My voice a little steadier and mind a little clearer, I snapped, "Talia, call security. *Now*." As she got out her phone and found the number, I added, keeping my eyes trained on her and not him, "Tell them there's an intruder, and he's dangerous. Possibly—"

He cut in. "Ellie, I don't mean you no harm."

Anger coursing through my veins, I exploded, "All you ever did was harm me, you sadistic asshole!"

Incensed, I took a step toward him, wanting nothing more than to claw his eyes out. But then the scared little voice inside my head reminded me how much bigger and stronger and meaner than me he always was. How I could never seem to get away from his viselike grip when he got it in his head he wanted to do some damage to me. I shrank back again.

He held out his hands. "I'm not going to hurt you."

"Oh, I've heard that one before," I breathed, circling around him until my podium was between us.

"Security is on the way," Talia said as she ended her call, eyes wide as she backed toward the rear door of the classroom.

I instructed her, "Now call 911 and tell them I have eyes on Marcus Copland, a wanted murder suspect."

Talia let out a cry and started dialing with shaking hands.

I added, "Tell them I have him in my classroom and security is on the way."

Marcus, my former stepfather, let out an anguished groan and said in a rush, "I didn't come here to fight—I need your help, and I can't get arrested right now. You have to call off security."

I barked out a laugh, finding some bravado. "Same old Marcus." I mimicked his hick accent, "'Don't tell no one what I done to you; I can't get arrested right now.' Well, you're getting arrested right now if it's the last thing I do, you sick son of a bitch."

As he made a move toward me, my bravado vanished. I didn't actually mean I was okay with this being the last thing I did. Damn him and his influence over my childhood I was clearly still holding on to.

He said, "I knew you wouldn't want to hear me out, so I wrote you a letter. Rachel, too." Instead of coming after me, he reached out and tossed two folded pieces of paper on the podium. His eyes darted toward the door. "Please read them. I need you to know I didn't—"

A scrawny security guard burst through the back door. "Ashmore College Security! I got a call about an intruder."

Marcus bolted for the other classroom door nearest me. The guard didn't make a move to follow him.

"That's the intruder!" I yelled. "Go after him!"

The guard shrugged. "Well, he left, so . . . problem solved?"

I gaped at him. "Are you shitting me? He's wanted in connection with a murder. Go after him!"

"That's not part of my job, ma'am."

I'd never be able to live with myself if I let Marcus get away. I guessed that meant it was up to me to figure out a way to at least slow him down until real law enforcement got here. Campus security was, as usual, going to be useless.

I ran to the door and shoved it open.

2

As Marcus fled the room, I'd seen him turn left, I assumed toward the nearest exit. I burst into the hallway in time to see him go through the exterior door. I dodged students, getting to the door in time to see him disappear down a walkway between the science building and the union building at a run. Getting out my phone, I took off after him, calling Talia to tell her to let security and the police know that Marcus was headed north on campus. My guess for his destination was the large parking lot on the far side of the library, the length of a city block away.

I ended the call and accelerated my pace. I began gaining on Marcus, who had considerably less spring in his step than he had when I was a teen.

I called, "Marcus! Security refused to come after you. I just want to talk."

Evidently he didn't believe my lies, because he only glanced over his shoulder to see me chasing him and turned up his own pace as well.

I didn't want to lose him. I sprinted as fast as I could, gaining ground again as I sped past dumbfounded students. It was approaching dinnertime, so there weren't tons of students wandering around, which was good considering a murderer was loose on campus and I, like a fool, was chasing him to . . . well, I didn't know exactly what my endgame was. Marcus wasn't slowing down. I supposed learning the make, model, and license number of his vehicle as I helplessly watched him drive away would be all I could hope to accomplish. That was, unless by some miracle security got off their collective asses and actually were of help in stopping and detaining him.

As we got to the courtyard between the library and Fenton Residence Hall, Marcus bellowed over his shoulder, "I'll find you later! Let me go!" This act slowed him enough I gained even more ground on him.

His words hit me, something about them triggering a reel in my mind of myself as an eleven-year-old child begging for him to let me go as he held me down on the dirty floor of our trailer with his weight. I saw him grin down evilly at me as he took a drag of his cigarette and then yanked up the front of my T-shirt. I screamed as the red-hot end of his cigarette made contact with the tender skin of my midriff, burning and searing as he held it against me and laughed as I cried.

Incensed by the memory, a flame of anger overtook me, far hotter than that cigarette. I found a burst of energy, my only urge in the moment being to stop him once and for all from hurting me or my sister ever again. Only feet behind him now, I jumped onto a low concrete bench for extra height and launched myself at him. My torso made direct contact with his back and knocked him forward, taking us both to the ground. He broke my fall, but barely, the wind whooshing out of my lungs. My palms, elbow, and knees took the brunt of me sliding off him and skidding to a stop across the concrete. Gasping for air, I looked over at him as we both lay there. I was happy to see he looked worse than I felt. Wheezing from having the wind knocked out of him as well, he grimaced, showing a gaping, bloody hole where his front tooth had been. The left side of his face was a mess of road rash.

I knew I needed to drag myself up and make sure he didn't get away, but I couldn't manage to do it. To my surprise, the unhelpful security guard came charging toward us, yelling into his walkie-talkie, "Intruder suspect and professor down in the library courtyard. Mayes responding." To me, he asked, "Are you all right, Professor?"

"I'm good," I choked out, hearing the sweet sound of sirens nearing us. "I need you to . . . cuff him . . . so he doesn't get away . . . Cops almost . . . here."

The guard's eyes grew wide. I bet he'd never subdued anyone in his life. He stammered, "I, uh, I—I'm not allowed to carry cuffs yet. I'm—"

I cut him off. "Then call . . . a real security guard . . . out here . . . to help!"

As he began speaking into his walkie-talkie, Marcus roused beside me and started getting up.

I began boosting myself up, crying, "Stop him!"

Marcus must have had a burst of adrenaline, because he scrambled to his feet and took off at a run. My useless security guard trailed after him, even in full health unable to keep up with Marcus's long strides.

I got out my phone and called 911. My breathing was beginning to return to normal, but it still felt like someone was sitting on my chest. When the operator answered, I said, "This is Ellie Matthews . . . criminalist for Hamilton County. Please let the deputies going to . . . Ashmore College know that Marcus Copland is . . . headed into the west end of the library parking lot on foot. He's six-two and wiry. . . blue shirt and jeans with blood on his face."

The dispatcher replied, "Deputies are already en route to that location. I'll let them know. Ms. Matthews, do you need assistance?"

I grunted. "No, I'm good."

"Do you need me to stay on the line with you?"

"No, thanks."

We ended the call, and I had just laid myself back down on the ground to rest when a couple of students rushed over and insisted on helping me. I allowed them to hoist me up and get me to the nearest bench. I sat for a minute or two, catching my breath again. The students made a good argument to transport me to the campus infirmary, but I managed to shake them off when I got a phone call from my friend Vic Manetti.

I had my breathing under control, finally. "Hello?"

"What the hell's going on?" Vic demanded, an edge of panic in his voice.

Confused, I asked, "How do you know something's going on?"

After a slight hesitation, he said, "Because I have an alert set up for the name Marcus Copland, and I just got a notification that he's at large somewhere on the Ashmore campus with law enforcement en route." Vic was an

FBI agent and had access to pretty much any information he wanted. "Are you in a safe location?"

"Yes." Technically true.

"How about Rachel?"

"She's not on campus." I frowned. "You put out an alert on Marcus?" I'd been relieved when Marcus had disappeared years ago. I'd never made any attempt to find him, not wanting him to have any reason to come after me or my family.

"I know you never wanted me to openly track him down, but this is different. I did it so if he ever got himself on law enforcement radar anywhere near you, I'd know about it. I called Nick to give him a heads-up. He's heading there now. Do you need me to come, too?"

My irritation vanished. After a rocky start, my two favorite men had actually become friends. "No, I'm good. Thanks, though."

"Did Copland try to contact you?"

I didn't have the energy to unpack my story right now, because Special Agent Vic Manetti would demand to know every detail while he berated me for my actions. Truth be told, I was more worried about telling him than I was about telling Baxter.

In the distance, I saw a young deputy I didn't know hurrying my way. "We'll have to talk later—I'm going to have to give my statement."

His tone grew dark. "You have a statement to give? What aren't you telling me?"

"I'll call you later. Promise."

"You better."

I hung up with Vic as the deputy approached me. He said, "Ellie Matthews?"

"That's me," I replied.

"I'm Deputy Jalen Walters. I wanted to let you know Marcus Copland was apprehended trying to leave the parking lot."

I sighed in utter relief. "Thank you. That's wonderful news."

Deputy Walters got out a notebook and pen from his pocket. "Can you tell me what happened, starting in your classroom?"

I launched into the whole sad story. As I did so, I noticed a couple of campus security guards heading our way, including my useless little friend.

They stopped several yards from us and made an exaggerated display of their visual perimeter sweep of the courtyard. I briefly wondered if miming and improv acting were part of their training program.

When I got to the part about my triumphant, if poorly thought-out, takedown, Deputy Walters frowned. "You just admitted to assaulting Mr. Copland."

I couldn't help but start laughing. "*Mr. Copland* assaulted me on a regular basis throughout my childhood. If he cries assault at me for what happened just now, that's straight bullshit."

"You ran after him and jumped on top of him, causing quite a bit of injury. The man's missing a tooth."

Was he seriously going there with me? I replied, "You know he's a suspect in a murder, right? He's been evading the police for years. I didn't want him getting away when I had the chance to stop him."

Deputy Walters shook his head. "You'd placed a call to security and to dispatch. Why did you feel the need to take it upon yourself to chase after him?"

I rolled my eyes and stabbed a finger in the security guards' direction. "Because bitch-ass Paul Blart over there refused to do jack shit about an intruder in a campus classroom." I raised my voice to address said bitch-ass Paul Blart. "Isn't that literally your job? To protect the students and faculty from unauthorized people coming onto campus to hurt them?"

Deputy Walters's frown deepened. "Stick to the events, Ms. Matthews."

I wrinkled my brow. "You know we're on the same side, right?"

"I think it would be best if you came with me to the station—"

I cut him off. "Can I just talk to the sheriff?" I hated to pull the *I want to speak to your manager* card, but Sheriff Jayne Walsh was like a mother to me and the person who knew the most about my past with Marcus. I couldn't imagine her being mad about my takedown—other than the fact that I'd put myself in danger to do it.

"Ellie!" called a strained voice from across the courtyard.

I felt a mixture of relief and apprehension as Baxter came running toward us, his face contorted with worry. He hurried over and kneeled down in front of me, his gaze roving over me, pausing briefly at my knees, elbows, hands, and finally my face.

Cradling my cheek in his hand, he asked, "Are you okay? What hurts?"

I hadn't taken the time to pay much attention to my wounds, but now that I gave them some thought, I noticed my knees, elbows, and palms were throbbing and burning. My new dress pants were completely ruined, shredded at the knees. But now that Baxter was here, I felt like there was nothing I couldn't handle.

I smiled. "You should see the other guy."

Deputy Walters cleared his throat and said gruffly, "Ms. Matthews, if you don't mind, we need to get back to our conversation. I want to take you to the station—"

Baxter cut him off. "Thanks for taking care of Ms. Matthews, Deputy Walters. I'll get her to the station for an official statement."

Walters nodded to Baxter and stalked away, scowling.

Once he was out of earshot, I murmured, "Thanks for getting him off my back. He was treating me like a common criminal."

Baxter grinned. "He's new. He doesn't know about the Ellie Matthews get-out-of-jail-free card."

"Seriously, Nick? You, too, with the assault thing?"

"I saw what you did to Marcus Copland. I got to the parking lot as they were loading him up and driving off."

"He had it coming."

He shook his head. "I'm not saying he didn't. I'm saying what you did was monumentally stupid and could have gotten you killed. And that's not to mention the panic attack I had when I got a call from Manetti about Copland being on campus. Of course I assumed you were involved and headed straight over. Luckily I was still in the area."

Frowning, I said, "So I get a lecture from you instead of a high-five for my efforts."

He leaned in and laid a soft kiss on my lips. "You get a trip to the station with me, where we'll have the staff medic get you bandaged up first. Then you'll have to answer to the sheriff for your crimes."

"She knows Marcus. She'll high-five me."

"I wouldn't hold my breath." His expression grew dark. "What was he even doing here?"

I shrugged. "He said he needed my help because someone's after him.

He's stupid, but surely he's not so stupid to think I'd lift a finger to help him."

Shaking his head, he said, "I don't like it that he's back in town, and I really don't like it that he tracked you down. Come on, let's get to the station."

My TA, Talia, found me in the parking lot as Baxter was helping me to his vehicle. Word of my incident had blazed around campus fast, so she'd gathered my things, including the two letters Marcus had tossed onto my podium, and brought them to me so I wouldn't have to trek back to my office. Still, the walk to Baxter's vehicle and then the twenty-minute drive from Ashmore College in Carmel to the sheriff's station in Noblesville was excruciating.

As my adrenaline waned, the pain from my injuries became all I could think about, even though Baxter tried valiantly to keep my mind off it. He kept up a steady stream of conversation, recounting every interview he'd had with the victims of his porch piracy case. When I barely laughed at his imitation of one woman's tearful monologue about her stolen twelve-pack of flavored seltzer with adaptogens that she was certain she could not live another day without, I saw his forehead crease with worry. I felt bad—he hadn't had to worry about me, even for a moment, in a very long time.

We finally got to the station. After we handed over the letters from Marcus as evidence, Baxter whisked me straight to the medic's office. Luckily, my favorite EMT, Aaron Richter, was on duty. He wouldn't care if I cursed at him while he was attending to my wounds.

Aaron looked up from his desk and whistled. "You look like you lost a fight with some concrete."

I replied proudly, "I helped apprehend a murder suspect."

Baxter added, "Which she's not trained or allowed to do."

Aaron burst out laughing. "Wait, the guy they just brought in? The one with the matching road rash and no front tooth? Nice." He held up a hand out of my reach. "Air-five for now 'til we get those hands of yours fixed up."

I air-fived Aaron and turned to Baxter. "See? He gets it."

Baxter rolled his eyes at Aaron. "Can you just patch her up and maybe not stroke her ego?"

"As you wish," Aaron said to him, giving me an exaggerated wink as he ushered me back to an exam table. He then disappeared into the nearby supply closet.

Baxter followed me, but I said, "You don't need to stay. I know you have work to do."

He frowned. "I'm not leaving you."

I'd counted seven tiny little gravel pieces lodged in the scrapes on my left palm and had been too afraid to study any of my other injuries. I wasn't sure I could hold it together while Aaron removed the debris. "Really not necessary," I said as Baxter helped me get up onto the table.

"I'm staying," he replied, pulling up a chair at the foot of the table.

Damn it. "You know what would be even more helpful to me? If you'd go find out what's going on with Marcus."

"I know what's going on with him. They're icing him so the chief has time to go over a years-old case file and decide what questions to ask. You'll be done here in plenty of time to watch the interrogation."

I sighed. "Look, if you must know, I'm planning to verbally assault Aaron every time he hurts me, so I'd rather not have any witnesses. He'll probably cry, and I don't want you to have to see that."

Aaron returned with an armful of medical supplies. "She's not wrong. I have a thin skin, what with the bulk of my job being to attend to the thugs in county who get into fistfights on the daily. They're so sweet and understanding when I have to yank their dislocated shoulders and broken fingers back into place. I'm a stranger to difficult patients with foul mouths."

Baxter laughed. "Okay, message received. I'll be at my desk. Find me when you're done."

"Thank you," I replied, relieved.

I laid back and closed my eyes as Aaron started working on me. He kept up a steady and hilarious monologue of stories about attending to the guests of the Hamilton County jail and their myriad injuries, which I punctuated with grunts, groans, and every last cuss word I knew. Once he was finally finished with me, I was beyond exhausted. I dragged myself through the building and dropped into the chair beside Baxter's desk.

Baxter spun around in his chair and zeroed in on my bandages. "All better?"

I sighed. "Everything hurts."

"That's what you get for going rogue."

"Agree to disagree," I grumbled.

He smiled. It was hard to be even a little miffed with him when he smiled at me. "That's probably our only option."

Sheriff Jayne Walsh approached the cubicle and stopped, eyeing my bandages. "Well, I bet you're pleased with yourself."

I flicked my eyes at Baxter and replied, "Deservedly so."

Both of them chuckled.

Jayne said, "I'd feel remiss if I didn't impress on you that physically taking down a suspect is something you should never do." The corner of her mouth pulled up. "But given that said suspect is a supreme piece of shit, I don't blame you. I know what you went through with him. That had to feel good."

I nodded. "It did."

Her expression became concerned. "If you want help breaking the news to Rachel that Marcus is back in town, I'm free this evening."

I closed my eyes. In all the frenzy, I hadn't given a thought to how my younger half-sister would react to finding out her father was back in town *and* that he'd sought me out for help.

I replied, "Thanks, Jayne. I'll let you know."

She nodded. "Well, what I really came by to say was that we're ready to interrogate our suspect if you're up to listening in from next door."

I broke into a smile. "Oh, yeah. This will make it all worth it."

3

I followed along with Jayne and Baxter to the interrogation rooms. They led me into a viewing room with a two-way mirror. In the next room, Marcus Copland, the bane of my existence, sat handcuffed to a metal table, working his tongue around the hole where his front tooth used to be. He looked sad and old. Not at all the rough and rode-hard monster I'd had to live with for several years of my life. But as the door opened and Deputy Chief Rick Esparza walked in, I saw that old persona suddenly click back into place.

A chill ran up my spine, and I sucked in a breath. Baxter rested his hand on my shoulder.

Chief Esparza slapped a file down on the table and took the seat across from Marcus. "Marcus Copland. Didn't think we'd ever see your face again."

Marcus shrugged and said nothing.

The chief went on. "Do you know why we brought you in today, Mr. Copland?"

Marcus shrugged again.

The chief leaned back in his chair, settling in for what I worried could be a long and frustratingly one-sided conversation. "You're a person of interest in the murder of Patty Copland. A suspect, really. You remember your ex-wife, Patty, right? Murdered, dismembered, stuffed in several garbage bags, and left strewn around this county to rot a few summers ago?"

I didn't realize I'd been holding my breath, but when the chief went into detail about my mother, I let it all out in a whoosh. Baxter gave my shoulder a squeeze and Jayne gave me a pat on the back. My mother and I had never been particularly close, so it wasn't grief that had me off balance about her remains. It was that I was the lead criminalist on the case and had processed bag after bag of some poor Jane Doe for over a month with no success at finding a clue to her identity or even a scrap of usable evidence in the sickening carnage. The case had driven me crazy and had me questioning why I put myself through that kind of hell on a daily basis. The nail in the coffin was the realization that it was my own mother I'd been studying all that time, and I hadn't had a clue.

Marcus said evenly, "I didn't kill Patty."

I huffed. "Not this bullshit again."

Marcus continued, a little edge creeping into his voice. "And since I didn't kill Patty, you have no reason to hold me. You're going to need to let me go."

Chief Esparza barked out a laugh. "You've been on the wrong side of the law enough times to know that's not how it works. Now tell me, why did you feel the need to kill your ex-wife? You had a new wife. Why not move on?"

"I didn't kill Patty."

"Okay, so it's just a coincidence that you'd been hooking up with her again right before she died and that you two had a big fight? You gave her a black eye, according to a witness."

"Whoever it is, they're lying."

I muttered, "Classic Marcus. Everyone's telling lies about him."

The chief looked through his notes. "A man named Jeff Morrow went on record that you barged into his home uninvited, grabbed Patty Copland by the arm, verbally assaulted her, and then hit her with a closed fist not once, but twice, in the face."

Marcus shook his head. "Doesn't sound like me."

My right hand—which had luckily survived my tumble with only a small scratch—reached out and hit the glass. "I've seen you do that to her dozens of times, you asshole!"

Jayne and Baxter both grabbed me and pulled me back as Marcus's head shot up. He wouldn't have been able to make out my words exactly, but I was sure the sentiment had come through.

Jayne said, "Ellie, I know you're angry, but you cannot do that. Come on, you know better. No more outbursts."

I nodded. Baxter had that worried look on his face again. I willed myself to rein it in.

His eyes fixed on the two-way glass, Marcus said in a kinder tone, "Ellie, I figured you'd be listening. Like I said, I didn't kill your mama."

The chief said sternly, "Mr. Copland, do not address anyone except me. If you insist you didn't kill Patty Copland, then who do you think did it?"

Marcus's expression went blank. "I don't know."

I recognized that look. I'd watched him lie to my mother more times than I could count. He was a decent liar, so my mother usually bought his bullshit, but I noticed he had a tell. His nose and mouth went uncharacteristically slack and his eyes seemed to defocus.

"He's lying," I said. "And I'm not saying that because I hate him. He's making his lying face. He knows something."

Jayne left the room, appearing a moment later in the doorway of the interrogation room. She called Chief Esparza outside.

After a moment, both of them returned to their respective rooms. The chief said to Marcus, "I think you do know."

Marcus shook his head, offering nothing else.

Chief Esparza took out the note Marcus had written to me. I'd glanced at both of the notes on the ride to the station and immediately passed them off to Baxter. The last thing I wanted was a keepsake from today.

Marcus's posture stiffened. "Why do you have that?"

"Ms. Matthews turned it over as evidence."

Marcus looked up at the glass again. "Ellie, I told you—"

The chief slammed his hand down on the table. "You will *not* address anyone except me, Mr. Copland. Are we clear?"

Marcus grunted, slipping back into his angry thug persona.

The chief said, "In your letter to Ms. Matthews, you insist you didn't kill her mother, but you do mention there's someone out there threatening to pin it on you if you don't leave town for good and stay gone this time. Who's that someone? Give us a name, and we'll look into it."

"I don't know," Marcus replied. Strangely, this time he didn't make his lying face.

"Where did the threat come from?"

He only shrugged in response.

The chief got out the letter for Rachel.

That really pissed Marcus off. He roared, "That is not for you. That is for my *daughter*."

The chief said evenly, "You should have mailed it. Now, in this letter you state that you've been getting anonymous threats to leave town since you came back. You're telling me you really don't know who would want to murder your ex-wife and pin it on you? Surely you know who your enemies are."

Again, a shrug was Marcus's only reply.

The chief came at it in a different way. "If you have some credible ideas on people who might have had a reason to kill your ex-wife, we'll run them all down. We want to be able to close this case and give Patty Copland the justice she deserves. Wouldn't you like for her to have that as well?"

No response from Marcus.

The chief blew out a breath. "Do you have anything more to say to me?"

Marcus stared at the chief, defiance written all over his face.

Chief Esparza got up and walked out of the room. He entered our room and looked at me with anguish in his eyes. "That went even worse than I'd expected. We don't have anything concrete on him aside from the altercation with Patty Copland roughly a week before she died. We don't know what day she died, so we can't get him with the alibi route. We never found any evidence on the body or the bags as to who handled them. We don't know where she was killed or where she was dismembered. The only way we can hold him is if he confesses, and it's clear he's not going to do that. I'm so sorry, Ellie. I'm afraid we're going to have to cut him loose."

I cast my eyes down. It was my fault that no one had realized my mother had gone missing and died. I'd left home the night of my high school graduation and had no more contact with her until the day I'd stormed in and taken seventeen-year-old pregnant Rachel away from her. I'd told her she'd never see us again or meet her future grandchild, and I kept that promise. It was on me that she'd been left alone with no one to care that she'd disappeared.

A tear slipped from my eye. I nodded and choked out, "Okay."

As the chief left, Jayne caught me in a hug. "I'm sorry, Ellie. It was such a long shot . . . finding him after all this time, plus all the roadblocks that had tanked the case already. If we can get our hands on any more information, I promise we'll do everything in our power to run it down."

I pulled back from her. "Thanks. I know you will."

She gave me a sad smile. "We'll get you those letters back. Give me a minute, okay?"

When she left the room, I allowed another tear to escape my eye. Baxter put his arms around me and held me. "I'm sorry, too. I know how much you wanted that monster locked up."

"It's not just that. This is going to make Rachel come unglued. Now that he's back, we'll both be looking over our shoulders. We're not safe at school. And if he can track me down there, he can track me home. I don't know what—"

He pulled away to look me in the eye. "I can keep you two safe in your home. We can have deputies watch out for both of you while you're on campus. I won't let him get to you again."

That setup had been the norm way too many times in the past year. Rachel and I tired easily of being trailed and driven around. And while I'd have loved nothing better than to have Baxter live in our home for the foreseeable future, I didn't want it on those terms.

I rubbed my aching forehead. "I need to talk to Rachel and find out what she wants. I'm sorry, but we're going to have to ditch our dinner plans."

Something flashed in his eyes, but he quickly put on a smile. "We'll try again tomorrow night."

～

As Baxter drove me home, I called Vic, bracing for a major lecture. Lucky for me, Baxter had already texted him the highlights, so he'd had a chance to cool off over my questionable choices. Vic ordered me to leave the dangerous stuff to the professionals and made me promise to call him if I felt the least bit unsafe for any reason. I agreed, relieved I'd dodged a bullet with him. Although he was a much more chill person after his brush with death last winter, Vic still got worked up when someone he cared about was in danger.

Baxter parked in my driveway and followed me inside my home, much to my four-year-old nephew Nate's delight. Those two were best buddies and had been for a while. Nate was over the moon when he heard that his favorite guy, Detective Nick, was Auntie Ellie's new boyfriend. Anytime Baxter came over to hang out with me, Nate commandeered most of his time. Not that I minded—I loved watching the two of them interact with each other.

The fact that Nate glommed onto Baxter the moment he entered the house made it easy for me to pull Rachel aside, safely away from little ears. I beckoned her to her bedroom and closed the door.

As her eyes landed on my bandages and torn pants, she gasped. "What the hell happened to you?"

I sat down on her bed. "I'm okay, just scraped up. I take it you weren't on campus late this afternoon."

"No, Nate had a soccer game."

Talia had said the news of my takedown of Marcus had traveled around campus, thanks to a highlight reel of the event posted on the campus newspaper's vlog. I was kind of surprised none of Rachel's friends had texted her the dirty details.

I said as nonchalantly as I could manage, "So, no one said anything to you about what happened there?"

She looked at me quizzically and walked over to her dresser. "My phone died. I haven't checked it in a while." She picked up her phone from the charger and blanched. "You tackled some guy? What the actual hell?" She jabbed her finger at the screen a couple of times, then her eyes grew wide. "There's a video?" Her jaw dropped as she stared at the phone, horrified. "Is that . . . ?" She drew in a ragged breath. "*Is that*—?"

I got up and enveloped her in a hug. "Marcus showed up in my classroom to talk to me. When I called security, he ran. There's still a warrant out for his arrest, so I wanted to make sure he got . . . detained."

She struggled away from me. "So you took it upon yourself to capture him? How dumb are you?"

I closed my eyes. "I know it wasn't the best idea. But he seemed a little more feeble than he used to be, so I went for it."

"Why do you even care anymore?"

I didn't know if I'd heard her right. "Why do I care *who killed our mother*?"

"Yeah. It doesn't make her any less dead, and he was leaving us alone. Why poke a bear?"

I was shocked to hear my sister say this. I'd always thought our mother's death haunted her way more than it did me. The two of them had been closer than I'd ever been with our mother.

"I mean, caring about who killed anyone is kind of what I do . . ."

She ran her hands through her hair, clearly frustrated. "Look, things were fine when we just left well enough alone and didn't pursue Marcus. I feel like you've put targets on our backs with your little stunt."

"He sought me out for help."

"And then when he was running away, possibly out of our lives forever, you decided it would be better if he stuck around?"

I shook my head. "He got brought into the station and questioned because of what I did. My little tackle move bought enough time for the deputies to arrive and stop him." Shrugging, I added, "And as a bonus, I skinned up his face and knocked out one of his front teeth. I won't lie—it felt good."

"But at what cost? Now you've pissed him off, and he's going to want revenge. He's going to find you and hurt you." Her voice broke. "Maybe me, too."

Taking her hands, I said, "I've already thought about that. Baxter's going to stay here for a while, and he's going to get a deputy to watch out for us while we're at school."

Rachel walked away and flopped down onto her bed. "Because that was so much fun the last couple of times."

"I know, and I'm sorry." There wasn't much else I could say on the matter. This was what we had to live with. I took Rachel's letter out of my pocket. "Um . . . Marcus gave me a letter to give to you. You don't have to read it if you don't want to."

She held out her hand. "Whatever. I'll read it." She took the paper from me and scanned it, then tossed it on the floor. "Old news."

Recalling what he'd written in her letter, I stared at her. "What do you mean, 'old news'? It says the reason he came back to town was to see Jack. You knew about that?"

Her response was a one-shoulder shrug.

Incensed, I raised my voice. "You knew he was in town and said *nothing* to me? What the hell, Rach?"

Rachel had another half-sibling besides me, Jack Copland. They'd gotten to know each other as kids when Marcus would occasionally try to be a father and do something with his two children. Jack was having health issues and wasn't doing well, which, according to the note, was the reason Marcus had come back to town.

Rachel wiped a hand down her face. "You know I keep in touch with Jack. He told me."

"And you didn't feel the need to give me a heads-up?"

Glaring at me, she spat back, "I didn't want to think about it, okay?"

I fought back an eyeroll. "Not thinking about something doesn't make it go away!"

"Look, I don't know what you want me to say here."

"I want you not to keep things from me."

Rachel had been doing really well with her mental health lately. She'd had a rough year, having been kidnapped and held by a serial killer, and had been working so hard at dealing with her issues. Add that to the constant fear we'd lived in for years that Marcus might come back and try to hurt us as well (Rachel had even changed her last name to better hide from him), she'd had an especially hard go.

Her expression softened. "I'm sorry, sis. Life has been so much better lately—for both of us—I didn't want to bring any negativity back into our lives. Jack knows not to tell Marcus that I live in town, so I figured even though he was around, he probably wouldn't bother trying to look me up.

According to Jack, he doesn't plan to stay long, so I didn't want to worry you over nothing. I never imagined he'd want to contact you."

I shook my head. "I get it, I guess. But from now on, it's safer for me to know everything. You don't need to try to protect me. It's my job to protect you, although I'm completely shit at it."

She smiled. "Not completely. Just mostly."

I smiled back, or at least tried to. "So you're good with this whole situation?"

"I'm good."

"Then full disclosure, Marcus swears up and down he didn't kill our mother."

"That's bullshit."

"Exactly what I said. I'm not sure what he's playing at. In the letters to us he insists there's an anonymous person out there who's threatening to set him up for her murder if he doesn't leave town for good. Why that's their one stipulation for not sticking him with a murder charge, I don't know. All I know is that he wants my help for some reason. I'm not clear whether he wants me to back him up on his alleged innocence or find out who's trying to frame him. I admit I didn't give him much time to talk, but when the chief questioned him, he clammed up. He wouldn't even comment on the threats he'd been supposedly receiving, even though the chief had our letters in front of him where Marcus had spelled it out. It was super weird."

She spread her hands. "My father is an idiot, so there you go."

"I know, but he's also not going to back off when he wants something. When I was chasing him and asked him to stop and talk to me, he said he'd find me later. They wouldn't let him talk to me at the station, so . . . I'm pretty sure he's going to try to get to me again."

"You owe him nothing. Don't agree to talk to him."

Something Jayne had said struck a chord with me: *If we can get our hands on any more information, I promise we'll do everything in our power to run it down.* I wondered if she intended to try to track down Marcus and badger some information out of him. Along that line, there could be some merit to me agreeing to hear Marcus out about his alleged innocence if he did in fact come back around to speak to me. Even if he planned to lie through his teeth, he was stupid enough that I might have a chance at getting him to blurt out something we could use to nail his dumb ass to the wall. It was dangerous for me to engage with him, but if Baxter and/or a deputy would be around to step in, what was the hurt? It would be kind of like an under-cover op, only I wouldn't have to pretend to be someone I wasn't. I'd still have to pretend—this time, I'd have to cover up the fact that I wanted nothing more than to kill Marcus with my bare hands.

I smiled at my sister. "I know I don't owe him anything. He might not want to talk to me anymore once he gets a good look at what I did to his face."

Rachel smiled. "I bet it felt amazing to dish back some of what he always did to Mom. Let's get dinner. I'm starving."

We ordered pizza and sat outside on the back patio to eat so Nate could run around with our golden retriever, Trixie. I didn't think it was possible after the day we'd had to feel any sense of normalcy, but I was able to relax and enjoy the evening.

After we'd finished, Baxter left to make a quick run to his house to pack a bag. Or at least I thought he'd left—less than a minute after I'd locked the door behind him, there was a knock.

Assuming it was him, I opened the door, saying, "Did you forget some-thing?" only to suck in a gasp as I found not Baxter, but Marcus, on my front porch.

4

Even through my shock, I knew I had to do whatever I could to alert Rachel so she wouldn't pop into the living room and run into her father—or worse, let Nate come bounding in. I said loudly, "Marcus, what the hell are you doing here?"

Marcus held out his hands. "I know I scare you, but I'm not here to hurt you, I swear."

Oddly enough, I believed him. However, I didn't trust he wouldn't change his mind, so I closed the door a bit and wedged my foot behind it, lest he try to barge inside.

"Then why are you here?" I demanded.

He sighed. I smelled liquor on his breath, not that it was any surprise to me. "You're the only one I trust to help me."

"Why in the hell would you trust me? You know I hate you, right? Hell, I jacked up your face a couple of hours ago. The only thing you can trust about me is that I wouldn't hesitate to do it again."

He grimaced. "It's because I know how much you hate me that I trust you . . . and because you was always the type of person who'd do the right thing, even if it meant breaking the rules. Like when you'd go steal formula for your sister because me and your mama were too screwed up to take care of our own kid."

I stared at him. "It's really disconcerting to hear kind words about me come out of your mouth. How drunk are you?"

"A little."

A little, my ass. To be fair, Marcus was a surprisingly high-functioning alcoholic and drug abuser. A good buzz always seemed to make him sound a bit smarter and more introspective.

I rolled my eyes. "Just get to the point."

Nodding, he said, "I need you to help to clear my name for your mama's murder, and I need you to do it off the books, without any of your cop buddies' help." He paused, not seeming to want to say the next part. He finally went on. "The people who are after me said they'd kill me if I went to the police."

I laughed. "So I should help you so you don't get killed. What's my motivation?"

He stared at me, then finally came up with, "Guilt, if I die."

Shaking my head, I replied, "Nope, don't think so."

"I didn't kill your mother, Ellie. I ain't never killed no one."

"Oh, so it makes you a good guy because you never let one of your brutal beatings get far enough out of hand to kill one of us?"

He rubbed his forehead. "I can't take back what I done in the past."

"No, you can't."

"I can say I'm sorry."

"You and I both know that's a lie." I shook my head, suddenly exhausted. "You know, Marcus, I don't really give a shit about what's happening to you. I'd love to find out who killed my mother, but it's pretty clear you don't actually want to help us find out who really did it. You could have been cooperative at the station, but instead you chose to be a dick."

"I don't like cops."

"Says every criminal ever."

He raised his hands and let them fall to his sides in a helpless gesture. "I couldn't name no names. I don't know who these people are."

"That is such bullshit. If you're not going to lift a finger to help yourself, I'm certainly not going to. Goodbye, Marcus."

I went to slam the door in his face, but he blurted out, "They threatened my kids' lives, too."

I froze, using all the strength I had left to try to read him. He had lied to me so many times over the years, I finally started assuming everything out of his mouth was the opposite of the truth. However, if there was a sliver of truth to this last statement he'd made, I couldn't not take action with my sister in possible danger.

Around my clenched jaw, I muttered, "You're serious about the threats on Rachel and Jack? You swear on their lives? On your life?"

"I swear it's the truth, Ellie. You know I wouldn't come to you for nothing if it wasn't my only option."

That much was probably true.

I let out a heavy sigh. "Okay. But I'm only going to help you because I don't want to see Rachel or Jack hurt, understand? You, I'll throw under the bus if I have to."

He nodded. "I figured as much."

"So talk. Start from the beginning."

Wiping his brow, he explained, "I knew it could be dangerous for me to show my face around here again, but . . . I had to see my boy. Right after I got back to town, I found a burner flip phone on the hood of my truck. The threatening calls started coming in on it. No way to know who it is because they use a voice changer."

I said, "The phone is some good evidence. Give it to me, and I'll process it. Maybe I can find out who's calling you."

"No can do. If I don't answer that thing, they'll know something's up."

"It's not like I'll have it forever. We're talking a couple of hours."

He clenched his jaw. "I'm not taking that chance."

I frowned. "I thought you said you were going to be helpful."

"I'm telling you the whole story, ain't I?"

"That remains to be seen." When he only gave me a blank look in response, I went on. "Tell me more about the caller. You keep saying 'these people' and 'they,' but is there only one person calling you?"

"When they call, they say stuff like 'we're going to kill you.' But it seems like only one person is doing the talking."

I nodded. "Did they tell you why they want you to leave town and not come back?"

"Only that I'm a piece of shit—"

"That's accurate," I interjected, unable to hold my tongue.

I saw a hint of a glare shoot through his eyes, but to my surprise it vanished quickly. He continued. "And they don't want me anywhere in this area."

"Okay, but *why*? I assume you're still dealing drugs because you have no other skills, so is it a territorial thing? Is there someone out there who wants you out of the way so they can have a monopoly or something?"

Marcus shrugged. "Could be, I suppose."

"Who has beef with you over territory, then?"

He wrinkled his brow, looking to be deep in thought. "Not sure. I've been gone a while."

I rolled my eyes. "I can't tell the difference between when you're playing dumb versus when you're being your normal amount of dumb. Or is it that you've finally become your best customer and your brain is fried?"

He got defensive. "I've cut back a lot since you knew me last. I don't do the hard stuff no more."

"Oh, you've cut back? Congrats. So you're high just under one hundred percent of the time, then?"

"Never did lose that smartass mouth of yours, did you?"

"Not even for a minute. Look, you're going to have to start coughing up some names, or I've got literally nothing to go on."

"Fine. Jake Campbell was always trying to shut me out of the trade when I lived around here. And Manny Ferrara shot me once."

I took out my phone and started a new note to make a list of criminals Marcus had pissed off. I dealt with lowlifes on a fairly regular basis, but knowing one of them so intimately and speaking so matter-of-factly about his illegal exploits was kind of sickening.

"Any others?" I prompted him.

"Not really."

"How about other types of enemies? I know you ran through women like it was going out of style, although I never did understand how. I'm sure you stole someone's wife or girlfriend at some point."

He smiled, which made my skin crawl. "Yeah, I did a lot of that."

"Which of those poor cuckolds might have wanted you miles away from their woman?"

"Too many to count."

I sneered. "Wrong answer. Make with the names."

Marcus scratched his head. "Earl Thompson, Mike Graves, Joe Novak . . . oh, and Tyrell Simpkins."

"Four is too many for you to count, Einstein?"

He huffed. "You're bitchy, you know that?"

I ignored him. "So which of all these guys you named knows you're back in town?"

"What?" he asked, seeming confused.

Maybe he'd given up "the hard stuff," but there was no doubt in my mind he was still using plenty of drugs. I explained, "There has to be a connection between your anonymous caller and whoever you've spoken to and seen since you returned, genius. Otherwise, whoever's supposedly after you would never know you're back. Who even knows you're here?"

"Oh, uh . . . none of them guys. I know to steer clear of 'em." He suddenly zeroed in on a point behind my shoulder. "I want to see Rachel."

My eyebrows shot up, and I said as evenly as I could, "She doesn't live in the area anymore."

Marcus's expression went dark, and his hands balled up into tight fists at his sides. Suddenly he looked a lot more menacing than the pathetic loser I'd been talking to. "Now *you're* the one who's lying! I know she's here! *Rachel!*" he roared.

Ice filled my veins, giving me the same sense of déjà vu I'd had when I first saw him earlier today. Worried it was only a matter of time before he lost control and got violent, I threw my weight against the door, slammed it shut, and locked it. While Marcus cursed me from outside, I called 911 and tried as calmly as I could to explain my situation. Upon hearing the commotion, Rachel peeked her head around the corner from the hallway, eyes wide and frightened. Suddenly, Marcus's screaming stopped, and a moment later headlights swung across the front window. I hurried to the window and peered out the crack between the curtains, nearly collapsing with relief when I saw Baxter heading toward our door. I finished up my 911 call and opened the door, flinging myself into his arms.

He caught me in a warm hug, but must have immediately sensed something, because his grip went tight as he demanded, "What's wrong?"

Rachel's shaky voice from behind me said, "Marcus was here. She was talking to him, and then he—"

When I heard her choke on a sob, I wiggled out of Baxter's grasp and went straight to console my sister. "It's going to be okay, Rach." I tried to take her hands, but she wasn't having it.

She cried, "It's *not* okay. He knows I live here!"

I tried to keep my face passive. "He's gone now, at least." I turned to Baxter. "Right? Did you see anyone running away from our house as you drove up?"

Baxter shook his head. "No, I didn't see anyone." His expression grew anguished. "I'm so sorry I wasn't here for you. I thought it would be okay to be gone a few minutes—"

I cut him off. "Don't blame yourself. I could have slammed the door in his face, but I didn't. This is on me."

I could tell by the look in his eyes that he blamed only himself. "That's why either a deputy or I will be with you *every moment* until that slimy son of a bitch is behind bars for good."

Angry tears leaking from her eyes, Rachel snapped, "I asked you not to talk to him, Ellie. Could you not do that one thing for me?"

I hung my head. I'd thought I was doing the best thing—getting Marcus to open up so I might be able to glean something from him that would ultimately be his undoing. Plus, if he wasn't lying about his anonymous caller threatening my sister's life, it was imperative we track down any leads we could get. Marcus did give up several names of people who likely wouldn't have any problem airing his dirty laundry, so I had hope things could work out in our favor.

I said to Rachel, "I'm sorry I made you feel betrayed. I didn't plan to have a whole conversation with Marcus, but when he said his anonymous caller threatened not only his life, but yours and Jack's, too, I felt like I should take any information he was willing to give."

"And how do you know that sack of shit wasn't lying to you?" she demanded.

"I don't. But I'm not willing to leave any stone unturned when your safety is at stake."

Baxter wiped a hand down his face. "That said, Rachel, I think you and

Nate should go stay with David for a while. Does Marcus have a reason to know where he lives?"

To my knowledge, Marcus had never crossed paths with our stepdad David, the one good man our mother ever brought into our life. Even after our mother had divorced him, David had always cared for us as if we were his own children and never hesitated to do whatever was necessary to keep us safe. He'd given Rachel and Nate a place to stay on more than one occasion, especially during the past year. He'd been relieved we'd gone so long without an incident, but I knew he would be more than happy to do anything he could to help.

"Not that I know of," I replied.

Baxter got out his phone and made a call as sirens began wailing in the distance. When the Noblesville PD cruiser pulled up in front of the house, he muttered to me that he'd take care of everything and went outside to meet the first responders. Rachel disappeared into her room, presumably where she'd left Nate and Trixie to be entertained by Nate's favorite cartoon playing loud enough to mask all the shouting. I collapsed onto the couch, using my last bit of energy to send the names and information Marcus gave me to Chief Esparza and Jayne, making sure to mention Marcus's allegations that his life and his kids' lives depended on them keeping any investigation into these people on the down low. I wanted nothing more than to wash my hands of Marcus for good.

BAXTER COORDINATED with Noblesville PD and the sheriff's office to get Rachel, Nate, and Trixie moved safely and hopefully invisibly to David's house. They stationed a deputy to watch over the house and accompany Rachel to her classes the next day. After I'd helped them pack and said my goodbyes, I packed my own bag and let Baxter take me to his house.

Again, the thought of living with Baxter was something I'd dreamed of for a while, but *again*, I didn't like the setup. It infuriated me that stupid Marcus Copland was deciding my fate and there was jack shit I could do about it.

As Baxter slid into his bed next to me, he said quietly, "Don't give that monster another thought tonight."

I looked over at him and smiled. "How did you know exactly what I was thinking?"

He smiled back. "Well, considering you always stew over your problems for days, it wasn't a stretch."

I chuckled. "Guilty."

His smile faded. "And you were touching the cigarette burn on your stomach."

Damned if I wasn't. I frowned. Baxter was the only person who knew the full story of the infamous cigarette burn Marcus had inflicted on me when I was eleven years old. I knew it haunted him because he'd brought it up several times.

"Guilty again."

He reached over and caressed my face. "I'm here. You're safe. Only good thoughts and sweet dreams tonight, okay?"

I nodded and snuggled into him, his mere presence taking away any lingering apprehension I had as I drifted off to sleep.

5

Baxter's phone started ringing long before my alarm was set to go off. As I tried to fall back asleep, I heard him say, "We'll be there soon."

Eyes scrunched shut, I muttered, "Who's we?"

He kissed my forehead and got out of bed, replying sleepily but with a definite touch of excitement in his voice, "You and me. Crime scene."

I groaned. "No. Can't I pass on this one?"

"The sheriff made sure to inform me you've run out of passes now that I'm back at a hundred percent. Plus it's a homicide, so everyone involved would prefer you be on it."

I sat up and rubbed the sleep from my eyes. "Damn. I guess that's what I get for being so amazing at my job."

Grinning at me, he said, "Less talk, more action. We should shower together. It'll save time."

I laughed. "That is absolutely untrue."

~

As Baxter drove us to the crime scene, located in the far southwest corner of the county, I contacted Talia to let her know she'd need to take over teaching my classes for most of the day. I emailed her my notes and any extra materials she'd need to get the job done. I got assigned a new grad student as my TA at the start of every school year, and since I'd yet to work a case so far this semester, Talia had yet to have to take over for me. I wasn't worried, though. She was one of the most focused and organized people I'd ever met.

Baxter pulled into a parking lot for a small doctor's office. Two cruisers, an SUV, and the criminalists' van were already here. I guessed we'd taken a little too much time getting ready this morning.

Baxter must have been thinking the same thing. "Sterling's going to have something to say about us being last to arrive."

His partner, Detective Jason Sterling, had a sharp tongue and an opinion about everything. After our rocky past, Sterling and I had finally buried the hatchet and quit being openly mean to each other. Baxter and I had even gone out to dinner a few times with Sterling and his girlfriend, my fellow criminalist Amanda Carmack, but that didn't keep us from sniping at each other on occasion like old times. Especially if one of us did something to warrant a snide remark.

I tried to keep it positive. "We're not dead last. No coroner's van yet, so we can't even do much besides stand around and speculate."

Smiling, Baxter put his SUV in park and said proudly, "You lobbed the first bad pun of our first case back. And just when I thought I couldn't fall more in love with you."

My face fell. "Yeah, about that. This isn't going to be weird, is it? Us working together now that we're . . . together?"

He shrugged. "Should be simpler, since we don't have to cover up the fact that we like each other."

"I guess," I replied uncertainly, knowing he didn't grasp the deeper meaning of my comment.

The idea of working alongside him wasn't my issue. I knew we could do that with pure professionalism. I was more concerned about how it was going to affect me to know he was going out pursuing criminals, especially the murderous kind. Yesterday I'd had a mild freak-out about his return to investigating, and that was over him going up against a couple of petty thieves. This was a homicide. I had the utmost faith in his skills and his intelligence. But having watched him nearly die, then struggle for months to regain his full strength, I had a real problem with the possibility of something similar happening again.

I had to lock all that down. In a crime scene investigation, there was no room for emotion or a clouded mind. I hadn't had to do this for a while. Taking a deep breath, I dug deep and flipped that switch to shut off my emotions. I hoped after yesterday I had enough energy to keep the switch firmly in place.

Sterling and Amanda were already inside the inner perimeter of the scene and seemed deep in conversation. Baxter and I signed the scene entry log and crossed the tape to join them. I kept my attention on my colleagues rather than on the scene. No sense in taking too close a look until I needed to. I still wasn't convinced I'd been able to rein in everything.

Sterling jeered at me, "Look who finally decided to show back up at work. Think you'll remember how to process a scene after your six-month vacay, Matthews?"

At least he hadn't gone after Baxter and me about arriving together and later than we should have. I replied, "'Vacay' is a stretch. But I've enjoyed not having to work with you for six months."

Instead of firing angrily back at me, he laughed. "Same."

Amanda said, "*I'm* happy to have you back." She turned to Baxter. "You, too, Nick."

Baxter nodded. "Thanks. What have we got here?"

His trademark smirk slipping into place, Sterling replied, "Roadkill."

Amanda groaned. "Jason, please."

He jerked a thumb over his shoulder. "My assessment is accurate. Someone mowed her down, decided she wasn't dead enough, and then ran her over some more."

I finally allowed myself a look at our scene. The crumpled remains of a woman lay in a pool of dried blood twenty feet from us, her body twisted and broken. Sterling's assessment was in fact accurate. Tire marks ran in a few different paths, as if the driver had backed up and taken another go or two at the victim. One set of the marks was bloody. A white van with DAVIS CLEANING SERVICE painted on the side was parked about twenty feet away from the body. No tire marks anywhere near it, so I assumed it was the victim's vehicle. I frowned, a feeling hitting me that this was not a simple hit-and-run accident.

A feeling must have been hitting Baxter as well, because he excused himself and hurried toward a strip of grass away from the scene. Decomp, especially with carnage like this, triggered his gag reflex. After he threw up, he'd be good to go.

"Where's Dr. Berg?" I asked.

"Meat wagon had a flat tire," Sterling replied. "He's fifteen minutes out."

Amanda turned to me. "I guess we can suit up and start with the outlying stuff."

I nodded. "Sounds like a plan."

As we stepped into our Tyvek suits and put on our booties, gloves, and masks, she ventured, "Are you feeling rusty?"

Chuckling, I replied, "Very. What would you think about officially taking lead on this one?" I shouldered my case of tools and the camera bag.

Her eyes widened as she grabbed her case and shut the van doors. "That would be amazing. Yes!"

Amanda was more than ready to serve as lead investigator for this scene, not to mention as head criminalist for the county. The only thing standing in her way was Beck Durant, the current head criminalist. The good news was that Beck was terrible at his job, which was why I got to consult on bigger cases and work with Amanda. The bad news was that Beck's mommy was a prominent county court judge who'd used her influence to secure the position for her little man, which meant Amanda had no way to move up.

The next thing out of Amanda's mouth as we walked back toward the scene was, "And let me just say how awful this case would have been if you hadn't come back today of all days. I can't even put into words how much worse Beck has been at his job the past week." Speak of the devil.

I laughed. "Only the past week?"

She rolled her eyes as we passed back under the caution tape and set our cases on the ground. "Yeah. Ever since he got this new girlfriend."

My jaw dropped. "Beck Durant managed to trick someone into going out with him?"

"Evidently. Her name's Carmen."

I got out the camera while Amanda took out the measuring wheel and a stack of evidence markers. "And she's real?"

She laughed. "Yes, I believe so."

"Have you seen her, though?"

"No. But I've heard enough about her."

"Hmm."

I lined up a few wide-angle shots of the taped-off area while my mind waffled between the Beck dating conundrum and the scene we were supposed to be considering. The doctor's office building was styled to look like a suburban colonial-style house. What remained of this poor woman was a gruesome and wildly out-of-place addition to the intentionally welcoming curb appeal of the setting. It felt surreal. In fact, it reminded me of our last homicide case, when a married couple met a violent end in their lavishly decorated bedroom. It was jarring when the contrast between the area and the carnage was so severe.

For that reason, it was nice to have something off-topic to discuss to keep my mind a little disconnected from the situation. I said, "Beck going on about her isn't enough to make me believe it's not some sort of online catfish situation. Has he met her in real life?"

Amanda nodded slowly as she set an evidence marker at the start of one of the black tire marks on the gray concrete of the parking lot. "Well . . . I think so. I overheard him yesterday leaving a voicemail for her finalizing their lunch plans. He came back to work happy enough after lunch, so I assume she showed up." Shuddering, she added, "He was doing a baby-talk voice over the phone. It was terrifying."

I snickered and took some mid-range shots of the deceased and of the Davis Cleaning Service van. "A lunch date and baby talk. Sounds pretty serious."

Baxter's voice from behind us said, "Lunch dates and baby talk? Shouldn't you be discussing evidence instead of gossiping?"

I turned and pulled my mask down so I could smile at him as he approached. "We're doing both. We're using our evidence-gathering skills to discern if Beck's new girlfriend is in fact real. It's very scientific."

"I meant evidence pertaining to this scene, but the other thing sounds important, too. What's your professional opinion?" he asked as he took the baseball cap off his head and placed it on mine.

My insides got all warm. I always had to borrow a hat from him to complete my head-to-toe protective gear, but the little gesture of him remembering to make sure I had one was comforting. Memories of our past cases flooded my mind—not only the bad ones this time, but also the good ones. It was then that I realized we were both where we needed to be. There would always be apprehension that came with this job. But at the end of the day, it was worth it.

I replied, "The evidence says she's real."

Baxter eyed me. "I feel a 'but' coming."

Amanda piped up, "But who in the actual hell would date Beck on purpose?"

I pointed at her. "There it is."

He shrugged and winked at me as he backed away from us. "Doesn't everyone have a soul mate out there somewhere?"

I shook my head and grinned, getting that warm feeling in my heart again. Baxter was the only person in the entire department who'd give Beck the benefit of the doubt.

Amanda took out the surveyor's wheel and began measuring the tire marks and plotting them on the rough sketch of the scene she'd started. She said, "I count four sets of marks. Whoever was driving the car wasn't dicking around. They made sure the job was done, and then some."

I ventured closer to the deceased and took some close-up shots, trying to focus the camera, rather than my thoughts, on this poor woman's wounds. I knew I'd become more sensitive to hurt and death over my six-month break, but automobile accidents had always been a tad more diffi-cult for me to stomach. Gunshot and knife wounds could be brutal, but the sheer force with which an automobile could do damage to the human body was mind-boggling. This particular incident couldn't have even involved high speeds, based on the short tire marks. It was simply machine, plus a hefty amount of vengeance, versus flesh.

The coroner's van pulled into the parking lot, so we abandoned our tasks to take a break and give Dr. Everett Berg plenty of space and quiet to make his initial assessment. Amanda and I joined Baxter and Sterling on the other side of the perimeter tape.

Sterling was saying, "I'll believe that when I see it."

"Believe what?" Amanda asked.

Sterling scoffed. "That Becky has a girlfriend."

I laughed and cuffed Baxter on the arm. "Now who's gossiping instead of doing their jobs?"

Baxter shrugged easily. "We've done all we can until we ID the victim. We're playing a waiting game between Dr. Berg going through the victim's pockets and Davis Cleaning Service returning our call about who was assigned to work here last night."

Watching Dr. Berg and his assistant, Kenny Strange, remove a gurney from the back of their van, Sterling grumbled, "Neither of them seems to be in any particular hurry."

Sterling shouldn't have expected anything different from Dr. Berg. He was everything you'd want in a coroner—calm, deliberate, and reverent. So reverent that he insisted on everyone in the general vicinity of the deceased adhere to the same rules he followed and would call you out if you weren't acting right. None of us were exempt from his admonitions—even the district attorney, whose temper often got him in hot water in Dr. Berg's cold, quiet morgue.

Dr. Berg and Kenny approached and rolled the gurney past our group, both greeting us with a quiet, "Good morning," before crossing the crime scene tape.

While we watched them begin their initial assessment of the body, Baxter said, "Do I see four sets of tire marks there?"

Amanda nodded. "That's what I determined." She handed him her rough sketch and pointed to a spot in the parking lot. "Looks like the vehicle—probably a car versus a truck, based on the smallish tire treads and the placement of the injuries I noted on the victim's legs—started there to make the initial hit. I'm thinking they must have floored it from a stopped position to leave that kind of rubber marks. I'm assuming the force from the initial impact knocked the victim to the ground. Then the driver backed up and . . ." She winced. "Probably ran over the victim while she was down . . . and then backed up over her. That must have done more damage than the initial hit, because the fourth set of tire marks were made of more blood than rubber." She shook her head. "Someone wanted this lady very dead." Flicking her eyes at Sterling, she added, "You guys be careful out there tracking down the psycho who did this."

Sterling puffed out his chest. "We know how to handle psychos."

It hadn't dawned on me that Amanda dealt with the same worries I did. She had the added stress of her boyfriend being a total hothead. Sterling was known to intentionally goad suspects to get a rise out of them.

After that exchange, we stood in silence, watching as Dr. Berg carefully searched the victim's pockets. He found a phone in a leather case and produced a driver's license from it. After making a note and placing the phone into a paper bag and sealing it, he approached us.

Smiling kindly at Baxter and me, Dr. Berg said, "Happy to have both of you back. I take it you're well, Detective?"

Baxter nodded. "Good as new. Thanks for asking."

Sterling, not unlike a child, was unable to control his impatience. "Who's the vic, Doc?"

A ghost of a frown passed over Dr. Berg's face, but he answered evenly, "Katherine Copland, fifty-two-year-old female from Noblesville."

Baxter's head snapped in my direction. "Copland? Any relation?"

A knot forming in the pit of my stomach, I removed my gloves and wiped a hand down my face. "Marcus's most recent ex-wife is named Katie, and to my knowledge, she lives in Noblesville."

Sterling stared at me. "The Marcus Copland you assaulted the shit out of last night?"

"That's the one."

Dr. Berg's jaw hit the ground as Sterling went on. "Do you know her? Would you recognize her from her license photo?"

I closed my eyes. "Yes." I refrained from saying *why* I knew what she looked like. I met Katie when I'd had to stop my mother from beating the shit out of her in Walmart after she found out Marcus had cheated with her. I guessed the assault apple didn't fall too far from the tree.

Still aghast, Dr. Berg hurried over to retrieve the victim's driver's license. He returned with it and showed it to me. Sure enough, Katie Copland, Marcus's latest ex-wife, stared back at me.

6

I threw my gloves on the ground and huffed. "Well, I'm out."

As I unzipped my Tyvek suit and began stepping out of it, Amanda balked. "Wait. Just because the victim is your, what . . . ex-stepdad's ex-wife, doesn't tie her to you that much. You can stay on, right?"

I shook my head. "It's more about who your lead suspect is inevitably going to be. No way I can give him the benefit of the doubt." More importantly, the less I knew about what Marcus was up to, the better I'd be able to sleep at night.

Baxter nodded. "Right, which means I'm out, too. It's way too coincidental to me that Copland shows back up in town—to visit this woman's son, no less—and she ends up murdered within days. I'm too close to Ellie and Rachel and the whole situation to be impartial, much less look impartial to the public."

Sterling shrugged. "Sounds like you've done my work for me, for the most part. If I play my cards right, I close this case all by myself in record time. Thanks for the easy win."

I gave him a fake smile. "Always happy to make *your* case closure record look better."

Sterling chuckled but didn't snipe back. He wasn't wrong—this case seemed like a no-brainer considering the circumstances. And I didn't care what Marcus got taken down for as long as he spent the rest of his life in prison. I was sorry, though, that Rachel's half-brother Jack had to lose his mom for it to happen. He seemed like a nice enough guy, and he certainly didn't need more on his plate right now.

Baxter turned to me. He tried to hide it, but I could see the disappointment in his eyes. "I guess this is our cue to leave."

Amanda frowned. "And my cue to call Beck."

Sterling put a hand on her shoulder and gave her a playful shake. "Aw, don't bother with that dumbass. I got you."

Her eyebrows shot up. "You'll help me collect evidence?" It was normally a cold day in hell before Sterling offered his help to anyone.

"Yeah, if Matthews can do it, how hard can it be?"

I rolled my eyes. "You two have fun."

Baxter and I said our goodbyes to the team and headed to his SUV. He was quiet as he drove me to campus.

I finally said, "I'm sorry you had to quit your first homicide because of me."

He looked over and smiled slightly. "It's not your fault."

"It's my fault that my life is a shit show that keeps biting *you* in the ass."

Shrugging, he replied, "I knew what I signed up for."

I gave him a mock scowl.

He chuckled. "I think we're pretty equal on life being a shit show the other one has to deal with. I've got no room to talk."

"Yours was one time. Mine is continual and never-ending."

"But mine was catastrophic. I managed to get myself shot and you almost shot."

"Only because you went hero mode when I had the situation clearly handled."

"Clearly handled? That's not how I remember it." He grinned. "But I don't mind being called a hero. I get that a lot, you know." I was happy he could finally joke about the situation. It hadn't always been the case. And other than a little broodiness at first, he was already joking about having to give up this investigation.

"I said you went hero *mode*. That's not a compliment."

"Hero mode," he said, throwing me an amused glance as he came to a stop in the parking lot next to the Ashmore College science building. "Isn't that what you did yesterday?"

"I'm woman enough to admit that's accurate, but I won't be sorry for it." Frowning, I looked down at the bandage on my left palm and added, "Other than being sorry I got hurt."

Baxter's face fell. "In all the excitement, I didn't even ask you how your wounds were doing after being out at the scene. I don't imagine wearing tight gloves and doing a lot of walking around felt too good."

I smiled. "I'm okay. My knees only hurt when I crouch down enough to stretch the skin, and I hadn't got to the crouching portion of the investigation before I quit. My hand and elbows are . . . better." Better in the way that the sensation was now more like a slow burn rather than my skin feeling like it was actively on fire.

Nothing got past him. "I didn't think about it before because the sheriff was adamant about you working the scene this morning, but maybe you should be resting today. If your TA is already set to teach your classes, let her."

"If I sit around and do nothing today after all the shit that's happened, I'll go nuts."

"I guess you have a point. At least teaching won't be physically demanding like working the scene would have been." He put his hand over mine. "But please take care of yourself otherwise. We left the scene before we had a chance to mentally process what we saw. It might hit you harder than you'd think. Give yourself some mental breaks throughout the day."

I squeezed his hand. "I will if you will."

"I will." He looked over as a sheriff's cruiser came pulling up beside us. "Right on time."

I made a face and griped, "Ugh. I appreciate the effort and money that's being spent on me, especially after this new wrinkle this morning, but I hate being followed around."

Baxter leaned over and gave me a quick kiss. "Too bad. Nonnegotiable."

I groaned as I saw Deputy Walters, the judgy first responder from my scuffle with Marcus yesterday, getting out of the cruiser. "That guy? Nooooo . . . What are the odds?"

Baxter chuckled. "Oh, damn. I think the cosmos hates you."

"I've believed that for a while."

Deputy Walters was standing practically at attention, dutifully, or maybe impatiently, waiting for me. It was hard to tell with him. He had a solid, unreadable cop face, but the disdain in his gaze was painfully evident.

Baxter said, "Play nice."

"Do I have to?"

"Yes, you do. But you can ditch him when I whisk you away to a quiet dinner tonight."

"I'll be counting the minutes."

He smiled. "Me, too."

I hopped out of Baxter's SUV and approached my babysitter. "Hi, Deputy Walters. Thank you for watching out for me today. I'm sure you'd rather be out doing something that matters."

Continuing to stand still as a statue, Walters nodded and said a little robotically, "Keeping the county's citizens safe matters. It's my job."

I bet he was fun at parties. Today was shaping up to be yet another shit show.

I ARRIVED partway through the first class of my day and hated to shove Talia aside, so I sat in the back of the classroom and observed. She did okay for her first time lecturing. She was stiff and seemed unsure of herself, but who could fault her after being given only a couple hours' notice? Besides, teaching wasn't what she wanted to do with her life. She wanted to work in a forensic lab as a firearms specialist. After the students left the room, I offered that she could teach the same class again during the next hour, but she politely refused.

I gave the lecture on the use of scanning electron microscopes to my second class. Specialized lab equipment was never my favorite topic. I found it boring because I never used any of it in what I did. Students like Talia who intended to make lab work their careers were quite interested and needed the instruction, so I always tried to make it as engaging as possible. Today I didn't hit the mark, because even my most enthusiastic students seemed checked out. Deputy Walters kept his unwavering attention on me, but I could tell he was bored as hell, too.

After class, I went to my office, my babysitter in tow. I said to him, "I've got office hours for the next hour and then lunch. Do you want to sit in my office with me or—"

He cut me off. "I'll stand guard outside your door."

I nodded. "Okay." At least I wouldn't be cooped up in my tiny office with Deputy No Personality.

I went through my emails and found one marked URGENT sent three hours ago from Dr. Thomas Graham, the head of the science department. The email had also been sent to the head of campus security. My heart sank as I opened it, knowing it couldn't be good news. It wasn't. I was due in Dr. Graham's office in five minutes for a meeting about the incident yesterday. Shit.

Hoisting myself out of my chair, I found my deputy "standing guard" outside and said to him, "I have to go to a meeting."

His only reply was a curt nod. He fell into step behind me as I trudged upstairs and knocked on Dr. Graham's office door.

Dr. Graham's voice called, "Come in."

I opened the door to find the head of campus security, Walt Franklin, seated in a chair across from Dr. Graham. I had to hold in a weary sigh as I sank into the chair next to him. I guessed it was a good thing I'd removed myself from the case this morning, otherwise I would have missed the email and stood up these very serious-looking men. Dr. Graham had a bad habit of scheduling last-minute meetings without professors' okay, assuming we had nothing better to do during our office hours than be at his beck and call. He got stood up a fair amount of time, but rather than changing his process to remedy that, he would instead send a strongly worded email to the professor who'd dared miss his meeting.

"Professor Matthews, this is Walt Franklin, head of Ashmore College security," Dr. Graham said.

I nodded at Franklin. "Nice to meet you," I lied.

Franklin only glared at me in response.

Dr. Graham went on. "Your incident in the courtyard yesterday made quite a stir on campus."

No shit.

Evidently unable to keep a lid on his temper, Franklin took over the conversation in a gruff tone. "It was more than a stir. Professor Matthews, you undermined the authority of campus security and verbally abused a campus security officer in front of students. Worse, there's a video of you doing so on our campus newspaper website. It's disgraceful."

I cared about what Dr. Graham thought of me. This guy, I couldn't give two shits about. I replied, "The outcome wasn't my intention, and it wasn't my fault I was being recorded."

Franklin scoffed. "That's a ridiculous excuse in this day and age. People should always assume they're being recorded."

I merely shrugged. I wouldn't have held back had I known I was being recorded. I said what I meant. I wasn't too worried about being the subject of a less-than-flattering video on the *Ashmore Voice* vlog. It wasn't my first time, and considering my penchant for outbursts, it wouldn't be my last. The student reporters were constantly filming around campus, hoping to catch faculty, staff, and students at their worst. No one was safe from getting caught saying or doing something that could take their status from unknown to infamous in a matter of minutes.

He went on. "It's all anyone is talking about, and now that security officer is being bullied by students."

"Then take it up with those students."

A vein popped in Franklin's forehead as he raised his voice. "No, *you're* to blame for this whole debacle for not exemplifying the standards expected of the faculty and staff of this institution."

I snorted. "Standards? The former president of this institution is currently serving out the remainder of her life in prison for the contract murder of one of our students. I should know, because I helped put her away. I hardly think me hurting your boy's feelings is a comparable offense."

Dr. Graham shifted uncomfortably in his chair and cleared his throat. For as much as he loved dishing out a good written reprimand, he didn't seem to enjoy face-to-face confrontations. He said tentatively, "I think we should stick to the facts of the situation."

Franklin smirked at me. "Here's a fact: You called my officer, and I quote, 'bitch-ass Paul Blart.' That was uncalled for and unprofessional."

I replied evenly, "I stand by my assessment of your so-called security guard. Here's a fact for you: He did nothing and let a murder suspect run away."

"It's not his job to apprehend murder suspects."

My eyebrows shot up. "But it's okay for him to allow murder suspects to run around campus, frightening your professors and being generally dangerous?"

Franklin's nostrils flared. "You didn't seem frightened. And from what I saw, you did more damage to the man in question than he did to you."

I bit back a bitter laugh at the ridiculous irony of that statement and managed to hold my tongue. It was one thing for my coworkers at the department to be apprised of my rocky past with Marcus Copland, but it would be quite another to air my family's dirty laundry to the stuck-up faculty and staff of Ashmore College. My lack of proper upbringing and decorum was in full view already. There was no need to fuel that fire.

Dr. Graham had evidently tired of our arguing. "I believe we've hashed this out enough. Professor Matthews, the proper course of action here is for you to apologize to the security guard."

I'd never had to work so hard to not roll my eyes. "Email or in person?"

Franklin snapped, "On the *Ashmore Voice* vlog."

Oh, *hell* no. I thought fast. "I could do that . . . if you want it to look like I was forced to apologize."

That idea didn't seem to bother Franklin, but it bothered Dr. Graham quite a bit. He shook his head. "No, no. That will never do. Apologize in person."

Franklin growled, "That doesn't get rid of our image problem."

It was then that I realized this was not even remotely about bitch-ass Paul Blart's hurt feelings. I actually started feeling sorry for the guy, because I imagined Franklin had made the whole incident about himself and his precious department and probably had ripped the poor security guard a new asshole for the bad publicity.

I sighed. "I have a good relationship with the editor of the *Ashmore Voice*. I'll get him to take down the video."

Franklin visibly relaxed but had to get in one last dig. "See that you do."

I stood. "Sounds like we're done here." Ignoring Franklin, I nodded at Dr. Graham. "Dr. Graham."

Dr. Graham seemed relieved. "Thank you, Professor Matthews."

When I left the office, my deputy tagalong fell into step beside me. He cleared his throat. "I, uh . . . heard what went on in there."

This time, I did roll my eyes. "I don't need a lecture about it from you."

Deputy Walters sighed. "I was going to say I agree with you that the security guard did not do his job. Him allowing someone you'd identified as a murder suspect to run around campus is unacceptable. I don't think you should have to apologize for being angry with him for that. He either needs to be retrained correctly or fired."

Wow. I didn't expect that. "Oh. Um . . . thank you."

"But it wouldn't hurt to apologize for the 'bitch-ass Paul Blart' comment."

He wasn't wrong. I nodded. "If you haven't already heard around the station, I tend to speak my mind and worry about the consequences later."

"I've heard."

"And now you've seen me in action."

He laughed, which surprised me. I'd never seen even a ghost of a smile on his face. "You lived up to the hype."

UPON RETURNING TO MY OFFICE, I contacted Al Nishimura, the editor of the *Ashmore Voice*, and managed to convince him to take down the video. It was going to cost me an exclusive interview about my next big case—Al was a true-crime junkie—but it was a small price to pay. I was also able to run down the security guard I'd berated and give him a fairly heartfelt apology for putting him in a position to get bullied. He was kind of a dick about it, but I hadn't expected him to be particularly receptive to anything I had to say. I also made a preemptive call to Vic to tell him he might get alerted to a BOLO or arrest warrant out for Marcus and that Rachel and I were under deputy supervision until he was apprehended. Vic kept a lid on his temper this time, barely, and told me to pass along to the department that he'd be happy to lend his expertise or resources if needed.

At exactly 1:00 p.m., Sam knocked on my open door. "Lunch?" she asked hopefully.

I nodded. "Oh, yeah. I need a break from my life."

Sam was always good at taking my mind off the tough stuff. She'd called me yesterday after seeing the infamous video, wanting to know if I was okay. I'd told her what I could about what had happened. I couldn't go into too much detail since I couldn't repeat anything I'd heard at Marcus's interrogation, but I'd told her enough that she was worried both for my safety and my mental health. After she made sure I was okay, she shifted the conversation to fill me in on the latest story in the faculty rumor mill—that one of Ashmore's biggest donors had pulled their monetary support over an argument he'd had with the dean of students over a pickleball game, of all things.

Grinning, Sam said, "I see you have a muscley new bodyguard. What are the odds he's single?"

"I'm not asking him that. But more importantly, he's very young. Probably the same age as our grad students. Which is too young for you."

She shrugged. "Not according to Professor Chambers. I heard he hooked up with his TA last semester."

Making a face, I said, "Gross. Really? Why do I never hear this stuff?"

"Because you spend all your free time either hanging out with your boyfriend or working crime scenes with your boyfriend." Not missing a beat, she added, "Speaking of boyfriends, you should set me up with someone. There's no shortage of age-appropriate hunky cops in your department."

I rolled my eyes. "Absolutely not. Thanks to me, you had a brilliant, adorable professor who thought you hung the moon, and you dumped his ass. I'm not setting you up with some other unsuspecting guy to hit and quit."

She feigned shock. "'Hit and quit'? How dare you?"

As expected, Sam's bubbly banter was already melting my stress away. I got up from my chair and walked toward the door, hoping a satisfying lunch would further improve my mood. "Remind me how many hours went by after you sealed the deal before you gave him the old 'it's not you, it's me.' Two? Maybe three?"

Snorting, she followed me out of my office. "Point noted."

As I opened my mouth to tell Deputy Walters that Sam and I were heading to lunch, my phone rang. It was Sterling. It was never a good sign when he called me. My heart seized as my thoughts went straight to Baxter, fearing something had happened to him. Even though I'd been able to come to terms with the idea that danger was a part of his job, my unconscious reaction to potential bad news might be something I'd always have to battle.

I answered breathlessly, "What's wrong?"

Sterling ignored my frantic question, barking, "Tell Deputy Dipshit to check his phone."

I heaved a sigh of relief that this call wasn't bad news, only Sterling being an ass. Although I replied "What am I, his secretary?", I dutifully relayed an edited version of the message to Deputy Walters, saying, "Sterling says to check your phone."

As the deputy got out his phone, Sterling said in a gentler tone, "Look, Matthews, you should watch your back. I sent deputies out to pick up Marcus Copland, but he wasn't at the address he'd listed at the station yesterday. The woman living there said she didn't know anyone named Marcus Copland, and based on what we know about his known associates and exes, I tend to believe her. We have a BOLO out and deputies actively searching for him, but he's nowhere."

My stomach started twisting again, but I managed to reply, "He's a dumb son of a bitch, but he's smart enough to know to get the hell out of Dodge after committing a murder. Did you look for him wherever he's been hiding for the last few years?"

"Yeah. We had the Terre Haute PD check the address we found on his truck's vehicle registration. No luck there, either." He cleared his throat. "Baxter said he might come looking for you, especially if he's going to try to cry innocent on this murder as well. Just . . . be careful."

I shivered. If Sterling was calling me to warn me to be safe, it was time to be worried.

Deputy Walters was back in full RoboCop mode. Returning his phone to his pocket and placing a hand on his holstered service pistol, he said, "Ms. Matthews, I'm afraid going out for lunch is out of the question today."

7

Much to our dismay, Sam and I had to order lunch and scarf it down in my office. I longed for some fresh air, but that wasn't in the cards for me today, or maybe for a while if Marcus didn't turn up soon. I finished out my classes and labs for the day with Deputy Walters practically stuck to my side. He did a great job, which I'd be sure to pass along to Jayne, but it made me feel more like a prisoner than a potential victim.

My own worries flew out of my head when Rachel called me as I was getting ready to leave for the day. Barely waiting for me to answer the phone, she snapped, "Jack called me and said his mom got murdered last night. I can't imagine you didn't know about this."

Shit. I'd purposely not contacted her because this conversation was certain to open up a whole can of worms. With me having been initially assigned to the case and knowing and seeing what I had, I couldn't discuss any aspect of it with her, especially before Katie Copland's family had been contacted. I didn't want to be put in that spot. So I'd kept quiet, hoping the case would progress enough as the day went on—and become common knowledge thanks to the media—that I could speak to my sister about it without breaking any rules.

Clearly the family had been notified, but since I'd gotten no word that Marcus had been apprehended, I still had to tread lightly. "I knew."

"And you said nothing to me?"

"I couldn't. I heard about it before the family was contacted. And I can't discuss anything I know with you, regardless. You know the rules."

She exploded, "Screw the rules! Marcus killed her. You know it. I know it. Is he in jail yet?"

I hated this. I said as diplomatically as I could, "I don't know."

"Call Nick and find out."

"It's not fair to put him in the middle of this."

"Then call Jayne."

Our conversation reminded me of the ones Rachel and I had while she was struggling to recover from her kidnapping. When she got nonsensical, there was no reasoning with her. I shifted her focus. "Rach, why do you need to know so badly?"

She suddenly let out a sob. "Because . . . what if I'm next?"

My heart broke for my sweet baby sister. I wanted nothing more than to go straight to her so I could throw my arms around her and comfort her, but I didn't dare. If Marcus was following me, the last thing I'd want was to lead him straight to her.

I said, "Don't think like that. You have your deputy watching out for you, right?"

"What if that's not enough?" she wailed.

I didn't know how to answer. I'd had the same kind of intrusive thoughts. What if Deputy Walters, as thorough as he was, wasn't seasoned enough to react properly in an intense situation? What if Marcus managed to get the drop on him? What if Walters had to resort to shooting at Marcus to keep him from hurting me and missed, leaving me vulnerable?

"I know you're scared. I am, too. You could ask Jayne if you can crash on the couch in her office tonight. No way he could get to you there."

She blew out a breath. "The sheriff's office would be the safest place in the county, that's for sure."

That much was true. I had an idea. "How about I meet you there? I'll bring dinner. I can even show you around if you want. The lab's pretty cool."

She let out a little chuckle. "Labs are not cool, you nerd."

Relief flooded through me upon hearing her make a joke. If camping out at the station made her feel safe, then that's what we were going to do tonight. "Damn. I was going to let you choose dinner, but after that comment, maybe not."

"No biggie. It's your turn to choose, anyway. Do you need anything from home? I forgot my curling iron. I had to resort to a messy bun today."

I replied, "Let me go get it for you. If by chance Marcus is watching, I don't want him seeing you coming and going."

"Oh, yeah. I guess that's true. See you soon."

THE DRIVE with Deputy Walters from campus to my home in Noblesville was no joyride. He might have spoken four words to me as he navigated the rush hour traffic snarling the roadways in Hamilton County. When we finally got to my house, he made sure to do a sweep of the area before allowing me out of his cruiser.

As I was locking up after retrieving Rachel's curling iron, I heard sirens, and they were heading this way fast. A Noblesville PD cruiser and a county sheriff's cruiser sped past my home and pulled to a stop a couple of blocks away behind a county-licensed sedan. I imagined my idiotic neighbors down the street were causing trouble again. Two families who lived next door to each other were always getting into fights. Sometimes it was the dads, sometimes it was the moms, and sometimes it was the kids. Their altercations almost always happened outside where the rest of us had to witness them, often spilling out in the street and blocking traffic. Welfare checks around here were a near-weekly occurrence.

My phone rang as I was getting into Deputy Walters' cruiser. Sterling again. I answered with, "This better not be another—"

"Ellie, we've been looking all day for Marcus Copland, and we . . . finally found him."

Although it worried me to hear Sterling call me by my first name, I focused on the important part of the sentence. "Fantastic. Did you get him to confess?"

"Uh . . . sort of. I'm sorry. I'm . . . Please pass on to Rachel that I tried . . ." He muttered a string of curses under his breath.

I prompted him, "What are you sorry about? And why are you being so weird?"

"Where are you now? Home?"

I had to wait for a screaming ambulance to pass so I could answer him. "Yeah." I'd never remembered an ambulance having to come out for one of my neighbors' epic fights. This one must have been serious.

"I'm headed your way. Stay put." The call ended.

Thoroughly confused, I looked over at Deputy Walters. "Sterling is coming here to pick me up."

Walters frowned. "Why?"

"He wouldn't say, but I guess it has something to do with Marcus Copland. He said he found him, but he wasn't making a lot of sense."

"We should probably wait inside."

I looked past Walters and was shocked to see Sterling jogging toward us from the direction of the growing circus down the block, now complete with neighbors blocking the street to try to see what was going on. "Um, looks like we're not going to have to wait."

Walters followed my gaze and then made another visual sweep of the area. I could tell he didn't like this little wrinkle in our evening plans. As Sterling got close enough for me to see his face, things started clicking into place for me. I didn't like the way the situation was unfolding.

I strode toward Sterling. "What do those first responders have to do with Marcus?"

Sterling stopped in front of me and shook his head. "He's unresponsive, but alive . . . well, barely. Looks like an OD."

"Oh," I replied, unimpressed. Marcus had overdosed twice during the time he'd lived with us. I hadn't cared then, and I didn't care now. I stared down the street. Between the extra vehicles clogging the street and people milling about, it was hard to see what was going on. "Where exactly did you find him? Was he camped out on my street in his vehicle, waiting for me to come home or something?" I shivered at the thought.

Sterling grimaced. "It's a little worse than that. I finally tracked him down to a foreclosed home on your street. Looks like he's been squatting there for a couple of weeks. Probably to keep an eye on you and Rachel."

"What?" I cried, the shiver turning into a full-on tremor that radiated through my body.

He laid a tentative hand on my shoulder. "I'm sure that's not what you wanted to hear, but at least for now there's literally no way he could come after you."

He had a point. Now I didn't have to worry. But that didn't make me any less furious. "I want to see this for myself."

"Fair enough." He led me down the street, Walters on our heels. "The chief took over for Baxter on the Katie Copland case since he was on your mom's case and it's a no-brainer to connect Copland to two dead ex-wives. When the chief and I arrived this evening to question him, we found him passed out in a chair surrounded by drug paraphernalia. He wasn't breathing, but he was hanging on with a weak pulse."

As we got closer, I glimpsed two EMTs wheeling an unconscious Marcus out of one of the houses on a gurney. I couldn't muster up the compassion to feel sorry for him.

Sterling went on quietly. "We tried to help him. We administered Narcan, and it did jack shit. The chief, the deputies, and I took turns performing CPR until the ambulance arrived. Oh, and I called Baxter for you. He's on his way." He said to Walters, "I guess this means you're off duty."

The deputy turned to me, his demeanor as serious as ever. "You're officially in Detective Sterling's care until Detective Baxter gets here?"

I replied, "Yes, and my stalker is pretty well out of commission. I'm good. Thanks for today."

Deputy Walters gave me a curt nod and headed back toward my house.

I could feel Sterling's gaze on me. It occurred to me that I'd never told him much of anything about my relationship with Marcus. He probably didn't realize how much hatred I had for the man. I turned to him. "I appreciate what you did to help Marcus. But if you're worried I'm upset about his condition, don't be. If they can't revive him, I won't lose sleep over it. He's a monster."

Sterling seemed slightly relieved, but still asked, "What about Rachel?"

I shrugged. "She's going to have mixed feelings since he's her bio dad, but she's been doing her best to hide from him for years. Her plan was to spend the night at the station because she's convinced he'd be coming after her next. I'm guessing she won't have to do that now."

We'd arrived at the scene, and Sterling had to bark at the neighbors to get us through to the perimeter. A combination of deputies and city officers had stationed themselves to keep looky-loos back from the dilapidated house, its yard, and the waiting ambulance. I got a look at Marcus as they were loading him into the ambulance. He looked bad. His skin was a ghastly grayish blue, likely from lack of oxygen considering one of the EMTs was pumping air into a manual resuscitator over his mouth and nose.

As they closed the ambulance doors, Chief Esparza walked up to us. "I'm sorry to be the one to break the news, Ellie, but it doesn't look good. I've seen enough overdoses to know that he's not likely to bounce back from this one."

I nodded. "I figured as much. Do you know what he took?"

The chief replied, "Based on what was on the table next to him, a combo of whiskey, heroin, marijuana, and Rohypnol."

I shook my head. What had been the point of him insisting to me he'd given up the hard stuff? Once a liar, always a liar.

Chief Esparza said to Sterling, "I think now would be a good time for a dinner break. I'll have our deputies secure the place. Pending Copland's prognosis, we may have to end up sharing our scene with another team, or at least shifting our focus a bit."

"Yes, Chief," Sterling replied as the chief strode away.

I heard some talking behind me and thought I recognized Baxter's voice. I turned and saw him heading straight for me, concern written all over his face. He caught me in a crushing hug.

"Are you okay?" he asked.

"Other than being pissed off and freaked out about Marcus literally moving in down the street from me," I replied.

"That's what I meant."

I smiled. I knew Baxter would get that Marcus's health was the least of my concerns.

"What did I tell you two about PDA?" Sterling griped.

Baxter and I released each other. I replied innocently, "That you find us adorable and want to see more of it?"

Sterling huffed. "Smartass." At least he was back to normal around me.

As Sterling stalked off, I said, "I have to get to Rachel. She needs to hear this in person."

Baxter put an arm around my waist and steered me toward the dispersing crowd. "Let's go."

~

WE FOUND Rachel in Jayne's office, her face red and blotchy. Jayne sat next to her on the couch, consoling her as the closest thing to a mother we had. When Rachel saw me, she bolted up, flinging herself into my arms. I held her tight, knowing she was anything but okay. I felt bad for being relieved that Jayne had already taken care of breaking the news to her, but I knew the rest of this night wasn't going to get any easier.

I asked my sister, "Would you like to go to the hospital to check on Marcus?"

She raised her head. "I probably should."

It was dead silent in Baxter's SUV as we drove to the hospital. After talking with the chief and seeing Marcus for myself, I couldn't in good conscience assure Rachel that her father was going to be okay. In fact, I didn't expect him to still be alive by the time we arrived.

I let Baxter take the lead at the ER check-in desk and put my focus on comforting my sister. We found out Marcus was still being treated and that the staff needed to confer with his family members. Not a good sign, in my opinion.

When we got to Marcus's room, Rachel wrenched away from me and hurried inside to hug the young man standing at Marcus's bedside. I recognized Jack Copland, her half-brother, who was the spitting image of his mother. My mind flashed back to seeing Katie Copland this morning. I found myself barely able to control my rage as I stared through the doorway at Marcus, who was hooked up to a bunch of tubes and wires. It angered me to think his children wept even a single tear over him, considering he'd brutally murdered both of their mothers.

I must have been exuding more emotion than I thought, because Baxter took my hand and murmured, "Settle down."

An errant tear leaked from one of my eyes. I brushed it away quickly. "Damn Marcus. No one should have to lose both parents in one day."

He squeezed my hand. "I agree."

We stepped out of the way as a doctor headed into the room and shut the door. Through the window, we could see her speaking to the Copland siblings. It couldn't have been good news based on the way they clung to each other. However, I did notice that Rachel was much more in control of her emotions, her focus seeming to be on consoling Jack rather than on herself. She did have the mothering instinct with people, although she hadn't had the strength to empathize quite as much since her kidnapping. I was happy to see that shining through again.

When the doctor left Marcus's room, Rachel came out to speak to us. She cleared her throat. "They ran a test that showed Marcus went without oxygen for too long. He's, um . . . he's brain-dead." I reached out to her, but she shook her head and went on. "As next of kin, Jack and I have to sign the papers to take him off life support."

Baxter said, "Rachel, I'm so sorry."

She shook her head again and took a deep breath. "It's okay. Right now I'm much more concerned about Jack than anything. I can't imagine what he's feeling today."

"What can we do for you?" I asked.

Rachel shrugged. "Leave, I guess. David has Nate, so I'm free for the evening. I thought I'd stay with Jack and make sure he's okay."

I smiled to cover the apprehension I was feeling over her quick emotional turnaround. "That's sweet of you. But . . . are *you* okay?"

When her chin jutted out ever-so-slightly, I knew she wasn't okay and was going to get defensive with me about it. "I'm fine, Ellie."

Baxter said, "We're only a call away if you need us."

"Would you like us to wait until . . . you're ready to go?" I asked. It broke my heart to leave her here to have to take care of this situation *and* feel like she had to be strong for Jack.

She shook her head. "No need. My brother and I need to do this together. Alone."

Baxter gave her a pat on the arm. "Like I said, if you need us, call."

Rachel began walking backward into the room. "Will do."

Baxter steered me away. "She's got this."

I sighed. "I know she's *capable* of handling it. I just hate that she has to. The last thing I want is for her to backslide. She's bottling something up."

"I know. But . . ." He gave me a contrite smile. "Maybe she doesn't want you there for this particular situation since your feelings about her father are so painfully obvious."

I slapped my forehead. "Ugh, you're right. I wouldn't want me here, either. I'm sure she'll talk about it when she's ready. Probably to you."

He squeezed my shoulder. "And I'll be ready to listen."

8

I had to admit I felt a giant weight lifted from my shoulders knowing Marcus would soon be taken off the machines and pronounced dead. I called David to let him know what was going on and to assure him that Rachel was safe staying with her brother. I then texted Jayne to let her know what had happened and how Rachel was holding up. Baxter's phone rang seconds later.

He answered the call, and Jayne's voice came through his vehicle's speakers. "Is Ellie there with you?"

"Yes, you're on speaker with both of us, Sheriff," he replied.

"First, Ellie, how are you?" she asked.

"I'm good. Sad for Rachel but relieved for all of us."

"Same. I realize you two have had a difficult day, but I wanted to offer the Marcus Copland homicide case to you. I only want you to take it if you're up for it, but I'm assuming it's going to be open-and-shut with very limited evidence-gathering and paperwork."

Baxter glanced over at me and raised his eyebrows. I knew he wanted it. Hell, he needed it. And maybe I needed it, too. Maybe processing the scene would give me some closure. It wasn't like Marcus could hurt me anymore. And overdoses were generally a cakewalk. The chief had already told me they'd found more than enough evidence to close the case.

Between that, the record of his hospital care, and the autopsy, it was a no-brainer.

I said, "I'm in."

Baxter said, "Me, too."

Jayne replied, "Good. Detective Baxter, I'll put you on as sole investigator. If you happen to run into a snag, I can have someone step in to help you. And Ellie . . . if you at any time feel like you need to pull back, say the word and I'll assign someone else. Okay?"

"Sounds good," I replied.

"I'll let you get to it, then," she said, ending the call.

Baxter said to me, "Don't hesitate to say something if it's even a little too much for you. You never know when something's going to hit you."

I assured him, "I will," hoping I could hold it together for long enough to put this whole fiasco to bed. I'd do damn near anything to purge Marcus from my life for good and get the closure I needed, even if I had to force it.

AFTER STOPPING by the station to get a field kit for me, we headed to the scene. Baxter parked in my driveway to help keep the street clear. I got out a protective suit and put it on over my clothes. I fully expected to get drug residue all over myself. Whenever Marcus had done drugs in my childhood home, he'd always made a ridiculous mess. Measuring out heroin was a lot like measuring out flour, in that it was difficult to do without the powder dusting every nearby surface. But Marcus took the mess a step further by crushing up (or making me crush up) his Rohypnol pills so he could snort them. This scene would probably bring back some bad memories from my childhood, but I hoped it would be worth it.

Once I had my suit zipped up, Baxter set one of his extra baseball caps on my head and shouldered my field case.

I eyed the case as I pulled my ponytail through the back of the cap and settled it on my head. "You don't have to baby me."

"I'm being a gentleman," he replied.

The two of us walked down my street, as we had nearly every evening during Baxter's recovery for some light exercise. This time was decidedly different. I wanted to kick myself for walking past this house on a regular basis and having no clue Marcus was squatting there. Had he sat inside watching us each night? I felt ill. I glanced over at Baxter, wondering if he was thinking the same thing. He appeared calm and even a little excited, so it was hard to tell. But knowing him, I imagined at some point he'd beat himself up over it, too.

Baxter and I signed the scene entry log and stopped on the porch to put on booties, gloves, and masks. I also got out some goggles and hung them around my neck to use once I began collecting drug samples. Even through my mask, a familiar scent hit me when we walked through the door. I pulled down my mask and inhaled to make sure I hadn't imagined it. Gross. The place smelled like Marcus. He had a particular odor about him that was a combination of the worst aromas—greasy hair, body odor, cigarettes, weed, stale brown liquor, and sweaty, soured clothing. I'd rather work in an enclosed space with the stench of days-old decomp than this.

Sterling approached us with a smirk, eyeing me. At least he was acting normal around me again. "It's usually Baxter who's looking green and pukey at a crime scene instead of you, Matthews."

That much was true. I had an iron stomach immune to pretty much any sight or smell, but with this odor triggering painful memories, I couldn't seem to control my body's reaction.

I replied, "This place smells like ten kinds of ass."

Sterling snorted. "You're not wrong. To bring you up to speed, we came in here earlier and found Copland unresponsive in that chair."

He pointed to a broken-down recliner in the middle of the room. Next to it was a table littered with random items I assumed included drug para-phernalia. It was getting dark outside, and with no electricity in the house, it wasn't easy to see clearly. We'd have to set up lighting in here before we started processing the place.

Baxter turned to me. "Didn't we see that chair on the street somewhere lately?"

I nodded. "A block down. It was at the curb on trash day."

I noticed a flicker of something in Baxter's eye, but he quickly put on his unreadable cop face, which he only used to mask his feelings when he was upset about something.

Sterling went on. "There's everything anyone would need to OD on the table next to him. We didn't move anything since we were pretty sure he wasn't going to make it." He flicked his eyes at me. "Your sister okay with all this?"

I was taken aback by Sterling trotting out his empathy again, but I appreciated the gesture. "She's . . . conflicted. She and her half-brother, Jack, had to give the order to take Marcus off life support."

He shook his head and muttered, "Damn. Jack Copland lost both parents in one day."

"At least he's not alone right now. Rachel is coping by concentrating on taking care of him."

Baxter changed the subject. He said to Sterling, "You said Marcus Copland gave you some sort of confession. How, since he was incapacitated by the time you got here?"

Sterling walked toward the table. He shined his flashlight on a torn piece of paper held in place by a burned heroin spoon. "This."

Written in blue ink, the note said, *I KILLED THEM ALL.*

I sucked in a breath, clamping my jaw as hard as I could to keep from breaking down. When I felt Baxter's hand grip my shoulder, I almost lost it.

Shaking his head, Sterling said, "There's one more thing."

He trained his flashlight on a small, red cooler under the table. *PATTY* was scrawled on the side of it. My mother's name. I felt my stomach lurch.

Sterling said, "Uh, Matthews, maybe you shouldn't . . ." He trailed off, seeming at a loss for words.

I had an awful feeling I already knew what was in the cooler without having to look. Baxter evidently hadn't had the same thought, because he crouched down and lifted the lid, only to recoil and let it slam back down.

Glancing from Baxter to me, Sterling muttered, "I'll let you two have a minute," and disappeared out the front door.

I said quietly, "Nick . . . is it . . . my mom's fingertips?"

Baxter nodded, too horrified to speak.

I choked out, "Just like in my nightmares."

He grabbed me and drew me into a hug. His voice was rough as he said, "Ellie, this particular evidence is not part of our case. You won't have to touch it or look at it or anything. But I totally support you if you want me to call Amanda out here to take over for you."

As I clung to him and focused on letting his presence work its calming magic on me, my thinking began to shift. As jarred as I was by the contents of the cooler, I felt a growing relief. My ongoing quest to find out once and for all who killed my mother had finally come to an end. All I'd ever wanted was for Marcus to confess to what I'd known to be true for years.

I let out the breath I'd been holding and felt a wave of frustration leave with it. I felt lighter than I had in years. I wasn't even angry.

I raised my head so I could look up at Baxter. His expression of worry and horror vanished as he regarded me. "You're . . . okay with this," he said slowly.

I nodded. "I'm more than okay. Marcus finally confessed—with evidence, no less—and he's out of my life for good. Rachel and I will never have to look over our shoulders again. It's over."

"I'm happy to hear you say that, but if processing this scene is going to tarnish that feeling in any way—"

"Nick, I need this."

He smiled at me. "Okay, then I won't leave your side."

I hugged him back hard, for the first time realizing how bright my future could be now that I could quit carrying around all the anger and fear and bitterness I'd let define me for so long. As much as I would have liked to revel in my newfound mindset, it would be in the best interest of our investigation to lock it down and work without letting my feelings cloud the issue. It was so much easier to put a lid on my positive feelings than to try to mash down anxiety or fear or fury.

I took a step back from him. "Let's get this party started."

While Baxter went outside to get Sterling, I retrieved my case from where he'd left it on the porch and brought it inside. I got out the camera and started off by taking some wide-angle shots of the living room, such as it was. The place was empty aside from Marcus's freecycled recliner, table, and several piles of trash and clothing strewn around the room. Had he not crapped it up, the house would have been decent enough. Now, the bank was going to have to pay someone to deep clean it. I'd bet Marcus had invited mice and roaches with all the fast food wrappers and takeout containers he hadn't bothered to throw out. He'd been a pig when he'd lived in my mother's trailer, and it didn't seem he'd changed his ways.

The two detectives returned to the house, but I ignored their conversation and stayed in my zone. I continued photographing the scene, taking plenty of close-ups of the table and the items on and around it. I focused on the evidence that pertained to my case, but my eyes kept wandering. The illegal drugs and paraphernalia were not nearly as interesting as the other items. My mother's fingertips apparently weren't the only trophies Marcus had kept of his kills. An expired driver's license belonging to a redheaded woman named Alice Graves and a fistful of long red hair were sealed in a Ziploc sandwich bag. Next to that sat an old iPhone with a bedazzled pink cover, which I couldn't imagine had ever belonged to Marcus, and a switchblade knife I remembered vividly as belonging to Marcus.

For a moment, the flashback of my encounter with that knife threatened to derail my Zen, but I quickly reframed it, reminding myself he was dead and gone and I was free of him. I continued my work, getting out a stack of evidence markers from my case and setting them next to the various drugs and accessories so I could properly photograph and log the items.

Baxter and Sterling walked toward me and began looking over my shoulder at the items on the table. With them that close, I could no longer tune out their conversation.

Sterling said, "I ran that driver's license for Alice Graves. She was murdered eight years ago down in Indy. Manual strangulation. They never caught her killer."

Baxter murmured, "Guess you have now."

"Matthews, you ever hear of her? Was she a former girlfriend or wife of his?"

I looked up from my evidence log form. "I don't recognize the name, but I never kept track of Marcus's other women. Rachel might know. I can ask her . . . but not tonight."

Sterling replied, "No rush. It's not like our suspect is going anywhere." He immediately backpedaled. "Whoa, sorry. Too soon?"

I smiled. "You're good. That old dirty bastard got what was coming to him. Well, minus the pound-me-in-the-ass prison time he truly deserved, but I'm not going to complain about him burning in hell for eternity."

His eyes bulged out. "Damn. Okay. One more question, then. Any idea who the phone belongs to?"

"Not a clue. But the switchblade is one of his prized possessions. He's had it for at least twenty years."

Baxter shot me a look. I was pretty sure he was wondering if Marcus had used the knife on me.

Hoping it would help both to set his mind at ease and un-demonize my memory of the incident, I said, "Don't worry, he didn't shank me with it. But he did use it to cut three inches off the end of my ponytail when I was ten."

Sterling stared at me. "Because you needed a haircut?"

"Because I ate the last slice of three-day-old pizza when my mother was off on a bender and there was no other food in the house besides Rachel's baby food. He wasn't planning to eat the pizza. He just didn't want me to have it."

While Baxter tried to mask his horror, Sterling let out a low whistle. "Yeah, I'd say he's burning in hell right now." Clapping his hands together, he changed the subject. "Well, I'm out of here. Amanda and Becky will be here soon to process the murder stuff. Have fun without me."

After we said our goodbyes, Baxter said to me, "I'm pretty sure our evidence is all in this room, but do you want me to look through the rest of the house to make sure there's nothing else?"

"That would be great."

While he disappeared into the back of the house, I measured the living room and began a rough sketch of the scene. I'd have to measure and sketch out the whole house regardless of whether there was any evidence in the remaining rooms. Even though this case wouldn't go to trial, we had to treat it like any other homicide until it was closed. Luckily, the house was tiny, so it took me little time to measure each of the rooms and sketch them out.

Baxter exited the kitchen and said, "The back of the house is empty except for a toothbrush, some soap, and a trash bag full of men's clothing in the bathroom. There's nothing in the kitchen besides some rotten food and trash. What's left to do?"

I stowed my sketch pad in my kit and got out some evidence containers, tape, and tags. "Only bagging and tagging the evidence on the table, all of which is covered in drug residue, which means you need to stay far away when I start moving stuff around. Outside would be best. Beat it."

With the sharp spike in the addition of the dangerous synthetic opioid fentanyl to an alarming number of street drugs, especially those in powder form, I had grown to hate handling drug evidence. Inhalation or skin contact with fentanyl could get a non-user high or even cause an acute health issue. I didn't have the time or energy for either.

Baxter said, "I told you I wouldn't leave your side, remember?"

"That's not a valid reason for you to stay in here."

He shook his head. "It is to me, and I think I can be of help. You handle the evidence—the dirty work—and I'll do the bagging and tagging. That way you won't have to change gloves a hundred times and won't run the risk of getting residue on the outside of the evidence containers."

He had a point. It would be safer for me and for anyone entering the scene after me if I had some assistance getting these heroin-dusted items packaged and sealed. "Okay, fine. But suit up first. There's an extra jumpsuit in the bottom of the kit. There should be a second set of goggles, too."

"Yes, ma'am."

9

As Baxter readied himself to assist me, he asked, "Other than the bad parts, how was your day? I can't imagine you enjoyed being followed around by Deputy Walters."

I put on a clean pair of gloves and adjusted my respirator mask. "I did not. Except for getting to have lunch with Sam, I've had an exceptionally shitty day. I got called into Dr. Graham's office so the head of security could yell at me."

"For what?"

I shrugged. "I kind of went off on a rant about the security guard who wouldn't help me apprehend Marcus. A student filmed it. And then the *Ashmore Voice* posted it on their vlog."

Throwing his head back and laughing, he got out his phone. "This, I have to see."

I put on my goggles. "Too late. I convinced Al Nishimura to take it down."

"Damn. But I could probably hit up my buddy Al to send me a copy of the video, right?"

"Considering the man crush he has on you, I'd say your chances are one hundred percent." After Baxter gave Al an exclusive interview regarding one of our cases last year, Al was convinced they were besties.

Chuckling to himself, Baxter sent a quick text and put on a pair of gloves.

Seeing him all suited up to help me reminded me of the first case we'd worked together, where he'd assisted me for hours in a cramped, dirty apartment. I'd taken a liking to him from the moment I'd met him, although it took me a while to admit it even to myself. He barely knew me at the time, but he'd made it his mission to push me to get back into field work. When I quit and ran to the safety of teaching, I never intended to return. Regardless of our relationship, which had had its fair share of ups and downs, he'd been there to encourage me every time I'd second-guessed my decision to consult for the department.

Luckily, my mask hid the goofy smile I was sure I was making. I set my mind back on the task ahead of us and handed him a flattened cardboard box, which he assembled and had for me at the ready. I went for the bottle of Seagram's 7. Evidently Marcus's beer budget tastes hadn't changed. First, I emptied the remainder of the liquor—most of the bottle—into a clean glass evidence jar and screwed the lid on tight. I then carefully placed the empty Seagram's bottle into the box. Baxter sealed the box and the jar shut with red evidence tape, scrawling his initials and the date across the tape. He then filled out evidence tags for both containers with the case number, item number, today's date, my name, and a brief description of the item, noting that there could be drug residue on the bottle.

I said, "I'll bag the Rohypnol blister pack next, if you'd get me a small plastic bag."

Most items we collected, especially anything even slightly wet or damp, were packaged in paper bags, envelopes, or boxes. Evidence often got stuck in storage for months to years before being used in a case. In that time, any moisture inside a plastic bag could cause mold, mildew, rust, or rot, any of which could damage the evidence beyond use. Drugs and their paraphernalia, however, went in sealed plastic bags that provided more protection to anyone handling them.

Baxter held open a small zip-top bag for me, and I dropped the blister pack into it. As he sealed the closure with evidence tape and completed the evidence tag, he mused, "Six missing tablets in the pack. Wonder if he took them all during this incident."

I replied, "I think he used to only take one or two per drug trip. If he took all six, he wasn't dicking around."

We continued collecting our evidence, including a bag of weed, a lighter, the heroin spoon holding the suicide/confession note in place, and a rubber strap Marcus would have used for tying off his injection arm. To package the red glass bong, I had to empty the gross bong water out of it first, collecting the stinky, sludgy liquid in a glass evidence jar. I then packaged the easily breakable bong itself in a cardboard box. As for the used needle, I took special precautions handling and packaging it, not even wanting to imagine the number of diseases Marcus had managed to contract over the years. I'd saved the heroin itself for last, in case I happened to spill some on the other evidence while collecting it.

I took a moment to regroup and steady my hands before diving in. Needing a release for my anxiety, I gestured to the busted balloon with a powder resembling dirty flour spilling out of it and joked, "Eww. You think this thing has been up Marcus's asshole?"

Baxter made a gagging noise. "Gross, and no. He's a dealer, not a mule."

I chuckled. "Oh, yeah."

He eyed me. "I thought I'd missed your gallows humor. Turns out I didn't."

I nodded slowly. "Hmm. If that's true, then were you lying to me this morning when you professed your love for me for coming up with the first gallows joke of the case?"

"Maybe I misspoke."

"Which time?"

He snorted. "You've learned interrogation tactics too well. I'm pleading the fifth."

Feeling sufficiently calmed down, I smiled and said, "Let's get back to work, then." I stopped to think for a moment about how I planned to collect the heroin and its less-than-sanitary packaging. "I'm going to need a medium-sized plastic bag and a medium-sized manila envelope."

He handed me the envelope and readied the bag by turning the opening inside-out so no powder could spill onto the outside of the bag. I slid the closed envelope, which I chose for its rigidity and sharp edge, under the open end of the drug-filled balloon and steadied the balloon itself with my free hand. I then carefully picked up the whole mess and deposited it neatly into Baxter's waiting bag without even a speck of errant powder escaping.

He quickly sealed the bag and wrote *BIOHAZARD* on it in big letters. When I let out a snicker, he conceded, "Odds are good the balloon was in *someone's* asshole at some point."

I carefully removed my gloves and disposed of them in a special trash bag, then I put on a fresh pair. "I think we're done, right? Normally I'd collect the suicide note, but I feel like this particular note is going to be huge in the other case."

"Yeah, Sterling would kill you if you tried to take it."

Amanda appeared in the doorway, all suited up and ready to work. "Knock, knock. You guys doing okay?" Her tone was light, but I could hear the concern lacing her voice as she approached us. I was sure Sterling clued her in to what was going on with me.

I nodded. "Yeah, just finishing up. We'll be out of your hair in no time."

Beck Durant, the county's head criminalist, who'd taken over my job when I quit, barged through the door behind her. He had no protective gear on at all. Idiot. "Amanda, we're not done with our discussion. Just because you already arbitrarily assigned yourself as lead on this morning's case doesn't mean you get to be lead on this case, whether they're related or not."

Beck had been my assistant when I'd had his job. He was completely useless, especially in a crime scene, where his lack of attention to detail turned him into an absolute liability. I always had to follow behind him and look for evidence he missed. Unfortunately, now he was not only Amanda's problem, but also her superior, so she had to tread lightly around him. I didn't.

I said, "She didn't arbitrarily assign herself as lead on this morning's case. I purposely assigned her as lead. If you want what's best for the department, you'll assign her as lead on this case as well. If you want to be a bitch about it, by all means, take the lead yourself."

I heard Baxter cough to cover up a laugh as Beck's face got all red, like it always did when he got upset. Beck complained, "I'm the head criminalist. I'm in charge."

I nodded. "Going the bitch route, then?" When he only growled at me in response, I added, "Well, if you're the lead, you should be the one to collect the most delicate piece of evidence."

"And what might that be?" he asked, crossing his arms and puffing himself up to appear bigger than his tiny frame.

I pointed to the cooler. "That cooler full of my mother's fingertips. You're going to have to work fast and smart to keep them from decomposing any more than I'm sure they already have." I approached him, letting some menace creep into my tone. "And if you screw this up and somehow manage to ruin key evidence in my mother's unsolved murder case, I will come after you."

Beck's haughty smirk faded as I spoke. He didn't have the strongest of stomachs. Between his squeamishness and lack of attention to detail, I didn't know why he'd chosen a career in criminalistics in the first place. Maybe it was because he knew he could count on his mommy to get him a job in law enforcement and use her political ties to ensure he kept the job whether he was good at it or not.

After staring at me like a deer in headlights for a good five seconds, he snapped, "Amanda, I'm assigning you as lead on this case. Get that cooler collected first and send it to the station with a deputy."

"I'm on it," she replied, giving me a wink.

Baxter and I gathered our things and exited the house. We then stripped off our gear and bagged it for disposal, replacing our gloves to protect our hands as we carted everything away. As we stepped onto the sidewalk, the chief pulled Baxter aside. While I waited for them to finish their conversation, I found myself staring at the house. I couldn't believe Marcus had been living only a few houses down from me and I'd been none the wiser. No wonder he'd lost it when I lied and said Rachel didn't live with me. He'd undoubtedly seen her coming and going from our home with his own eyes. And that meant he'd seen Nate. I shivered but quickly shook it off, secure in the knowledge that Marcus was dead and could never lay a finger on my precious nephew. Who knew what kind of destruction he could have wreaked on my family if he hadn't decided to take his own life? I didn't even want to think about the possibilities his evil mind could cook up.

My gaze landed on a vehicle covered with a dirty blue plastic tarp sitting under a freestanding carport. Something triggered in my memory. Sterling had mentioned they'd run Marcus's vehicle registration—which had been for a truck. Although fully covered by the tarp, the vehicle was clearly car-shaped. I didn't imagine the former owners of this home would have left a car here. I walked closer and went around to the front of the vehicle. The tarp was hitched up enough that the dented front bumper was exposed. The driver's side wheel well and front quarter panel were covered with dark splotches that looked a lot like blood.

"Sterling!" I yelled.

Sterling halted his conversation with one of the deputies to look my way and make a face. "What? I'm busy."

"Too busy to take a look at the car that ran over Katie Copland?"

His eyes nearly bugged out of his head. He hurried toward me. "How in the hell do you know . . ." He took one look at the blood-spattered bumper and said, "Oh. I see. Even more fuel for our fire. I honestly wish that son of a bitch had pulled through so I could have the pleasure of nailing his ass to the wall."

I shook my head. "Trust me, we're all better off with him dead."

ON THE SHORT ride to the station, my mind was reeling over the sheer volume of evidence Marcus had left behind. It struck me that he'd brought little to town with him besides a bag of clothes, his knife, his drugs, and his murder trophies. Maybe he'd left some things in his vehicle. I texted Sterling to ask if there was still a BOLO out for Marcus's truck now that he was dead. Sterling's reply was, *Yes, I'm not stupid.* Well, that cleared that up. As I continued down my rabbit hole, I wracked my brain for what I remembered about him from living with him all those years.

I snapped my fingers. "I finally figured out what was missing from that scene."

Baxter glanced over at me and joked, "Good choices?"

I laughed. "Definitely. But I meant I didn't see Marcus's lucky two-dollar bill."

"Not following."

"He always used it to snort stuff. Like the roofies he used to boost his heroin high. Or coke when he was in a festive mood. He liked to keep it on our coffee table so it was always at the ready, but after the time I'd had to stop toddler Rachel from putting the nasty thing in her mouth, I started relocating it to higher ground. Which of course got me slapped a few times before stupid Marcus got it through his head that drug residue could kill his daughter and started keeping his paraphernalia in a safer spot."

He shook his head. "I don't think your sister would have survived childhood without you."

"Possibly not." I frowned. "Speaking of drug paraphernalia, there was also no mirror or credit card to line the powder up for snorting. Come to think of it, no powder residue from the Rohypnol anywhere, either."

"Then he must have swallowed the pills whole." He thought for a moment. "Why snort roofies, anyway? I mean, sure, snorting drugs makes them kick in a little faster, but the potency wouldn't be affected. And snorting is hell on the nose."

"Roofies give Marcus a tummy ache."

"Oh." He shrugged. "Maybe this time he didn't care, since he was planning to die anyway."

I considered that idea but wasn't convinced. "He was such a little bitch, though. I don't think he'd run the risk of even a little stomach pain from the roofies while waiting for everything to work its magic."

"Where are you going with this?"

"I don't know. It feels off that he would change his habits. But then again, I haven't been around him in over a decade. Things change."

Baxter reached across the console to take my hand. "If this is still bothering you once we've gathered all our evidence, I'll help you get to the bottom of it before we close the case. Deal?"

I smiled. "Deal."

~

WHEN WE GOT to the station, Baxter insisted I go to the breakroom and decompress while he checked in our evidence and spent a little time following up on his porch piracy case. I did as instructed, not completely loving the mothering/smothering thing he'd been doing ever since we'd found out Marcus was back in town. Granted, I was a complete wreck and probably needed as much moral support as I could get. I shouldn't have faulted him for being the supportive boyfriend he always was, but I felt like I dealt with things better if given a minimal amount of coddling.

Speaking of supportive people in my life, I figured it was only a matter of time before Vic caught wind of all that had happened tonight and started calling me and demanding answers. If I was lucky, once he knew Marcus was dead, he'd quit worrying about my safety and be more interested in discussing the case than my feelings. I knew he'd appreciate me breaking the latest news on Marcus personally this time.

When I called Vic, he answered with, "Hey, how's it going? Did Marcus ever turn up?"

"It's been a day, and Marcus turned up, all right. He's dead from an OD, and Baxter and I got put on his homicide case."

"Damn, you have had a day."

"But wait, there's more. When we processed the scene, we found he'd left a note confessing to killing my mother and some other women . . . right next to my mother's fingertips that he'd cut off and various trophies from his other kills."

After a moment of hesitation, he whistled. "Holy shit. That's a lot. You okay?"

"I'm getting there." I sighed. "But there is something bugging me, and I need your beautiful mind."

"My beautiful mind is blown at the moment, but I'll certainly try."

"Riddle me this . . . Marcus has always used roofies to boost his heroin high. As far as I know, he never swallowed them—he crushed and snorted them instead—because they hurt his stomach. Pretty violently, if I recall. So why, when he's overdosing on them and probably taking way more than usual, did I find no evidence of him snorting them this time?"

Vic paused a moment before answering, "If he's going to die anyway, what's a little stomach discomfort?"

I frowned. "That's what Baxter said."

"Great minds." When I didn't reply, Vic added, "Why do you care? He's dead. You should be leading a parade through the streets or something."

I huffed out a snicker. "I suppose so."

"Something else bugging you about the case?"

"Kind of. When he came to my house last night and insisted I help him clear his name to get the mysterious people off his back, he made it a point to tell me how he'd quit using hard drugs. I could tell he still drank and smoked weed—I could smell both on him, and his mind was even duller than before. So why OD on 'the hard stuff' after supposedly getting off it?"

"Well, he's a coward, right? Serial abusers generally are."

Nodding to myself, I said, "He was nothing if not a coward."

"So he took the easier way out. The act of killing oneself with a weapon or by a fall takes some real determination in the moment. You can sometimes back out of an OD—make yourself vomit, call 911—if you change your mind. He probably assumed that a lethal amount of drugs would mask most of the pain of death or knock him out so he faded away peacefully. The act of snorting Rohypnol would cause some acute pain, so maybe he opted for swallowing the pills whole, hoping he'd be unconscious by the time his stomach got irritated. He also didn't have to worry about waking up to any consequences, so maybe that was a good enough reason to risk it."

I let out the breath I didn't know I'd been holding. "Oh. I didn't think of it that way."

Marcus was stupid as hell, but he was an experienced drug addict. He knew what and how much to take to get the kind of high he wanted, and I rarely saw him nursing a hangover. He didn't like lingering consequences, hence the snorting of the roofies. But consequences didn't matter to a dead man.

I could hear the smile in Vic's voice. "Take the win. You're used to having this crazy weight on your shoulders, so I'm sure it's not easy to let it go. But it's time. The universe owes you and Rachel some easier days."

I laughed. "It certainly does."

"Get some rest. I'll check in on you tomorrow."

As I ended the call, Baxter stuck his head in the doorway. "Time for the coroner's meeting."

Rest would have to wait.

10

Baxter and I met Dr. Berg in the morgue, which exuded its usual somber stillness. I was happy to see that our often-angry district attorney Wade McAlister didn't bother to show—he didn't waste his time on homicides that weren't going to trial. Not having to deal with him was good, considering how unnerving it was going to be to have to stand there and participate in a professional discussion over Marcus's lifeless body lying on the slab. Thankfully, it was covered head-to-toe in a crisp white sheet, at least for now.

I still didn't have my head wrapped around Marcus's death. Without his body at the scene, it had been easy enough to process it and keep my cool. I didn't know how I'd fare during this meeting, but luckily they were usually short and sweet.

Dr. Berg said, "Hello, again." He studied me for a moment. "From what I've gathered, Ellie, you weren't close with the deceased, but please offer my condolences to Rachel."

I tried to smile, but I didn't quite make it. "Thank you, Dr. Berg. I will."

"Let's begin. The autopsy for Marcus Copland will begin at nine o'clock tomorrow morning. Detective Baxter, I'll see you there."

Baxter nodded.

Dr. Berg went on. "I've determined the preliminary cause of death to be cardiac arrest. The hospital's drug analysis showed benzodiazepines, cannabis, and opioids in the deceased's system, along with a blood alcohol level of .15. These results are consistent with the investigators' incident report. However, I am also performing a full toxicology screen for my own report." He hesitated and looked my way. "I did notice something inconsistent with the fact that the deceased's alleged drug of choice was heroin." He pulled back the sheet from Marcus's left arm and raised it so we could see its underside. "Other than this single track mark, which was made not long antemortem, the deceased presents no skin irritation, infection, or abscesses. There is some old scarring—in my estimation, years-old—but no skin lesions that might suggest current or ongoing intravenous heroin use. The toxicity screening can substantiate my hypothesis, but as you know, it won't be completed for some time."

I flicked a look at Baxter, whose eyes were already on me. Marcus must have been telling the truth about his drug use, but that didn't negate the fact that when the going got tough, he slipped back into his old habits. I guessed it made sense—once an addict, always an addict. This whole situation had me unsettled. I'd forgotten what life around Marcus Copland was like. You never knew what gut punch was coming next that would upend your world.

When neither of us replied, Dr. Berg went on. "I've sent the deceased's clothing and personal effects to the station. Do either of you have questions for me?"

I didn't want to hear another word about Marcus. I shook my head.

Baxter replied, "I'm good."

We removed our protective gear and headed back to the station in silence. I figured I was radiating the vibe that I didn't want to dissect Dr. Berg's information, which was what we normally did on the ride back. I hated to feel this way about a case, but I just didn't have the capacity to care anymore.

Unfortunately, once we got back to the station, we had to meet with Jayne for the requisite initial meeting to brief her on our progress. Since it was only the three of us, we went to her office rather than meeting formally in the conference room.

After taking one look at me, she said, "We're going to keep this short and sweet, and you're both going to go home and get some rest."

I smiled. Jayne always knew what I needed.

She said, "First, have you heard from Rachel since we last spoke? Is she doing okay now that she's had a little time to process things?"

Shaking my head, I replied, "No. I'm trying to give her some space from me."

"Fair enough." She consulted her notepad. "I thought you both might want to know that the vehicle you found tonight is very likely the one used in Katie Copland's homicide. Ms. Carmack found blood matching the victim's type on the front bumper. The vehicle was reported stolen yesterday."

I nodded slowly. Everything was falling into place, but I still couldn't feel good about any of it.

Baxter filled Jayne in on everything we found at the scene and what Dr. Berg had told us at the morgue. I had to admit I only half-listened, and I was sure both of them knew it.

When he was finished, Jayne finally said, "Ellie, I know it's been a difficult day, and I appreciate your willingness to power through and work the case. Let's get you rested up and we'll talk tomorrow, okay?"

I stood from my chair, feeling a partial sense of relief now that this day was over. "Sounds good."

I CALLED Rachel on the way to Baxter's home, but got no answer from her. I hoped she wasn't still upset with me over my feelings toward her father. It wasn't like she didn't know why I felt the way I did, but it had to have been disconcerting for Rachel that her own sister didn't care that her father had died. I cared how his death affected her, of course, and she knew that, but my feelings made me the least empathetic choice to offer her comfort. I left a message and then also texted her, asking that she at least let me know she was somewhere safe. She replied back immediately that she and Jack were at his house looking through his mother's old photo albums.

After pulling into his driveway, Baxter reached over and wiped a tear from my cheek I hadn't felt fall. "Rachel okay?"

I sighed. "I guess. She and Jack are looking through old photos. I can't imagine the day he's having."

His face was stuck in a worried frown. "I wouldn't sell short what you've gone through over the past few days." After a slight hesitation, he continued. "I've been debating whether I should tell you this tonight or not, but I figured you wouldn't appreciate me keeping information from you."

I didn't know if I could take much more, but he wasn't wrong. I simply nodded.

He said gently, "Amanda made it a point to check the prints on the fingertips in the cooler first. She said to tell you they definitely belong to your mother."

I nodded again, figuring I couldn't hold it together if I spoke.

"Between that and the confession note. . . I feel like there's probably going to be enough evidence to close your mother's case."

My breath hitched in my throat. I'd felt a sense of victory having laid eyes on Marcus's suicide/confession note and his collection of morbid trophies, having my suspicions finally confirmed. I hadn't continued the thought of what it meant in terms of justice being served. My mother's cold case finally being closed after years of limbo was huge for Rachel and me. At the moment, I was too spent to wrap my mind around it and feel a full sense of resolution.

He grabbed my hand. "I don't know how you managed to do what you did today."

I did. I was able to give him a genuine smile. "I have some really great support."

He smiled back. "Let's get you some rest."

～

THE NEXT MORNING, Baxter shook me awake. "You need to see this."

I opened one eye and saw him standing next to the bed, his attention focused on the TV on his dresser. I followed his gaze and saw footage of Beck carrying an evidence tote out of the house where Marcus had been found. "I don't need or want to see Beck's ugly mug, especially at the ass crack of dawn."

"It's eight-thirty," he pointed out.

"Still."

"Just listen."

I caught the WIND-TV Channel 7 morning news anchor mid-sentence. ". . . found at the scene, the most gruesome of all being the severed fingertips of a cold case murder victim. The license, phone, and fingertips have all been able to be tied to women who were either married to or involved with Marcus Copland over the past couple of decades."

I bolted upright. "What the hell? Who blabbed?"

"I don't know," Baxter replied, his face stuck in a worried scowl.

The anchor went on. "Area residents shouldn't fear for their safety. Alleged serial killer Marcus Copland died last night of an apparent self-inflicted drug overdose. His final words to the world were a haunting written message: 'I killed them all.' Our exclusive coverage of this explosive story continues after the break."

I growled. "I've seen enough."

Baxter turned off the TV. "This is bad."

"You think?" I grabbed my forehead, which was already throbbing. Not a good sign for the rest of my day. "It's obvious who the license belonged to. We know Amanda verified my mother's prints last night. But do we think the phone belonged to yet another of his victims, like the news suggested?"

"That's the general consensus."

"Have they figured out who yet? I mean, if Marcus kept it for years, the service plan is long expired. They'd have to get a warrant *and* get the carrier to cough up old information. Have they had that kind of time?"

"That's not the problem. The phone's screen is busted all to hell and the SIM card is suspiciously missing. It's kind of a brick unless the tech guys can work actual magic on it." He shook his head. "For that fact alone, it shouldn't have been mentioned to the press. Plus the autopsy isn't for another thirty minutes, so we have no official cause of death yet. I've got a bad feeling someone's getting fired today, and my money's on your buddy Walters."

My jaw dropped. "No freaking way."

Baxter nodded. "It's his first time riding solo. He's green. You noticed it."

"Yeah, but surely it wasn't him. He's such a stickler for the rules."

"On duty, yes. But sometimes it takes deputies a minute to figure out how to decompress in a healthy way. Reporters love to follow newbies to their favorite bar, get them all liquored up, and trick them into spilling their guts."

"That's frightening."

"It's also how bullshit stories like this one originate." He looked at his phone and frowned. "And since I'm lead on the Marcus Copland homicide, I'm already being inundated with calls, texts, and emails. I plan to ignore them as long as I can."

I grabbed his hand. "Sorry. Anything I can do?"

He leaned over and planted a kiss on top of my head. "Use the back door to the station so you don't get waylaid by the press. We all know how you come off on camera sometimes."

"Hardy-har-har, Baxter."

AFTER I AGREED to take Marcus's case, I'd contacted Talia to get her set up to take over my classes for today. I knew I wouldn't be at one hundred percent, plus I wanted to be available for Rachel. When I texted my sister and offered to meet her for coffee this morning, she replied that she and Jack would be busy making arrangements for both parents' funerals. I held my tongue, or rather my fingers, from replying that I couldn't imagine anyone wanting to attend a funeral for Marcus, especially now that he was a newly branded serial killer. I assumed she hadn't seen the news coverage yet, and I wasn't going to be the one to point her to it.

Baxter had been right about using the back door to the station. I managed to slip past the crush of reporters and camera operators lining the sidewalk at the front entrance. As I entered the building, I got a call from Vic.

When I answered, he said, "Will you be at the station this morning?"

"Yep, just got here."

"Do me a favor. Go to the conference room."

I turned a corner to head that way. "Why?"

He chuckled. "Why do you always have to ask so many questions?"

Frowning, I replied, "I'll warn you, my fuse is already short this morning."

"Right. I saw the news. Who's the snitch?"

"Hell if I know."

I walked into the open conference room to find Vic in the flesh. He was dressed in one of his sharp G-man suits, pawing through a stack of files. "Hey," I said in person, ending our phone call.

He looked up when I entered the room and hung up his phone. Throwing his arms out wide, he announced, "I'm back, baby!"

I chuckled and went over to give him a hug. But when I got close enough to see the names on the files, I shrank back. "Oh. You're back for . . ."

Vic's face fell. "I thought you'd be more psyched about me leading a multi-agency task force to nail Marcus Copland's dead-but-still-sorry ass to the wall."

Smiling, I said, "I am. I just . . . I've been so mired in how this whole mess has affected me and my sister, I haven't given much thought to the bigger picture. Marcus managed to leave the county a true-crime podcast's worth of shit to deal with, and now the Feds are involved?"

He nodded. "Given the trophies left behind, we're definitely veering into serial killer territory, plus at least one of the homicide cases crossed county lines. So, here I am."

"Lucky for us, you're the one Fed no one minds working with."

"Does that mean you'd like to work with me?"

"I do like to work with you. But if you're asking if I'd like to work with you on this investigation specifically, it's a hard no."

Vic frowned. "Oh, come on, Ellie. You know you won't be able to put this behind you until you find out every detail of what happened."

I shrugged. "Eh. There are a lot of details I've learned over the past couple of days I'd like to forget."

Giving me a friendly pat on the back, he relented and backed off. "I don't blame you. You'll get no more peer pressure from me to join the team."

"Thank you. Now I've got to go deal with the details for just a little longer while I wrap up my paperwork, and then I'm officially done with Marcus Copland. Forever."

11

I worked on my scene notes and other reports at Baxter's desk, then moved the party to the lab office to complete a professional-looking final sketch of the scene with the use of a CAD program. The lab was quiet this morning. I assumed Amanda and Beck had worked well into last night to get a jump on processing some of the more pertinent evidence. I put off processing any physical evidence, hoping there wouldn't be a revelation at the autopsy to prompt further investigation into Marcus's death. After finishing up the last of my clerical tasks, I returned to Baxter's desk to gather my things and found him just arriving.

"Hey," he said, still the slightest bit pale from being cooped up in a morgue with an open body cavity all morning. As much as Marcus stunk on the outside, I couldn't imagine he smelled any better on the inside.

"Looks like you had fun at the autopsy," I joked.

"You know it," he said with a groan as he dropped into his chair. He looked up at me with that worried expression again. "I learned a couple of interesting things. Marcus was in fact telling the truth about his drug use. Dr. Berg found no collapsed or scarred veins, a healthy enough heart, and no irritation in the nasal cavity. If he was using, it wasn't anything he injected or snorted. He did have significant lung damage and his liver was shot, but you said he was a smoker and an alcoholic. Dr. Berg saw some chalky drug residue in his stomach. He'll get back to us later today on stomach contents."

So Marcus had told me one truth. Not sure why he bothered. Not sure that I cared about it enough to give it any more thought. I shrugged. "Cool, whatever. So did you hear Vic's assembling a task force to investigate Marcus's many sins?"

Baxter nodded, still eying me. "He asked me to be on it. Will you be okay if I—?"

I winced and cut him off. "I never want you to think you have to ask me for permission to do your job."

"I'm not."

"You literally just did."

"I meant . . ." He sighed. "Manetti told me you don't want any part of it. I didn't know if you had a reason other than wanting to get on with your life, and I didn't want to agree to anything that might stand in the way of that before I spoke to you."

Tears sprang to my eyes at his unending kindness toward me. "Thank you for putting me first. I told Vic no because I don't want to give this situation any more of my time and energy, but I absolutely think you should be part of the task force if you want to. And I'll be happy to help you if you need any insight or information I might have. I just don't want to be in the trenches this time."

"I think that's a good idea." He stood. "I'll let Manetti know."

"I'm heading out. I'm finished on my end unless there's a development in Marcus's homicide case that would require a full process of his evidence for further information."

Baxter's face fell. "Oh. Well, then I guess I'll see you . . . sometime?"

We'd been used to spending practically every waking moment together during his recovery time, and since he'd gone back to work, we'd still been together a lot between him protecting me from Marcus and us investigating together again. I knew he was bummed our case was over so quickly.

I took his hand. "Being back on the job with you was fun, and I'll miss getting to spend so much time with you. But I think I'm really going to enjoy my new-and-improved normal. Rachel and I have some fear-free living to do, starting right now."

He squeezed my hand. "You both deserve it."

I COLLECTED my nephew and my dog from David's house, got them their favorite treats (a chocolate chip cookie and a pup cup) and lunch, and took them home for some outdoor playtime in our backyard. We ran and wrestled and played until the three of us collapsed on the grass in a heap, enjoying the perfect combination of autumn sun and cool breeze. Aside from the day Nate was born and the minute I knew Baxter was going to pull through from his gunshot wound, I couldn't remember being so happy and at peace. All was right with the world.

When Rachel stepped onto the patio, Nate and Trixie raced to get to her first. Trixie was faster, but after greeting the dog with a quick head scratch, Rachel scooped her little boy into her arms and held him close. My throat tightened at the sight of them. We were all going to be okay. We'd never have to worry again about Nate running across Marcus. The only monsters in his life would be silly ones in cartoons.

Rachel set Nate back onto the ground, and he ran to happily play with his dog again. To my surprise, my sister launched herself into my arms. She whispered into my neck, "It's over." I held her as tightly as she'd held her son, feeling like I was finally in a good enough place that I could help her heal. Before I could say anything, she pulled back from me and wiped a hand across her face. She never wanted Nate to see her upset, but after the year she'd had, it had been hard to hide it from him. He'd noticed her distress on occasion, and we'd tried our best to use it to teach him it was normal for everyone to be sad sometimes.

She said, "I guess you've seen the news."

I nodded. "I have. I'm sorry . . . it can't be easy for you and Jack to stomach on top of everything else."

"It's not, but at least my connection to Marcus isn't public knowledge. Jack had to leave town. He went to go stay with a friend in Muncie."

"Poor guy. Is his health okay enough to do that?"

"Not really. I made sure he ate and took his medication, but he couldn't sleep. Maybe being away from the situation for a night or two will help."

"I hope so." I studied her face, which was drawn and pale, like she hadn't slept herself. "How are you feeling?"

She shrugged and dropped into one of our patio chairs. "Like I've been run over by a truck." She looked up at me. "Do you believe the news?"

Again, I couldn't share case details, but the fact that the news was still running the story with no retractions meant the department wasn't contesting their claims. And that meant I could talk about anything that had been said on the news.

I said, as diplomatically as I could, "The news mentioned items found at the scene . . . and their list is accurate. Those items are pretty damning evidence."

Barely above a whisper, she asked, "Did you see Mom's . . ."

"I didn't look."

"Good." Her pretty face twisted into a sad frown. "I guess what I'm getting at is . . . you know when Marcus told you someone was trying to pin Mom's murder on him? Do you think there's any truth to that? I mean, after what you saw last night?"

I let out a hard sigh. "Before last night, sort of. Now, not so much. There was a time I'd started to believe he was telling some form of the truth. I figured he was involved in our mother's death but . . . maybe hadn't done the actual deed. My goal was to get him to give up whatever he was holding back about himself in the process of trying to throw someone else under the bus."

"I just . . ." She glanced over at Nate, who was giggling as Trixie gave him a sloppy doggy kiss on the cheek, and lowered her voice. "I don't want him to be guilty. My DNA combo is bad enough without my father being a serial killer."

I took her hand. "That's not genetic, Rach. The increased possibility of substance abuse, yes, but not the predisposition to be a monster. For what it's worth, I don't want him to be guilty, either."

"You don't? But the reason you hate him so much is because you believe he killed Mom."

I closed my eyes. It was time to come clean with her. Clearing my throat, I announced, "Nate, naptime!"

"Aww," Nate whined, the corners of his mouth drooping downward.

I replied, "I'll make you your favorite dinner if you go without complaining." His favorite dinner was chicken nuggets and mac and cheese, not exactly a difficult culinary undertaking. I was already planning on making it, anyway.

His eyes got wide. "Okay!" He whizzed past us and disappeared into the house.

Once we were alone, I turned to my sister. "Rach, the reason I hate Marcus has nothing to do with Mom."

She seemed confused. "I know he was always super shitty to you and you guys butted heads constantly when we all lived together. He was never a good stepdad to you, but you and I have both had worse."

I blew out a breath. "No, that's not true. He hid his true self from you."

"He hit Mom in front of me, and he yelled at both of us all the time. You, especially. Hell, he did drugs in front of us. What was there to hide?"

"He abused me, Rachel. You were too little to know what was going on or to remember for a lot of it."

Her eyes grew wide. "What did he do to you?"

"He hit me and kicked me. He'd lock me out of the house and tell Mom I stayed out all night whoring around." Gritting my teeth, I lifted the hem of my shirt and showed her my scar. "He put out a lit cigarette on me."

Horror evident on her face, she cried, "He did that? You told me it was a chicken pox scar."

"I told everyone that. He said if I told anyone the truth, including you, that everything he did to me . . . he'd do it all to you, too."

My sister's eyes filled with tears as she stared at me. "You took all this abuse and kept it hidden all this time . . . for me?"

I shrugged. "There was no reason for us both to have to go through it."

Clasping my hands, she said, "You could have told a teacher and got the police after him."

"All that would have accomplished was for me to be taken away from you." I smiled. "You were the only person in the world I loved, and the only person in the world who loved me. I wasn't going to give that up for anything."

She grabbed me and hugged me with all her might. She held me, sobbing, for several minutes. When she finally let me go, she whispered,

"Now I get it. And now I'm glad he's dead, and I'm glad I got to be the one to pull his plug."

My phone buzzed on the table, but I ignored it. "I didn't tell you this so you'd hate him, too. I told you because I think you deserve to know the truth." I frowned. "And given the scope of this investigation into the murders, I'm sure his life—and probably ours—is going to be picked apart piece by piece. Vic and Baxter are on the task force, so you know they're going to come to us for answers. We probably know things about these women we don't even realize. You especially, if Marcus had any amount of custody of you while he was with them."

She eyed me. "Are you not on this task force?"

"No. I declined Vic's offer."

"Why? You've wanted for years to run across some kind of proof that Marcus killed our mom. Now you have the chance to be part of the team that puts the whole puzzle together, and you turn it down?"

Shrugging, I replied, "Marcus is already dead. It's not like me being on the task force will make a difference in his punishment."

"Ellie, I know you. And I know that working through a case—especially a personal one—is the one thing that can give you some serious closure. You still need it with Marcus. I can see it in your eyes. Sure, he's dead, and you know that. But to really put him to rest, I think you're going to have to do this."

Sometimes my little sister was so insightful, I felt like the younger one. I smiled at her. "Vic said the exact same thing. You really think I need to make this all about me?"

She smiled back. "Agreeing to consult on a case is not making it about you, even if you get some psychological benefit out of it. Besides, Vic asked you to be on his team because you're the best at what you do, not out of pity because he thinks you need fixing."

"Okay, but do I really want to know all the dirty details about Marcus? Will I be able to sleep at night?"

"Again, he's dead, so he's no longer a threat you should lose sleep over. Could you really hate him more than you already do? I seriously doubt it."

"Fair point."

She took my hands again. "If there's even a slight chance he was telling the truth about someone setting him up, don't you want to get to the bottom of it? And if he actually didn't kill Mom, don't you want to figure out who did? Or if he did and had help, who's out there running around unpunished? I want to know all of that, Ellie. At this point, I don't care if the news is good or bad. I just want the whole truth. And I know you want that, too." She glanced over at the table. My phone was buzzing again. "You gonna get that?"

I hadn't wanted to ruin our discussion, but I'd noticed Baxter had called a couple of times. Multiple calls meant it was something important. I assured Rachel, "I'll be quick, I promise," and picked up the call before he got my voicemail again. "Hey."

"Hey," Baxter replied, his tone tentative.

"You okay?" I asked, my automatic response of worry taking over.

"I'm fine . . . I, uh . . . may have some news."

"Well, spit it out," I replied, a little more tersely than I'd intended.

"With joining the task force, I'm back in the loop for the Katie Copland investigation. They were able to pinpoint her TOD at 8:45 p.m. The office's security system logged the time she'd set the alarm upon leaving. Do you remember exactly what time Marcus was at your place that night?"

"No, but I can figure it out. Hang on a sec." I switched over to view the recent call list on my phone. My jaw dropped as I noted the time I'd placed my 911 call. "Uh . . . he was standing on my doorstep at 8:38."

"That's what I thought. Which means—"

I looked at Rachel. "Marcus didn't kill Katie Copland."

12

Rachel gasped. "Are you sure?"

Nodding, I replied to both her and Baxter, "There's no way he could have made a thirty-minute drive in seven minutes. He didn't kill her."

While Rachel sat quietly processing this, Baxter said, "That's the timeframe I thought it was, but I wanted to verify it with you before taking it to the task force. This is going to turn the investigation on its ear."

The news had certainly thrown me for a loop. "I guess they'll have to separate the Katie Copland case back out . . . and if Marcus is no longer a suspect, I could step back in and work on that case. I'm sure the task force has the criminalists tied up, so another set of hands wouldn't hurt."

"True, but I've got a gut feeling it's become a little more complex than that. The more I think about the evidence we saw belonging to Marcus's alleged murder victims all laid out next to him with a confession note, plus the vehicle that killed Katie conveniently sitting out in the open . . ." He blew out a breath. "I don't like it. It's all too neat. Too tidy."

"What are you saying?" I asked, again getting that nagging sensation I'd kept having last night.

"I'm saying I'm beginning to believe Marcus's story about being set up for your mother's murder and possibly the others as well." He hesitated.

"And I think you're thinking it, too. Yesterday you couldn't quite put your finger on it, but I know you believed something was off about his overdose. Maybe because there *is* something off about it."

I didn't want to believe Marcus could be innocent of anything, especially killing my mother, but I'd bet on Baxter's gut even over hard evidence. Rachel was still sitting there staring off into space. I felt like she looked—dazed and in disbelief, not knowing what to make of everything I'd just heard.

At a loss, I asked, "So now what?"

He replied, "Now the task force is going to have a hell of a long meeting and basically have to rethink every aspect of every case, including Marcus's homicide. That said, I'm going to need you to come in and process the evidence we collected last night."

I felt my brain finally let go and come to terms with what my subconscious had been struggling with for a while. "Like it's a murder-homicide instead of a suicide-homicide."

"Yes." After a pause, he added gently, "And I hope you'll reconsider joining the task force. If nothing else, you'll be a great sounding board. If we can convince you, of all people, that someone who's not Marcus Copland committed all these murders, we can convince anyone."

He wasn't wrong. I laughed. "What's in it for me?"

I could hear the smile in his voice. "The fortune and fame, of course."

"The fortune part is laughable. And you know I hate the fame."

"How about the adrenaline highs and palpable suspense?"

"I can get that from eating gas station sushi."

He chuckled. "You'll get to hang out with me."

"Now you're talking."

"So I can officially put you down as my plus-one at the upcoming task force meeting?"

I sighed. I guessed I was doing this. "Yes."

～

When I got to the sheriff's station, I headed to the conference room to find Vic. I could tell from his rigid posture that Baxter had dropped the bomb on him. Vic was flitting around the room, rearranging crime scene photos between a couple of different whiteboards.

I said quietly, "Is there still a spot open for me on your team?"

He spun around. When he saw me, his shoulders relaxed a bit and he smiled. "For you? Always. What do you make of this new wrinkle?"

I threw up my hands. "I think it's bananas, because it means I'm going to have to seriously consider believing all the crazy shit Marcus said to me over the past few days. It's against character for him to tell the truth, you know."

"So I've heard." He ran a hand through his hair as his gaze swept the now disorganized whiteboards. I hadn't seen him this agitated since the old days, before a near-death experience had chilled him out considerably.

I asked, "Are *you* okay?"

He smiled. "I'm fine. I hate it when a case gets so upended you practically have to start over. It's frustrating to think we've wasted a day, especially since we now know Katie Copland's murderer is running loose out there and not safely contained in cold storage at the morgue."

"I'm sure it wasn't completely wasted. The evidence is the same. You just have to look at it from a different perspective. I have no doubt this team can get to the bottom of it. Anything Marcus was involved in can't be that complex. He's too stupid."

Chuckling, Vic said, "Shouldn't I be the one giving you the 'keep your chin up' speech?"

"Keep it in your back pocket. I'm sure I'll need it at some point."

THE TASK FORCE meeting wasn't scheduled to begin for another hour, so I figured I'd better use my spare time wisely. I checked out the Seagram's 7 bottle, the Rohypnol blister pack, and the personal effects Dr. Berg had collected from Marcus's pockets from evidence and took them with me to the lab.

To my delight, I found Amanda in the lab office and Beck conspicuously absent. "Guess who's back?"

Amanda looked up from the computer, a smile lighting up her face. "Ellie! I'm thrilled you're here. Beck is driving me up a wall." She quickly sobered. "I'm sure this won't be easy on you, but I really appreciate your help."

I got a fresh lab coat out of the closet and put it on. "It won't be, but it'll be worth it."

A peal of feminine laughter rang through the lab.

Amanda scowled and jumped up from her chair. "I'm going to kill that little shit," she muttered as she brushed past me.

I followed her out into the lab to find Beck with a stunning young woman on his arm. She was mid-twenties and quite stylish. Miles out of Beck's league.

I was still trying to shake off my disbelief as Amanda bellowed at Beck, "You know we can't bring non-employees into the lab when we have evidence out." She stabbed a finger at the two pieces of evidence I'd placed on one of the worktables.

Beck scoffed. "Settle down, Beavis. That evidence isn't 'out.' It's still packaged up."

"Doesn't matter, and you should know better, *Butthead*," she fired back.

He puffed out his chest and drew himself up to his full height, which still didn't make him as tall as Amanda. "Have you forgotten that I'm your boss?"

This argument was going nowhere fast, and I was way more interested in how in the actual hell Beck snagged this lovely young woman. I cut in. "Beck, is this your new girlfriend?" When a sneer in my direction was his only response, I turned to the woman and introduced myself. "Hi, I'm Ellie Matthews. I work with Beck."

Her expression turned haughty. "Oh, I've heard all about you."

I managed to hold in a snicker but couldn't hold back a grin. "All good things, I hope."

She rolled her perfectly made-up eyes. "No. Not at all."

Still fighting the urge to laugh, I went on. "So, where did you two meet?"

"Ellie, shut up," Beck snapped.

"I'm just making conversation."

"No, you're not."

I huffed. "Come on, Beck. You brought her in here so you could parade her around. I'm playing along. Isn't that what you wanted?"

Beck put his arm around his girlfriend's shoulders and steered her toward the door. "Come on, Carmen. I'll walk you out."

As the door swung shut, Amanda griped, "He's such an asshole."

I smiled. "Don't worry. I'd bet money on the fact that Vic will kick him off the task force now that I'm on it. Vic doesn't care for Beck's work."

She brightened. "I didn't even think about that. Sounds like it's my lucky day. I'm going to get a snack before the meeting. Want anything?"

"I'm good."

Amanda left the lab, and I dug into the box of Marcus's personal effects. I'd put the burner phone he'd mentioned out of my mind until Baxter pointed out that Marcus's bullshit story about the people trying to frame him may not have been so bullshit after all. Unfortunately, there was no phone in this box—it contained only a pack of cigarettes, a lighter, a set of keys, and a wallet with a couple of credit cards and a fake ID that weren't in Marcus's name. Maybe Amanda and Beck had found the burner in the house during their sweep, but that would mean Baxter and I had missed it, and I highly doubted that. The only other place I imagined it could have been was in Marcus's truck, wherever that had ended up.

Still stewing over the missing phone, I readied myself and the workstation for processing the bottle of Seagram's 7. I put on a pair of gloves and cut the tape on the cardboard box, then gently removed the clear glass bottle from the box. I set the bottle on the workstation and used the bench magnifier to look for signs of latent prints. None were noticeable. I found that odd, considering I was normally able to see smudges on glass from finger oils. Not to mention that I'd never seen Marcus with clean hands—his dirty fingers would have made all kinds of prints on the bottle.

Since I had access to the lab's cyanoacrylate fuming chamber, I figured this was the perfect time to put it to use. Much of the time, I used fingerprint powder to lift prints from evidence at crime scenes to avoid the possibility of the prints getting smudged during packaging and transport. This time I'd waited, hoping not to have to delve so far into Marcus's homicide investigation that I'd need to collect prints as evidence of foul play.

I placed the bottle and a test strip inside the main chamber. I then added the proper amount of cyanoacrylate to its tray, which I transferred to the lower hot-plate chamber. I turned on the machine and waited for the liquid cyanoacrylate to begin vaporizing. Once it started to work its magic, I kept an eye on the test strip so as not to overdevelop the bottle. Cyanoacrylate, or superglue, fuming was an amazing tool for preserving fingerprints, but it could destroy them if you didn't pay attention. If the layer of cyanoacrylate became too thick and filled in the voids in between the ridges of fingerprints, you were left with nothing. Although that was generally a rookie mistake I never made, I still watched the progress through the glass door like a hawk. Once the machine got to the end of its cycle, it turned itself off and purged the chamber of excess vapor.

I removed the bottle, which was now covered in a barely visible white film, from the chamber. No prints jumped out at me. I got a sinking feeling in my gut as I took the bottle back over to the bench magnifier for a closer look, again finding no prints. I got out the black fingerprint dust and brushed down the entire bottle. I finally saw a couple of swipe marks and took several photos to document my paltry find. Damn. Someone had wiped down this bottle, and there were zero reasons for it to have been Marcus. A suspicion forming in my gut I didn't like, I used the same fuming procedure on the Rohypnol blister pack and got the exact same result. No prints—just a couple of smudges.

It was time for the meeting, so I repackaged the evidence and cleaned up the workspace. Ditching my lab coat, mask, and gloves, I headed to the conference room. The rest of the team was already there—Vic, Sterling, Baxter, Chief Esparza, Jayne, Amanda, Beck, and, to my surprise, Shane Carlisle, an old college buddy of mine. Shane was a detective with the Indianapolis Metropolitan Police Department who'd helped us out several months ago on the last big case we all worked together. I ran over and greeted him with a quick hug as everyone was settling into their seats, then took my place next to Baxter in the chair he'd saved for me.

I was elated to be a part of this team again, and it felt even better this time. During our last case, Baxter and I were barely speaking to each other. Vic had still been on medical leave and could only help in an unofficial capacity. Granted, what we had ahead of us was going to be grueling and frustrating, but it would be worth it to get to work with such amazing people again. Except Beck, of course, but there was no question in my mind his days were numbered.

Vic said, "Okay, everyone, let's get started. Detective Baxter, would you like to share your new theory with the class?"

Baxter chuckled. "Sorry to be the bearer of news that's going to blow up this investigation, but we have an alibi for Marcus Copland for Katie Copland's TOD. He can't be our guy because he was at Ellie's front door at 8:38 PM."

The task force members who hadn't already heard the news stared at him wide-eyed.

Sterling shook his head. "No, no, no, no. No freaking way. He's the guy. There's so damn much evidence against him. Evidence that he laid out next to a *confession* note." He turned to me. "Matthews, you sure you got your time right?"

I replied, "I'd like him to be guilty more than anyone at this table, but I can say without a doubt it was exactly 8:38 PM. That was the time my phone logged my 911 call to get him removed from my property. Go listen to the first few minutes of the recording of the call. I'm sure you'll hear him screaming at me through the door."

Sterling swore under his breath.

Baxter said, "That said, the fact that the vehicle used to run down Katie Copland was found where Copland was squatting seems a little suspicious. I'm not saying he wasn't involved in the crime in some way, but I do think there's a possibility the vehicle was planted there to make him look guilty."

Sterling pinched the bridge of his nose. "I don't like where you're going with this, dude."

As per usual, Sterling was viewing the evidence in his normal straightforward manner and Baxter was pissing him off by thinking outside the box.

Baxter went on. "Given the effort Marcus Copland put into contacting Ellie—not to mention finding a place to stay near her home—I think we need to put a little credence in what he had to say to her."

Vic said, "Ellie, you want to give us a quick rundown of what Copland told you?"

And there it was, the thing I'd been dreading the most. I knew at some point I'd have to start airing my dirty laundry to my fellow task force members, but I'd hoped it wouldn't be this soon. I took a deep breath.

13

While recounting my conversation with Marcus from two nights ago to the task force, I didn't end up feeling as vulnerable as I'd feared I would. But then again, there had been nothing too personal said between the two of us. We'd traded a few barbs and some information, but no old wounds had been reopened that I had to explain to the team.

When I was finished, I asked, "Did anyone find the burner phone he mentioned to me at his place? He said it was a flip phone."

Amanda shook her head. "No. The only phone we found was that iPhone in the jeweled case."

I frowned. "How about his truck? Where did it end up?"

Chief Esparza said, "We found out earlier today it got towed for a parking violation. We're having it brought over so we can search it. We'll make sure to look specifically for that burner since it wasn't on his person or at the scene. Sounds like a solid piece of evidence."

Jayne eyed me. "What do you think of Marcus's insistence that he was being set up for your mother's murder and that his life was in danger?"

I shrugged. "I mean . . . I guess there's enough reasonable doubt out there to support his claims. For example, I just processed the bottle of Seagram's 7 and the Rohypnol blister pack that were sitting on the table next to where Marcus was found. There were no prints on either item, but I did find a couple of smudges on the bottle. I'm pretty confident it was wiped clean."

Amanda said, "We're finding the same thing as we've been processing the other evidence from that table. The phone and the driver's license—both of which should have been super easy to pull prints from—had zero prints on them. Smudges, yes, like you said, but devoid of even a single partial, which makes no sense unless they'd been wiped."

Beck rolled his eyes. "Except that those items are several years old, so any prints could have been smeared off at any point."

Amanda didn't back down. "As for the license, yes. It was in a plastic bag. But whoever placed the phone on that table for us to find would have left at least a partial behind unless they purposely wiped it down *last night*."

Beck looked like he was gearing up to start an argument, so Jayne cut in. "It makes enough sense that Marcus might have wiped off the evidence even years ago so none of it could be tied to him. And yes, it stands to reason there should be at least one print somewhere on the phone if Marcus had been the one to place it on the table. But what I don't like is the fact that the whiskey bottle looks to have been wiped off. Based on the crime scene photos, it was about a quarter empty, which means Marcus would have touched it at least a couple of times to drink out of it. He'd have no reason to wipe it off."

Shane whistled. "So a very plausible explanation is that he wasn't the last person to handle it, and whoever did handle it didn't want anyone to know they'd handled it . . . and probably didn't want anyone to know they were there on the night in question."

Vic asked, "Ellie, what about the other items on the table you collected? The drug paraphernalia. Was it all wiped clean, too?"

"I haven't had time to process the rest yet," I replied.

"That's Job Number One."

I nodded.

He paused for a moment before asking, "And you found no glass, cup, or mug that might have been used to drink the whiskey?"

I replied, "No drink containers of any kind on the table, but that doesn't surprise me. I assumed he drank straight from the bottle like he always did. You get drunk faster that way."

"What about elsewhere in the room? Did you find any item that could have been used as a drinking glass?"

I glanced at Baxter. He shook his head and said, "None anywhere near him. There was random trash here and there, but unless he chucked his drink container all the way across the room for some reason, I'd say he didn't use one."

A frown marring his face, Vic went on. "Let's talk about the Rohypnol. Ellie, when we talked after you processed the scene, you struggled with believing Copland had ingested the Rohypnol orally, citing the fact that you'd never known him to ingest it that way because of the stomach discomfort it caused."

I said, "Right. He always crushed it up and snorted it."

"And there was no evidence of that at the scene?"

"I didn't find any of his snorting paraphernalia, no."

Vic turned to Baxter. "Detective Baxter, did the autopsy shed any light on this?

Baxter replied, "Yes. We know from hospital testing before Copland's death that he had high levels of benzodiazepine in his system. During the autopsy, Dr. Berg found no irritation in the nasal cavity and no drug residue there, so he's positive the Rohypnol wasn't snorted." He shot me a worried look. "He got back to me on stomach contents just before we started this meeting. All he found was whiskey and benzodiazepine drug residue." He shot me another look. "Dr. Berg believes that if Copland had ingested any Rohypnol tablets whole, there would still have been partially digested remnants left in his stomach."

Vic mused, "So the only way the Rohypnol could have gotten from point A to point B would be for Copland to have either swallowed them in powder form—which is highly unlikely—or to have dissolved them in the whiskey he drank. Ellie, you haven't processed the whiskey itself yet, have you?"

"Not yet."

"That's Job Number Two."

I nodded.

Vic addressed the room. "I don't know about the rest of you, but I think we've got enough evidence to start coming at these cases from a different angle. If some lowlife drug dealer or equivalent wanted Marcus Copland dead, I firmly believe we'd be looking at a pop-and-drop right now. But if this alleged suicide was in fact a hit, someone did a hell of a lot of planning and spin control to orchestrate it. That could color every facet of our other homicide cases. Did anyone find evidence of a struggle at the scene?"

Sterling said, "The place he was living was a sty, but I saw no signs of struggle."

Baxter added, "I asked Dr. Berg to do a thorough recheck for defensive and offensive wounds on the body. He found no perimortem injury."

Chief Esparza frowned. "The more I think about it, the more I'm not buying Copland's grand gesture at an eleventh-hour confession with all of his trophies laid at his feet. I've tangled with the guy enough to know he's not one to admit to anything, especially considering his deep-seated hatred for law enforcement and the fact that he's a world-class asshole. Ellie, what's your take on the trophies?"

I replied, "I'm not seeing Marcus being organized enough to keep tabs on those items all these years, much less being capable of preserving human remains for so long."

Amanda cleared her throat. "Not to interrupt, but I agree with you there. The . . . human remains . . . have been well cared for. I had Dr. Berg look at them, and he believes they've been in a deep freeze for years. Considering the house Marcus Copland was squatting in had no electricity and Jason believes he was there for a couple of weeks, it would have been impossible for him to have kept the remains there with him. The tiny cooler, even with a never-ending supply of ice, would have allowed them to deteriorate fairly quickly. Someone else had possession of them, at least for the past two weeks." She said to me apologetically, "Sorry. Go on."

After that last bit of information, I was a little thrown off. I shook my head to clear it and managed to go on with my thought. "Um . . . as for Marcus dragging all his trophies around from place to place . . . I'm not so sure. He was homeless a lot, which I think is why he was such a big-time womanizer—so he could mooch off his conquests. He moved in and out of our place a few times, and not once did he bring more than a duffel bag's worth of stuff with him. I heard him say to his buddies on more than one occasion that he traveled light so he could 'leave a ho at a moment's notice if shit gets too real.'"

Amanda shot me a sympathetic look. We'd become pretty close friends over the past year, but I'd never breathed a word about Marcus to her. She knew the basics of my mother's homicide, as did many of the people in the department, but I kept a tight lid on the personal stuff that was no one's business. Except now my personal stuff had become everyone's business.

Shane asked, "I suppose it's possible he had a friend here in town store his trophies for him while he bounced around, right?"

Jayne nodded. "It's possible, and that could be a good lead if we can figure out who he might have trusted to hold several prized possessions like those."

Vic said, "Sounds like we have plenty of leads to chase. Given the new information we've discerned today and the fact that these cases might now be related in a different way, I'm going to change our game plan. I'm assigning two investigators to each homicide so we can work separate theories as we see fit. Then we'll meet to collaborate and hopefully find connections between the cases. Chief Esparza and Detective Sterling will remain on Katie Copland's case. Detective Carlisle and I will work on Alice Graves's case, Sheriff Walsh and Ms. Carmack will take Patty Copland's case, and Detective Baxter and Ms. Matthews will remain on Marcus Copland's homicide. Any questions?"

Beck huffed. "Yeah, I got a question. Why am I not included?"

Vic smiled. "I guess it's your lucky day, pal. We have enough investigators to go around, so we can let you get back to your usual responsibilities."

"You mean your girlfriend's here, so I get shoved aside like usual," Beck fired back, throwing a sneer in my direction.

Vic's expression went unreadable. You did not want to mess with him when that happened. "I was trying to say it nicely, but now I don't feel like I have to. You're a liability, so I want you off the task force. Get the hell out of my command center."

Slamming his notebook shut, Beck shoved his chair out so hard it banged against the wall several feet behind him. He let out a string of curses under his breath as he stormed out of the room. Amanda and Sterling made the mistake of sharing an amused glance and had to struggle to hold in their laughter.

Back to his usual positive self, Vic said, "Good luck out there, and stay safe."

14

We all stood and gathered our things.

I said to Baxter, "I won't be of any help to you for a few hours while I process our evidence."

He smiled. "Not a problem. I think the evidence is the most important part at the moment. Let me know if you find anything. I'm going to canvass your street to find out if any of your neighbors saw anyone coming or going from Marcus's place last night."

"Ooh, have fun with that. They're not the most neighborly bunch."

Baxter headed toward his cubicle, and Amanda and I fell into step together on the way to the lab. She could barely contain her glee. "Vic wasted no time kicking Beck to the curb. That was epic."

I chuckled. "Beck didn't think so. His mother will be hearing about this."

"Luckily her connections don't extend all the way to the FBI."

Beck was indeed a liability. It had become Jayne's problem to keep him from screwing up the more complex cases, which was why she'd been so insistent to get me back on the payroll. For straightforward, everyday cases, it was Amanda's problem to keep him in check, which meant extra work for her without extra pay or a better job title. Since he had the lead criminalist position locked down, she had no chance of a promotion. I'd been surprised she hadn't taken a better job elsewhere, but I had a feeling getting to work with her boyfriend was overriding her desire to move up the ladder. In fact, I'd been surprised to hear her mention that Sterling had brought her in to do some actual investigating with him—the same unconventional choice he'd given Baxter a lot of grief for when he'd initially partnered with me—on a couple of cases while Baxter had been out on leave. She'd had a little experience broadening her investigative horizons by being part of a few task forces, but she was thrilled to have the chance to get out in the field with Sterling. Her extra work and new skills must not have gone unnoticed, because Vic had set her up to work with Jayne on my mother's case.

Once we got to the lab, the two of us got down to business with our separate piles of evidence. Figuring I needed to get the team some answers as quickly as possible, I got the lighter, the heroin spoon, and the rubber strap out at the same time to examine them for fingerprints. Since these all had the potential to be covered in heroin residue, I took extra precautions, including wearing a Tyvek suit and every piece of protective equipment I could find and performing the whole task of unboxing and examining the items under a ventilation hood. Just like with the bottle and blister pack, I wasn't able to discern any traces of fingerprints on these items under the bench magnifier.

I commandeered the cyanoacrylate fuming chamber again, and this time I put all three items in at once, hanging the rubber strap up on a rack for better cyanoacrylate coverage. Once the fuming process was complete, it was back to the bench magnifier for a closer look. And yet again, these pieces were all clean. I went through the process of applying black fingerprint powder, knowing it was an exercise in futility. Upon a final and thorough examination, I found no prints on the lighter, spoon, or strap—not even a tiny sliver of a partial or any signs of swipes. I sighed. If Marcus had used these items to administer the heroin to himself, they would have been riddled with his fingerprints. With having injected enough heroin to kill him straight into a vein, I doubted he would have had enough time in a lucid state to have wiped off these three items. I took photos of the items to show no prints were found and then repackaged them to await Amanda's second examination.

I had the needle and the balloon full of heroin left. As much as I didn't want to deal with either of them for the sake of my own health and safety, it had to be done. I used extreme care in removing the needle, which of course had had no protective cover for the sharp end, from the slender cardboard tube I'd used to package it. For the third time today, I did an initial check for prints, progressed to the fuming chamber and fingerprint powder, searched in vain for prints, and took several photos of nothing.

I moved on to the balloon. Because it was made of rubber, a porous surface, the fuming chamber was a no-go. I skipped that step and went straight for the fingerprint kit. After emptying the heroin powder into a new plastic evidence bag and shaking as much of the residue from the balloon into the bag as I could, I laid the empty, busted balloon out flat on a piece of butcher paper on the work surface under the ventilation hood, changed my gloves, and started brushing.

Bingo. Finally, I'd found a single decent print. I backed slowly away from the table so as not to disturb my find, removed my gloves, and grabbed the camera. I took way too many photos of the print, but I wasn't about to let this piece of evidence slide by with anything less than thorough, bordering on over-the-top, documentation. The print wasn't perfect by any means and it would take some skill to get it onto a tape lift, but it was enough for me to work with. I changed my gloves again, got out a tape lift, and carefully smoothed the tape over the print I'd found. Holding my breath, I peeled the tape back, hoping the whole print would come with it and the tape wouldn't stick *too* well to the rubbery balloon material. The tape came up as well as could be expected, and I smoothed it onto the attached backing of the lift card.

I stared at the print. Such a seemingly small piece of evidence, but it had the potential to blow the lid off the investigation—or it could just as easily be of no use. I took more photos of the lift card for good measure and forced my excited self to clean up my workstation and myself before heading to the lab office to process the print.

I scanned the print and pulled it up on the computer setup we used for processing fingerprints. With the aid of the comically enormous monitor, I was able to plot out all the bifurcations and ridge endings and even found a lesser-seen minutia called a spur, which was a short ridge jutting off a main ridge. The core pattern was a plain arch, super common. Once I was finished, I ran my plotted print through the AFIS database and waited impatiently for my list of possible matches. It popped up with an eighty-one percent match to someone named Jared Wesson, who had a hefty criminal record for, no surprise, drug charges. I performed the same ridge examination of Wesson's index finger print from the AFIS system, noting the minutiae and then cross-referencing each one with my heroin balloon print. It was indeed a match. Jared Wesson had the potential to become a viable suspect.

As I texted and emailed Baxter and Vic the information I'd gathered, Amanda and Jayne entered the office.

Jayne smiled at me. "It's good to see you back doing what you do best."

I replied, "I'm not going to lie—I do miss fingerprinting when I don't get to do it all the time."

Amanda got out two jumpsuits from the closet and handed one to the sheriff. To me, she offered, "You're more than welcome to come in and plot out fingerprints anytime your heart desires. I *don't* miss fingerprinting when I don't get to do it all the time. We're headed out to search Copland's truck. I'll be sure to look for some prints for you."

I knew she'd rather get her hands dirty, so to speak, out in the field or even in the lab than sit and stare at a computer screen. I could tell she was extra excited for this particular search, since she would get to work alongside the sheriff. On run-of-the-mill cases, Jayne worked as a coordinator. But on task force investigations, she was on the front lines, her sleeves rolled up with the rest of us. It would be a great learning experience for Amanda to get to work so closely with Jayne, which I imagined was Vic's master plan when he partnered them for this investigation. It would also be an amazing resume builder for when she decided to go for the career move she deserved.

As they left the office, I called, "Have fun."

Only moments later, Baxter appeared at the door. "Hey, nice work finding that print. The guy is a known drug dealer with enough priors that if we lean on him right, we should be able to get him to give something up. Manetti and I are headed out to talk to him."

I huffed. "I coaxed his print off the ass balloon full of heroin for you, and I don't even get to go along to harass the guy?"

He grinned. "Take it up with Manetti. He said your time is better served processing evidence."

"Boo." Tensing, I asked, "You think this dealer is our guy?"

"He could be, but I find it hard to believe he'd be so meticulous about wiping everything down only to leave one big thumbprint on the bag of heroin. What I do think is that he could have sold the drugs to our guy."

"Either way, be careful."

"Always." After glancing around, he gave me a quick kiss. "Dinner later? Just you and me?"

I nodded. "Sounds perfect."

Once he left, I put on a clean lab coat, gloves, and mask and went back out into the lab. Being especially careful, I got out the evidence jar of liquor I'd poured from the Seagram's bottle and placed it on a clean worktable. I searched the cabinet where the presumptive drug testing kits were kept. I selected one that detected benzodiazepines and grabbed a couple of clean pipettes. First, I picked up the jar, trying my best not to jostle it around, and looked for drug residue. I held the jar under the bench magnifier and studied the liquid near the bottom. It was brown and quite clear, free from any bits or residue. After taking a couple of photos, I put on some protective goggles and opened the jar.

Using a pipette, I sucked up some whiskey from the bottom of the jar, where the largest concentration of added drug particles should have settled. I snapped the top off the test ampoule and placed a drop of the whiskey into the tube, then replaced the test's cap and set it aside. While I waited for the reagent granules in the ampoule to do their thing, I resealed the jar of whiskey. After one minute, the granules in the test ampoule were still the same brownish color they had been originally. I waited another minute. Again, no change. I frowned. The reagent should have turned purple if there'd been even a little Rohypnol present in the sample.

Thoroughly flummoxed, I took photos of my findings and made a couple of notes. I labeled the spent test and boxed it back up for evidence, stewing over the fact that I'd again run into the issue of no evidence where there should have been some. If Marcus hadn't swallowed the roofie pills the normal way, he had to have dissolved them in a drink—which had to have been the whiskey, since that was all that was found in his stomach. Had he poured his whiskey into a glass to drink it (and to add his roofies), we would have found said glass at the scene. As per usual, thinking about Marcus for too long gave me a headache, so I threw myself back into my work.

I removed the glass bong from its box and set it on my workstation. Under the bench magnifier, I could see plenty of latent prints and smudges on the dirty red glass. Finally, some evidence to collect. In theory, the prints likely all belonged to Marcus, so it wouldn't prove much aside from the fact that he was a pothead. There were enough visible prints that I didn't bother with cyanoacrylate fuming. I took some photos, used a cotton swab to collect DNA from one of the unusable smudges, and then brushed fingerprint powder over the surface of the bong. I took more photos and began lifting the prints. I ended up with four full prints and three partials. While I had the fingerprinting tools out, I also processed the plastic bag that held the marijuana. I found several smudged prints, but also managed to find two viable full prints. To collect these prints without risking ripping the flimsy plastic, I cut away the area of the baggie containing the print, positioned it in a tape lift card, and smoothed the tape down over the top.

I returned to the lab office, plotted the prints I'd collected, and ran them through AFIS. Marcus's name was at the top of each print's list of potential matches. No surprise there, but I did my due diligence and compared his collected prints in the system to the ones I'd found on the bong. Feeling like I was spinning my wheels, I returned to the lab to find Amanda and Jayne returning with a cardboard box.

I asked hopefully, "Did you find a burner phone?"

Jayne replied, "We found a phone, but it's a low-end smartphone, not a flip phone. We were able to turn it on, and it seems to be Marcus's personal phone. It's got quite a few contacts in it. Detective Baxter is looking at it now. Should be very helpful."

I shook my head. "That's not it."

"Are you sure the burner is a flip? Did you see it, or did he only tell you about it?"

Frowning, I replied, "He only told me about it." I thought back to our conversation. He'd seemed sincere, and I didn't think he was lying. "But I do believe it exists."

She shrugged. "I hope we'll run across it, although I don't know of anywhere else to search. In the meantime, the phone we did find should net us most of what we need to know about Marcus's movements and communications leading up to his death."

I relaxed a bit. That was one good thing.

Amanda chimed in, "Aside from that, we found a bunch of receipts, so that can help flesh out his timeline as well. And then we found his drug stash." She opened the lid so I could see the contents.

Jayne explained, "His stash of drugs to sell, I believe. Multiple bags of small amounts of the same drugs, divvied up and ready to pass out."

I nodded absently, still mired in the mixed bag of information I'd gleaned over the course of my afternoon.

"What? I know that look."

Amanda murmured, "I know it, too."

Sighing, I said, "I hate to sound like a broken record, but I'm stuck on those roofies. The whiskey from the bottle on the table tested negative for Rohypnol, so Marcus didn't dissolve it in his drink. He didn't swallow the pills whole, either, because all Dr. Berg found in his stomach was residue. How in the hell did Rohypnol get in his stomach?"

Jayne furrowed her brow. "Would he crush them up to swallow them for any reason?"

"Again, there's the issue of no evidence of that. There would have been white pill powder all over that table, and there was none. There was some heroin on the table, but it's easy to distinguish because of how dingy it is." This investigation was going to force me to share one embarrassing and painful memory after another. I hoped I could remain detached enough to get my job done. I explained, "In the old days, when Marcus would deign to crush his own roofies, he did it with the bottom of a shot glass, and he'd get the powder everywhere. I know, because I was the only one who'd clean it up so Rachel wouldn't accidentally get into it. He knew he sucked at it, so he stuck me with the task of crushing up the pills for him. He'd whine that he was too drunk to do it, but he was never too drunk to hit me if I refused."

As Amanda tried to mask her expression, one somewhere between pity and horror, Jayne said to me gently, "Okay, I agree the lack of white pill powder doesn't make a lot of sense. What's your theory?"

I took a moment to gather my thoughts, taking into account the additional information I'd learned this afternoon. "Every item on the table I processed was wiped clean except for the weed bag, the bong, and the heroin balloon. The balloon would have been difficult to wipe off. Then there's the mystery of how the Rohypnol got from the pill pack into his stomach. There's also the missing burner phone, which is the one thing that could suggest someone set Marcus up." I blew out a breath. "What if he was telling the truth about the person or people out to get him—whoever kept threatening him over the burner phone? They could have killed him and shot him full of heroin to make it look like an overdose, figuring the cops wouldn't think anything was amiss. Had Marcus not reached out to me, I wouldn't have thought twice about it. At first, I wasn't even going to process the evidence I gathered for his homicide investigation. It was only after Baxter figured out Marcus had an alibi for Katie Copland's death that things started seeming fishy."

Jayne nodded. "Let's follow that. The night he died, Marcus is sitting there alone—toking up, we can assume, considering the hospital found marijuana in his system. The killer or killers show up at his door . . . What does he do?"

Amanda chimed in, "He's scared of them, right?"

"Right," I said.

She went on. "Even so, is he going to invite them in, sit down, and let them shove a needle in his arm without a fight?" She paused for a moment to think. "Well, maybe if they had him at gunpoint."

Imagining the scenario, I shook my head. "No, not Marcus. Even high and at gunpoint, he'd either fight back or try to run. There was no sign of defensive or offensive wounding on his body."

Amanda said, "Then it couldn't have been any kind of hostile takeover. He let them into the house . . . maybe because he *wasn't* scared of them."

Jayne mused, "You said he told you they'd used a voice changer during their calls to him and that he had no idea who was doing the calling. He could have had no idea he was inviting in the enemy. Maybe he even considered the person or persons as friends."

I said, "Wait, that's very possible, especially if they brought the Seagram's. It's Marcus's favorite. Say this 'friend' brought the booze to share. Also say this friend was thoughtful enough to bring along a couple of glasses for them to use . . . and while Marcus wasn't looking, they slipped some roofies in his drink."

Amanda's eyes widened. "So once he became pliable, or possibly even blacked out, they could hit him with the heroin." She gasped. "And *then* they'd have all the time in the world to wipe down the Seagram's bottle and the heroin paraphernalia they touched. To leave without a trace, all they'd have left to do is grab the glasses—one of which would have had the Rohypnol residue we've been looking for—and the burner phone."

I added, "And that's why the bong and baggie had Marcus's prints on them but nothing else did, including the lighter. The killer would have been the last to touch everything *except* the bong and the weed."

Amanda said, "Wait, we're forgetting the heroin balloon." She thought for a moment. "If the killer was smart enough to concoct this plan and make sure to leave no evidence of themselves behind . . . maybe they're smart enough to protect their hands while handling drugs. At best, that balloon has fecal matter all over it. At worst, the heroin could have been cut with fentanyl or even carfentanyl. If I were going to handle heroin, whether during a purchase from a drug dealer or while I was using it to kill some-one, I'd for damn sure have some kind of gloves on. That said, there'd be no need to bother to wipe prints from something you never touched with bare hands."

Jayne couldn't contain her smile. "I believe you criminalists may have just out-investigated my detectives."

Amanda and I high-fived each other.

Jayne's smile faded. "Now the real work begins."

15

Amanda and I spent the rest of the afternoon performing second passes on evidence either she or I had already processed. It was a necessary evil of the job, even though we'd never had an instance where the second pass on anything either of us had processed revealed new information. Today was no different.

Sterling and Baxter entered the lab as we were cleaning up our workstations.

Sterling jeered, "I hear you two have been forming theories behind our backs."

Amanda removed her gloves and pulled down her mask so he could get the full effect of her proud smirk. "We have. Sheriff Walsh was quite impressed with us."

He replied, "Since you think you have this case all figured out, maybe you'll want to watch while I interrogate the owner of the stolen vehicle that ran over Katie Copland. Should be interesting."

Amanda tried to hide her glee, but couldn't quite suppress her smile. "Sure." She ripped off her lab coat and practically skipped toward him.

"I'll even take you for coffee on the way to the interrogation room." He held the door open for her.

"You're too good to me," she said, pinching his cheek as she walked past him.

Baxter and I shared a chuckle. Considering my history with Sterling, I never thought I'd be anything but disgusted watching him flirt with someone. But he and Amanda made such a great couple, I didn't mind.

Baxter said, "I was able to put together a timeline of Copland's interactions and movements over the past couple of weeks from the phone and receipts that were found in his truck. I've got a whole list of people for us to interview."

"Fan-freaking-tastic. I've been patiently waiting for the part where I get to reconnect with Marcus's asshat friends."

"Only the less dangerous ones. Full offense, but I'm taking official backup to talk to some of these clowns."

"I'd be offended if I didn't want to avoid this part of the investigation."

Smiling, he changed the subject. "In other news, Manetti and I went looking for your drug dealer. No luck. According to his girlfriend, he's out of town, which we didn't believe for a minute. Manetti's writing up a warrant to ping his cell phone. While we're waiting, do you want to listen in on the interrogation, too? The car's owner is an ex-con with a hefty criminal record, so it should be fun to watch Sterling pick a fight with him."

I smiled. "That does sound like fun."

BAXTER and I stopped for a moment in the breakroom to get coffee. The viewing room next to the interrogation room was full by the time we got there. Shane, Amanda, Jayne, and Vic were conferring about the case, but halted their conversation to greet us. Vic pulled me aside, and the rest of them began a new conversation about the disconcerting appearance of the man waiting to be interrogated. There wasn't a square inch of skin on his hands, arms, neck, face, or bald head that wasn't covered in tattoos or impaled by piercings. Just then, he nervously licked his lips, revealing a tattooed and forked tongue.

I managed to pry my attention from the Lizard Man as Vic said to me quietly, "Hey, tech is having no luck getting into that busted iPhone. I hope you can help with it."

"What can I do? Amanda said there were no prints on it."

He scratched at the five o'clock shadow on his cheek. He did that when he was gearing up to say something I wouldn't like and was wracking his brain for a diplomatic way to say it.

My face fell. "Just say it, Manetti."

"Okay, I need you to come up with a list of Marcus's exes. I'm assuming it belonged to one of them. With a starting point, maybe we can find a way to back into figuring out whose it is."

I frowned. "I don't know any of them except Katie, but that was mostly from what Rachel told me about her. Oh, I guess I do know one other—a frenemy of my mother's."

Again with the face scratching. "Well, I was hoping Rachel might help you come up with the list. I'm sure she was around him a lot more than you were."

I blew out a breath. "Vic, you don't know what you're asking."

"No, unfortunately I do know exactly what I'm asking, and it sucks. But we need a reliable source who's an expert on Marcus Copland's life. You two are his only known associates I trust farther than I could throw."

"Yeah, he ran with some real pieces of shit."

Sterling and Chief Esparza entered the room next door and took seats across from Lizard Man. The rest of us quieted down and crowded around the two-way mirror.

Chief Esparza slid a photo across the table to the man. "This your car?"

Lizard Man stared down at the photo, his hands balling into fists. "Yeah. I want it back."

The chief said, "We want some answers first."

"I'm not giving you jack shit."

Sterling shrugged. "Then we're not giving *you* jack shit."

Lizard Man's nostrils flared as he turned on Sterling. "I know my rights. You can't hold me, because I didn't do anything. And you can't hold my car, either. Cough it up, pig."

Baxter and I shared a worried glance. The one thing you didn't call Sterling was a pig.

To my surprise, Sterling kept his cool. "What day was your vehicle stolen?"

Lizard Man rolled his eyes. "I already went over this with some other cops. You're wasting my time, especially if you have my car and are just being dicks about giving it back."

"Where were you Monday night at 8:45 p.m.?"

Lizard Man threw up his hands. "I don't know. Waiting for a ride home from work because my friggin' car was stolen, maybe? What is it you're accusing me of, asshole?"

Chief Esparza said, "Settle down, Mr. Meyer. Can someone you work with verify that you were still at work at 8:45 that night?"

"Yeah, my boss and another coworker. Why do I feel like I need an alibi for something?"

Vic said, "I'm going to run that down," and left the room.

The chief pressed, "How do you know Marcus Copland?"

Lizard Man stared at him. "Who? Is that the asshole who stole my car?"

"We have no proof he took it, but it was found on the property where he was living."

"Good enough for me. I want to file charges."

Sterling said, "Well, he's dead, so you're SOL."

Lizard Man sat back in his chair. "What the hell's going on here, and what does any of it have to do with me?"

"We'll get to that. How do you know Katie Copland?"

"I don't know anyone named that," Lizard Man ground out. "Answer my damn question."

The chief explained, "Your vehicle was used in a hit-and-run homicide. Based on the fact that you have a lengthy criminal record, we felt it necessary to thoroughly question you."

"So I'm being profiled. Typical cop bullshit, you people deciding I'm a criminal because of the way I look."

The chief snickered. "How you look? You mean, like a white guy crying for attention? No. We're profiling you because of your history of committing felonies."

"But this time I'm the victim. I'm the one whose car got stolen."

Sterling shrugged. "What better way to cover your ass than to say the car you used to run someone over was stolen before the incident occurred? It's a common tactic." Vic slipped into the interrogation room and passed

Sterling a folded note. As Vic left the room, Sterling added, "But not this time. Looks like you have a solid alibi for the hit-and-run. You're free to go."

Lizard Man stared at him. "That's it, after all the shit you just put me through?"

Sterling and the chief stood and gathered their files. Sterling replied, "Yeah. We'll contact you when your vehicle is released from evidence. I wouldn't hold my breath." He opened the door. "After you."

Lizard Man, incensed to the point where his face was turning a purplish color under all those tattoos, shoved his chair back so hard it tipped over. His expression of pure rage made me worry about our investigators' safety —until he puffed himself up to his full height. He was easily a foot shorter than Sterling and posed no physical threat. All of us in the viewing room chuckled as he stomped out of the interrogation room like a toddler. Granted, this incident had left him without a vehicle for a while, which would have angered me as well, but at least it hadn't left him with a murder charge.

As we filed out of the viewing room, I pulled Baxter aside and gave him a contrite smile. "Vic needs Rachel and me to come up with a list of Marcus's exes. Rather than the fun dinner date you and I had planned tonight, I feel like we should spend our break time forcing my sister to relive her painful childhood memories. Bribing her with takeout from her favorite restaurant, of course."

He smiled. "Say no more. It'll be much less stressful for her to come up with that list in the comfort of her home versus having to come in and do it here. Raincheck on our dinner date. We'll try again tomorrow. Maybe the fourth time's the charm."

BAXTER and I grabbed a family-style Italian meal from a local restaurant and went to my house. We dished up dinner for ourselves and Rachel and Nate and didn't mention a word about the investigation while we enjoyed a relaxing meal.

Once it was time to clean up, Rachel sidled over to me. "Okay, sis. What the hell's up?"

I chuckled. "Am I that transparent?"

She glanced over her shoulder at Baxter, who was trying to convince Nate he needed to wash the spaghetti sauce off his hands *before* petting the dog. "Nick is that transparent."

"Oh, true. So . . . Vic asked me if the two of us would sit down and delve into our past."

"Always a good time."

"And come up with a list of Marcus's exes."

She made a face. "That'll take forever. He was a total man-whore."

"I know, and I'm sorry. For what it's worth, Vic is sorry about having to ask."

"He should be."

Rachel and I sat on the couch, her with the mug of hot chocolate I made her for some extra comfort and me with a notebook. Nate was only too happy to drag Baxter outside for a game of kickball.

I said, "Okay, I guess I'll have to get the ball rolling, because you were nothing more than a twinkle in Marcus's eye when he and our mom met. He wasn't around for terribly long before he knocked her up with you."

She nodded. "Ah, yes. Theirs is a love story for the ages. A tale as old as time."

Snickering, I said, "Ooh, you're snarky tonight."

"It happens when you become an orphan," she snapped.

I winced inwardly. This was how Rachel got when she was trying to put on a brave face and cope with something. She'd lash out with biting comments, anything ranging from simple sarcasm to purposely hurtful truths. As difficult as it was sometimes for me to not snap back, I handled this much better than when she retreated into herself and wouldn't let me near her. If she was at this stage so soon after Marcus's death, she was well on her way to healing.

I went on. "At least he 'made an honest woman out of her,' his words, before you made your appearance." Pausing to recall that particular day from hell, I felt a frown form on my face. "I remember our mom crying on their wedding day over the fact that she looked like a blimp in her dress. I don't know if she wanted us to suffer together or what, but she made me wear the ugliest purple dress I'd ever seen to be the flower girl."

A moment from that day flashed into my head. I'd complained to my mother about the dress, which Marcus overheard. He took his first chance to "be a father figure" and slapped me across the cheek. The image of my mother's jaw dropping in horror was something I'd never forget. She'd assured me on several occasions that he was different than the other losers she'd been with, including my own father. I remembered her turning to Marcus, I assumed to defend me or kick him to the curb or something. But then she suddenly pasted on a smirk and let out a bark of laughter. She told me that's what happened to little girls who were ungrateful. Needless to say, I was in no mood to participate in their wedding after getting a glimpse of what their marriage was going to mean for me. But Rachel didn't need to hear that story right now.

I cleared my throat. "Um . . . and then of course he starts cheating on Mom with Katie and knocks her up as well."

Rachel nodded. "Some of my first memories, unfortunately. Mom and Marcus get divorced, then he marries Katie, who he later turns around and cheats on with Mom."

I frowned. "Which breaks up Mom's marriage to David because Marcus got her to start using again." I thought for a moment. "Isn't it around this time that Marcus was also nailing Mom's friend Ava?"

"I was only six at the time, so it's fuzzy for me. But I think you're right, according to a few way too detailed conversations I overheard between Mom and Ava over the years."

Ava Donatelli was our mother's best friend and worst enemy. The Marcus thing was the catalyst for one of their frequent enemy phases. During another, I had to physically break up a fistfight between the two of them, which netted me a black eye at the tender age of fifteen.

She went on. "I guess Mom won that battle, because she and Marcus got remarried when I was seven." She looked down at her mug of hot chocolate, but not quickly enough that I missed the tears pooling in her eyes. "And then two years later, you left."

I put down my notebook and took one of her hands. "I couldn't stay there and keep getting abused."

"I know that now." She raised her sad eyes to meet mine. "But I didn't then, and I kind of hated you for it."

16

My heart hurt for nine-year-old Rachel. It had taken all I had to walk away from that sweet child, knowing the situation I was leaving her in. The only hope I held onto was that I'd never known Marcus to physically abuse her —he reserved his unbridled anger for our mother and me. He was a shitty dad and didn't hold back on the emotional or verbal abuse, but he at least did one thing right by his daughter. I wouldn't have left her otherwise.

I said quietly, "I know you did. I'm sorry I made you feel abandoned."

Rachel squeezed my hand. "It's okay. There was honestly a better vibe in the house once you were gone. Marcus really hated your guts."

"Don't I know it." I picked the notebook back up, hoping to steer our conversation to something hopefully a little less painful. "Since I wasn't around after that, the rest of this list is going to have to be all you."

After pausing to think for a moment, she said, "Their second marriage lasted four years, and I want to say his next conquest was either . . . Michelle or Amy."

"Do you remember last names?"

"Sorry, not for them." She paused again, closing her eyes. "Oh, yeah. It was Michelle *then* Amy. He knocked up Amy, too."

I stared at her. "Uh . . . you have another sibling out there I don't know about?"

She scoffed. "Come on, I wouldn't hide that from you. Amy lost the baby pretty early. I remember her coming home one night when I was staying with Marcus. She barely got inside before she collapsed. She looked all roughed up. He rushed her to the hospital, and when they came back, she was catatonic, but I remember him being oddly upbeat."

"Because he'd dodged a bullet."

She huffed out a mirthless laugh. "Something like that."

"Did Mom know he'd gotten another woman pregnant? Seems like something she'd have taken issue with."

"I don't think she knew, at least not at the time. *I* certainly didn't tell her. I was only thirteen, but I knew that kind of bombshell would lead to the bender to end all benders."

She wasn't wrong. I'd been around that age when Katie got pregnant with Jack, well before our mother and Marcus's divorce was final. When our mother found out about the baby, she disappeared for over a week, leaving me in charge of three-year-old Rachel. Not that I'd minded—I'd been Rachel's primary caregiver since birth, so it was business as usual. I cut school for the week and did nothing but hang out with my adorable little sister in the peace and quiet of a home that was devoid of cigarette smoke and conflict for the first time in my life. It was glorious, and I remembered telling my mother when she returned that Rachel and I had been much better off without her. That comment earned me a slap across the face, but the look in her eye told me she couldn't disagree with my assessment.

Rachel went on. "After Amy . . . I'm going to say it had to have been the stuck-up redheaded chick. She had a good job and a nice house. Not quite his usual type, but now that I think about it, she may have been a closeted coke user. She was offputtingly energetic, and I'm pretty sure she had a jeweled coke nail. Anyway, she already had two kids, and I assume she either didn't want any more or thought Jack and I were heathens. So when Marcus had custody of us, he had to take us out to a park or something. We went to her house maybe twice, and she never let us stay overnight. I think the only thing she ever said to me was, 'Take your dirty shoes off when you come into my home.'" Shaking her head, she added, "Bitch."

I said, "That was Alice Graves. She was one of his exes who got murdered."

Rachel shrugged. "Whatever. Like I said, she was kind of a bitch."

Again with a cutting remark. I let this one go as well. "Do you know how long he lived with her?"

Wrinkling her nose, she replied, "I don't know. We saw him so infrequently around that time it was hard to keep up."

"I wonder if he was still living with her when she was killed."

"Not sure on that one."

"Do you remember him mourning the loss of a girlfriend?"

She snorted. "Can you imagine Marcus caring about anyone enough to mourn them? He replaced women like you'd replace a tire. When one got worn out, he'd ditch her and get a new one. Or if he was feeling lazy, he'd go back and slum it with an old one."

I nodded. She wasn't wrong. When Marcus and our mother would fight, his words would wound her deep. In my opinion, the awful things he said weren't the kind you could walk back, but our mother allowed herself to be reeled back in by him every time. Although I could never fathom why, the only explanation was that she was truly in love with him. I didn't believe he ever felt the same way about her.

Rachel went on. "So after Alice, it was a couple of years before I remember another woman in the picture." She huffed out a laugh. "This girl was completely different than the others. For starters, she was closer to my age than his. In fact, I think she was your age."

"Gross."

"It wasn't like that. She'd immigrated here and was having some kind of trouble with her green card. She paid him to marry her."

I made a face. "Someone *paid* Marcus to marry her?"

Shrugging, she replied, "She didn't have a lot of other choices. Most people are too smart to agree to take a risk like that. Marcus saw the money and didn't worry about the potential prison time if they got busted."

"Which is exactly why you don't choose the dumbest man alive as your partner in crime."

"Well, they never ended up sealing the deal. One day she just . . . disappeared. We never saw her again."

This story suddenly sounded very familiar. "Wait. What was her name?"

"Jihyo Yoon."

My eyes bugged out. "Holy shit. She's not missing; she's dead. I worked her case." I thought for a moment. "There was never a mention of Marcus's name in relation to her. Jayne and I would have been all over that if there'd been any kind of tie."

Rachel frowned. "I think I know why. Surprisingly, he wasn't totally stupid about it. He used a fake identity to protect himself in case they did actually get caught. Only Jihyo knew his real name. She introduced him to her sister and her friends as James Albright. He had identities for Jack and me, too. We were . . ." She scrunched up her face to think. "Heidi and Tim Albright. Marcus bought us both brand-new iPhones if we promised not to tell our moms it was a sham marriage."

Now it all came flooding back. A farmer in Sheridan found a skeleton buried on his property and called it in. We went out to investigate the scene, such as it was. Beck and I dug around for the better part of a day, and all we found was a skeleton with some degraded clothing. Could have been there a year or several years. Dr. Berg couldn't come close to determining the date of death, so Jayne called in an anthropologist from Ashmore, which was how I met Sam. She studied the bones and was able to come up with a timeframe of death at roughly a year. Sam also used the skull to recreate the face of the victim, which Sterling was able to match with Jihyo's missing persons report. Although we finally had a disappearance date, there was still no concrete date of death, so it was impossible to work any alibi angles. It was the same issue that had plagued the investigation of my mother's death. We had no primary scene, and after a year, we weren't going to find one. Sterling and his former partner worked their asses off, but they were never able to gather enough evidence to charge anyone for her death.

I vividly remembered seeing Jihyo's poor sister, Hana, the day she showed up in our department to formally ID her sister and give her statement to Sterling and his partner. She was only a couple of years older than I'd been at the time, but she was a shell of a woman. She'd spent every waking moment over the previous year searching for her sister. She'd done most of the work on her own because the IMPD hadn't given Jihyo's missing persons case much priority, considering her tenuous immigration status. I couldn't imagine hanging onto hope for that long, only to find out her little sister had been dead and buried the whole time. The one thing Hana did manage to get the IMPD investigators to do was to look into the man Jihyo was engaged to—James Albright—who was, unsurprisingly, nowhere to be found. The cops told her it was more likely the two of them had run away together than that James had done something to Jihyo.

That particular case had hit me hard. Rachel had been seventeen at the time, completely left to her own devices by our worthless mother. I knew she'd taken up with a new guy who was way too old for her. I'd tried to reason with her and talk her into dating someone her own age and who wasn't a known drug dealer, but she was in love. I was gearing up to do something drastic—calling CPS was on the table, even though I knew it could make Rachel's already shitty life even worse. Hell, I'd even contacted Marcus, of all people, for help. Of course, he refused to lift a finger to help me, even though it was his daughter's safety at stake. Luckily, all Rachel ended up with from the situation was a baby, which was the most wonderful thing that had ever happened to either of us. The news of her pregnancy prompted me to take her in myself rather than trusting someone else to take care of her and her child, which ended up being the best decision I'd ever made.

But Rachel didn't need to be mired down with the specifics of Jihyo's case. It was technically still active since it had gone unsolved, but once I shared this particular bit of information with the task force, the case was going to be fully reopened and thrown in with our investigation. I let my sister keep talking and didn't share what I knew.

Rachel went on. "It sucks that she died, but it makes sense. People like her don't just up and leave town. She loved her job, she had plenty of friends, and she was super close with her sister. As far as I could tell, Marcus really did think she was missing, so I don't think he was to blame. He looked for her at her work and her apartment, and he checked with her sister, who actually did go to the cops about it. I'm betting his interest was more about not getting his money than her safety, though. The one thing he said to me about her disappearance was that he bet it was the 'friggin' North Koreans,' his words, stealing her back."

I rolled my eyes. Marcus was so damn stupid. "He didn't even know which Korea his green card fiancée was from? Why did he ever think he had the capacity to fool federal immigration officials?"

"You know him—always scheming. He insisted I learn things about Jihyo and spend time with her to make it look like they were a real couple. I didn't mind. She was really sweet—one of the kindest people I'd ever met. It was nice getting to hang out with an adult who wasn't more screwed up than I was."

I handed her my notebook and pen. "Write down every detail you remember about her, especially any of Marcus's friends or associates she might have come in contact with." I thought for a moment as Rachel began writing. "Speaking of details, I don't suppose you remember anything about the phone she had, do you?"

Not taking her eyes off her task, she smiled. "Oh, yeah. Her phone case was freakin' sweet. A little extra for someone in their mid-twenties, but sixteen-year-old me coveted it so hard."

My hope rising, I said, "Describe it."

"Hot pink and comically jewel-encrusted. I think it had a crown on it and a built-in ring. Don't get me wrong—Jihyo wasn't materialistic or pretentious or immature. She just had a thing for bling."

That description certainly matched the iPhone in evidence from Marcus's OD/confession scene. Vic was going to be happy to hear the good news.

Rachel finished writing and handed me the notebook. "This has certainly been a trip down memory lane. To my knowledge, Jihyo is the last of the new women. Marcus eventually went back to Katie and married her again. Right around that time, I came here to live with you, so I didn't see anyone from my old life again except Jack. According to him, Marcus had yet another fling with Mom that was supposed to be a big secret, except it wasn't."

I nodded. "Definitely not a secret. It's even in Marcus's police file."

"Oh, wow. Must have been one hell of a fling."

"Um, so that takes us up to the time when..."

She closed her eyes. "I know."

"I hate to ask you to think about this, but do you have any ideas about anyone from Mom's and Marcus's past who'd want to kill Mom and pin it on Marcus? Or who'd want to try to make Marcus suffer by killing his exes and holding it over his head?"

My sister rubbed her forehead. "The only people I knew from his life were his women and his loser friends. Those guys were all real dicks, so I'd usually try to hide when they'd come over. I mean, I guess it could be one of them. They'd fight on occasion—I'd watch out the window of my room while they had hilarious drunken punching matches." She sat up straighter and looked me in the eye. "Wait a minute. What about that asshole Earl? Didn't he live with us for a while until Marcus beat the shit out of him? That's another one of my earliest memories. I feel like those two had beef on and off as long as I can remember. And Mom for some reason found him irresistible. I lost count of the number of times I came home after school to find them doing it on the kitchen table."

I made a gagging noise. "TMI, Rach. But he's a great suspect. Good thinking." I added Earl's name to the list and jotted a few notes about him.

I'd almost forgotten about Earl Thompson. One of Marcus's oldest friends, Earl was a real piece of work. He used to come over to our place way too much. At first I'd thought he had some kind of bromance with Marcus, but then I started noticing how much time he spent leering at my mother. She'd noticed too. And in true Patty fashion, she'd use Earl's crush on her to make Marcus jealous so he'd pay more attention to her. It worked, but not before Marcus would kick Earl's ass and send him packing for a month or so. Then Marcus would forget he was mad at Earl and the cycle would start all over again. When Marcus left my mother for the first of many times, good old Earl was right there to slide into his place. He was nearly as abusive to me as Marcus had been, which Marcus wouldn't have cared about. But Earl made a fatal mistake—he hit three-year-old Rachel. I knew Marcus would lose his shit over that, and I wanted Earl gone. So, the next time Marcus came over to pick Rachel up for visitation, I narced on Earl. Marcus did in fact lose his shit, beat Earl nearly to death, and tossed him out on his ass. We didn't see Earl again until Marcus moved back in with us a few years later, but the two men weren't tight like before. Marcus tolerated Earl coming around occasionally with their friend Jimmy, but things were never the same between them.

She chuckled. "Speaking of beef, I know you have nearly as much with Earl as Marcus did. Don't try to knock out his teeth, too. People won't believe this one is an accident."

I smiled at her, relieved at her resilience in the face of dredging up our bitter past. "I was worried about making you relive all this stuff, but you seem okay. Are you okay?"

She nodded. "I'm good. It was kind of nice to relive some of the better moments with Marcus."

I reached over and hugged her. "I'm happy to hear it. Seriously, thanks, Rach. This list is going to be essential to our investigation."

My sister pulled back, tears shining in her eyes. "I'm expecting you guys to put it to good use to find out who killed Jihyo and Katie, and who really killed Mom."

"I promise we will."

WHEN BAXTER and I returned to the station, we found Vic in the conference room hunched over his laptop. I was beginning to get a little worried about him. Ever since his near-death experience, he hadn't been such a slave to his job. This investigation had him looking a little too much like the old Vic. And I was afraid it was because of me.

I dropped into the chair next to him. "Did you take a dinner break?"

Vic flicked his eyes at me, then returned his attention to his screen. "Not yet."

Baxter, who'd taken the seat next to mine, joked, "Are we going to have to drag you out of here and force you to take care of yourself, Manetti?"

Vic looked up and smiled, shutting his laptop. "No, Dad. I'm meeting Steve for dinner so I can bounce some ideas off him."

I made a face and said in a loud aside to Baxter, "That doesn't sound like any fun."

Baxter chuckled as Vic shot me a reproachful look. Special Agent Steve

Griffin wasn't my favorite person. He'd been our FBI liaison on a prior case and had let the giant stick up his ass nearly ruin our investigation, not to mention Vic's and my careers. Vic had forgiven his longtime friend for his shortsightedness, but I hadn't.

To Vic, I said, "Let it be known that I think you're on the verge of sliding back into Old Vic's habits. And Old Vic was kind of a dick."

"I'm well aware of your formerly poor opinion of me, not to mention your unfunny middle school jokes about my name," he replied dryly.

"I made fun of your name one time. And Sterling started it."

He laughed. "Did you come in here to bust my balls or do you actually have something of use for me? A list, perhaps?"

"Courtesy of my very kind and cooperative sister, I have the mother of all lists for you. Behold, Marcus Copland's list of conquests." I pulled the paper from my bag with a flourish. "I'll warn you, it's a lot. He was quite a dirty skank."

Vic ran his eyes down the list and whistled. "Damn. The man got around."

Baxter shook his head. "I don't get what they all saw in him."

I shrugged. "It's one of life's great mysteries."

Vic mused, "Well, he dealt drugs, right? Maybe he comped his wives' and girlfriends' scores. To some women, that alone could make him irresistible."

"It could account for why my mother kept going back to him."

She'd had no problem exchanging sex for drugs. I supposed it was safest for her, theoretically at least, to do it with Marcus. He was the devil she knew. Plus since she'd always harbored feelings for him, I imagined "paying" him for drugs was much more appealing than "paying" some stranger.

Vic tapped the paper with his finger. "You wrote 'phone' next to the name Jihyo Yoon. You think she's the owner of the bedazzled phone?"

"Rachel knew Jihyo well and was able to describe the phone case in detail without prompting."

"Hot damn. Now we're getting somewhere." He opened his laptop and started typing.

I said, "Don't get too excited. Sterling and I worked her case five years ago. It went—"

"Cold." He finished for me, slouching back in his chair. He spun his laptop to show us a scanned copy of the first page of Jihyo Yoon's homicide report. "This her?"

Baxter chimed in, "I don't imagine there are a lot of HamCo homicide reports for women named Jihyo Yoon for you to get mixed up."

"Smartass," Vic muttered. "So we have another wild goose chase to add to the pile."

"I'm afraid so," I replied. "Talk to Sterling, though. He may have a strong opinion on a potential suspect—I remember he and his old partner had some nasty arguments over this one. I think this case is the reason they broke up, not that Sterling ever needs much of a reason to end a partnership." I nodded at Baxter. "You've lasted longer than most."

He grinned. "Because I'm the perfect partner."

Winking at my boyfriend, I replied, "Yeah, you are."

Vic said, "Focus, please, lovebirds. You two want to run point on this case? I know you're already on the Marcus Copland homicide, but let's face it—whoever killed these women is likely his killer as well. I don't think it will involve a lot of extra work."

Baxter winced. "You think Sterling will get pissy if you don't give it to him?"

Vic shrugged. "He's had five years to figure it out. I say a set of fresh eyes is a good thing."

"I agree," I said. "I'll have Amanda take another pass at the evidence from that case. And by evidence, I mean the scraps left from clothing that absorbed a dozen gallons of human stew over the course of a year."

Both men groaned, "Ellie," at the same time.

"What? That's *so* less gross than the fact that there are multiple women out there who chose to have sex with Marcus Copland. I'd bathe in human stew before I'd let Marcus—"

Baxter cut me off. "Please don't finish that sentence."

Vic said, "And also get the hell out of here. Both of you. I need peace and quiet to study this list so I can divide it up and dish out assignments."

As Baxter and I stood, I eyed my friend. "Fine, but after that, it's break time for you, pal. Oh, and don't tell Steve I said hi."

Vic chuckled as we left the room.

As we walked down the hallway, Baxter said, "So . . . you ready to track Marcus's last couple of weeks with me?"

I made a face. "I suppose I can't put it off any longer."

"Nope."

17

As Baxter drove, I perused the timeline he'd put together for Marcus. "Impressive work, Detective. Too impressive, I'm afraid. It's going to take us days to visit all the places Marcus went in the last couple of weeks." Marcus had made the rounds in town to his favorite liquor store, pizza joint, and bar, plus several stores and fast food places for day-to-day items.

Baxter shrugged. "It's not like we need to hit up McDonald's and Walmart and the gas stations he went to. But I do think we need to visit the liquor store near your house. Ava Donatelli happens to be on shift—"

I muttered, "Like that drunk old whore will be of any help."

"Damn. I take it you don't care for her."

Clenching my jaw, I shrugged, knowing I needed to sack up and prepare myself to dive back into my old life. I'd worked so hard to distance myself from the world I'd grown up in, and most of the time I felt like I'd succeeded. All on my own, I'd managed to buy a nicer house than I'd ever lived in. I was a respected professor at one of the most prestigious private colleges in the state. My friend circle consisted of pillars of the community. I'd managed to pull myself and my sister out of the self-sabotaging cycle our mother had raised us in. But the further I delved into this investigation, the more I felt like my current life was a sham that could unravel at any moment, landing me right back where I started.

"Ellie?"

I started. "What?'

Baxter cast me a worried glance. "I said, Marcus and Ava had several phone and text conversations. I think she could be very helpful, especially since she was so close to your mother. Then I asked you to look at the next page and tell me if you recognize any names. Only first names are listed for the contacts, but I think it won't be too hard to figure out who these people are."

"Right. Sorry." I flipped to the next page. My heart sank as I recognized names of people I'd thought I'd never have to lay eyes on again. I shook my head to clear it and got down to business. "Um . . . 'Jimmy' would be Marcus's buddy, Jimmy Belzer. He's a tool."

"A dangerous tool with a record, so you won't be talking to him."

I wasn't afraid of Jimmy Belzer. "He's more stupid than dangerous." I continued down the list. "'Katie' and 'Jack' are obviously the Coplands. 'Michelle' is an old girlfriend Rachel mentioned but didn't know her last name. 'Ava,' we know. The name 'Tyrell' isn't super common, so I'd assume he's the Tyrell Simpkins Marcus told me was one of his cuckholds."

"He's also a known drug supplier, so I'll speak to him without you."

The next name actually brought a smile to my face. "'Rick' is probably Rick Palmer. I think I mentioned him to you during our first case together. We lived with him for a hot minute when I was little."

Baxter's eyebrows shot up. "The drug dealer from that scary neighborhood in Indy?"

"Yeah."

"Yet another one you'll be sitting out."

I frowned. "Boo. I wouldn't mind seeing Rick again."

He wasn't going to budge on this. "No. Go on."

"The last name is 'Bobby,' which doesn't ring a bell with me."

"Katie Copland's neighbor, Bobby Harper. Sterling had a visit from him yesterday demanding answers about Katie's death. Seems like the two of them were close from how distraught the guy was. I think we should interview him now that we know he was in contact with Marcus as well," Baxter said as he pulled up in front of the liquor store where Ava and my mother used to work together.

I grunted. "Ah, memories. I've reconciled many a cash drawer at this fine establishment."

His eyebrows shot up. "You worked here, too? When?"

"When I was in high school. Off the books, of course, since I was painfully underage. My mother would summon me here after midnight to count the drawer and do the end-of-day reconciling when she and Ava would get too drunk and/or high during their shifts. Once I left, Rachel got the job."

He frowned and changed the subject. "I guess Ava Donatelli never had any aspirations of moving up the corporate ladder. At least she's easy to find."

"The fact that she's held down this shitty job for so long is a win for her."

"What are we walking into here? You said Marcus was cheating on Katie Copland with your mother and this woman at the same time, but that was a while ago. How did it all shake out?"

Feeling uneasy, I said, "As for what we're walking into . . . it might not be pretty. It all depends on whether or not my mother told Ava about me taking Rachel away from her. I could see it going either way. She might have spilled her guts and cried on Ava's shoulder, in which case Ava will try to scratch my eyes out the second I walk in the door. It's equally possible my mother made up a bullshit story about how she kicked Rachel out of the house or how Rachel ran off with her baby daddy to save face. To answer the other part of your question, my mother and Ava always had a volatile relationship. They'd be besties and hang out every waking moment, then one would stab the other in the back, usually over some loser like Marcus . . . or even sometimes over scoring or selling drugs. It was weird. I mean, I've had to break up actual fistfights between them. Women generally don't resort to that."

He nodded. "Huh. But they have no problem tackling men twice their size?"

I gave him the stink-eye. "You're lucky you're cute, because I'm getting real tired of hearing about that."

He chuckled all the way to the door. His lightheartedness, if a little forced, was welcome. Not only did I have to dredge up memories of my mother with the person who'd always been closest to her, but I had to do it surrounded by enough liquor to fill a swimming pool. I'd been committed to my sobriety long enough that drinking was no longer my go-to instinct, even in difficult situations. My issue was that this place, especially its poisonous contents, was a painful reminder of my mother's nasty habit that I, despite my best efforts to not turn out like her, had managed to replicate.

Ava glanced our way as we entered the store. The moment she laid eyes on me, her jaw dropped. She whispered, "Patty?" and stared at me like she'd seen a ghost. And I knew why. As much as I'd like to deny it, I was the spitting image of my mother. More accurately, I was the image of her I vaguely remembered from when I was very young, before half a lifetime of hard living had ruined her body, mind, and soul.

Ava wasn't the only one caught off guard by a specter of her past. Her appearance had me disconcerted, too. Aside from all of their fighting and backstabbing, she and my mother had been two peas in a pod. They'd dressed alike, fixed their hair alike, and had the same taste in men, booze, and drugs. My mom always said Ava copied everything she did, but it was mutual. The two of them were eerily similar, down to their sallow, scarred skin and perpetual dark undereye circles from decades of drug abuse. Worse, when I walked up to Ava at the counter, I caught a whiff of an unmistakable stink that triggered a jarring scent memory. I could have been convinced that my mother was in the room with us—the mix of cigarettes, unwashed hair, and the Chanel No. 5 knockoff perfume both women called their "signature scent" hit me like a ton of bricks. I exhaled a ragged breath.

Baxter shot a concerned glance my way and said, "Ms. Donatelli, this is Patty Copland's daughter, Ellie Matthews, and I'm Detective Nick Baxter. We're here on behalf of the Hamilton County sheriff's office to ask you a few questions about Patty and Marcus Copland."

Ava relaxed and slipped on a sneer in place of her shock. "Well, Ellie, ain't you all growed up? Last time I seen you, you was a teenage delinquent. Now you're a cop?" She scoffed. "No daughter of Patty's would ever side with the enemy. You working a long con or are you dirty?"

Evidently my mother had chosen to lie about why Rachel had left her home, which was good news for me. I managed to shake off my initial shock to reply, "We'll be asking the questions, Ava. You and Marcus were close. Did he ever mention anything to you about my mother's death or the deaths of any of his other girlfriends?"

She narrowed her bloodshot eyes at me. "Why you coming around now asking about this? Patty's been dead for years."

Baxter said, "Her case has been reopened. When's the last time you talked to Marcus?"

Flicking her eyes away, she replied, "Not since Patty died."

I shook my head. "Try again."

She huffed. "Fine. This week. He come in a couple of times around the end of my shift and drove me home."

Baxter asked, "Did he mention running into any of his old buddies lately? Or enemies?"

Winking at him, she replied, "Me and Marcus never did much talking when we was together."

I rubbed my forehead, trying to stave off the mental image our conversation was conjuring in my head. "We don't want gory details, Ava. We want to know if you're aware of any run-ins, altercations, or arguments he had since he got back. Any threats he might have received."

"If he did, he didn't tell me nothing."

"Did he take any calls when you were together?"

She shrugged. "I don't remember. We was high most of the time."

"Shocker," I muttered. It was time for a change of subject. "You know he's dead, right?"

Frowning, she said, "I seen that on the TV." She shook her head. "But I don't believe a word of that other horseshit they said about him. Marcus was a lot of things, but a killer ain't one of them."

Baxter asked, "Why do you say that?"

Ava grinned at him. Ooh. She'd lost some teeth since the last time I'd seen her. She softened her tone and purred, "I've been with a lot of dangerous men, honey. The killers are . . . different. Marcus never gave off that vibe." She pulled a lighter and a pack of menthols from her pocket and eye-boned Baxter as she lit a cigarette and took a puff. "You look like you got a little danger in you, sweetcheeks, but I bet I could still show you a thing or two."

"Gross," I blurted out before I could stop myself. To cover my horror at

Ava propositioning my boyfriend, I added, "You can't smoke inside a business."

Unfazed, she blew a billow of smoke my way. "I can't believe Patty's kid is a friggin' goody-two-shoes. Your mother would roll over in her grave if she could see you now."

Ava could get under my mother's skin like no one else, and now she was directing her superpower my way. Unfortunately, it was working. I snapped, "Roll over in her grave? And how might she do that, Ava? Surely you remember she was hacked into several pieces, some of which were a pile of human soup by the time we found them. Soup can't roll."

Baxter muttered to me, "You have *got* to stop using that phrase."

Ava's face fell, and her complexion got even grayer. "Look, me and your mom didn't always get along, but she was . . . the only real friend I ever had." Tears pooled in her eyes. "I miss her."

Baxter jumped in, using a tactic I'd never seen him use before—flirting. He rested his elbow on the counter and leaned toward her. "I'm sure you miss her a lot, Ava. And being such a close friend, you could be one of the most important people we talk to in this investigation."

Straightening a little, she said, "Me? I'm important?"

He gave her the sweet grin he usually reserved for me. "Of course you are. For instance, what do you remember about the last time you saw Patty? Was she acting normally? Did she give any indication she thought she was in danger?"

"No. Things was pretty normal. She missed a couple of shifts in a row, but that wasn't too surprising for Patty. She went on benders, as you know." She looked at me, this time with some actual compassion in her eyes. "But then she was just gone. Never came back to work. Never returned my calls. The last time I seen her before that was at her place. That loser Jeff was there, and they was fighting. Over Marcus . . ." She frowned. "And some other shit that was going down."

I said impatiently, "She was cheating on Jeff with Marcus. We know. What else was going down?"

Ava acted like she didn't want to talk about this part. "She'd, uh . . . been helping . . . facilitate deals for this guy, Dante, who—"

"What do you mean, 'facilitate'?" I butted in.

"Talking up Dante to anyone who'd listen. Bringing him new customers. Feeding him names of other dealers in the area so he knew who to intimidate into giving him their turf."

Figuring I probably didn't want to hear the answer, I asked anyway, "And how was she reimbursed for her trouble?"

She looked away from me and sucked on her awful cigarette. "With product. Dante didn't want the kind of payment she usually gave her dealers, so he figured out another way for her to earn some credit with him."

I'd been hoping for a different answer. My mother had indeed been a crack whore, and a well-known one at that. I nodded at Baxter to take back over.

He flashed Ava another smile and asked, "Did Jeff have a problem with Patty's relationship with Dante?"

She replied, "Yeah. He was one of them dealers Dante liked to intimidate."

"If her boyfriend was a dealer, why didn't she work for him instead?"

"She was already working for Dante when she met Jeff. You don't screw Dante over and live to tell about it."

Baxter and I shared a glance. He asked, "Did she ever mention Dante being unhappy with her? Did he ever give her a specific reason to be scared of him?"

"Not that I know of. Patty wasn't stupid. She knew how to keep people off her ass."

I asked, "Back to Marcus. Do you know why he went to Jeff's house the week before she died and beat her up? Using her as a punching bag was always a pastime of his, but for him to seek her out to do it, something must have gone down between the two of them."

Ava nodded. "Oh, yeah. That was because she sent a bunch of his regular customers Dante's way."

I clicked my tongue. "That'd be more than enough ammunition for a good Marcus beatdown."

"Sure enough," she agreed. I assumed she'd been on the receiving end of a good Marcus beatdown at one point or another.

I figured it was time to get down to business. "So did you kill my mother?"

Her jaw dropped. "No! Why would I—" She shook her head and appeared to be taken aback. "How could you even think that?"

"You were a person of interest back in the day. There had to be a reason for it."

Her lip curling in disgust, she spat, "Because I'm poor white trash, that's why."

I shook my head. "That's a cop-out. I know the people who investigated the case. That wouldn't have been enough for them."

She looked away. "I wasn't too cooperative when they questioned me. I might have . . . been a little high and . . . pulled a knife."

I snorted. "You're lucky you didn't get yourself shot."

"Lucky? I lost a damn tooth when they knocked my ass on the ground to take my knife away."

"To be fair, that tooth was probably going to fall out on its own."

She stared daggers at me. "You watch your mouth, smartass."

I fired back, "Maybe you should watch yours. It's kind of a nightmare in there."

Baxter stepped in to smooth things over before they got out of control. "Ava, we don't think you killed Patty. I'd like to know, though . . . who do you think killed her?"

Shrugging, Ava said, "Probably Marcus's wife. He was cheating on Katie with Patty and Katie knew it."

I shook my head. "Katie Copland did not have the upper body strength to cut up a corpse and transport it. Who else?"

"Jeff, maybe. He was a fool."

"You think her boyfriend wasn't one of the suspects the cops came up with? Think harder, Ava. You have to have a couple of brain cells left."

She smirked at me. "Why do you think I should know something the cops ain't been able to figure out in four years?"

I slammed my hand on the counter between us, making her flinch. "Seriously? You were her best friend, and you have no idea who could have killed her? Or maybe you know damn well who killed her and are covering for them. Was it Dante?"

Ava shook her head slightly, looking like a deer in headlights. "I don't . . . I ain't narcing on someone like Dante Romero. That's suicide."

Baxter shifted the conversation. "Ava, let's dial it back. Can you think of some of Marcus's friends, business associates, or enemies who'd want to set him up for murder or at least run him out of town?"

She took another drag from her cigarette. "Marcus wasn't what you'd call popular. Everyone had their reasons for hating him enough to want to ruin his life."

"Can you give us names of some of those people who hated him?" Baxter gave her another of his winning smiles. "It would really help me out, and I'd be very grateful to you."

Ava raised one of her badly drawn-on eyebrows. "How grateful? Like, take me in the back room for some hand stuff, grateful?"

His smile faded, and his eyes registered fear as he backed away from the counter. Ooh. My poor sweet Baxter couldn't handle sex talk of any kind. He was in way over his head.

I rolled my eyes at her and pulled a twenty out of my purse. Tossing it across the counter, I said, "He's younger than your kid. Let's say we're two dime bags grateful."

She shrugged and swiped the bill, tucking it safely under her dingy bra strap. "That's old enough."

As Baxter worked to hold in a retch, I barked, "Start talking."

Ava said, "Fine. Marcus and Hector Torres was always into it over one thing or another. Same with Jake Campbell. Joe . . . somebody . . . beat the shit out of him once. I think it was over his whore wife, Michelle." She paused for a moment. "Come to think of it, put Michelle on that list, too. She's a bitch."

"You know her personally?"

"Nah, not really. Me and Patty tracked her down once so Patty could convince her to stay away from Marcus."

I looked her in the eye. "So my mother had a heart-to-heart conversation with this woman?"

Smiling, Ava said, "You knew your mama. It was more of a fist-to-face conversation."

I held in a weary sigh. "Do you know Michelle's last name?"

"Mmm . . . it was Kovak . . . no, wait. Kojak."

"Novak?" I supplied, pulling a name I remembered from my conversation with Marcus when he showed up at my house.

"That's it. She left her husband for Marcus." She laughed. "By the time the ink was dry on the divorce papers, Marcus was already tired of her. Serves her right. She busted up Marcus and Patty's second marriage."

If that was true, the woman deserved a medal. If only she'd come into Marcus's life and turned his head a little sooner, my last couple of years living at home might not have been such a torturous hell.

I asked, "Any other people you can think of with something against Marcus? Friends or family? He was the type who'd screw over anyone."

"He didn't have no family besides Rachel and that kid he had with Katie." She shot me a glare. "And he *wasn't* the type who'd screw over his buddies."

"Whatever." I turned to Baxter. "You good?"

He nodded, still looking a little ill.

I said to Ava, "Thanks for the info. I'd say it's been fun catching up, but we both know it wasn't."

She surprised me by breaking into a proud smile. "You're Patty's kid, all right. Full of the same sass and fire. You, uh . . . ever see Rachel?"

"I do. We're close."

Her eyes filled with tears. "Patty'd be so happy to know that. You tell Rachel I said hi."

"I will."

Once Baxter and I got outside, he let out a long breath. "That was the weirdest interview we've ever done, and that's saying something."

I couldn't keep the grin from my face. "You were the one who made it weird. You never flirt with women to get them to talk. That's a Vic thing."

Baxter threw up his hands. "I thought I'd give it a try. Never again, though." He hesitated, his eyes pleading. "Don't you dare tell him I tried it and failed."

I burst out laughing. He and Vic had surprised me over the last few months by becoming friends. I didn't think it would ever have happened, but they'd bonded over having both been wounded on the job and on medical leave for a good chunk of the past year. And although they were no longer at odds, they had no problem pointing out each other's faults, especially if it got a laugh out of me.

Taking his hand, I promised, "I won't."

18

With my attention on a text to Talia about the next day's lab, I hadn't been paying attention to where Baxter was driving us until he pulled to a stop in my driveway.

I said, "Surely we're not calling it a night already."

He smiled. "Oh, you're not even close to being off the hook for today. I thought we might ask Rachel if she'd help us speak to Jack Copland. Show him a friendlier face than either of ours and maybe put him more at ease."

"Great idea."

We entered my house to find Rachel sitting on the couch with a bowl of popcorn in hand, bingeing yet another old comedy series. She'd given up on her lifelong favorite genre—horror—after being kidnapped and held by a serial killer. I didn't blame her one bit.

As Trixie greeted Baxter and me, Rachel joked, "You guys wrap up the investigation already? It was my list that cracked the case wide open, wasn't it?" My sister knew from experience that investigations took a lot of my time. My lengthy absences from home put a strain on her to keep the house in decent order, take care of Nate on her own, and keep up with her school-work, but she never complained too much.

I laughed and gave my dog a kiss on the head. "We wish. But seriously, your list is invaluable, and Vic is thrilled you were able to tie his mystery phone to Jihyo. He wasted a lot of his day on it."

"Cool." She eyed us, sensing something was up. "So why are you back?"

Plopping down next to her on our comfy couch, I helped myself to a handful of her popcorn. "Baxter has something to ask you."

Baxter shot me a mock frown and said to Rachel, "I realize you've done more than enough for us, but I want to ask another favor. Would you contact Jack Copland and ease him into our interview? We need to ask him about his and his mother's interactions with your father this week, plus I'd like him to go over your list. We know it's going to be a tough conversation."

Her expression turned sad. "It will be, but I'm happy to do anything to help him and you. Phone call or FaceTime?"

He sat down on the other side of me. "It would be best to be able to see his reactions."

Rachel put down her popcorn bowl and grabbed her laptop from the coffee table. "FaceTime it is." She pulled up the FaceTime app and initiated the video call. After a few moments, Jack's face filled her screen, illuminated only by the light of his phone screen. Poor kid looked so sad sitting there in the dark, though I hadn't expected anything different. Rachel said, "Hey, bro. How you holding up?"

Jack sighed. "Not great. The change of scenery is helping a little, but I know it's all going to come crashing back when I go home to an empty house."

Rachel gave him an encouraging smile. "You're not alone. I'm here for you. You know that."

"I know." He blew out a breath. "So what's up? FaceTime isn't your style."

Her smile faded. "Yeah, about that . . . You know my sister, Ellie?"

"Sort of."

"She and her partner need to ask you some questions about Marcus."

Jack wiped a hand down his face. "I don't even want to think about him, Rachel. And I don't know what I can tell her. I suddenly feel like I didn't know our dad at all. I mean, you thought he was a murderer, but . . . I really didn't believe it . . . I guess I didn't *want* to believe it. Until now."

Rachel glanced at me. "Um, there's a new development there . . . Ellie and her partner figured out there's no way Marcus could have killed your mom. He was actually here at our house at the time. We're his alibi."

Jack's eyes bugged out. "He didn't kill my mom? Who did?"

"That's what they're trying to figure out, and that's why they need your help."

"Oh . . . okay . . ." He let out a breath. "So you're sure he didn't kill my mom?"

She nodded. "Yes."

"But . . . did he still kill your mom?"

"Possibly not."

"Damn. That's a lot to take in." He rubbed his forehead for a few moments and then sighed. "Okay, I'll talk to them."

"They'll make it quick so you can get some rest." My sister gave Baxter and me a pointed look. "Right, guys?"

Baxter and I both nodded.

Swiveling the laptop our way, I said, "Jack, I'm sorry about your mom . . . and dad. It's a terrible time, but we really appreciate you talking to us. This is my partner, Detective Nick Baxter."

Jack nodded.

Baxter said, "We heard Marcus came to town specifically to visit you. Is that what he told you as well?"

"Yeah," Jack replied.

"Did he say he had other business here?"

"You mean work business?"

Baxter replied, "Yes, and any other type of connections or interactions he might have wanted to make with people he hadn't spoken to in a while."

Jack shook his head. "He never talked about any work stuff around me." Probably because Marcus's only "work" was dealing drugs. He went on. "Um . . . he did say he wanted to try to reconnect with Rachel."

My stomach clenched. I asked, "What made him think she was here in town?"

He stared back at us, his eyes strained. "I'm sorry, you guys . . . Rachel . . . My mom let it slip to him one night when he came to our house. She didn't know it was supposed to be kept a secret."

Next to me, Rachel went rigid. I could feel barely controlled anger rolling off of her. Evidently Jack hadn't come clean about this to her yet.

He went on. "That's on me. I never told her that you guys thought Dad killed your mom. I didn't want to give her another reason to hate him or for her to worry her about her safety . . . Now I wish I'd said something." He hung his head. "I didn't think it mattered that she knew about Rachel still living here because . . . I never imagined she'd speak to Dad again after he left us like that. Again." Looking up at the screen with tears in his eyes, he said, "Rachel, can you forgive me?"

I turned the laptop so Rachel was in his view.

She cleared her throat and said tightly, "Yes. It's over now." That was Rachel-speak for "I love you, but I'm still pissed at you and will be for a while." I'd received plenty of that sentiment over the last year as my sister struggled to recover from her trauma.

Baxter stepped in and smoothly changed the subject, so I turned the laptop back toward us. "Marcus told Ellie he'd received threats over the phone. Did he mention that to you or your mom?"

Jack replied, "Not to me. If Mom knew, she didn't say anything about it. She probably wouldn't have, though. She treated me like I was made of glass."

Out of the corner of my eye, I noticed Rachel's posture relax. I stole a glance at her. Her anger had morphed into sadness. According to what I'd heard, Jack's health was bad enough that I wasn't surprised his mother did everything in her power to not put additional stress on him.

I said to Jack, "How about him getting into a fight or argument with anyone, or someone being angry with him?"

He shrugged. "You knew him. He was always pissing someone off."

Baxter asked, "Can you give us some specifics?"

"Well . . . someone kicked his ass pretty hard a couple of days ago. He wouldn't tell me who."

Baxter and Rachel nudged me from both sides. I probably should have 'fessed up to that "someone" being me, but I figured Jack would be less receptive to my questions if he knew the truth.

Jack went on. "And a week or so before that, he got into it with Earl and ended up with a black eye. I think it happened at a bar."

I said, "The two of them hadn't gotten along for decades. Was it worse this time?"

"I'm not sure."

Baxter asked, "Can you think of anyone Marcus knew who might have wanted him to leave town? Did anyone threaten him or your family back when he lived with you?"

Jack blew out a breath. "I was only fifteen . . . I was kind of wrapped up in my own stuff."

I said, "You and I were at a similar age when we lived with Marcus. At that time in my life, I was doing my own stuff as well." I paused to frame this as best I could. "But it was hard not to notice what Marcus was up to. At least with me, he never bothered to hide his transgressions or arguments or drug use. He didn't care what I saw. He didn't try to protect me from himself or his drugs or his sketchy friends or his even sketchier customers. I'm sure you've seen things that might not have registered at the time. But the one thing we do know is that you and your mom were the last people he lived with and some of the last people he saw before he split town. We need to know what spooked him."

He thought for a moment. "Right before he left, I remember him flipping out over your mom's death. Like, bad."

When Jack didn't elaborate, Baxter asked, "Out of grief or anger? Or was he scared he'd be the prime suspect?"

"He was crushed. I'd never seen him cry before. He practically drank and drugged himself into a coma, which my mom got pissed about because he'd promised to cut back. And it only made things worse when Dad started calling out Patty's name and muttering about how much he always loved her."

My eyebrows shot up. "Really? Is that why you found it hard to believe Rachel when said she thought he'd killed our mother?"

"Partially."

I wondered if he and Rachel had ever discussed this, but that was a topic for another time. "Sorry for the interruption, Jack. Go on."

"So while he spent the weekend getting blitzed out of his mind, my mom figured out he'd been cheating on her with Patty. When he finally sobered up enough for her to confront him, they had the mother of all fights about it. Dad left that night, and I never saw him again until a couple of weeks ago. He didn't even say goodbye to me." He sighed. "Mom blamed herself for driving him away. She was a wreck. She'd be mad as hell, then suddenly get terrified that something bad happened to him, considering the type of people he hung around with. Not knowing was driving her crazy. Without our neighbor, Bobby, she might have actually gone nuts. He stepped in to take care of us the first time Dad left, and he stepped right back in again this time. Bobby looked for Dad for weeks. He went to the police, checked with all the hospitals, tracked down all of Dad's friends, and went around to all the places he liked to hang out. Dad had disappeared into thin air. My mom finally gave up and moved on. A few months ago, Dad calls her out of the blue. Mom was done being mad at him, so she made sure he and I reconnected. It was a weird relationship, but at least I had my dad sort of back in my life."

I said gently, "I'm sorry that happened to you, Jack. Thank you for being open with us. If you don't mind me asking, did your parents ever get divorced?"

"No, they were still technically married." He huffed out a sheepish laugh. "I know this sounds dumb, but I was kind of hoping once they saw each other again they'd, I don't know . . . fall back in love or something. And maybe he'd stick around for a while." His voice broke.

Rachel turned the laptop back so it faced her. "Jack, that doesn't sound dumb. I know you had some good times when our dad and your mom were together. She was good for him. She evened out his rough edges. I'm sorry they didn't get one more chance to try to make it work."

"Me, too," he choked out.

Rachel looked at me. "Time to wrap this up."

I replied, "You're right." I leaned over so Jack could see me on the screen. "Thank you, Jack. We really appreciate this."

He nodded.

I looked at Rachel pleadingly. "Could you guys take a quick look together at our list of Marcus's exes to see if there are any we missed?"

My sister frowned at me. "I think we've done enough for one night."

Jack said, "It's okay. If you think it'll help find my parents' and your mom's killer, then I'm in."

"Thank you," I said.

I pulled up a photo of the list we'd put together and handed Rachel my phone. Baxter and I left her and Jack alone as she began reading the list of names of the women their father had loved and left.

I pulled Baxter into my bedroom and shut the door. "What do you think about the neighbor, Bobby Harper?"

He slid his arms around my waist. "I thought you were bringing me in here for a more fun reason than to talk shop."

"Sorry. Tick, tock."

He shrugged and released me. "I think he's someone we need to have on our radar. If he's the one who swoops in to rescue Katie Copland every time Marcus breaks her heart, he's got to have a pretty strong opinion about him."

"Strong enough to drive Marcus out of town so he could have Katie all to himself?"

"Maybe." He stroked his beard. "The thing that doesn't add up in that scenario is Katie's death. He already had her all to himself."

I countered, "Until a couple of weeks ago when Marcus came back to town. If Bobby thought Katie was choosing Marcus over him—again—then maybe he snapped and killed them both. He's got a screw loose in there somewhere if he wants Marcus's sloppy seconds, right?"

His mouth pulling up in the corner, he said, "Fair point, but what reason would he have to kill Marcus's other exes?"

"The obvious one." When his reaction was a perplexed stare, I explained, "Katie would have hated those women for taking and/or keeping Marcus away from her and her son and busting up their little family. She was certainly no fan of my mother for that very reason. Bobby was head over heels for Katie, so he wanted to please her, and it didn't hurt that he could screw Marcus in the process. By keeping the trophies, he threw in some extra insurance for himself, and he got Marcus out of his way by holding the murders over his head."

"I don't hate your idea, but I'm still stuck on why he'd kill Katie if he loved her so much that he killed three people to make her happy."

"Nobody likes getting cuckolded."

"I'm going to need a little more than that to be convinced."

"Okay, fine. You asked for it." I cleared my throat and made a theatrical sweeping motion with my hands. "Picture this: Marcus suddenly shows back up at Katie's house, probably acting like he owns the place and angling to get in her pants. They're still married, after all, so he has his husbandly rights. Jack's thrilled about the possibility of them being a family again. There's no room for Bobby in this scenario, and he becomes wild with jealousy. But if he cries about it to Katie, she might decide he's a little bitch and run back into the arms of her favorite bad boy forever. If he opts to have a man-to-man chat with Marcus, he could get his ass handed to him. He ends up going total chickenshit and starts anonymously threatening Marcus over that burner phone, insisting he leave town again, but Marcus is too stupid to back down. Bobby decides he's finally had enough and that Katie isn't worth the trouble. He ends both of them. To cover his ass, he plays the concerned friend card and makes a big deal at the station about the status of Katie's investigation. He's an evil freaking genius."

Baxter grinned at me. "You know you're especially beautiful when you play devil's advocate and think like a delinquent?"

I winked at him and opened the door. "Let's keep this professional, Detective."

"To be clear, you're the one who lured me into your bedroom."

We returned to my living room, where Rachel and Jack were wrapping up their conversation. She closed the lid on her laptop and collapsed into the couch cushions.

I gave my sister a contrite smile. "Sorry we roped you into that, but we think Jack gave us plenty to work with. Thank you."

"No sweat," she replied, her tone implying the opposite of her words.

I perched near her on the arm of the couch. "Do you know Jack's neighbor, Bobby Harper?"

"Yeah, I've known him since I was a kid. He's really nice. A way better father figure to Jack than Marcus could ever have hoped to be."

As nonchalantly as possible, I asked, "What was he to Katie?"

She barked out a laugh. "You mean were they doing it?"

"Yes, we unfortunately need to know all the gory details you can tell us."

"Yeah, they were doing it. He treated her like a queen. I don't understand why she didn't kick Marcus to the curb permanently the second she met Bobby."

Baxter asked, "How did she treat him?"

Rachel shrugged. "Kind of like a doormat, like Marcus treated her."

"So Bobby had to work for her affection?"

"Pretty much."

Nodding, he asked, "What was Bobby's relationship with Marcus like?"

"Bobby was always really friendly toward Marcus when Katie or Jack was around, but I remember overhearing them argue a few times. Sometimes when Jack and I would play or hang out in his backyard, we could hear their voices from Bobby's house next door. The two of them would sit in Bobby's garage and drink beer in the evenings. Most of the time it was all joking around . . . but then someone would start some shit that would escalate into an actual fight. Marcus would come back with a bloody nose, and we'd see Bobby the next day with a black eye. Typical Marcus bullshit. You know how he and his friends rolled."

I said, "Can you remember what they fought about? Katie, perhaps?"

"Oh, yeah, Katie for sure. You know, when I was little, I thought Bobby was Katie's older brother. He was super protective of her, and Jack called him 'Uncle Bobby' until he was a teenager." She chuckled. "I walked in on Katie and Bobby kissing one day and still didn't realize my mistake. I asked them if siblings who really loved each other kissed on the lips instead of just hugging. They said yes, and then Katie gave me two enormous home-made cookies to agree not to tell Marcus. She didn't give me a reason why he couldn't know, but a cookie in each hand was reason enough for me."

I smiled sadly. "I bet it was. Mom never made us cookies." I had a sudden flash of memory. "Wait, how old were you then? Seven?"

She furrowed her brow. "I think."

"I remember you coming home one day asking me if we could kiss on the lips. I said absolutely not, and you burst into tears. You said Katie and her brother kiss on the lips because they really love each other, and that you really love me so we should lip-kiss, too. I was afraid there was some weird shit happening at that house, so I told Mom I didn't want you going over there anymore."

Rachel scoffed. "I bet she did what she always did when our welfare was at stake—nothing."

"I figured that would be the case, so instead of making the situation about your welfare, I framed it as an opportunity for her to out Katie Copland for being a freak. That seemed to interest her, so I guess she ratted Katie out to Marcus, because . . ." I thought for a moment. "Huh. Marcus moved back in with us right around that time. And the minute he divorced Katie . . ."

"He remarried Mom." My sister's eyes widened. "Did we bust up Marcus and Katie's first marriage and *Parent Trap* my parents?"

I put my head in my hands. "Shit." Why had I never put all that together before?

Baxter cut in. "You absolutely did not. Katie was clearly cheating on Marcus with Bobby, and Marcus was cheating on Katie with Ava and your mom. They busted up their own marriage. Don't put this on yourselves."

I raised my head. "I couldn't care less that I had a hand in Marcus and Katie's divorce. What I'm upset about is the fact that I had a *giant* hand in bringing Marcus back to torture me. Why didn't I realize Marcus would drop Katie like a bad habit and latch onto the nearest thing with boobs?"

Rachel reached over to grab my hand. "Because when my safety is at stake, you never half-ass anything. You go beast mode and never worry about the consequences you'll have to face for the crazy shit you always do to protect me."

Baxter smiled at me. "It's your best and worst quality."

They weren't wrong, and I literally had the scars to prove it. I was surprised Baxter didn't bring that up (again), but this conversation was lighthearted and needed to be kept that way.

I said to him, "On that note, can we be done walking down memory lane for today? I much prefer interviewing criminals and lowlife dickbags."

"Yeah, I think we're done here." He said to Rachel, "Thanks for letting us ruin your day. Twice. We appreciate the help."

She smiled. "Anything for you guys."

Baxter took my hand and pulled me to a standing position. "Time to track down some criminals and lowlife dickbags."

19

Baxter and I found Bobby Harper sitting alone in his garage, whittling a piece of wood and drinking his fifth beer, judging by the number of empty bottles at his feet. He didn't even get up from his tattered lawn chair as we approached.

"What do you want?" he bellowed, shielding his eyes from the lights of Baxter's SUV as we got out and approached him.

Baxter flashed his badge. "Mr. Harper, I'm Detective Nick Baxter and this is Ellie Matthews from the county sheriff's office. We have some questions for you about Marcus Copland."

Bobby set his whittling knife and piece of wood aside to take a long pull from his beer bottle. "I got nothing to say about that sack of shit."

Baxter set his hands on his hips, making sure to rest his right hand on the service pistol strapped to his belt. "We'll be happy to escort you to the station and talk there."

"Fine, I'll talk," Bobby groaned. "Don't you already have a confession, though? And that son of a bitch is dead, so why does it even matter?"

Baxter replied, "What you've seen on the news isn't necessarily the whole story. Let's start with you, though. Can you tell us where you were Monday night at 8:45 p.m.?"

His knuckles going white as he gripped his beer bottle, Bobby glared at us. "You mean when Katie was killed?"

"Yes."

"I was here."

"Alone?"

Bobby ground out, "Yes. Why the hell does it matter where *I* was when Marcus was running down Katie?"

I replied, "Because Marcus didn't run down Katie."

He scoffed. "Says who?"

"Me. I was interviewing him at the time."

Bobby's face fell. He removed his dirty trucker hat to wipe his forehead with an even dirtier bandana handkerchief. He shook his head.

Baxter asked, "What was your relationship like with Marcus Copland?"

Seeming dazed, Bobby replied, "Uh . . . we was . . . neighbors. We used to hang out and . . . we was friendly enough."

"How about after he found out Katie was cheating on him with you?" I asked.

His eyes widened. "We had a falling out." He waved a hand. "Ah, that was fifteen years ago, though. Once he moved on, he quit being pissed at me. We was okay after that." Narrowing his eyes at me, he said, "You look awful familiar."

"I get that a lot."

Continuing to stare at me, he muttered, "I know I seen you somewhere . . ."

I ignored him. "Can you tell us where you were yesterday between five and six p.m.?"

Bobby's expression turned suspicious. "Why?"

Baxter said, "Answer the question."

"Driving home from work and then over at Katie's tending to Jack, making sure he ate something." He shook his head and muttered, "Poor kid."

No alibi for part of the time when Marcus was ingesting all the drugs that killed him. Interesting. I asked, "Did you talk to Marcus in the past couple of weeks?"

"A little."

"Did he mention anyone threatening him? Was he afraid someone was out to get him?"

Grunting, Bobby replied, "Somebody or other was always out to get him, seems like."

"Did he name names?" Baxter asked.

"He didn't say nothing about it to me. Or Katie, as far as I know."

Baxter went on. "Someone ran him out of town four years ago, and it sounds like they knew he was back and gave him an ultimatum. You know anything about that?"

Bobby shook his head and peeled at the label on his beer.

Taking a couple of steps toward our interviewee so he could tower over him, Baxter said, "I think you might."

Raising his eyes to meet Baxter's, Bobby said, "I think unless you want to arrest me for something, pretty boy, you need to get the hell off my property."

I said, "Spoken like a man with something to hide. I wouldn't be surprised if you were the one who ran Marcus out of town in the first place. Your sweet Katie was heartbroken because he was cheating on her yet again, and you saw your chance to get her back. Maybe you're smarter than you look and you figured the police would be looking at Marcus for Patty Copland's murder. So you threatened to pin the murder on him if he didn't leave town for good."

Bobby tried to jump up from his chair at us, but it was too rickety and he was too old and too buzzed. The chair slid, its frame bent, and he landed on his side with a grunt on the grease-stained concrete. He wheezed, "That's horseshit! You got two seconds to get off my property before I get my shotgun and start shooting!"

Baxter was working to hold back a laugh. He head-nodded toward a nearby pegboard, where a sawed-off shotgun hung prominently in a disturbing display of semi-legal weaponry. "I figure we got a good five minutes before you can haul your sorry ass up and limp across the room. We'll be in touch, Mr. Harper." Belying his nonchalant tone and words, he steered me purposely to his SUV and wasted no time peeling out of the driveway.

I said, "So *now* what do you think about Bobby Harper?"

"He's definitely mixed up in this cluster."

"I agree. So who's he mixed up with? Katie?"

He threw an amused glance at me. "You really do think Katie Copland could have had a hand in some of this, don't you?"

"She married Marcus twice. That makes her at least as crazy as my mother. So, yes, I could see her going to certain lengths to make him pay for what he did to her. She certainly hated my mother enough to kill her . . . and if I'm being honest, the same goes for my mother." A chilling thought hit me. "Wait. My mother . . . she never let a chance go by to exact revenge on the skanks she thought were responsible for turning Marcus's head and breaking them up." I looked over at him. "You don't think she'd—"

He reached over and put a hand over mine. "Ellie, this whole investigation is so convoluted. At this point, nearly everyone involved is a potential suspect. It's not unfair of you or a slight against your mother's memory to—"

I gaped at him. "You'd already come to that conclusion about my mother! How long has she been on your suspect list, and when were you planning to clue me in?"

He pulled over to the side of the road and put his vehicle in park. "You know I like to think outside the box. I've gone through every player we know about—including the murder victims—and asked myself what lengths they'd go to get back at Marcus." His expression turning apologetic, he went on. "Your mom had a staggering amount of motive to have played a part in the deaths of Alice Graves and Jihyo Yoon."

I nodded, trying to keep my tears at bay. My heart broke as I thought about how this development would affect Rachel if even a small detail of it turned to be true. She already thought her father was a monster. What would it do to her to find out our mother was one as well? My opinion of our mother was already so low it was practically nonexistent, but the idea of her having anything to do with murder made me ill. If Rachel had felt like this for years about Marcus, I didn't know how she stood it.

As if reading my mind, Baxter reached out and enveloped me in a hug. I leaned into him, hoping his calming presence would dissipate the storm inside me. He said, "I could be totally off base here. A lot of other people have tons more motive than your mother—it's just that I can't look past the fact that she doesn't have zero motive. The last thing I ever want to do is worry or upset you, so that's why I kept this idea to myself. I was hoping to prove myself wrong and never have to bring it up."

I pulled back and tried to smile. I was sure it was more of a grimace. "That's a fair assessment. And thank you for letting me come to it on my own."

He leaned in for a quick kiss. "Well, I knew better than to drop that kind of a bomb on you, especially after the week you've had."

"If you don't mind, can we table discussing it until tomorrow?"

"How about we table it forever and let someone else dig into it?"

I hesitated, hating to dump this on someone else *and* sit back and watch while they took all the skeletons out of my mother's very crowded closet.

Again with the mind reading, Baxter said, "The sheriff is assigned to your mother's homicide case. She already knows more of your family's history than anyone. I'll mention it to her, and she can run with it how she sees fit. You know she'll be discreet."

I nodded, the knot in my gut beginning to unravel. "That's perfect."

NEXT ON OUR list was Michelle Novak, who according to her driver's license was now Michelle Rutkowski. She was the manager of Marcus's favorite pizza parlor, which we were considering visiting anyway. When we arrived, we found her behind the small bar washing glasses. She looked like Marcus's type—rode hard and put up wet, but at one time probably quite pretty.

Baxter showed her his badge. "Mrs. Rutkowski?"

Michelle seemed to be having a hard time deciding whether to be defensive or flirt with Baxter. She ultimately chose flirting. "It's Ms. I'm newly divorced."

He smiled. "Nice to meet you, Ms. Rutkowski. I'm Detective Nick Baxter and this is Ellie Matthews. We'd like to speak to you about Marcus Copland."

She made a sign of the cross, which I was pretty sure she did backward. "Rest his soul."

"Yes. We found your contact information in his phone and—"

Michelle was completely ignoring him to stare at me. "Look at you," she drawled. "You've got to be Patty Copland's spawn."

I nodded. "I am."

"You look just like her. That is, without the meth mouth and needle tracks." She leaned over the counter, giving my body a once-over. "And if she ate a toddler or something."

Offended to my core, I snapped back, "Patty only kept it tight because all she ever put in her body was booze, drugs, and diseased dicks."

Baxter just about choked on a snort of laughter, but managed to hold it together.

Michelle, on the other hand, threw her head back and laughed like a hyena. When she finally sobered, she said, "Yep, you're Patty's kid, all right. Beer's on me. What'll you have?"

Baxter said, "Nothing for us, thanks. We only want information."

She shrugged. "I don't know what I can tell you. I haven't talked to Marcus in forever."

I said, "Are you using 'forever' in a hyperbolic sense?"

All I got was a blank look from her. "A what, now?"

"Do you consider 'forever' to be three days ago when you had a four-minute phone conversation with him? Or the three times in the past two weeks when he was here drowning his sorrows?"

Her eyes widened only slightly when I busted her in a lie. Laughing easily, she said, "Yeah, I was being anabolic."

Baxter shot me an amused grin before he asked her, "Did he mention to you about anyone threatening him?"

Turning her attention toward drying a glass, she replied, "Not that I remember."

"We know he had enemies in the area. Did he talk about any altercations he had with anyone in the couple of weeks he'd been back?"

"Mmm . . . nope."

This wasn't going well.

I said, "You've known Marcus for quite a while. Who has he pissed off enough in the last several years to make them want to run him out of town?"

She eyed me. "You mean when he split after your mom got murdered?"

"Yes."

"Well, duh. The cops were circling him like sharks. It would've been stupid to stick around and let them catch him."

I studied her for a moment, trying to decide if anything she'd said remotely resembled the truth. I wasn't sure it had. "So does that mean you believe he killed my mother?"

She shrugged. "Who can say? Your mom wasn't exactly Miss Congeniality. Nobody really liked her that much."

I nodded. "I suppose you could say the same thing about Marcus."

"I suppose."

"It's possible someone killed him as well."

Her nonchalant expression faltered for a moment. "He died of an OD. The news said so."

Baxter said, "The news gets things wrong sometimes."

Michelle had regained control of herself. "Hmm. Who'd want to kill Marcus?"

"That's what we're here to find out. You knew him. You know his friends and his associates. Surely you could come up with a couple of ideas."

I could see the wheels turning in her head. It was impossible to tell whether she was conjuring up a lie to cover for someone or was actually giving Baxter's question some thought.

She finally said, "Ten years ago, I would have said my ex. He beat Marcus all to hell. As much as I hate to put in a good word for Joe, it couldn't have been him. He's in jail."

I said, "He blamed Marcus for ending your marriage."

"Big time."

"Not for nothing, but my mother credited you with ending her marriage to Marcus."

Michelle sneered, "I remember. I lost a molar because of it."

"Well, I appreciate what you did. My little sister was better off with Marcus out of their household."

She gave me a strange look. "You're welcome, I guess."

Baxter got us back on track. "After you and Marcus split—"

Cutting in, Michelle spat, "Thanks to that whore, Amy."

"Right. Not long after that, he was with a woman named Alice Graves. Did you ever meet her?"

"No."

"She was murdered right after they split up."

"So?"

This was going nowhere again. I jumped back in. "Let's circle back around to that whore, Amy. What can you tell us about her?"

Her expression going sour, Michelle said, "She weaseled her way back into Marcus's life and got herself knocked up on purpose. I'm not convinced the kid was even his."

I asked, "Because you don't want to have to stomach the fact that he'd been cheating on you, or because Amy's the type of person who'd lie about the identity of her baby daddy?"

"I don't know. Both?"

"Do you remember her last name?"

Shrugging, she ground out, "No. Never cared enough to learn it."

Clearly.

Baxter again tried to get our interview back on track. "Look, four of Marcus's exes were pretty brutally murdered, and we think he was, too. You knew him well. You were one of the few people he reconnected with when he came back to town. We believe it's possible that someone was intent on setting him up for murder and running him out of town. Who in his life would have gone to those lengths to get him to leave and never come back? And then when he did come back, to murder him and brand him a serial killer?"

She blew out a breath. "Look, Marcus had no short supply of enemies, and they're not the kind of people you want to screw around with. I wouldn't know where to start."

I said, "Start with the ones you think are the craziest. Surely you have an opinion."

"I hate to say it, but if we're talking crazy, your mom was the worst of the worst. Her and her weird friend."

I assumed she was talking about Ava, considering Ava's story about their "fist-to-face conversation" with Michelle. "I can't argue with you there. Who else?"

"That whore, Amy, was pretty batshit, too. She was obsessed with Marcus. Like, boil-a-rabbit obsessed."

Baxter and I shared a glance.

She went on. "And I always hated his friend, Jimmy Belzer. He tried to get handsy with me once, but I clocked him and shut that shit down."

"While you were with Marcus?" Baxter asked.

"No, after. He was the one-man clean-up crew for Marcus's sloppy seconds."

I frowned. "He went after *all* of Marcus's exes?"

"I said what I meant: sloppy seconds, not selective seconds. He didn't discriminate."

Baxter's expression had gone dark. "Do you happen to know if Alice Graves was one of the exes he tried to clean up?"

"I already told you I didn't know her."

"My question wasn't whether or not you knew her."

Michelle put a hand on her hip and scowled. Evidently she was done flirting with Baxter. "I don't know anything about her. Marcus never mentioned her to me."

He nodded. "Okay, then did he ever mention a woman named Jihyo Yoon? He agreed to a green card marriage with her, but she ended up dead before they made it down the aisle."

"That name doesn't ring a bell, either."

The question I'd been itching to ask technically pertained to our case, but my reason for asking didn't. "Did Jimmy try to get with my mother? He was always coming around our place, even when Marcus wasn't in the picture."

She snickered. "Yeah. He tapped that. But then again, who didn't?"

A fair statement, but I never enjoyed hearing other people say it out loud.

Baxter quickly changed the subject. "I was under the impression Marcus and Jimmy were friends, but I can't imagine the dynamic between them could have been that great if Jimmy was scooping up the women Marcus tossed aside. Do you believe Jimmy had an axe to grind with Marcus, or did you just throw his name in the ring because you don't like him?"

"Mostly because I hate him, but he's slimy as shit. I wouldn't put anything past him."

"Even murder?"

Shrugging, she said, "I could see it."

Baxter and I got a text notification at the same time. I looked at the message from Vic on my screen and sucked in a ragged breath.

911. Task force report to pinned location. Sheriff stable but wounded in drive-by shooting. Bring any equipment needed to work the scene.

20

Baxter shot Michelle a "Thanks for your time," over his shoulder and steered me out of the pizza parlor. To me, he said quietly, "Manetti said she's stable, so that's good news."

"Sure," I breathed, a lump forming in my throat. For years, Jayne had been high up enough on the department food chain that being in the line of fire was a thing of the past. Why now?

I got another text from Vic, this one only to me rather than to the whole task force: *Sheriff Walsh is fine. She just got grazed. She insisted I text you to tell you not to worry. So don't worry.*

I breathed a sigh of relief and said to Baxter, "Vic said she just got grazed, and she's evidently more worried about me being worried than she is about herself."

Baxter smiled. "Sounds about right." His smile faded as he plugged his phone into his SUV and pulled up the pinned location on the vehicle's screen. "The shooting happened at her house."

And my stomach dropped again. "At her house? Drive-bys do *not* happen in her neighborhood."

In my neighborhood, maybe. But Jayne lived in a lovely area where her neighbors had monthly block parties and their kids played outside freely without a care in the world. She'd invited Baxter and me to the last block party. It wasn't quite our scene—her neighbors were nice, but way too chatty and in my business. They wanted to know all about how Jayne and I met, which wasn't my finest moment considering our first interaction was her arresting me for shoplifting when I was a wayward teenager.

Baxter must have been thinking the same thing I was. "Her subdivision is going to be a circus. I hope Manetti had the foresight to mobilize an army of deputies to keep her nosy neighbors from injecting themselves into our investigation."

Even though I'd been told not to worry, it wasn't that simple to turn off my head. The drive over to Jayne's house and the hoops we had to jump through to get to the scene were a blur, up until I spied Jayne being loaded into an ambulance, a large bandage covering her left upper arm, which was in a sling. I jolted back to reality, scribbled my signature on the scene entry log, and rushed to Jayne's side.

Before I could even utter a word, she held up her good hand and said, "I'm fine."

I frowned at her. "You got shot, Jayne. You're anything but fine."

"It's just a flesh wound. I need a significant number of stitches, but I'll be good as new after that. I'll be back at it tomorrow morning."

"Getting shot isn't all about the physical wound. How's your head?"

She smiled proudly at me. "That sounds like something I would normally say to you."

Smiling back, I said, "And you're a smart cookie, so take your own advice. You should rest tomorrow rather than diving back in."

"We have five active homicides. I can't afford a day off."

Raising one eyebrow, I said, "That sounds like something I would normally say to you."

She rolled her eyes. "Okay, you've made your point. I promise to take care of myself."

I hoisted myself into the back of the ambulance. "You're not doing it alone."

Jayne put on her serious sheriff face. "I want you on this scene. That's an order."

"What, seriously? You're going to play the boss card on me?"

"Damn straight. Get the hell out of my ambulance."

The EMT who'd been securing the gurney gave me an apologetic look. "We can't let you ride along if the patient doesn't agree to it."

Jayne said, "I don't agree to it."

I hopped down from the back of the ambulance. "Fine. But the moment I'm done here, I'm going straight to the hospital to check on you."

"I'll probably be done before you are."

"How many shots did they fire at you? How many bullets am I looking for?"

"Just the one."

I nodded. "Then I'll be done long before you are. It's a full moon. The ER will be insane. Have fun with that."

I left Jayne and headed toward where the task force had congregated on Jayne's lawn.

Vic asked me, "How's the sheriff feeling?"

"Full of piss and vinegar, evidently," I replied. "She didn't want any coddling."

Sterling chuckled. "That's what we want to hear."

Vic said, "To bring everyone up to speed, earlier this evening, Sheriff Walsh made a comment to the press about the task force taking a harder look into Marcus Copland's death based on new information. She also said the person responsible for running down Katie Copland is still at large. After her soundbite aired, she received an anonymous phone threat of more violence if we don't back off."

Shane shook his head. "If that's not proof the killer is still out there, I don't know what is."

"Is there a recording of the call?" Baxter asked.

"Yes," Vic replied. "The sheriff thought fast and began recording when she heard the caller using a voice changer. I've got a couple of my guys dissecting it now. It's a short call, so there won't be a lot to glean, but we might get something."

A chill ripped up my spine when I heard the words "voice changer." Yet another point in Marcus's favor that he was actually telling me the truth.

Vic went on. "As the sheriff got out of her vehicle here in her driveway thirty minutes ago, about two hours after the call, a vehicle drove by and fired one shot. The sheriff's upper arm was grazed, and she said the sheer shock of the incident had her on the ground. She guesses the killer thought they'd either finished the job or gotten their message across, because they left in a hurry."

Amanda said uneasily, "This killer isn't afraid of much if they came after the sheriff, of all people. Didn't they know that would cause a war and a full-scale manhunt?"

The chief, who looked as broody as I felt, said, "In my mind, this is an escalation. Even though this incident seemed poorly planned and was left unfinished, the target being so high-profile makes it a bigger deal. We can't afford to back down from this act of violence, threat or not."

Vic said, "I agree, which is why I'm assigning an FBI security detail to each member of the task force."

His news was met with groans and grumbling all around.

He held up a hand. "That includes me, so I fully understand how much you all are not excited about this. But if the killer is gunning for us, we need to be prepared. Deputies should be here any minute with vests. I want everyone wearing one while we're out here in the open working this scene. After we wrap this up, everyone goes home to rest. I've emailed you a list of interviewees we've put together who had various dealings with Marcus Copland throughout the years. It's a long list, so we need to divide and conquer. Your individual assignments are marked, and I've tried to match them up with the cases you're working so we're not duplicating interviews. We'll meet tomorrow afternoon to go over our progress. Let's get to work."

Amanda and I broke off to get our kits out of the crime scene unit's van. Baxter and Sterling fell into step a few feet behind us.

She glanced back at them. "Are you following along to help process the scene? I think we're only looking for one bullet and maybe some tire marks. No offense, but we don't need two more sets of hands."

One look at their stony expressions spoke volumes to me. I explained, "They're filling in as our security detail until our assigned G-men get here."

Amanda smiled at Sterling. "Aww, that's so sweet."

I murmured to her, "Give it time. It'll grate on you before long."

Baxter had gone into hero mode guarding my safety often enough that we'd had words multiple times about him not giving me my space. It wasn't that I was ungrateful, it just got old being herded around like a child and having every decision about where I went and how I got there made for me.

We didn't bother suiting up except strapping into the bulletproof vests a deputy brought over to us as we were grabbing our field kits out of the back of the van. It had been a while since I'd had to work in a bulky vest, and I didn't enjoy hauling around the added weight. The detectives followed several paces behind us as Amanda and I began our scene examination by running through the drive-by shooting scenario to find the general search area for the bullet. Based on the small bloodstain on the concrete of the driveway, which showed us where Jayne fell, we were going to be looking at the portion of brick and trim to the left of her garage doors.

As we approached the house, Amanda shined her flashlight on our search area. The drive-by reenactment had me a little off my game, having to mentally envision my mentor and friend being gunned down over this stupid case. I couldn't help but think if I'd let Marcus get away that first day at Ashmore, maybe the rest of the events that followed wouldn't have unfolded the way they did or even have happened at all. Before I could get my bearings, Amanda cheered, "Yes!" and began taking photos of a bullet lodged in the wooden garage door casing.

I snapped out of it and held a scale and an evidence marker next to the bullet so she could get photos with our usual visual documentation. Once she was done with the photos, she got out a large pair of tweezers and gently worked the bullet free from the wood. I got her a small manila envelope out of the field kit to contain the bullet.

Before she dropped it into the envelope, she showed it to me and said, "Ooh, this is a big boy. Forty-five?"

I studied the base of the bullet, trying not to think about how much damage a large caliber bullet like this one could have done to Jayne if it hadn't hit her where it did. "Looks like it." I held up the scale to measure the bullet's diameter. It was roughly eleven millimeters across, or .45 inches, hence the name. "Yep. Good eye."

As Amanda dropped the fired bullet into the envelope, I noticed that there was some blood on the mangled business end of it. Jayne's blood. My stomach rolled. I usually had no trouble at crime scenes, even gross ones. I could look at horrific wounds on dead people all day, but there was something about even non-life-threatening wounds on live people that I found very unsettling. I hadn't even seen Jayne's wound; it was my mental image of it that haunted me.

Worse than my issue with wounds was the thought that the person we were actively chasing wasn't bothering to run—they were fighting back. Any one of us could be next on their hit list. Vic went on camera all the time to give press updates during our task force investigations, and he had a bad habit of being excessively blunt and not sugar-coating the facts for the viewers at home. What if he said something the killer didn't like and they shot him, too? I'd thought I'd watched him die once, and I never wanted to have to go through that hell again.

Ripping off my gloves, I marched out of the scene, ducked under the crime tape, and grabbed Vic by the arm. Unceremoniously ending his conversation with the chief, I dragged him several feet away as he griped, "What the hell, Ellie?"

I looked up at him. "No press. Promise me."

Vic gave me a strange look. "What?"

"You have to promise me you won't talk to the press, especially on camera, about the case. In fact, promise me you'll put a gag on everyone on the task force and in the department. Hell, gag the whole FBI while you're at it. I don't care for Steve, but I also don't want to see him shot."

His expression softened. "I get it."

"Then you'll blindly agree to everything I just said."

He smiled. "I agree that a gag order is our best bet at this time, especially since we assume the killer believes they hit the sheriff in a more vulnerable spot, and we don't want them thinking otherwise. But eventually we're going to have to talk."

That wasn't close enough to my terms for my liking. "You can talk all you want after the killer is behind bars. I'm not budging on this, Vic."

He gave me a mock punch on the arm. "Okay, I agree to your terms. I know how important every member of this task force is to you. Except maybe for Sterling."

I sighed. "He's important to me, too. He saved my ass, and he's trying really hard not to be so terrible anymore."

Vic's expression became concerned. "You look like hell. Why don't you head home? It's late, and this investigation has to be emotionally tougher on you than anyone."

"We're not done processing the scene. I'm not dumping this on Amanda. She's been at it as long as I have the past few days."

"She didn't have to support her sister through losing her father and dredge up a bunch of old wounds." He took my left hand and inspected the now scabby scrape on my palm. "While trying to heal from a bunch of new ones." He grimaced. "Honestly, I don't know how you're even functioning after finding your mother's fingertips in a freaking cooler. Damn, Ellie, you need a vacation."

I frowned. "Yeah, but from my life. Vacations don't work that way."

He took me by the shoulders. "We're going to figure this out and put all these cases to rest. When that happens, I truly believe you'll finally find some peace."

"That's a lovely thought, but I'm having to walk through hell to get there. And since I'd like to do that as quickly as possible, I'm going to get back to work." I shrugged him off.

"Wait. How about this? I know you're going to want to check on the sheriff tonight. Why don't you and Nick go to the hospital and have her reiterate tonight's events? She should no longer be in shock, and maybe she'll recall something she didn't tell us earlier."

I gave him a mock frown. "Fine, Agent Bossypants. I'll go."

"And you'll happily take your FBI security detail with you."

Rolling my eyes, I added, "Because that's going to be as fun as it sounds."

Vic gave me a pointed look. "Says the woman who ordered her superior to gag every law enforcement official in the county out of concern for their safety."

I had no rebuttal for that. I smiled. "See you tomorrow."

IT WAS a bit crowded in Jayne's hospital room with Baxter, me, our two FBI bodyguards, and Jayne's FBI bodyguard. She was being kept overnight and was anything but happy about it. The ER doctor was concerned about her elevated blood pressure and insisted she be monitored for several hours to determine whether it was due to the trauma or if there was an underlying issue.

She grudgingly shared with us only the bare minimum information about her physical state. However, when we told her we were technically there in an official capacity to follow up about her earlier statement, she became much more eager to talk.

Baxter asked, "Tell us about your drive home. Did you stop anywhere after leaving the station or notice anyone following you?"

Sitting up straighter in the bed, Jayne replied, "I went straight home using the same route I always take. No stops. To be honest, I was so beat, I paid little attention to anything besides the road directly in front of me. Even in broad daylight, I might not have noticed someone tailing me. In hindsight, I should have been more attentive a couple of hours after receiving a threatening phone call. The way they phrased it, 'There will be more bloodshed if you don't back off,' made me assume they were talking about another civilian victim. I didn't expect them to be referring to me." She let out a mirthless laugh. "We all know what happens when we assume."

I said, "If it was intended as a personal threat against you, they missed the mark. 'More bloodshed' isn't strong enough language to make someone think they're in imminent danger."

She frowned. "Regardless, I was being lax about my safety. It's my fault for allowing this to occur, but I'm thankful it was directed at me rather than another task force member."

I considered reaching out to try to console her, but thought better of it. Like me, Jayne didn't respond well to coddling of any kind, even if she seemed to need it. I knew her well enough to know that she'd appreciate our efforts to get justice for her over all else.

Baxter steered the conversation back to the facts. "Sheriff, once you pulled into your driveway, how long was it before you were shot? Walk me through that timeframe."

She was deliberate in listing each minuscule event. "I put my vehicle in park, turned it off, unbuckled my seatbelt, and reached for my purse and phone. I sat there for a few seconds to reply to a text from Agent Manetti. I opened the door and got out. I noticed headlights coming closer but thought nothing of it. I closed the door. Next thing I knew, I felt my arm burning and heard the shot. Between being exhausted, the sheer shock of realizing I'd been shot, and the searing pain, my knees buckled under me, and I was down. I didn't pass out, but I'm a little foggy as to how long I was on the ground before I called 911. But I do remember a vehicle tearing down the street the other way before I roused up and started dialing."

I said, "Which could have been your shooter after having turned around in your cul-de-sac?"

"That's what I thought. None of my neighbors would ever drive that fast. We're all very careful to watch out for our kids and pets as we drive, especially since they don't always watch out for themselves." I wished people on my street would do that. I lived in constant fear of Trixie slipping out the front door and bumbling into the road with Nate running blindly after her.

Baxter said, "Your house is so near the cul-de-sac, that was probably only a few seconds. Did you catch a glimpse of the vehicle itself, or was it too dark to see anything but its lights?"

"I've been wracking my brain about that. I *think* it could have been a white sedan. I remember a flash of white, and I hope that's not me getting paint color confused with headlights. But it wasn't a truck or SUV. It was low to the ground. I'm certain of that."

"Every little bit helps," he replied, shooting a text to Sterling.

I said, "You want us to swing by and pick you up tomorrow morning?"

Jayne gave a little salute to her FBI shadow. "I'm sure I can find a ride."

"I suppose you can." I turned to address the four men in the room. "Could you all give us a minute?"

Frowning, they all trooped outside, essentially barring the door.

Once Jayne and I were alone, I said, "How long have you known you had shitty blood pressure?"

She barked out a laugh. "Nothing gets by you, does it?"

"Jayne—"

"Listen, I've tried blood pressure medication, and I don't like the way it makes me feel. I need to be sharp to do my job."

"You also need to be alive," I pointed out dryly. "Knowing you, you tried exactly one type of blood pressure medication, decided you didn't like it, and told your doctor to go to hell."

Shrugging, she admitted, "It went a little like that, yes."

"Will you please go back to your doctor, beg forgiveness, and ask nicely to try another type of medication?"

"If it will make you get the hell out of here so I can sleep, then yes."

I grinned at her. "My work here is done."

21

When I emerged from my bedroom the next morning, I found Rachel in our living room flirting with a very young-looking FBI agent. Evidently, at some point during the night our original agent left and we got a fresh one. I'd woken up Rachel when I got home from the hospital to break the news about my new security detail. I didn't want her to find a strange man in our house this morning and freak out. In explaining why I'd been assigned my own personal FBI agent, I had to drop the bomb on her that Jayne had been shot. She'd been upset, but was able to take comfort in the fact that Jayne wasn't badly hurt.

The agent cleared his throat when he saw me. "You must be Ms. Matthews. I'm Agent Liam Davis. I'll be providing security for you today."

"Hello, Agent Davis. Please call me Ellie."

Agent Davis nodded, trying valiantly to keep his attention on me, but having a tough time not sneaking glances at my pretty sister. He was only a few years older than her, at most. I hadn't seen this adorable enamored expression on Rachel's face in a long time. She'd agreed to go out on a couple of dates over the summer, but hadn't had much interest in actively pursuing romance since her abduction.

I had a brilliant idea. "I'm going to spend the day with my partner, Detective Baxter, who has his own security detail. Would you be willing to look out for Rachel instead? Considering our suspect's threat was so vague and she's as much a part of this investigation as anyone, I think someone should have her back."

Agent Davis worked to hold back a grin. "Agent Manetti assigned me to you, but if he signs off on it, I'd be happy to—"

I waved a hand. "Consider it done. Manetti and I are pals." My phone buzzed with a text from Baxter saying he was here to pick me up. "Gotta go. I'll see you guys later."

As I headed out the door, I texted Vic, letting him know there was a new game plan and that Agent Davis was waiting on the word to come from him. I received back a text that only said *K*, followed by another text with a middle finger emoji and a snippy remark about me not being the boss of him. I hopped into Baxter's SUV, still chuckling.

"What's so funny?" Baxter asked, pulling me in for a kiss.

"Vic's response to me informing him I reassigned my FBI detail to hang with Rachel for the day."

He smiled. "I'm sure that went over well. But it's a good idea to get Rachel some protection. Between me and my broody FBI shadow, you're covered." He jerked his thumb behind him toward a nondescript sedan idling at the curb.

"Ooh, broody. That ought to be fun. Speaking of fun, what delinquent are we going to start with this morning? "

"Manny Ferrara. He's the one who shot Marcus—"

"Enough said. I like him already."

THE DIRECTOR of the halfway house where Manny lived led Baxter, me, and our FBI babysitter *du jour* out back to a shaded area with a few picnic tables. Manny Ferrara was seated at one of them looking like he didn't want to be there. The director made our introductions and left us alone. Agent Broshears stood to the side, stoically at the ready in case anyone tried to jump us in this secure location.

As Baxter and I sat down across from Manny, he stared at me and asked, "Do I know you?"

I held back a sigh. Manny Ferrara had been in the drug scene for a long time. No way my mother hadn't bought from him at one point. I didn't want my identity to skew this interview, so I replied curtly, "No."

"I feel like I should know you."

"You shouldn't," I snapped.

Baxter cut in and began the interview. "Mr. Ferrara, what was your relationship like with Marcus Copland?"

"Well, I shot him, so what do you think it was like?"

Baxter nodded. "Right. Did you shoot him for business or pleasure?"

Manny barked out a laugh. "It did give me a lot of pleasure to shoot that piece of shit."

That wasn't a straight answer. I asked more pointedly, "Was it over a drug territory or simply because he was a piece of shit to you?"

He looked uncomfortable. "Look, I did my time for shooting Marcus. I'm still paying for it. I lost everything."

"Including your territory?" I pressed.

After hesitating for a moment, he nodded.

Baxter said, "I assume since you're in a halfway house that you're not currently pursuing a career in dealing?"

Manny shook his head. "I'm done with that. I, uh . . . I have a kid now, so I need to stay away from the violence. And I don't want to go back to jail. I've missed enough of my son's life as it is."

This guy was difficult to interview. He kept veering us slightly off track, and I couldn't tell if it was intentional or not. "Who took over your territory while you were in jail?"

That question, he had no trouble answering clearly. He spat out, "Jake Campbell."

Baxter said, "Ouch. Hurts when a friend stabs you in the back. At least I assume he was a friend ten years ago when he signed your marriage license as a witness."

Manny's eye twitched, but he said nothing.

Baxter went on. "Back to Marcus . . . why did you shoot him? You had to have a reason."

Manny's expression turned dark. "He beat the hell out of my sister."

"That tracks," I muttered. When he turned his angry gaze on me, I said, "Hey, I think you deserved a medal instead of a sentence for retaliating on behalf of your sister. I'm sure the dozens of women Marcus abused during his lifetime would agree. Unfortunately for you, you're the only person who ever attempted to kill him—or the only one who got caught. So we have to ask, did you kill Marcus Copland Tuesday night?" I didn't believe Manny was involved in the murders—especially since he'd been in county when my mother was killed—but I wanted to see if agitating him would make him any chattier.

Seeming unoffended by my blunt question, he replied calmly, "No. I haven't even seen the guy since my trial. But I hear he hasn't been around for a while."

"Did you know he was back in the area lately?"

"Not until I saw it on the news."

Baxter said, "Can you tell us where you were Tuesday night between five and six p.m.?"

"At work," Manny replied. "I work seconds at the sewer plant."

I asked, "When was the last time you talked to Marcus?"

He shrugged. "Would've had to be when I was shooting him."

Baxter bit back a grin. "How did you know him originally?"

"You get to know your competition."

To clarify, Baxter said, "But you were never friends."

"Never."

"Then how did he meet your sister?" I asked.

He ground out, "Jake friggin' Campbell."

I frowned. "Jake introduced them? Why would he do that? He wasn't friends with Marcus, either."

"Exactly. If you ask me, he was trying to kill two birds with one stone. He knew I had beef with Marcus from way back. He also knew I'd go ballistic if I found out that no-good son of a bitch was sniffing around my baby sister. And he knew my sister loved bad boys. It was the perfect plan: I kill Marcus . . . he's dead, I'm in jail, and both of our territories and customers are suddenly Jake's for the taking."

"That's diabolical," I said uneasily.

"Jake Campbell is one greedy, sadistic bastard."

Baxter asked, "Sadistic enough to kill some of Marcus's exes and use that to run Marcus out of town?"

Nodding, Manny replied, "Absolutely. Jake wouldn't think twice about it."

Baxter and I shared a glance. I asked, "Did he ever threaten Marcus to try to make him leave town?"

"Probably. He did it to everyone. Me included, after he decided he didn't give a shit who he stepped on to come out on top."

Baxter asked, "What was the threat? Violence against you? Your family?"

"Just me."

I said, "The first murder occurred eight years ago. Do you know if something went down between Jake and Marcus around that time?"

Manny started fidgeting, his knee bouncing enough to shake the whole table. "A year before I shot Marcus . . . I can't think of anything that stands out."

"What about the rest of the local drug scene? Anything big happen there?"

Eyes widening, he looked like he was going to be sick. "Nah. Nothing."

Baxter scoffed. "Dude, you're freaking out. You clearly know something."

"I'm done talking. I was being cooperative so you'd put in a good word with my PO, but I don't need it that bad." Manny got up and hurried toward the door.

Baxter turned to me. "Well, it's painfully obvious something big happened eight years ago, and Manny is too scared to talk about it."

I stood. "Great. Add that to the list of things we don't know."

WE HEADED BACK to the station, which meant as soon as we walked in the door we were rid of broody Agent Broshears for a while. Baxter had made plans to have Hector Torres brought over from the adjacent county jail to wait for us in an interrogation room. I remembered Hector being around a decent amount of time during my childhood. He and Marcus had an odd friendship, not that any of Marcus's relationships were healthy ones. Hector constantly tried to impress Marcus, often to the point of one-upmanship and always to the point of cringe. Their relationship ran hot and cold in no discernable pattern. Sometimes Marcus tired of Hector's shenanigans and told him to get lost. Sometimes it was Hector who had enough of Marcus's meanness and ran away butthurt. I was pretty sure my mother had something to do with Hector's one-sided pissing contest. Regardless, I didn't like Hector. He was an asshole. Worse, I'd testified at the trial that finally put his sorry ass away for chopping cars, so he really hated me.

When I entered the room, he started jawing in true Hector form. "Oh, no. No friggin' way am I saying shit to this bitch. I wanna go back to my cell. Guard!"

Even though I'd told Baxter all about Hector and warned him about this very type of reaction, I saw him tense up. Before my sweet boyfriend could fire something back on my behalf, I gave Hector a fake smile and said, "Long time no see, Hector. How's county treating you?" I gestured toward his black eye. "Evidently not too well. Looks like you're the one who's the bitch."

Hector spat back, "Screw you, you sanctimonious whore. I know where you came from. You ain't shit. You—"

Baxter slammed his hands down on the table. "*Enough.*" He didn't say it loudly, but his tone made Hector's big mouth clamp shut. "We need you to answer some questions about Marcus Copland."

Hector leaned back in his chair as far as the shackles that chained him to the table would allow. Shaking his head slowly, he said, "I'm not talking to her."

Baxter narrowed his eyes at him. "Well, you're gonna talk to me."

Shifting his gaze from Baxter to me and back, Hector said, "I'll talk to you. *If* she leaves, *and* I get an extra thirty minutes of TV time per day."

I rolled my eyes. "What are you, five?"

He crossed his arms, not unlike my nephew when he dug in his heels and insisted he get his way. "Those are my demands."

I shrugged and headed for the door. I called to Baxter over my shoulder, "Send him back. We don't need him. He's too dumb to accurately remember what happened in the last decade, anyway. Plus Marcus didn't trust him. He wouldn't have told this douche anything we don't already know."

I swung the door open. As Baxter followed me out, Hector started whining about how he knew all kinds of stuff no one else would know about Marcus. As the door closed behind us, I heard him yell, "Bitch, I know who killed your mom!"

I sucked in a breath and snapped my head toward Baxter, whose jaw was slack with shock. "Uh, did he just say . . ."

Baxter ran a hand over his beard and said gently, "That was probably a desperate attempt for attention, so I wouldn't get my hopes up." He paused. "However, I'm going back in there, and I will get to the bottom of it."

I nodded, all kinds of emotions swirling around inside me.

He steered me down the hall. "Let's grab some comm gear, and you can watch from next door. If there are any questions you want to ask him, all you have to do is whisper sweet nothings in my earpiece."

I nodded again, but I only had one question: Did Hector really know who killed my mother?

22

From the viewing room, I watched Baxter ask Hector the general questions we asked everyone about their relationship with Marcus: when they'd last seen him (both lately and before he'd split town) and where they'd been when he was being killed. Hector didn't have much current information to give, since he'd been in lockup for the past three years. When it got interesting was when Baxter started asking him about who had a major grudge against Marcus.

Hector said, "Dante Romero. He came to town and tried to squeeze a bunch of the dealers out of their territories, but Marcus wasn't having it. Him, Tyrell Simkins, and Jake Campbell were the only ones with the balls to fight back against Dante. Everybody else bitched out."

Baxter asked, "When did that happen?"

Hector thought for a moment. "Like seven or eight years ago. Their turf war went on for months, and they finally got Dante to back off. Or so they thought, because then Marcus got popped. We all thought Dante put a hit out on him because it was his bitch-boy Manny who did the popping. Turns out Manny could actually think for himself once in a while and wasn't following Dante's orders that time."

I said into the mic that went to Baxter's earpiece, "Holy shit. No wonder Manny clammed up on us. He was working for Dante. Maybe still is. Ask

Hector if Manny siding with Dante instead of Jake was what ruined their friendship."

Baxter said to Hector, "Manny told us he shot Marcus because Marcus beat up his sister. He also said Jake was the one who set up Marcus and the sister in the first place. Do you know if that was in retaliation for Manny siding with Dante against him?"

Hector guffawed. "That whole thing was because Jake and Marcus thought it'd be hilarious to screw with Manny."

"Those two weren't friends, though. There was a serious rivalry between them."

Shrugging, Hector mused, "'The enemy of my enemy is my friend.'"

I was appalled. "Is he saying Marcus beat up Manny's poor sister as part of some kind of joke? I mean, there's no acceptable reason to hit a woman, but damn."

Baxter said, "Marcus beat up an innocent woman as a joke?"

Hector waved one shackled hand. "He slapped her around was all. Not even that hard. Jake told him to make it just enough to get her to run crying to big brother so he'd lose his shit and do something stupid."

"Mission accomplished, but did Marcus not realize the retaliation would be directed at him?"

I muttered, "I'm sure Jake did."

Chuckling, Hector said, "Manny was a little bitch, and Marcus could kick his ass any day of the week. Manny never liked guns and didn't even own one. That's why we assumed it was Dante's doing at first. It's also why Marcus only brought a knife to a gunfight."

Baxter asked him, "Did you witness it?"

"No, but Marcus's old lady did. Well, I guess she was technically Tyrell's old lady."

Baxter stood and started pacing so he could shoot me a covert glance through the window. "Tyrell Simpkins?"

"Yeah, Marcus was giving it to Tyrell's wife behind his back. Dick move to pull against your supplier, but that was how Marcus rolled."

"What was her name?"

"Shanice."

Frowning, Baxter said, "And she was a witness to the shooting? There were no witnesses listed on the incident report."

"That's because she dumped Marcus's bloody ass at the ER and ran so Tyrell wouldn't find out she was stepping out on him."

I pointed out to Baxter, "He found out eventually."

Baxter asked him, "Speaking of Marcus's lady friends, do you remember a woman named Amy?"

Hector snorted. "That chick was friggin' nuts."

"So we've heard. Do you know her last name?"

"Johnson."

I got out my phone and Googled "Amy Johnson Indiana," but it was way too common a name to glean any specific information. We'd have to get on the department system and check her name against Marcus and his known associates and hope she was mixed up in some of his shenanigans.

Baxter asked, "What happened between her and Marcus? Michelle Rutkowski said the woman was obsessed with him."

Guffawing, Hector said, "Michelle's nuts, too. But she's not wrong. Marcus and Amy knew each other from way back. He was never that into her, but she was rich and she kept turning up like a bad penny, DTF, so Marcus would get with her once in a while if he was broke and bored."

"So broke and bored he got her pregnant?"

Hector's eyebrows shot up. "That's news to me."

I said, "I guess he wasn't handing out cigars to his buddies for his third unwanted child."

Baxter asked, "Do you know when they were together last?"

"It's been a while. I think she like, died or something."

I sucked in a breath, taking my phone back out and this time Googling "Amy Johnson death Indiana."

Baxter stopped pacing. "Think hard. Is she dead or not?"

"Dead."

There were two Amy Johnson obituaries from the last decade, one of them on an Indianapolis funeral home's website. I clicked on the link and found this Amy Johnson had died nine years ago, which according to Rachel would have been roughly around the time she miscarried Marcus's baby. There was a wide-angle shot of a woman looking out over a gorgeous mountain panorama rather than the usual headshot of the deceased. There wasn't a lot of personal info in the obituary other than that Amy enjoyed traveling and hiking. If she had family, they weren't listed, aside from the fact that she was "preceded in death by an angel baby."

"You got any details?" Baxter demanded.

I piped up, "If I have the right obit, which I think I do, she died nine years ago. Looking now to see if there's a homicide to go with it." I Googled "Amy Johnson homicide Indiana."

Hector made a face. "I don't know, man. All I know is Marcus said she died, but it was like, years ago."

Poor Baxter was so done with this guy. I could tell by the tone of his voice. "Did he mention how she died? Was she sick? Was she in an accident? Did she get murdered like most of the women he was with after her?"

While Hector stared blankly at the ceiling, either thinking or stalling, I said to Baxter, "No news reports of any homicide, and no clues in the obit for COD."

Hector finally said, "Nah. I don't think he cared that much."

I could tell from his posture that Baxter was frustrated. I said gently, "We'll figure it out. You can move on."

He sank tiredly into his chair. "Okay, Hector. Let's cut to the chase. Did you know Alice Graves, Jihyo Yoon, Patty Copland, and Katie Copland?"

"Sure, knew them all." He wiggled his eyebrows. "I knew Patty intimately. She gave me the clap once."

"Of course she did," I muttered. I was itching to find out what Hector allegedly knew about my mother's murder, but I knew Baxter needed to work up to it.

Baxter went on. "Then I'm sure you know they were all Marcus's wives or girlfriends and also murder victims."

Hector nodded solemnly. "Yeah, Marcus was actually torn up about a couple of them."

"But he chose to run only after Patty Copland's murder. Why?"

After a brief hesitation, Hector admitted, "He never told me. Never said goodbye, either. I mean, I guess I'm not surprised . . . we got into a fight earlier that week."

"What about?"

"Same old. We were both drunk, and that's how our fights usually started. I couldn't even tell you what it was about."

Leaning back in his chair, Baxter crossed his arms. "Maybe about him accusing you of having something to do with Patty's disappearance?"

Hector held out his hands. "Whoa, whoa. That took a turn. You saying you think I had something to do with Patty's murder? Or even those other skanks?"

"You weren't as good of friends with Marcus as you'd like me to believe."

"Yes I was," he protested. "Hold on, now, is that what that bitch Ellie told you? Because she was a kid and wouldn't know shit about what went on back then. And she wasn't even *his* kid. She wasn't around him that much. Only when he lived with Patty, and that wasn't for very long."

Maybe not to him, but it might as well have been an eternity for me. Marcus was far and away the worst of my mother's many exes I'd had to stomach living with.

I couldn't see his expression, but I noticed Baxter's hands ball into fists as Hector was talking about me. Although his voice got low and dangerous again, it was controlled as he said, "You're not the first person we've talked to regarding this case. Help me understand why you think you're Marcus Copland's bestie, and yet not one person has mentioned you to us."

Hector scoffed, although it was painfully obvious his bravado was dwindling fast. "Who did you talk to? Because a lot of people claimed to be Marcus's friends who weren't."

"You mean like you?"

"No! I'm the real deal. Listen, you want to know something not everyone knows? His former friend Earl is a stalker. Yeah, that's right. He stalked that Alice Graves chick after she dumped Marcus. He stalked your girl Ellie's mom, too."

That was certainly interesting, but I didn't know if I bought it. Earl wouldn't have needed to stalk my mother—Patty Copland never played hard-to-get, especially with him.

Baxter was already on it. "Who told you this?"

"Marcus."

"How did he know?"

"Alice called and bitched him out one day for sending his creepy friend to bother her, but he didn't tell Earl to do shit. Marcus cut Earl loose twenty years ago for diddling his kid or something."

So Baxter wouldn't lose his mind completely, I clarified, "Earl didn't diddle any kids, that I know of. He hit Rachel, I told Marcus, and Marcus nearly killed him."

His voice a bit tight, Baxter asked Hector, "When did Earl stalk Patty?"

Shrugging, Hector replied, "On and off for years. Marcus caught him doing it one day and made an impression on him. Gave him the scar on his right cheek."

"And when did this happen?"

"Not too long before Marcus left town."

My breath hitched in my throat.

Realizing what I had, Baxter said, "In other words, Earl stalked Patty Copland for years, including just before she was murdered. And he stalked Alice Graves right before she got murdered as well."

Hector sat back in his chair. "Huh. Never thought of it that way. If I had, I'd have turned Earl's dumb ass in for the hell of it. He's a dick."

I frowned. "Not the brightest bulb."

Baxter pressed, "How about the other two women—Jihyo Yoon and Katie Copland? Did you ever hear of Earl stalking them?"

"Nope."

"You said earlier you know who killed Patty Copland. Is that true?"

Hector frowned. "I always figured it was Dante Romero. Patty was working for him at the time. But now with the thing about Earl, I'm not so sure anymore."

Baxter said, "You were basing your statement solely on the fact that Patty was working for Romero?"

"Well, yeah. Patty wasn't good at anything besides giving head, so it's not exactly a stretch to assume she screwed something up and he got pissed. Dante doesn't dick around when it comes to his business. You make a mistake, he makes an example out of you."

I didn't know why I'd gotten my hopes up that Hector, of all people, would have the insight no one else seemed to have about how my mother met her untimely end. Regardless, I felt deflated and was relieved I wasn't in the next room fighting to keep a brave face in front of Hector.

Baxter veered their conversation back to the track they'd been on. "We heard Earl and Marcus got in a bar fight last week. What do you know about that?"

Curling his lip, Hector spat, "I don't know jack shit. In case you hadn't noticed, I'm stuck in here. I don't know what goes on in the real world."

I noticed Baxter's head cock to the side and imagined the usual expression of annoyance that crossed his face when people were trying to blow smoke up his ass. "County isn't in a bubble. Inmates are worse than teenage girls when it comes to gossip, and it doesn't matter if the incident happened on the inside or outside. Surely you heard something."

Hector raised his hands and shrugged. That bastard definitely knew something.

Baxter sighed tiredly. "Is this the part where you're waiting for me to offer you something for your information?"

"That's generally how bribes work."

I assumed in an effort to waste a little time and let Hector sweat it, Baxter slowly rose from his chair and pushed it in, then turned enough that I could see his profile. "Here's my offer: You tell me what you know, and I won't let it slip to your fellow inmates that we've spent some quality time chatting this morning."

Hector's face fell, but he couldn't resist countering with what little bravado he had left. "They won't believe it. I'm no snitch."

Baxter snorted. "You're literally sitting here snitching right now." He pointed to the camera mounted in the corner. "I could pump the audio of this conversation through the jail's speaker system if you think it would help them believe it."

"You wouldn't."

Baxter's handsome face twisted into a devilish grin. "Try me."

Hector's words tumbled out in a rush. "Word is Earl had some unfinished business with Marcus."

"What kind?"

"Earl never got the chance to retaliate after Marcus roughed him up that last time. Earl can hold a grudge like nobody's business."

Furrowing his brow, Baxter said, "So it was simply four-year-old revenge for a beatdown?"

"Yeah. That's all I heard. I swear."

"Maybe you could find out more for us."

Hector's jaw dropped. "Hell no. I'm no snitch."

Baxter nodded. "You mentioned that."

"Going around asking too many questions is exactly how snitches get stitches." He gestured to his black eye. "I'm already not one of the popular kids. Pass."

"So you don't want the extra thirty minutes of TV time?"

"Not that bad."

"Suit yourself." Baxter wasted no time picking up his notes from the table and leaving the room. A moment later, he walked into the viewing room. "You think he'll change his mind?"

I'd kept a close eye on Hector once the subject of snitching came up. His posture had stiffened, and it wasn't difficult to feel the fear radiating from him. Physically, he'd covered it well, doing a lot of head shaking and uttering a few "pffts" and grunts as Baxter left him alone in the room, no doubt unhappy with how things had turned out.

"I doubt it," I replied. "But I imagine we could get as much or more information at the bar where the fight went down."

"True." His expression turned to one of concern. "You okay? He didn't pull any punches when he spoke about your mother."

I huffed out a mirthless laugh. "He didn't say anything I didn't already know."

23

Baxter and I returned to his desk to do a deep dive on Amy Johnson to try to find some useful information. I snagged his chair and made him sit in my usual seat next to his desk to decompress from his interview. It took a bit longer than usual to track down Amy Marie Johnson's death certificate. When I pulled up the PDF of the document, I understood why. I turned to Baxter, who hadn't taken a break at all, studiously making notes in his file and pausing only to send intermittent text messages.

"Get this—Amy Johnson died in Mexico, and her cause of death was exsanguination due to some kind of trauma." I kept reading, hunting for words I recognized. Hard to mistake the word *suicidio* for anything else. "It was ruled a suicide."

Baxter looked up. "That's interesting, and possibly alarming, given the fact that this case already includes one staged suicide."

"True." I took another look at the death certificate, barely any of which was in English. "Uh . . . location of death is listed as La Quebrada in Acapulco. Not a ton of info here, aside from the mention of Eleazar Funeral Home in Indy, which was where her remains were sent. My three years of high school Spanish didn't cover a lot of words one might find on a death certificate."

Furrowing his brow, he said, "But you know the word for 'exsan-guination'?"

"Well, *sangre* means 'blood,' and this says *desangramiento*. In many languages, the prefix 'de' generally means some kind of lessening or taking away, like 'dehydrate.' And I think the suffix 'iento' is like a state of being or something like that. So . . . 'blood being lessened' is pretty much the definition of exsanguination."

Grinning, he said, "You're cute when you nerd out, Professor."

I shot him a glare. "I am not a nerd. And I'm way too salty to pass for cute."

He laughed. "My mistake. Hey, if you print that, I'll take it to someone who knows a little more Spanish and get the rest of it translated."

I did as he asked and gave him the printout. He headed down the hall-way, and I took a moment to rub my aching temples. When that only made my head hurt worse, I popped a couple of Tylenol and ran to the break-room for coffee. Shane was in there staring at the wall, drinking deeply from a steaming cup.

I said, "Hey, Shane. This case has me so busy I've barely had the chance to say two words to you. How are Kaitlyn and the baby?"

Shane smiled. "They're great. Olive isn't a baby anymore. She turned one last week."

"Ooh, fun. Is she walking?"

"Yes. Life got exponentially harder about three weeks ago."

I laughed. "I'm sure it did."

He set his coffee cup on the counter behind him. "Ellie, are you doing okay with this case? I know it can't be easy on you."

Smiling, I remembered the time I finally broke down and told someone I trusted at college about my home life. That someone had been Shane, my closest friend. He knew nearly everything about my childhood, except a few stories that were too painful to share.

I replied, "I won't say it doesn't suck when I have to get up in front of the task force and give everyone a peek into my screwed-up life. But since so many of you are like family to me, if I have to bare my soul, I'm thankful it's to this group."

"Good attitude. I was hoping it isn't taking too much of a toll." He gave me a pat on the back. "Since you're feeling decent, would you like to listen from the next room while Manetti and I question Earl Thompson? Baxter told us what your last interviewee said about him. I'd love to tap into your stellar bullshit meter, and considering your history with this guy, you're bound to have some insight."

I snorted. "'History' is such a nice word for what Earl put me through."

Shane grinned at me. "So if I were to stumble and my fist somehow landed on his face, that might make you happy?"

Vic entered the room and made a beeline for the coffee. "I didn't hear that."

I said, "Funny story, Marcus already did that to Earl for me. Well, he did it for Rachel, but I was the one who tattled on Earl for hitting us. And Earl knows it. Which is why I'm not going anywhere near that asshat."

Vic nodded. "Good plan." He glanced at his watch. "Deputies are en route with him and should be here in ten. Meet us at Interrogation Three in fifteen."

"Yes, sir."

~

I RETURNED to Baxter's desk. "Want to watch a Vic/Shane/Earl cage match in fifteen minutes?"

Baxter spun around in his chair. "Hell yeah." He reached for a paper on his desk and handed it to me. "Here you go. Translation courtesy of the chief."

I took Amy Johnson's death certificate from him and sat down. Struggling a bit to read the chief's messy handwriting in the margins, I murmured, "Exsanguination by *blunt force* trauma. Ah, makes sense. Identified by a US driver's license found in a bag discarded by the deceased, per witnesses. Sent to a crematorium in Acapulco. Remains shipped to Eleazar Funeral Home per emergency instructions found with ID." I looked up. "I found her obituary on Eleazar's website, so that part checks out."

"For me, it's the only thing about this death that checks out. I looked up La Quebrada. It's the name of a famous cliff diving spot."

My eyebrows shot up. "Oh. A tumble off a cliff would definitely net you some exsanguination by blunt force trauma. Do you think she tried to cliff dive and missed, or did she literally go jump off a cliff?"

He mused, "That's a great question. Here's another one: If you're going to kill yourself, why go all the way to Mexico to do it? There are plenty of cliffs here."

I shrugged. "Her obituary said she enjoyed traveling."

"If you were enjoying yourself at your travel destination, would you jump off a cliff?"

"Probably wouldn't do it no matter what mood I was in. I don't love heights."

Smiling, he said, "We can look into this later."

Baxter and I spent the rest of our wait time writing up reports on our interviews from this morning and last night, then headed to the interrogation rooms. I felt apprehensive about seeing Earl again, even though he wouldn't even know I was there. Something about his voice always put me on edge. Probably because the only time he ever spoke to me was right before he started swinging.

Vic and Shane were already in the viewing room when Baxter and I arrived. I purposely turned my back to the two-way glass to delay my first glimpse of Earl.

Vic said, "Nick, thanks for the heads-up about the stalking and the recent bar fight. Anything else we should know about this piece of shit before we start?"

I said, "Only that it doesn't make a lot of sense to me that Earl would have stalked my mother. She hooked up with him numerous times over the years. Don't stalkers creep on people because they're unable to interact with them in person?"

"Usually, yes," Vic replied. "But there are a lot of instances where people in relationships will stalk their partners as a sex and dominance thing. It can also be part of gaslighting and emotional abuse. And then it's only a hop, skip, and a jump to physical violence, which is why I'm ready to get cracking on this interrogation."

I smiled, knowing if anyone could hold their own against Earl, it was Vic and Shane. "Get cracking, then."

As the two of them left, it was time for me to face my past, again. I turned and saw a much older man than I remembered. Like Marcus, Earl didn't seem so intimidating after over a decade, especially with the head of gray hair and thirty pounds of beer gut he'd amassed.

Too bad his sneer was still as ugly as ever. As Vic and Shane entered the room, Earl bellowed, "I know my rights. You can't just haul me in whenever you damn well please. I ain't done nothin'."

Vic took the chair across from him. "Well, if you 'ain't done nothin',' you've got nothing to worry about."

Shane flipped through the file in front of him. "Does 'nothin'' include getting into a fistfight with Marcus Copland last week at Ace's Bar?"

Earl scoffed. "Bar fights don't count. And last I checked, dead men can't press charges."

"Victims don't press charges, genius. Prosecutors do." When Earl's expression turned worried, Shane added, "But maybe we can talk the DA out of it if you answer some questions for us."

"What kind of questions?"

"For starters, did you kill Marcus Copland?"

Baxter huffed out a laugh. "He certainly wasted no time going for the throat."

Earl rolled his eyes. "Drugs is what killed Marcus Copland. It was only a matter of time."

Shane said, "Okay, then where were you Tuesday between five and six p.m.?"

"At work."

"Where?"

"The high school."

My jaw dropped. "They let him around kids?

Baxter snickered as Shane also remarked, "You're allowed near kids?"

Earl sneered again. "After-hours maintenance."

"How about Monday at eight-forty-five p.m.?"

"Same."

Vic asked, "What did you and your buddy Marcus talk about at Ace's before you started punching each other?"

Barking out a laugh, Earl said, "What a sack of shit he always was."

Vic shrugged. "We can't dispute that, but do you have a specific reason for your assessment of him?"

Earl gave him a blank look. "Huh?"

Vic dumbed down his question. "Why was he a sack of shit? What did he do to you?"

His expression growing dark, Earl ground out, "Last time I seen him, he jumped me, beat me senseless, then left town. Anything I did to him, he had coming."

"Like threatening him to leave town?"

"I never gave a shit if he lived here or not. It's not like we was still friends."

"So you were enemies?"

Earl shook his head. "We went our separate ways a long time ago."

Shane, knowing exactly what went down, asked, innocently, "What happened?"

"Misunderstanding."

I growled under my breath. Baxter squeezed my shoulder.

Shane's voice took on an edge. "Which misunderstanding was that? The time you abused his child or when you stalked his exes?"

Earl's face practically turned purple as he spat, "Whoever told you that is a liar."

Vic stepped in, his tone as harsh as Shane's. "Multiple people told us that. It's impossible for people who don't know each other to separately make up the same lie. You're the common denominator here. What was your reasoning for stalking Alice Graves?"

"Who?" Earl tried for nonchalant but wasn't a good enough actor.

"The woman you stalked after she and Marcus Copland ended their relationship eight years ago. She was found murdered a few weeks later."

"I don't know her."

Vic scoffed. "That's funny, because we spoke to two people this morning who said Alice complained of you harassing her. She was considering filing a restraining order against you only days before she was killed."

"They lied."

Barking out a laugh, Shane said, "Look, dude, you're not nearly as smart as you think you are. Did you think we wouldn't look at Alice Graves's file and find out you were investigated as a person of interest in her murder?" He held up a sheet of paper. "This is a report detailing you having a similarly stupid conversation with an IMPD detective. We know you're the one who's lying. And if you don't knock it off, an assault charge is the best thing you could hope to happen to you today."

Finally, Earl accepted that he'd been had. His shoulders slumped. He muttered, "Fine. I might have showed up a few times at a few places Alice went."

"And the last time you showed up where she was, you killed her?"

Earl's eyes bugged out. "No! I didn't kill her. I just . . ." He set his jaw and looked away.

His tone dripping with mockery, Shane said, "Oh, buddy. You thought she was pretty and liked to look at her. Is that it?"

Earl snapped, "Screw you, asshole."

Vic asked, "Did you stalk Alice Graves for the same reason you stalked Patty Copland for years?"

His mouth pulled up in the corner, making my skin crawl. "Naw, that was a game me and Patty played."

"Gross," I complained, taking out my phone. I texted Vic and Shane, *Please don't make him elaborate.*

Vic glanced at his phone before going on. "I might be inclined to believe you, but your timing sucks. The last time you stalked Patty Copland was right before she died. You see how this looks like a pattern for you?"

Earl crossed his arms and leaned back in his chair. "Prove it."

"We know Marcus Copland caught you stalking her and did something about it."

"Says who?"

Shane replied, "Says you, according to the report the hospital filed when you showed up there that night all beat to hell. Once they pumped you full of pain meds so they could stitch up that ugly-ass scar on your face, you told your whole sad story to anyone who'd listen."

At the mention of his scar, Earl lost his shit. Hopping up from his chair and slinging it toward the far wall, he raged, "I did *not* kill Patty. I loved Patty, and she got taken away from me. I even came to you pigs after all those bags of her got found—" He paused for a moment, looking a little ill, then went on a little more calmly, "I knew it was Dante Romero who killed her, but nobody would listen to me. I got told I was a 'known associate' of Marcus's, so nothing I said mattered. They'd already decided he was guilty, and that meant I was lying to cover for him. I didn't give a shit whether or not Marcus looked guilty. I wanted that sadistic bastard Dante punished for what he did to Patty."

When Earl mentioned Dante Romero's name, Baxter got out his phone and started texting, I assumed to let the guys know we'd heard an earful from both Ava and Hector about him.

Vic said evenly, "You'll need to take a seat again, Mr. Thompson." He checked his phone while Earl grudgingly retrieved his chair and sat back down. "Thank you. Why do you believe Dante Romero killed Patty Copland?"

Earl shook his head. "When she told me she was working for him, I tried to talk her out of it. I told her he's bad news and lots of people around him die. She didn't listen." He choked back what sounded like a sob. "I seen them together a couple of times when I'd watch her. Dante handled her way too rough. I even seen him pull a gun on her once." He hung his head. "I should've done something, but . . . I wasn't tough enough to go up against Dante Romero and live to talk about it. If I made any kind of move on him, he'd kill Patty and me both. So I turned our little stalking game into a way to look out for her until I could figure out a way to convince her to walk away from him. But I didn't . . ." He sighed hard. "I failed."

His words hit me like a ton of bricks. Earl was being truthful.

I'd known Earl for a long time, and he'd always been in a constant state of putting on an act. He strutted around in front of my mother like a bull in heat, desperate to make her think he was a big man. Despite his large stature, Earl was, as he'd said, not tough. I saw through it and pointed it out once, only to get a slap across my "sassy mouth" from him. Besides today, the only other time I'd seen realness out of him was one of the times my mother nearly ODed. He'd barged into our place raring to hook up and found her on the couch next to me, unconscious, as I watched TV. Assuming she was sleeping, he came over and started kissing her and whispering some pretty gross stuff in her ear loud enough that I could hear. When I informed him she'd taken some pills and passed out—which was a monthly occurrence, so I thought nothing of it—he looked honestly frightened. Then he got mad. He started screaming about what a horrible daughter I was to let this happen. By that point, I'd had enough altercations with him to know I'd better get out of his reach and stay there. When he tired of chasing me around the room, he scooped up my mother and rushed her to the hospital.

Hours later, I heard them return. Wanting to be prepared in case he decided to take another stab at trying to punish me for "allowing" my mother to take too many drugs—like anyone could have stopped her—I eavesdropped on their conversation from my room. I was shocked to hear how kind he was being to her. He was telling her he wished she cared about herself as much as he cared about her, and that he was there for her anytime she needed him. What I wasn't shocked to hear was my mother swooning over the fact that a man was paying attention to her, followed by a lengthy pause that was my cue to put my headphones on and fall asleep as quickly as I could so I didn't hear the sounds that inevitably came afterward.

A text from Shane broke me out of my thoughts: *What does your bullshit meter say about this?*

I texted back, *I believe every word he said after he went batshit on you.*

Shane said to Earl, "I appreciate you being candid, finally. Let's talk more about Dante Romero. You think he killed Patty Copland. Do you think he might have killed Alice Graves as well, possibly in an effort to get at Marcus? Romero was also a person of interest in the Graves homicide."

I turned to Baxter. "What? Dante Romero was a person of interest in two of the cases? Why the hell are we not focusing all our energy on him?"

Baxter frowned. "There's never been a shred of evidence against him for anything. Aside from that, he's got the sleaziest lawyers around on his payroll, not to mention a few politicians and judges, so he's basically untouchable unless we have him dead to rights. The lawyers already informed Sterling that Romero won't be doing any police interviews unless there's a warrant out for his arrest *and* enough to charge him."

"That sucks."

Earl, who'd taken a moment to ponder Shane's question, said, "I wouldn't put it past that psycho to kill his own mother. I guess it's possible. I know that one of Marcus's ladies made herself scarce after getting a death threat around the time Manny Ferrara shot Marcus."

I perked up. "Ooh. That's new news."

Shane asked, "Do you know who the woman was?"

"Valerie Hale, my buddy Jimmy's cousin."

"Valerie Hale?" I echoed. "I know her." I texted Vic and Shane, *Ask if she and my mother were friends.*

Vic said, "You're talking about Jimmy Belzer?"

Earl nodded.

After glancing at his phone, Vic asked, "Who made the death threat to Valerie Hale? Was it in person or through a note or phone call?"

"Phone call. Me and Jimmy always figured it was either Dante or the girl Marcus was two-timing with Val, but Val had no idea. She said the voice was garbled, and all's they said was 'stay away from Marcus or you're dead.'"

Baxter mused, "If Valerie Hale got the threat to quit dating Marcus around the time he got shot, then the woman being two-timed would have to be Shanice Simpkins, right?"

"That's right," I replied.

Vic asked Earl, "Did she know Dante Romero or any of Marcus's other enemies? Or his friends or exes, for that matter?"

Earl replied, "I don't know if she knew the enemies, but she was in the original group of us who used to do everything together—me, Jimmy, Val, Marcus, Patty, and Rick Palmer."

Vic nodded. "To wrap up, I want to ask you about Jihyo Yoon and Katie Copland, two other women in Marcus's life who were brutally murdered. Is there a connection between them and Patty Copland and Alice Graves we're not seeing? Would anyone connected to Marcus have a reason to kill these four specific women and frame Marcus for it?"

Earl stared off into space for a few moments. "Dante Romero killed Patty, and no one's gonna change my mind about that. Alice . . . could have been Dante, I reckon. I think she died sometime during that turf war, so maybe she was collateral damage. Now, Katie . . . I didn't know her too good. She showed up when me and Marcus was parting ways. But that Chinese mail order bride—"

"Korean green card bride," Shane corrected him.

"Whatever. She's the wild card in that list of women. I don't think any of Marcus's friends—or enemies—even knew about her besides Jimmy, who's his best friend, and who told me. To pass all them government tests get the okay for their sham marriage, Marcus had to look like an upstanding citizen, so he had to make sure his life didn't creep over into hers, and vice versa. That girl was a business agreement, not the love of his life. Someone killing her to get at Marcus would have been a waste. He may not have even knew she died. Jimmy said something about her going back home." Earl blew out a heavy breath. "Marcus is the connection between them women. If you think someone killed all them to frame him, it's Dante Romero."

24

Earl's interview ran longer than any of us expected, especially after his sudden urge to spill his guts and be helpful. The four of us had to rush straight to the task force meeting without getting to discuss any of the highlights of Earl's soul-bearing.

Amanda, Chief Esparza, Sterling, and Jayne were waiting for us in the conference room. Baxter, Vic, Shane and I all stopped in our tracks to stare at our sheriff sitting there. She seemed no worse for wear despite having survived a murder attempt mere hours earlier. The only telltale sign of her brush with death was the sling supporting her left arm.

She saw our expressions and held up her free hand. "I'm only here for the meeting and to finish some urgent paperwork on my desk. After that, I'm headed home, so you can all save your sermons on how I should be handling my recovery."

As the four of us obediently offered her no rebuttal and took our seats, Vic said, "On that subject, where are we with finding the shooter?"

Sterling said, "We were able to pull together enough video footage from neighborhood smart doorbells to see the license plate of the vehicle used in the shooting. As with the Katie Copland case, the vehicle was reported stolen last night. Deputies are locating the owner and picking him up as we speak. The chief and I will have a little chat with him as soon as we're done here." He turned to Jayne. "Sheriff, with any luck we'll have a lead on the son of a bitch who shot you before lunch."

She smiled. "Thank you, Detective."

Vic said, "I'd like each set of investigators to give a rundown of interviews so far and share any potential suspects. If anyone has information to add, please speak up and we'll discuss it before moving on. Detective Carlisle, you want to start?"

Shane said, "Agent Manetti and I spoke to Alice Graves's ex-husband, daughter, and best friend. If Marcus Copland is no longer being considered a suspect, they're pretty confident about Earl Thompson being to blame for her death, considering he was stalking her in the weeks prior. I've got someone from IMPD bringing over the evidence this afternoon from the Alice Graves homicide case as well as from the home invasion that occurred at her house a little over a month before she died."

I knew nothing about a home invasion. Based on a few surprised faces around the table, I wasn't the only one.

Jayne said, "Can you brief us on the home invasion?"

Shane nodded. "One evening when Alice and her kids were out, two men broke into her home and roughed up Marcus. She came back and interrupted them, and they ran. IMPD came out and took statements and searched the place, but they never caught who did it. Marcus played dumb when asked who the intruders were, and the investigators thought he was lying. They assumed it was one of his enemies sending a message, considering there was a big turf war going on during that time."

"The one Dante Romero started," I said. "Was their theory about Romero's possible involvement in the home invasion why he was a person of interest in Alice's homicide case?"

"Yes. There was never any evidence against him in either case, but given his open aggression toward Marcus Copland at the time, it was a safe assumption he could have been involved. Any other questions on that?" When no one spoke up, Shane went on. "Back to the interviews. Agent Manetti and I spoke to Rick Palmer, Marcus's oldest friend who shares an identical list of known associates, but he was stoned out of his mind and very uncooperative."

Hearing that about Rick made me sad. He'd been a decent man when I knew him, aside from the drug dealing, of course. And I'd never known him to be a user. I guessed if you were in that world long enough, you eventually gave in and joined the insanity.

Shane continued. "Jimmy Belzer, Marcus's closest friend, had a lot to say about Jake Campbell, a dealer who'd fought with Marcus for decades. He believed Jake double-crossed Marcus during the turf war and masterminded the events leading to him being shot by Manny Ferrara. He also said Jake had tried several times to take over Marcus's territory through coercion and threats. In his opinion, if anyone wanted Marcus out of town, it was Jake."

Baxter said, "It checks out that Jake Campbell masterminded the shooting. We interviewed Manny Ferrara and Hector Torres this morning, and both said Jake was the driving force behind the events leading up to the shooting. Basically, Jake put Marcus up to going out with Manny's sister and then abusing her, which he knew would make Manny go nuts and retaliate. If Manny had been a better shot, Jake could have taken over both of their territories instead of only Manny's."

Vic asked, "Chief Esparza, what did Jake Campbell have to say when you interviewed him?"

The chief replied, "He stonewalled us for a good ten minutes until Detective Sterling got a text from Detective Baxter saying Manny Ferrara had thrown him under the bus. Then he suddenly got real chatty about Manny Ferrara and how he agreed to becoming one of Dante Romero's minions in exchange for keeping his territory—with a hefty sales tax, of course. He gave up nothing on himself, so the interview was kind of a waste."

Baxter added, "Manny Ferrara nearly stroked out when we started asking about what went on in the drug scene in the year before he shot Marcus. At the time we talked to him, we didn't know about the turf war and Manny joining Team Romero. We'll pay him a second visit now that we know where to put the pressure."

Nodding, Vic said, "Let's move on to Joe Novak."

Shane shuffled some papers in his file. "We interviewed Joe Novak from an Illinois prison. He has a history of altercations with Marcus over his now ex-wife, Michelle Rutkowski. All he would talk about was how much of a liar Michelle was, warning us several times not to believe a word she says. He was in prison during two of the four homicides, so we don't consider him a person of interest. He also wanted it noted he thinks Michelle is a great candidate for our prime suspect because she's 'a crazy succubus,' or possibly Rick Palmer, for the reason that he's 'a dick.'"

Sterling chuckled. "The people on your list sound way more fun than ours."

Shane shook his head. "Oh, I saved the best for last. Earl Thompson, former friend of Marcus's, former flame of Patty's. Detective Baxter and Ms. Matthews listened in on this one and fed us questions from next door."

I tuned out Shane's reiteration of Earl's interview, telling myself my time was better spent skimming over my notes before Baxter and I had to share our information. If I was honest with myself, my tune-out was more because I didn't want to relive that part of today. I'd been fine during the interview, with a wall and three armed badasses to protect me from a monster who haunted my childhood. But now, parts of the interview were stuck on repeat in my head with no one to protect me. At the moment, the featured clip was Earl's sneer as he spoke about his stalking game with my mother segueing into his anguish over failing to protect her. I wanted to hate him. I *did* hate him for the abuse he dished out to me and to my sister. But now that I thought about it, aside from David, Earl had treated our mother the best. I'd had no idea he'd continued to love her and had tried to watch out for her the rest of her life. It was so much easier to fully despise him. I didn't want the complication of my mixed emotions.

I broke out of my thoughts when Baxter said my name. "Ellie believes he was telling the truth about not killing Patty Copland. He was close to Patty while she was on Dante Romero's payroll and allegedly begged her to get away from him for her own safety. Earl Thompson is convinced Dante Romero is her killer, and I don't know that I disagree. The state in which her body was found feels like something an aspiring drug lord would do."

I looked over at Baxter. His bright blue eyes were on me, sincere and at the same time sad.

No one seemed to notice our exchange, since Chief Esparza began bringing us up to speed on his and Sterling's interviews. "We have a couple of leads, but I'm not going so far as to say they're solid ones. Katie

Copland's neighbor, Bobby Harper, was in a relationship with her. That's not the main reason he's of interest to us, though. He showed up at the station not long after her body was found and started demanding answers and pointing his finger at Marcus Copland. But it was his demeanor that was of concern. He was scattered. Angry one moment and unhinged the next, then suddenly he'd be muttering 'I'm sorry, Katie.' We didn't have any evidence on him, so we couldn't hold him. We're looking into his known associates to find out if he might've passed the task of killing her to someone else, because the worst thing on his record is a drunk and disorderly over ten years ago. He had a rocky relationship with Marcus Copland, dating back a couple of decades. Long enough that he could be mixed up in any of our homicides."

Baxter said, "Ellie and I spoke to him last night about the Marcus Copland case and got the feeling he was hiding something about Marcus being forced out of town four years ago. According to Rachel Miller, the dynamic between Katie and Bobby was unbalanced. He seemed to put more into the relationship than she did, and he'd gone back to her after she'd left him for Marcus once already."

I added, "Bobby had a lot to lose with Marcus back in town. Marcus didn't bother to divorce Katie when he left. Even though she'd moved on to Bobby, legally she was still Marcus's wife. If I were Bobby, I'd feel like the odd man out, my only option to wait and see if the third time's the charm for the Coplands. Maybe he got sick of waiting for her to get her head out of her ass."

Shane said, "I could be convinced he killed the other three women, ran Copland out of town, set him up to take the fall, and killed him. What I don't buy is him mowing down the love of his life after doing all that work to bust up her marriage. Why kill her if he was planning to get rid of her husband permanently this time?"

I conceded, "That's the part of my theory that doesn't make sense."

Sterling snorted. "The *motive* is the part of your theory that doesn't make sense? That's the part that *has* to make sense, Matthews. Without motive, you don't have a theory."

Rolling my eyes, I said, "Thank you for mansplaining motive to me, Detective."

Vic cut in. "Let's move on before you two get into one of your legendary fights."

Sterling and I looked at each other and then turned to Vic with confused expressions.

Sterling said, "We're past that, man."

I nodded. "Yeah, we're buds now."

The chief, only moderately amused, said, "I'll move this along. We've made an effort to work the Katie Copland case like any other homicide instead of looking at it through the lens of our overall investigation. We spoke to several of Katie Copland's family members, friends, and co-workers, and none of them, except her son, were fans of her husband. They were relieved to see the news story about him confessing and killing himself. They all agreed that aside from Marcus being back in town, nothing in her life had changed lately. She'd received no threats, had no altercations, and made no mention of feeling unsafe. Her phone records and financials don't indicate any unusual activity. No threatening emails, texts, or voicemails. Based on those factors, I would lean toward her killer being someone who was close to her rather than someone who had an issue with her."

I muttered, "Like Bobby Harper."

The chief went on. "However, we can't put blinders on to the fact that the vehicle used to hit her was one piece of a set of carefully laid out evidence that was intended to nail Marcus Copland's coffin shut. With that in mind, I believe her death had little to do with her and was instead a fourth attempt to put Marcus Copland away by someone who was desperate to get him out of their life for good."

Sterling chuckled and glanced my way. "Like Bobby Harper. And by the way, Matthews, we're both wrong about your theory. As the significant other, he doesn't need a motive. Love gone wrong, even if it's only perceived, is enough to put anyone away. Your theory's solid. I like it."

Vic had been fairly quiet during our discussion, jotting notes on the whiteboard behind him as the task force members spoke. While the rest of us sat there dumbfounded by Sterling's glowing compliment, Vic said, "Let's back up to the beginning and assume the killer's original plan of attack against Marcus Copland was simply to frame him for the death of Alice Graves. Copland had motive coming out his ears because she dumped him, and he had a record of being violent toward women. He was the perfect suspect, and it should have been a slam dunk considering he had no alibi for her TOD. However, the killer did too good a job at covering their tracks and left no evidence whatsoever at the scene. With zero evidence, Marcus Copland couldn't be tied to the murder, either, so he couldn't be charged."

He paused for a moment and tapped the end of his marker against the board. "Here's my issue: the killer had evidence they'd taken from the scene —Alice Graves's license and hair. Had they planted that on Marcus Copland at the time, he'd still have decades left in prison. Why allow yourself to fumble the ball at the end zone when you only had one more step to take? While we're talking fails, if you're forced to make a second stab at pinning a murder on someone, why would you transport your victim to the middle of nowhere and bury them where they aren't likely to be found? No body, no crime. Same for the third victim—why let the body degrade and wait weeks before allowing it all to surface? All that accomplished was making it impossible to determine the time and date of death, which made it even more impossible to determine a single suspect because nobody could alibi out." He shook his head, a look of confusion marring his face. "It's like they quit trying to make Marcus look guilty, with the exception of victim choice, until they decided to kill him and pulled out all the stops."

Amanda said, "The only one of our four victims we know for a fact Marcus Copland didn't kill is Katie. I looked at the evidence and reports we had from the other cases and compared them to Katie Copland's. The first three were all hands-on incidents—manual strangulation, knife attack, and blunt force trauma. Katie Copland was killed in a very different manner. Equally brutal and terrible, but not personal or intimate. That feels important to me."

Vic smiled. "Nice insight, Ms. Carmack. What do you think could be the reason for that?"

She took a deep breath and replied, "Maybe someone else killed her. I think we may be trying too hard to attribute five homicides over nine years to the same person."

25

Amanda flicked her eyes at me, her expression apologetic as she went on. "Marcus Copland could have killed the first three women, and . . . it's possible that someone could have figured it out and decided to punish him by killing his wife and then him."

I said to my friend, "Never feel like you have to hold back about Marcus in front of me. I know he's capable of terrible things. The one and only reason I believe he didn't kill Katie is that I saw him with my own eyes only minutes before."

When a look of relief crossed Amanda's face, I added, "And to build on your clever theory, Baxter and I were discussing the idea that one of Marcus's women might have been involved in some of these homicides—maybe with Marcus or maybe with someone else. For example, Katie herself. Losing Marcus meant her only child lost his father. He left her for my mother, and she was not happy about that. Granted, it happened over a decade before my mother died, but it wasn't a huge secret Marcus was hooking up with my mother again before she disappeared . . . while he was married to Katie."

I was getting a lot of stares from around the room, but I pushed forward. Regardless of my feelings, I had to treat every possible person of interest equally. "And I'd be remiss if I didn't also name my mother as another possible example. She never passed up an opportunity to accost Marcus's latest conquest and start something, especially the women he'd left her for. I had to pull her back once when she started physically assaulting Katie. I was twelve. We got confirmation from two different people yesterday that my mother also assaulted Michelle Rutkowski over Marcus. I'm sure there were others. I'll be honest—if my mother were still alive, she'd be one of the first people I'd look at for Katie's murder."

Jayne smiled kindly at me. She of all people knew what it had taken for me to be the one to bring that up. She'd probably come to the same conclusion even before Baxter brought his idea to her. She hadn't been my mother's biggest fan, and for good reason. Jayne had tried multiple times to counsel my mother on taking care of her daughters' safety. She'd offered more times than I could count to take my mother to AA or NA, but of course Patty Copland's response to all of it was that she "didn't need help from some childless bitch cop."

Jayne said, "I think these theories all have merit. While I believe the chances of it being a duo or the killer having an accomplice are good, I'd like to see us pare down this lengthy list we already have before we start adding an exponential number of possibilities. We've learned from experience that adding a second suspect tacks on a lot more moving parts to an already complicated case."

Vic shot me a wink and said, "Don't we know it. The sheriff's right. Let's keep doing what we're doing—eliminating everyone we can until we're down to the most likely individuals. When we get close, we can reevaluate. Now, where were we before this crazy train got derailed?"

The chief said, "I think I was ready to talk about our last interview. We made the mistake of tracking down Tyrell Simpkins at home rather than having him brought here. When Detective Sterling showed Simpkins his badge, Simpkins pulled a gun on him. I arrested him, and he took his Miranda rights very literally." He shook his head. "So damn much time wasted today."

Vic said, "I know I gave you all a lot to work on. I appreciate your perseverance even when things get tough. Let's keep moving on. Sheriff, can you and Ms. Carmack bring us up to speed on your investigation?"

Jayne had been researching my mother's case file and trying to run down persons of interest who'd all but disappeared. "We're waiting to get in touch with Jeff Morrow, Patty Copland's boyfriend at the time of her death. Turns out he was an IMPD narcotics officer on the trail of Dante Romero."

My jaw dropped. My mother's last boyfriend was a vice cop? No way she knew about that. And what in the hell was he thinking getting *that* close to my mother? Gross. She wasn't into taking it slow with men. That guy must have been okay with being deep undercover. And STDs.

Jayne went on. "He and the Noblesville PD managed to take down part of Romero's operation and had charges brought on Romero himself, but Romero's lawyers found a way to get him off. Morrow's cover got blown during the operation, so he's currently in a different state. He's still working vice, and we're waiting until he can safely get away to get on a Zoom call with us."

Amanda gave her report, and it was clear she had been working her ass off. She'd had a mountain of evidence to collect and process between Katie's death scene, the vehicle that hit her, the trophies left at Marcus's death scene, Marcus's truck, and Jayne's shooting, not to mention the documentation and sketches she didn't trust Beck to do. Plus she'd found time somewhere to look over the old case files *and* come up with a brilliant theory of her own.

Vic said, "Detective Baxter and Ms. Matthews, you're next."

As Baxter launched into regurgitating our interviews, starting with Ava's from last night, I tuned out again. Reminiscing with my mother's bestie hadn't been a good time. Ava hadn't been particularly nice to me when I was young—not that any of my mother's cohorts had—so I'd gone in expecting the worst. Ava didn't disappoint. Baxter had moved on to the Michelle Rutkowski interview, and I perked up as the discussion turned to Amy Johnson and her unusual death.

Sterling perused the death certificate and guffawed as he tossed it back across the table toward Baxter. "That looks fake. I bet she paid someone fifty bucks to file the thing and send some bonfire ash back to the States."

Baxter said, "I agree there's something off about it. Amy Johnson was living with Marcus Copland—and was pregnant with his child—right before he started dating Alice Graves."

Jayne sat up straighter. "What? He has another child out there?"

I replied, "No, Amy lost the baby. Rachel remembers the night it happened."

"How did she lose it?"

"Rachel didn't say, but she did mention Amy looked like she'd been roughed up."

Sterling opened his laptop. "I'll see if there was a report filed."

Chief Esparza said, "Detective Baxter, are you thinking Amy Johnson could be another victim for our case?"

"Unfortunately, she could be," he replied. "The situation is suspicious enough that I think someone could have killed her and orchestrated the coverup all from here. I doubt anyone even had to set foot in Mexico to get it done."

Sterling said, "Ding, ding. There's a police report from nine years ago detailing an assault on Amy Johnson. She showed up at the ER with multiple contusions, a sprained ankle, and vaginal bleeding. She said she was pushed down a flight of stairs by . . ." He glanced around to make sure everyone's attention was on him. "Katie Copland."

I cuffed Baxter on the arm. "See?"

Not ready to give up the spotlight, Sterling held up one finger. "*But* . . . after a thorough investigation, Katie Copland was not charged with assault. Her alibi was solid, and the investigating officers did not believe there was any evidence—aside from Amy Johnson's accusations—to prove wrongdoing. In the notes, it says Amy Johnson was extremely agitated and had to be sedated by the hospital staff during her police interview."

Baxter eyed me. "We've heard multiple accounts that Amy Johnson acted irrationally a lot of the time."

My jaw dropped. "Yes, but *this* time she was allowed to be irrational. She'd just lost her baby."

Sterling said, "Matthews, quit interrupting me. Another interesting note here states that Katie Copland's alibi was that she was at the high school football game with . . . Bobby Harper."

I rolled my eyes at Baxter but said nothing, knowing Sterling wasn't done hearing himself talk.

He went on. "This was confirmed by multiple witnesses. As much as I'd love to heap obstruction on top of my boy Bobby's other sins, I don't think I can."

Vic said, "I think it's worthwhile to add Amy Johnson to our list of victims as a possibility. I'd like us to contact the law enforcement branch in Acapulco who investigated her death and obtain the incident report that backs up the death certificate."

Sterling cut in. "If any of that exists."

Vic said, "If it doesn't, we'll open an official case for her. Let's keep going."

Baxter said, "I think we've discussed everything we learned from speaking to Hector Torres and listening in on Earl Thompson's interview."

Vic nodded. I'd noticed his expression had been troubled for most of the meeting as he listened and tried to digest everything we talked about. "You guys have really done some top-notch work on this investigation. We've got a lot of information to wade through, but I feel like we have two and a half decent suspects we should be running with: Bobby Harper and Dante Romero, with Manny Ferrara as Romero's errand boy for the Graves and Yoon homicides. Anyone disagree?"

"What about Jake Campbell?" Jayne asked.

Shrugging, Vic said, "I know Jimmy Belzer and Manny Ferrara said Campbell would do anything to get ahead, but I'm not convinced he fits our profile. Sounds to me like his aggressions are straightforward and calculated to do the most damage. He blatantly pitted Manny Ferrara and Marcus Copland against each other to take out both of them or at least keep them occupied for long enough to make a grab for their territories. He openly bullied and threatened dealers to try to take what was theirs. Killing these women and hoping Marcus Copland would either get charged or go into hiding is too arbitrary a plan for someone like him. There were too many variables to guarantee him what he wanted when there was a simpler solution. I think if he were to make a major move involving committing murder himself, he would have offed Marcus Copland and been done with it. I also think his threats were, for the most part, empty. According to vice, he hasn't expanded his operation since taking over Manny Ferrara's turf, and he's had zero assault charges since then. Doesn't sound like he successfully intimidated anyone."

Jayne asked, "Can the same not be said for Dante Romero in regard to our victims?"

Vic replied, "Not exactly. Dante Romero came to the area intent on making a name for himself. He didn't just want to take over territories. He wanted power. He wanted an army. He wanted to be feared. So when he kills someone or has them killed, it's going to be in a manner that causes pain and suffering and feels personal even though it probably isn't. It's intended to provoke terror and keep people in line. It may not even have anything to do with the victim. The first three murders were violent, and the close manner of attack made them seem personal. We know Dante Romero was directly linked to Patty Copland in a way that had a good probability of ending in disaster for her. I know Romero is going to be a tough one to nail, but if any group can do it, it's this one." He gave us a proud but tired smile. "We've discussed Bobby Harper ad nauseam, so I'm not revisiting that. Also, if you get a hot lead that has nothing to do with our Three Stooges, absolutely go ahead and follow it. The last thing I'd want to do is stifle your investigative process. I'm only trying to help sharpen our focus and save us all some time. Anyone have any final thoughts?"

Sterling joked, "Yeah, Manetti, I think this meeting could have been an email."

Laughter erupted from around the table. As we all got up and exited the room, I could feel a lighter vibe from the group. We were so close. We only needed one decent break to bring it all together.

BAXTER and I went to lunch and managed not to speak a word about the investigation the entire time. We mostly talked about how much we missed restful sleep, not having to work every waking hour, and what series to choose for a Netflix and chill day once we solved this thing and were rewarded with time off. We parted ways once we got back to the station. I wanted to have a look at the evidence Amanda had processed from the various scenes, plus I wanted to get my hands on the evidence Shane had requested from the two Alice Graves cases.

I checked out the two Graves boxes from evidence and took them to the lab. Beck was puttering around near the fume hood with his back to me, so I didn't bother greeting him. I set the boxes on a worktable and found Amanda in the lab office, typing fast and furiously on a laptop.

I leaned against the doorframe and asked, "Want to look through the Alice Graves evidence with me?"

Smiling, she jumped up and came my way. "I'd love to. These scene notes are going to be the death of me."

I shook my head as I walked toward the table where I'd left the boxes. "Nope. One more crime scene this week, and I quit."

Beck muttered, "If only."

I asked innocently, "What's got your panties in a wad, Beck? Have a spat with your girlfriend?"

He snapped his head up. "What did you hear?"

Snickering, I replied, "Nothing. Chill."

Amanda kept walking, her gaze zeroed in on the fume hood. "Why is that in there? You and I both processed it. I sealed it up for long-term storage myself."

Beck's eyes darted from Amanda to the hood, then to me and back to the hood. Something was up with him. When Beck got agitated, things got very interesting. I didn't want to miss a minute of the action, so I strolled over to look at what Amanda was studying. A chill crept up my spine. Hanging from the drying clips in the fume hood was Marcus's alleged confession note saying, *I KILLED THEM ALL*. Only it looked different than I remembered. The blue ink was badly smudged, and the paper was rumpled and dingy.

Amanda leaned into the chamber for a closer look. "Why is it wet?" she demanded, her expression thunderous. "And *brown*?"

Beck's face went white. I didn't know whether to laugh or be appalled.

She took a deep sniff. "You spilled your *coffee* on it?"

"Oh, shit," I breathed.

Beck protested, "It wasn't my fault. It was an accident."

I'd never seen Amanda furious like this. "Doesn't matter! You ruined a key piece of evidence in a multi-departmental quintuple homicide investigation!"

I added, "That you got dismissed from."

"Shut up, Ellie," he sneered. To Amanda, he said, "Like I said, this wasn't even my fault. My now ex-girlfriend was the one who spilled her stupid latte all over the place, which I had to clean up."

I didn't think Amanda could get any madder, but she did. Her jaw dropped, as did her tone. Her voice laced with danger, she said, "You brought a civilian in here while you had evidence out? Again? We've had this discussion once already this week. Do you think you're above the rules because of who your mommy is?"

Beck did not appreciate it when anyone brought up his mommy, Judge Ferguson, or as she was not-so-affectionately nicknamed, the Dragon Lady. She was horrible to everyone except her sweet baby boy, who I was pretty sure still lived with her at the ripe old age of twenty-eight.

He crossed his arms and huffed. "I am your boss, and you can't talk to me that way. I can fire you—"

"No you can't," I interjected.

He went on. "Then I can have you fired—"

"No you can't," I interjected again.

"Would you shut the hell up?" he screeched. "I'm the lead criminalist, and I'm in charge of this lab. So if I want to show off some murder memorabilia once in a while, I can do that."

I gaped at him. "You and your 'murder memorabilia' again? I feel like you should have learned your lesson when Agent Griffin chucked your phone into the Woodland Gardens woods for sharing crime scene photos. When is your dumb ass going to grasp the meaning of the word 'memorabilia'? The gist is literally within the word. What makes an object memorabilia is that it embodies the *memory* of a past historical event, its value and importance hinging on the fact that it's old and rare. New stuff doesn't qualify. And most importantly, *all evidence from active investigations is confidential.* Period."

Sterling's laugh cut through the tension. "Now who's mansplaining, Matthews?" He swaggered over to us. "I want to see some murder memorabilia."

Amanda stabbed a finger toward the note. "There you go. Coffee stains and all."

Sterling's eyes bulged out. He turned to Beck. "You did this?"

I said, "No, his girlfriend—oh, excuse me, *ex*-girlfriend—did."

Shaking his head, Sterling got out his phone. "Oh, Becky, Becky, Becky. What are we going to do with you? Oh, wait. I know. We're gonna get you shitcanned." He scrolled through his contacts, making sure Beck could see his screen. "There's the sheriff's number." He tapped his screen and put the phone to his ear.

Beck's voice went up an octave. "You're *tattling* on me?"

"You bet your ass I'm tattling on—Hello, Sheriff Walsh. We have a situation in the lab that needs your assistance. It's urgent."

As Sterling put his phone away, Beck looked like he was weighing his escape route options. He started nonchalantly slinking toward the door, but nothing got past Sterling. His hand shot out and grabbed Beck by the back of his shirt. Beck tried to wriggle away, which any of us could have told him was an exercise in futility. Sterling had fifty pounds of muscle on him, and in one move had Beck seated in a nearby chair, his hands resting heavily on Beck's scrawny shoulders.

Jayne's eyes narrowed in on Sterling and Beck as she entered the lab. "What is it this time?" She didn't have much patience for the war of words that had been raging between the two of them for as long as they'd worked together.

Figuring I was the only one without a dog in this fight, I gestured toward the note and explained calmly, "Marcus's alleged confession note has been damaged. It's inadmissible now. It had been logged back into storage, but Beck retrieved it to show to a civilian. Her coffee overturned on the note, stained and degraded the paper, and smudged the ink."

Jayne stared at the note for a few moments and then shifted her disgusted gaze to Beck. "Mr. Durant, you're fired." She turned to Amanda. "Ms. Carmack, you're promoted. Congratulations."

Sterling shot Amanda an excited grin and mouthed, "That's awesome, babe."

Beck sputtered, "What? My mother—"

Jayne talked over him. "Won't be able to help you this time. Detective, escort Mr. Durant out of the building."

Sterling was clenching his jaw so hard to conceal his glee, I worried he might crack a molar. Gripping Beck's upper arm, he hoisted him up from the chair and swept him out the door.

Jayne sighed wearily. "Can we please wrap up this investigation quickly and with no more stupidity or bodily harm?"

"We will certainly try," I said.

26

Once Jayne left the lab, Amanda let out a squeal. "Do you think she was serious about my promotion?"

I smiled. "Of course. The woman never says anything she doesn't mean." I reached out and gave my friend a hug. "Congratulations, *boss*! I'm thrilled for you."

"Me, too," she said, a look of utter happiness on her face. Then she suddenly deflated before my eyes. "Wait. I don't know how to do this job. Beck was actually very conscientious about doing his administrative tasks, even staying late sometimes to finish them. And he was oddly secretive about them, so I have no clue where to start."

"I know how to do this job. I'll show you whatever you need to know. And don't worry about the admin stuff. There's not that much, and it's way easier than the real work we do. I'm betting Beck was spending the bulk of his supposed 'admin time' playing online nerd games and didn't want you to know."

She let out a sigh of relief. "Good."

I assured her, "Trust me, you can do this job in your sleep. Don't stress. Accept the title and the raise, and enjoy being Beck-free."

Her eyes lit up. "A Beck-free workplace is a dream come true."

Properly celebrating Amanda's good news would unfortunately have to wait until after we wrapped the case. She and I got back to work, each putting on gloves and opening a box. Hers was the box from Alice Graves's home invasion, which contained several fingerprint lift cards, strips of used duct tape affixed to a thick sheet of plastic, and a butterfly knife.

Amanda brandished the butterfly knife. "Ooh, I wonder if the intruders did a bunch of lame tricks with this knife to try to scare Marcus."

I thought for a moment. "When I envision this particular home invasion scenario, I'm not sure who I consider the 'bad guys.'"

She laughed. "I understand your dilemma. If the intruders are the bad guys, does that make Marcus the good guy or the worse guy?"

"He's the worse guy. Always."

She gingerly opened the knife. "Fingerprint dust. Looks like someone may have found a print or two on here. That's decent news." She shuffled through the print cards while I unboxed and unbagged the contents of the homicide evidence box.

I said, "This is just the usual stuff: victim's clothing, purse, and shoes. No murder weapon since it was a manual strangulation. Boo."

She held up a print card. "This one is marked 'print from butterfly knife,' with a note that says, 'no match in AFIS.' Boo to that, too."

Shrugging, I said, "It's been eight years. Once a criminal, always a criminal, so chances are decent this 'bad guy' decided to do more stupid stuff. I'd run it through again and see if you get a hit."

Amanda disappeared into the office to use the AFIS computer. Much more intrigued by the home invasion evidence than the murder stuff, I picked up the remaining print cards and looked through them. These were mostly prints gathered from doorframes, and they were all marked as belonging to either Alice Graves or Marcus.

"Ellie!" Amanda cried.

I hurried into the office. "What?"

She was grinning ear to ear. "The print from the butterfly knife belongs to Manny Ferrara."

I hurried behind Amanda to look at her screen. "No freaking way," I said, excitement rippling through me.

"Yes!" Amanda cheered, ripping off her gloves to get out her phone. "I love it when we crack the case before the detectives." She started typing, I assumed a text to Sterling to share her second bit of amazing news.

I smiled. "Don't celebrate just yet. You haven't verified it."

She waved a hand and continued typing her text. "The match percentage is eighty-nine. I'll risk it."

I bumped her aside. "You keep gloating to your boyfriend. I'll verify it." I quickly replotted Manny Ferrara's print from AFIS and verified it was a match as Baxter and Sterling showed up at our door.

Sterling grinned at Amanda. "There's my badass lead criminalist girlfriend."

Baxter said, "Congratulations, Amanda. You've deserved this promotion for a long time."

All smiles, Amanda said, "Thank you."

Winking at her, Sterling said, "You said you had something waiting for me that would blow my mind. I don't get why you asked me to bring Baxter along, though. You know I wouldn't be down for that."

"Eww," I complained. "She meant a work thing that will blow your mind, you perv."

He shrugged, unaffected, murmuring to Amanda, "My idea will have to wait until later, then."

She shook her head with a flirty smile. "Down, boy. We may have just done your jobs for you. Again."

I had to hold in a snicker. I loved that Amanda's confidence in her work was growing.

I could tell from Baxter's expression that he was growing a tad impatient with us. He cared so much about this case because of Rachel and me, and I felt like he didn't want to waste a moment of time on anything not case-related.

I explained, "There was a butterfly knife collected from the Graves home invasion. The print lifted from it belongs to . . . Amanda, you do the honors."

She announced proudly, "Manny Ferrara."

Both detectives looked stunned. Baxter found his voice first. "That's an amazing find, and it means there's a very good chance he had something to do with Alice Graves's death."

I nodded.

He went on. "Which means I'm going to talk to him without you."

I knew this was going to happen, but I still felt like complaining about it. "I talked to him this morning and made it through unscathed."

"We didn't accuse him of murder this morning."

Sterling said to me, "Let the men handle it, Matthews."

Amanda stared him down. "Would you like to rephrase that, Jason?"

He blanched. "That was a joke. Matthews knows it was a joke. We're buds." He looked at me pleadingly. "Right, Matthews?"

I replied sweetly, "Of course we're buds. And you know what buds do when they go out and leave their other buds behind at the station, right?"

Sterling shook his head, seeming flummoxed.

"They bring back coffee. And not the gas station or the drive-thru kind. I'm talking local, preferably roasted in-house, and made with love."

Amanda chimed in, "They also bring back coffee for their badass lead criminalist girlfriends."

Our antics had both of them grumbling on their way out, but the spring in their steps was unmistakable.

Amanda and I returned to the main area of the lab to keep working on the evidence. After a while, she ventured, "I meant to ask you this earlier, but with all the excitement this afternoon, I kept forgetting. How much evidence from your mother's case did you examine?"

"Too much." She seemed to be getting at something rather than making small talk, so I explained, "I processed all the . . . bags of her up until I got to her head, which was the last bag. When we opened it, I immediately recognized her earrings and bolted. Anything that was found after that, I didn't lay eyes on. And I'll be honest, I've never gone back to look through her case file or the evidence or anything. I probably should, but I really don't want to."

"I don't blame you. I would have done the same thing." She added tentatively, "Would you mind talking about it with me, though?"

"Go ahead."

"Like I mentioned at the meeting, I looked through all the cases' evidence. And I noticed something about your mom's evidence that I didn't see noted in the file."

I frowned. "What's that?"

"There was a bag of various things that were found tangled in her hair. There were leaves and twigs and general organic matter you'd find outdoors in the woods or in a field, which makes sense since the bags were shredded enough to let debris in. The interesting part was that there were also these little wood pieces that reminded me of the pine shavings we used to line the cattle stalls on our farm when I was a kid. I wonder if maybe your mother was in a barn around the time of her death. That detail may be insignificant, but I didn't want to keep anything from you."

I nodded, wondering whether it was worth our time to try to chase down another vague lead. My phone started buzzing incessantly in my pocket, so I took off my gloves to see what was up. Rachel was blowing up my phone with a rapid succession of text messages:

I can't find Jack.

I'm at his house to pick him up to take him to his doctor's appointment.

He's not here.

The front door was unlocked, so I went inside.

He won't answer any of my texts or calls, either.

His mom's car is here, and he couldn't have walked far on his own.

I'm worried.

I said to Amanda, "I need to deal with a Rachel crisis. She's okay. I'll be back." I left the lab and called my sister.

She picked up on the first ring. "Something's not right."

I gathered that. I said calmly, "Tell me what you know."

"I already texted you what I know, and it's not a lot," she snapped. "That would be why I said I was worried."

If it had been one of my students not being where they'd said they'd be and not answering their phone, I wouldn't worry that much. College-aged kids were flaky sometimes, and other times they went off the grid for a bit to decompress. But given Jack's special circumstances, this wasn't one of those times you could pass it off as no big deal.

I went with the basics first. "Did he make it home from Muncie?"

Rachel replied, "Yes, he texted me this morning to let me know his friend dropped him off."

"Might he have found another way to get to his appointment and forgot to tell you?"

"I called the doctor's office, and they said he wasn't there, either." Her voice broke on the last word.

In an even calmer tone, I asked, "Okay. What can I do to help you?"

"Find Jack. Isn't that what you do?" she wailed.

"Text me his address, and I'll call dispatch to get someone over there right away." An eerie thought striking me, I began hurrying toward the conference room, hoping to find Vic there. "Is Agent Davis still with you?"

"Yes."

I wondered why he wasn't being of more use in this situation, like calling for help, but that was the least of my worries. "Stay in the vehicle with him, doors locked. I'll head there now."

Her tone more even, she said, "Okay. Thanks."

I made a quick call to dispatch to get someone out to Jack's house ASAP. When I entered the conference room and found both Vic and Shane there, my anxiety waned, but my face must have given up my feelings. They both demanded, "What's wrong?"

I replied, "I don't want to alarm you, but Jack Copland may be missing."

They both snapped into action, standing and gathering their jackets and keys.

Vic said, "First things first—have deputies been sent to his last known location?"

I nodded. "Yes, I just called dispatch. Jack should have been waiting at his home for Rachel to pick him up for an appointment. He's not answering her calls or texts. She tried the door and it was open, but he's not there."

"Is his vehicle there?"

"I don't think he's able to drive right now. She mentioned his mom's car was there, so he's not off somewhere on his own unless he's on foot. Which is even more unlikely."

Vic's expression turned to a grimace. "Between his health being compromised and both parents being recent homicide victims, I'm not waiting the customary forty-eight hours to start an official search for him. I'm calling an all hands on deck for this one. Let's move out."

As SHANE DROVE, Vic and I were on our phones mobilizing the task force to meet us at Jack Copland's home.

The moment I put my phone away, Shane said gently, "Ellie, I've been thinking. Now, I don't want to freak you out, but we might want to consider the possibility that—"

Full of adrenaline, I blurted out in one breath, and way more harshly than I intended, "We've clearly not backed off our investigation, so the killer is ramping up the violence—again—and there's a decent chance they're being violent against Jack as we speak, so what's to stop them from picking off Marcus's family members one by one, and the only ones left are Rachel and Nate, so they need to go somewhere safe, miles away from this hellscape?"

Flicking his eyes my way, he replied, "Yes. If this is actual worst-case scenario, they need to be in a secure location."

Vic said from the back seat, "I'm already on it."

My stomach twisted at the words "worst-case scenario." If something happened to Jack, it would destroy Rachel. Aside from being worried about Jack's safety and my sister's safety and mental health, I was pissed. Pissed at the killer for taking Jack's mom when he needed her, possibly hurting Jack, terrorizing my sister, shooting Jayne . . . not to mention killing my mother, which indirectly derailed my entire career. I might never have even met this person, yet they were responsible for the trajectory my adult life had taken.

Shane put his hand on my arm. "You okay? You zoned out on me."

"I'm not okay, but I'm handling it."

"We got your back. You know that, don't you?"

Vic's head appeared between us. "He's right. But if this gets to be too much and you need out, we'll get you out."

I knew with these guys by my side I could get through anything. Shane had supported me in college when I'd struck out on my own for the first time, and Vic and I had been to hell and back together multiple times. "I'll get through this. We've been through worse."

Vic smiled. "Damn straight. We'll get Rachel and Nate secure first. Then we catch this son of a bitch. I've got a safe house being set up for them as we speak."

I breathed an audible sigh of relief.

Shane joked, "Hey, at least working with the FBI is good for something."

BY THE TIME we reached Jack's house, first responders from the city and county were already there and had the home and yard secured and cordoned off. Vic informed me that agents were already en route to David's house to secure Nate's location so Agent Davis could escort Rachel there to pick him up on their way out of town. The only thing they were waiting on was me, because Rachel had refused to leave until we got to say goodbye.

My sister rushed me the moment I stepped out of Shane's SUV. She flung her arms around me, and I hugged her back tightly. I knew she was choked up, because she didn't utter a word. She was worried and sad and scared, and it killed me to see her that way again after how much she'd struggled the past year to put her life back together. And it wasn't like I'd made it any easier, with our safety being compromised by me openly chasing killers around the county. I was so sick and tired of forcing my poor sister and nephew to endure security details and to have to leave our home, even though it was for their own safety. I always felt it was my fault they became targets. I harbored those thoughts now as well, although this time Rachel's connection to my case wasn't through me.

I worked to keep my voice steady as I said, "We'll find Jack. You go and spend some quality time with Nate. I'll speak to your professors, so don't give school another thought. You take care of yourself and leave the rest to us. We're getting close. We just got a break that could be the key to taking down this piece of shit."

She leaned back to look at me. "What about you?"

"For starters, I'm not allowed anywhere near anyone who's considered the least bit dangerous, because literally everyone on the task force thinks I need protecting."

"They're right. You need protecting from all the dumb shit you do."

"That was hurtful . . . but fair."

Rachel smiled through her tears. "I'll call you when we get there, okay? Keep me posted on Jack."

I smiled back. "I will. I love you."

"I love you, too."

As my baby sister was escorted away by Agent Davis, I took a moment to compose myself. I spotted Baxter getting out of his SUV at the curb and waved.

He hurried toward me and enveloped me in his arms. "You hanging in there? Manetti said the team escorting Rachel and Nate to the safe house is top-notch. You won't have to worry about their safety one bit."

Against his chest, I said, "I'm okay."

He released me and lowered his voice. "I don't like this. Now, I don't know this kid. His disappearance and radio silence could be from him having some kind of mental break. He's had an extremely difficult few days on top of dealing with chronic poor health. Not that I hope this is the case, but the alternative is even more dangerous for him."

"I know."

Baxter steered me toward Vic, who was ending a call on his phone.

Baxter asked him, "Did you get a location from the cell trace?"

Vic replied, "It's showing that it's right around here somewhere. The signal is currently offline, but the last ping was an hour ago on the cell tower nearest here. He, or at least his phone, has to be close. We have people checking door-to-door to find out if anyone saw him on foot."

I held back a shiver. This scenario felt eerily like the time we searched for Jayne's missing niece at Ashmore.

Baxter said encouragingly to me, "Hey, we'll find him, we'll take down the killer, and then this nightmare will be over once and for all for you and Rachel."

I nodded, blowing out a slow breath and digging deep to lock down my emotions so I could do my job. It wasn't fair to the rest of the task force and especially to Jack if people had to waste precious time coddling me. As I latched onto Baxter's words, *this nightmare will be over once and for all for you and Rachel,* and repeated them in my head, I gained the determination to flip that switch inside me and pour all of my energy into the investigation.

I looked up at them. "Let's do this."

27

Grinning, Vic said, "There she is. We'll start by taking a sweep through the house and seeing what we can see."

Vic, Baxter, and I walked to the house, pulling on gloves as we went. Sterling, Amanda, and Shane were already inside having a look around.

Vic said to them, "Please tell me one of you found a big, glaring clue that will tell us exactly what happened here."

Amanda smiled. "Sorry, nothing yet."

Shane added, "No signs of struggle, though. If Jack Copland's disappearance is courtesy of our killer, they didn't hurt him here, nor did they drag him away kicking and screaming."

Baxter turned to me. "Do you know exactly how bad his health is? I mean, could he physically fight back in a hostile situation?"

I replied, "I don't know exactly how bad off he is, but he's unwell enough that he doesn't drive. And you heard Bobby Harper last night—he said he went over and 'tended to' Jack and made sure he ate. I'll be honest, though, I don't know what his health issue is. Jack was always a sore subject in our household growing up. Even now, Rachel rarely talks about him."

For once, I'd been on my mother's side about something. Neither of us wanted to hear about how great Rachel's little brother was. My mother was jealous that Jack had come along and busted up her marriage, and I was jealous I had to share my only sibling with someone else. I admittedly still harbored a bit of that feeling.

Amanda was busy studying the prescription pill bottles on the table next to her. "Some kind of pain and inflammation, plus depression. I've got Percocet, Lortab, Xanax, a corticosteroid—"

Sterling interrupted her. "Are those medications he'd have to take throughout the day or once a day?"

If she noticed him slipping into his signature rude behavior, as he did when cases got tough, she didn't react. "Some of both."

Shane said, "If he's not just out for a walk—which we don't believe he's able to do—and he's planning to be away from home for a while, shouldn't he have taken his medications with him?"

Baxter nodded. "Yes, unless he's had some kind of mental health incident or was lured or forced away from here."

Shane glanced around the small living room. "I suppose if someone came to his door and pointed a gun in his face, he might have left with them without a struggle."

Amanda was still concentrating on the bottles. "There's something shady going on with these meds. There are almost a dozen fairly aggressive drugs here that don't all play well together. Besides the ones I already named, we've got Lexapro, Wellbutrin, deracoxib—wait, that drug is for dogs . . ." She looked around. "Do they even have a dog?"

I glanced around for the telltale signs common in my own home—dog toys strewn about, dirty paw prints by the door, and clouds of fur in every corner. None of that here. "I'm going to say no."

She went on. "There's also Prozac, gabapentin—wait, that's prescribed to a dog, too—and holy shit . . . Dilaudid? They only hand that out for severe pain."

Shane asked, "Besides the dog ones, are those all prescribed to Jack Copland?"

"They are," Amanda replied. "But by several different doctors."

"Sounds like our boy is a drug seeker to me," Sterling said.

Vic said, "Drug seeker or not, he's still missing and at risk. Here's the plan. Ms. Carmack, I want you to dust all the doors for fingerprints and get them processed immediately. Detectives, split up tasks and work this as a missing persons case. Ms. Matthews and I will stay and look through the rest of the house and join you after we're done."

Baxter, Sterling, and Shane left, and Amanda went outside to get her kit, leaving Vic and me alone in the home.

I blew out a breath and looked around again. The place wasn't exactly messy, but it wasn't neat, either. I couldn't imagine Jack, if he was as sick as we'd thought, had the energy or the drive to keep things tidy after losing his mother and father back-to-back. If he was a drug seeker, as Sterling surmised, he might have spent most of his free time getting high rather than cleaning.

"Where do you want to start?" I asked Vic.

He replied, "I'll take the back door. You take the front door. Then we can go around to all the windows. If we find a sign of forced entry, we can rule out a lot of theories."

I remembered something from Rachel's texts. "Rachel said the front door was unlocked when she got here, so she came inside to look for Jack. I don't know if the Coplands were big on locking up, but in this neighbor-hood . . . I think I would. It reminds me too much of my neighborhood."

"Good to know."

Amanda was working on printing the doorframe as I studied the door itself with a flashlight. She said quietly, "I saw your sister being escorted away by the FBI. I'm sorry she has to go into protective custody—I can't imagine how scared she must be. And you, too."

"She's having a tough time, but she's incredibly strong. As long as this doesn't drag on too long, she'll be fine."

"The same could be said for you." She stopped brushing fingerprint powder on the doorframe to smile at me. "You know we're all here for you anytime you need anything."

I nodded. "I know. It helps when the people I'm working with 24/7 are the ones I go to when I need support. And even though Rachel and Nate aren't necessarily having a great time, if they're in FBI protective custody, their safety is the one thing I don't have to worry about. It's amazing how much of my energy that frees up."

Chuckling, she joked as she went back to her task, "Look at you finding the silver lining. Are you feeling okay?"

I laughed. "You know me too well."

Finding no sign of forced entry on the door, I moved on to the two windows of the living room. They were painted shut, and likely had been for decades from the look of them. I scanned the kitchen next—same situation. I found Vic in what had to have been Katie's bedroom.

I said, "No sign of anyone messing with the front door. So far all the windows I've checked are painted shut."

He came my way. "Same here. I only have to check the ones in the other bedroom. Then we can move on to sifting through a teenage boy's crap."

"You saved the best for last."

We entered what was clearly Jack's room, given the male clothes and shoes scattered about, youth sports trophies gathering dust on shelves, and a well-used baseball bat and glove propped in the corner.

Vic inhaled sharply through his nose. "You smell pot?"

Making a face, I said, "Yeah. And he's only nineteen. I don't think even quack doctors can get away with prescribing it to patients who can't legally buy it." Vic checked the windows while I perused the personal items strewn across the dresser. "He seems to be a connoisseur of shitty body spray. And terrible art." I picked up a well-worn sketchbook and flipped through it. The drawings were pretty talentless, not that I'd know art if it bit me in the ass. As I kept flipping, they got increasingly graphic. The figures got more and more distorted, then they started losing body parts and dripping blood. I held the last page up for Vic to see. "Dude's got some issues."

Vic stared at the drawing of a naked woman whose throat had been slit deep. "That's messed up."

"Yeah it is. It's not a reaction to the last couple of days, either," I replied, thumbing through a couple more sketchbooks on the dresser. One culminated in a woman being strangled by a pair of hands, the perspective being what the person doing the strangling would see. "Creepy. This has been going on for a while." I got to one of the more well-worn sketchpads and glanced at several pages before a gut punch had me gasping for air. All I could utter was a strangled cry.

Vic was next to me in less than a second. "What's the matter?"

I pointed at the drawing as a cold, tingly chill snaked up my spine.

Vic removed the book from my hands and set it down. He then ripped off his gloves and took me by the shoulders. "Let's get you out of here for a bit."

I shook my head and found my voice. "No, this can't wait. We need to figure out what possessed him to draw that. And how he knew exactly what it looked like. Now."

"Ellie, you need a minute."

I twisted away from him. "Vic, no. This kid drew an accurate depiction of how my mother's remains were found. The tattered garbage bags . . . the body parts bagged separately . . . the blood and goo oozing out . . . It's frighteningly exact. He had to have seen it, and that means . . ." One horrible thought after another slammed through my brain. I squeezed my eyes shut and focused on my breathing in an effort to get hold of myself.

His voice as gentle as I'd ever heard it, Vic replied, "Let's not make that jump just yet. He could easily have drawn these from what was shown on the news. I remember being appalled that WIND-TV was allowed to show everything they did, but it was a live feed. As soon as the FCC figured out what was going on, they made them halt their broadcast and fined the hell out of them, but the damage had been done."

Between my breathing exercise and Vic's solid reasoning, I was able to regain a decent amount of my composure. Frowning, I said, "Oh. Right. I'd forgotten about that." I dug deep and unearthed some old repressed memories. "The press got really aggressive with us. There was a leak about the anonymous tips we kept getting about the locations of the bags, so we had news vans tailing us every time we left the station. The bags were left in rural areas, and we had to hunt around for some of them. It's next to impossible to secure a perimeter when you can't pinpoint a location, so the press kept running amok in our secondary scenes. Our deputies did their best to chase down everyone with a camera, but then they got tricky and started using concealed GoPros to live stream. The day of that particular broadcast, the WIND-TV guys found the bag before we did. That's how they got such an unobstructed shot." I shook my head in disgust. "I've never seen the chief so pissed. I was convinced we were going to have another murder on our hands."

"I don't blame him," Vic said. "Back to the artwork . . . I read Nick's report about your interview with Jack. He mentioned to you about his father going on a raging bender after your mother's death and how crushed he seemed. Maybe the violent artwork was how Jack dealt with witnessing his father's grief over the situation. If Marcus was drunk rambling about the details, a mental picture might have gotten stuck in Jack's head until he found a way to purge it."

As he spoke, I began forming another theory. I picked up one of the sketchbooks and flipped to the woman being strangled and held it out to him. "If the body parts in the bags are supposed to be my mother, who does that make this?"

Vic's expression went grim. "Alice Graves."

"And the one with her throat slit?"

"Jihyo Yoon."

"Bingo."

He shook his head. "Wait, Alice Graves died eight years ago. Jack would have been eleven. I don't feel like it's realistic that he was involved in any way."

"It's realistic if his shitty single mom needed someone to help her. Or if she couldn't find a sitter, so he had to tag along on her murderous rampages."

Letting out a snicker, he said, "I'm happy to see you've progressed to gallows humor."

I wasn't trying to be particularly funny. When my mother was between boyfriends and needed help doing something shady, I was her go-to, being someone she could easily coerce into keeping their mouth shut. While she'd never made me an accomplice to murder, she'd had me steal for her, be her lookout while she broke into various places, and help her smash up her exes' and their new girlfriends' vehicles. The vehicle-smashing part was admittedly kind of fun, but I hated her for making me do the other stuff.

I said, "I still say Katie Copland had a lot to lose with Marcus hopping from woman to woman. According to Rachel, Alice wanted nothing to do with Marcus's kids, which meant he didn't see them as much when he was with her. I'm sure that upset Jack, which Katie didn't like. Then he was going to marry Jihyo, which meant he'd be locked down for a while. Katie probably didn't like that, either. And don't forget that both times Marcus and Katie got married, their relationship ended because of him nailing my mother on the side."

He nodded slowly. "I hadn't framed the other two victims that way. Your mother, yes. I could see Katie Copland going after her. The only problem with your theory is that Katie didn't run over herself."

"But a troubled young man with mental and physical issues who'd been unwillingly involved in or witness to three murders might snap and try to hurt the person who put him through it. And then snuff out the absentee father who put his mother on the bus to Crazytown."

Vic's eyes widened, then he grinned at me. "You sure you don't want to come work for me at the Bureau? You'd make a fantastic profiler. You think like a Fed."

"I think like a Fed? That's not a compliment."

"It was intended to be. I think like a Fed."

I wrinkled my nose. "It's not a flex either, Manetti."

He snorted. "All right, smartass. You've got a great theory, but there's no evidence to back it up. And let's not forget our drive-by. Wasn't Jack Copland at a friend's place in Muncie last night? How'd he shoot the sheriff from there?"

"Muncie's not that far. In under three hours he could have come here, stolen a car, done the deed, and gone back. Or he could have lied to Rachel about when he got back to town to give himself an alibi. In fact, the whole trip could have been a sham to stay off our radar."

"There you go thinking like a Fed again."

I scowled at him. "Seriously, stop saying that."

He chuckled. "If you think Jack Copland is guilty of something, find me some proof."

"Get me a warrant, Agent. We can't collect jack shit—or any of Jack's shit—without it." I laughed heartily at my own joke while Vic rolled his eyes. "You see what I did there?"

"Yes, you're a comedic genius. Sit tight while I go secure your warrant."

I wandered out to the living room and spotted Amanda at the open back door dusting for prints. "Have you been able to lift any usable prints?" I asked her.

"A few," she replied. "But I'm not convinced any of them are going to belong to Jack's would-be kidnapper. Since there was no struggle or forced entry, I don't know that the killer would have touched the door. They probably knocked, Jack opened the door, and they . . . I suppose shoved a gun in his face and forced him to leave?" She thought for a moment. "Although if the door was closed when your sister got here, then it's likely the kidnapper would have been the one to pull it shut. So the single unsmudged print I found on the outside knob could in fact belong to them."

"Way to reason it out, Mademoiselle Lead Criminalist."

She blushed. "I've been so into the scene, I keep forgetting about my promotion. Then I remember and agonize over whether I've done or said something unprofessional. I'm afraid I'm developing imposter syndrome."

I shook my head. "You're always way more professional than the rest of us, and you're more than qualified to do this job. Vic obviously thinks so, given how much investigative work he threw your way."

"I hoped that was the case. I've really enjoyed getting to be more involved."

"Well, he wouldn't have done it if he didn't believe in you. We all do." I added kindly, "After you did such a stellar job on the first case we worked together, I made it a point to push more and more of the lead investigator tasks your way. I wanted you to gain experience so you could move up to a lead position, even though you might have to leave us to do it. Lucky for us, now you don't have to."

She gave me a quick but tight hug. "I had no idea. I thought you were passing me those tasks because you were busy investigating with Nick or stretched too thin with school or simply overwhelmed with the nature of some of our cases."

I eyed her. "Or that I was lazy?"

"The one thing you're not is lazy." She turned her head to the side. "Do you hear that?"

I stepped outside the house to stand next to her on the tiny deck and listened. "Is it . . . some dogs fighting down the street?"

She stood very still. "No, I think it's closer, but muffled. It sounds more to me like a wounded dog. Maybe the Coplands have one after all. Does this house have a basement?"

"If it does, there's no interior door." I hopped down from the deck and began walking along the back perimeter of the house. "I'd say no. I see crawlspace vents, but no windows. And no doors back here besides the one you've been dusting. I'll check around the side." I walked around to the side of the house, finding only another crawlspace vent. I turned around and headed back.

As I rounded the corner of the house, I saw the top of Amanda's head bobbing down some stairs leading to the basement of the house next door. "Amanda, don't! That's Bobby Harper's house!" I yelled, taking off after her. It wouldn't be a good look for one of the task force members to break into the house of a suspect, even if it was to try to rescue a hurt dog.

I heard her scream. I got to the top of the stairs in time to catch a glimpse of Jack Copland's face before the door slammed shut.

28

My whole body began quaking. I turned to go get help and stumbled, catching myself before I went down. Luckily, two deputies were already rushing my way.

"We heard yelling," one of them said. "Everyone okay?"

"No," I croaked, working to keep my voice steady as I pointed next door. "Jack Copland just pulled Amanda Carmack inside the basement of that house against her will. She's who screamed."

One of the deputies seized me by the arm and ushered me back into the yard behind the Copland house.

My phone rang. I was going to let it go to voicemail, but when I saw the call was coming from Amanda's phone, I immediately answered and put it on speaker so the deputy could listen. "Amanda? Are you okay?" I choked out.

"Hey, Ellie. It's Jack." He sounded disturbingly upbeat and conversational.

"Where's Amanda?" I demanded, fear gripping me.

"Hanging with me." His voice suddenly got dark. "Hey, buddy, tell your pig friend to get the hell out of this yard, or Amanda here gets cut. Nobody approaches this house. Got it?"

The deputy snapped into action, rushing over to his colleague. Obviously Jack could see at least the backyard out the basement windows, which was creepy at best. I hurried back inside his house to get out of his line of sight.

"Got it," I griped.

Snickering, Jack said, "What's the matter? Don't like being watched?"

I ignored him. "Put Amanda on the phone."

Jack scoffed. "Don't tell me what to do, bitch. I call the shots."

Vic and Sterling barreled through the front door. I clutched the phone to my chest to cover the speaker and pressed my index finger to my lips in a shushing gesture. Thankfully, they understood and stayed silent. Vic took out his phone and started recording. I glanced at Sterling. One look at his face and I could tell he was in anguish. I'd never seen him scared before—not even when he and I were being held by a dangerous killer ourselves.

I was finally more angry than frightened and was able to gain control over my voice again. I asked innocently, "Why would you need to call any shots, Jack? So far as we know, you're a poor sick little orphan boy who went missing. All anyone wants is for you to get home safe."

"I saw you go in my house earlier. I'm sure you found my drawings and put two and two together. Our sister is always telling me how wicked smart you are."

I frowned. "Yeah. I found them."

Sterling came my way, holding out his phone. He'd typed, *Is Amanda okay? Have you heard her voice?*

I held out a hand in what I hoped he'd understand was a "calm the hell down" gesture. I was going to have to try another tactic to get Jack to let Amanda speak.

Jack said, "I blame my shitty upbringing."

"I had the same shitty upbringing as you, thanks to your shitty dad, and I didn't go on a killing spree that included my parents."

He barked out a laugh. "Two isn't a spree. Well, I guess I did get to kill my dear old dad twice. That was pretty cool."

Hmm. If he only killed Katie and Marcus, who killed everyone else? Time to use my unfortunate gift of persuading batshit crazy people to open up to me.

I said, "Hey, if it were up to me, I'd give you a pass for killing Marcus. He had it coming. But your mom didn't seem that bad. Hell, she was a way better mom than mine, according to Rachel."

Jack laughed. "I wondered when the psychoanalyzing and fake bonding was going to start. Nice try."

Shit. That couldn't have gone worse. "Fine, you caught me. But you haven't hung up yet. And let's not forget you called me, assclown. The only reason you'd do that is to make a deal, and I'm not dealing until I know Amanda's okay."

As I was speaking, Vic started frowning and shaking his head at me and typed something into his phone. He held the screen out to me. It said, *YOU don't deal with a killer. Negotiator en route.*

Jack muttered something, then Amanda's frightened voice said, "Ellie? I'm . . . okay. He's got me tied—"

Jack interrupted her. "See? She's fine, and she'll stay fine—enough—if you play nice."

I'd made the mistake of glancing at Sterling while Amanda was speaking. The tears in his eyes gutted me. I shook it off. "So you've escalated this to a full hostage situation. Dipshit move, man. We'll be sure to add it to your list of felonies."

"Call it what you want. I'm calling it my free ticket out of here. I got out of Bobby's lame-ass attempt to tie me up and was about to take off until I saw cops swarming my place. I saw your friend out the window and came up with an even better plan. First, you're going to get all the cops the hell off my lawn and out of my neighborhood. I smell even a whiff of bacon, and pretty Amanda loses a pretty body part. Kind of like your mom."

Even though I'd had no problem taunting him, now that he'd made a specific—and graphic *and* personal—threat of what he'd do to Amanda if we made a misstep, I was back to being terrified. I looked at Vic for guidance. Vic shook his head vehemently, typing rapidly on his phone. Next to him, Sterling was nodding his head, his eyes pleading. I was conflicted. I needed to buy time.

I said, "If we agree to that, then what? What's next after we vacate the area?"

"I want a car."

There went Vic again with the head shaking. I knew there was no way anyone would let Jack take Amanda to a secondary location. However, I thought it best to play along and keep him talking to me as long as possible.

I said, "You watch too many movies. The sheriff's department does not have the budget to pass out cars. Why can't you use your mom's car?"

"That piece of shit? I won't get to the county line in that thing."

I had an idea. If for some reason we couldn't safely extract Amanda from the house, we could hide someone in the back of the CSU van to take Jack down. "How about Amanda's wheels? Her crime scene van is pretty sick. It's got lights and a siren so you could make a fast getaway and not have to worry about speed limits." It had neither lights nor a siren. I was hoping he wouldn't know that.

Jack was quiet for a moment, I assumed to mull it over. "I'll consider it."

"So if we can come to an agreement about your demands, you have to give Amanda back unharmed."

He corrected me, "If you *follow through with* my demands, I'll give Amanda back unharmed. She'll have to go along for the ride for a while to make sure no one follows me out of town. Once I'm safely away, I'll dump her on the side of the road."

Now both Vic and Sterling were shaking their heads.

I said, "I don't like that plan."

"Tough shit. You have fifteen minutes to call me back with your answer. And don't pass me off to some smartass FBI hostage negotiator. I'm only talking to you, Ellie. You get me."

I stared at Vic. He nodded and started a countdown timer on his phone.

I replied, "Okay. I'll take this to the powers-that-be and get you an answer about what we're able to do."

Jack said, "I'll make it easy for you. Agree, and Amanda gets to keep all her fingers and toes. Disagree, and—"

The call ended.

"Damn it," I spat out, chucking my phone at the couch.

Sterling bellowed, "Disagree and what? How about I go over there and rip that son of a bitch apart with my bare hands?"

Vic put a hand on Sterling's shoulder. "I think you should go outside and get some air, Jason. I know you don't want to become a liability in this situation."

Looking like he was going to cry again, Sterling stormed out of the house, leaving Vic and me alone.

Vic came over and enveloped me in a hug. "You did great, Ellie. That was amazing."

I let out a pent-up breath. "You know what would be amazing? If crazy dickbags would quit holding the people I love hostage."

"Yeah, that would be good, too." He let me go and started backing toward the door. "I have to go confer with the sheriff and the brass. I think Nick's on his way here. He cut his interview short when I sent the alert about Amanda and he heard you were on hostage negotiation duty."

I collapsed onto the couch, too exhausted to be repulsed about how dingy it was, agonizing over how frightened I knew Amanda was. I could only hope that Jack wasn't hurting or terrorizing her during the fifteen-minute wait.

"Ellie?"

When I heard Baxter's voice, I jumped up and vaulted over the couch, straight into his arms. "Nick, thank you for dropping everything to check on me."

"Always," he replied, holding me tightly. "When I got the alert that there was a hostage situation out here, I was terrified I was going to open it up and see your name." He let out a breath and let me go. "But I have to say, when I saw it was Amanda, I kind of wished she had you in there with her."

My eyebrows shot up. "Come again?"

Baxter shook his head. "I only mean that she has to be scared out of her mind right now, never having been in a situation like this before. You, on the other hand, are fantastic in a crisis and can talk and think your way out of damn near anything." Taking my hand, he added, "And your first aid skills? Literally a lifesaver."

I smiled up at him. "I wasn't sure where you were going with that, but I'll take the compliment."

"Now that the mushy stuff is out of the way, I need to fill you in on some other stuff that I think will give us leverage to get Amanda away from Jack safely."

"Let's hear it."

"You know how Earl said that Valerie Hale got a death threat around the time Marcus was shot, but didn't know who it was because the caller's voice was garbled?"

I nodded.

"I spoke to Shanice Simpkins right before I came here. She got the same death threat, only in person. From Katie Copland."

My eyes grew wide.

He went on. "Oh, it gets better. Shanice admitted that in her younger years she never backed down from a fight. She threw the first punch and clocked Katie. Katie retaliated by knocking her down and strangling her . . . during which she told Shanice she was going to kill her just like she killed 'that redheaded whore.'"

"Oh, snap. Who's got two thumbs and was right about Katie Copland all along?" I pointed both my thumbs toward myself. "This girl!"

Baxter frowned at me. "That's your takeaway? I haven't even finished the story."

I shrugged. "Spoiler alert—Shanice makes it."

"Only because 'some redneck in a dirty trucker cap' pulled Katie off her kicking and screaming. Then he warned Shanice if she ever breathed a word of this to anyone, he'd come after her and finish the job."

My jaw dropped. "Bobby Harper wasn't Katie's partner or accomplice . . . he was her cleaner."

He nodded. "Shanice also said that when Bobby drove away, she noticed a freaked-out-looking kid in the backseat of the truck who'd had a front-row seat to the whole thing."

I felt ill. "Ruining his childhood, his mental health, and the rest of his life."

"Pretty much," he said. "In even weirder news, Bobby Harper has been hiding in plain sight in the crowd outside. When the deputies ran out front and announced there was a hostage situation next door, he turned himself in on the spot. He knew Jack killed Marcus and covered for him to us when we asked for his alibi."

"Clever."

"Well, he's not terribly clever, because he didn't put it all together until about an hour ago that Jack killed Katie. In a panic, he invites the kid over and proceeds to knock him out and tie him up in his basement while he decides how to handle the situation. Then we all show up here, so he blends in with his looky-loo neighbors to find out what's going on. When he hears Jack has Amanda, he decides he's to blame for backing Jack into a corner. Bobby was just beginning to spill his guts when I pulled up, so I got to hear most of the story straight from the horse's mouth."

It took me a moment to let all that sink in. I wanted desperately to finally know the real story about my mother's death, but I knew I had to keep it together for Amanda's sake. I had a job to do, and her life was riding on it. As I put all my effort into sharpening my focus to come at this situation objectively, an idea came to me.

I locked my feelings down, all except my growing confidence. "I think you're right about having the leverage we need now. Can you go ask Vic if we can have Bobby in here when we call Jack?"

Baxter made a face. "He's not gonna like that."

"I know, but I think they have a weirdly strong bond . . . the whole unlawful imprisonment thing aside. Bobby was torn between being angry at Jack for killing Katie and wanting to protect him from getting caught."

"Sounds a lot like what he did for Katie all those years."

"Which is why if there's one person who can talk Jack Copland down from the ledge, it's Bobby Harper. I think Jack was done after he killed Marcus. I don't think he ever had plans to hurt Bobby."

Baxter nodded. "Okay."

When he left, I glanced at the time. We had six minutes. I rushed into Jack's room, grabbed his sketchbooks, and brought them out to the living room. I opened each of them to the most accurate depiction of each murder —Alice, or possibly Shanice, given what Baxter said, being strangled, Jihyo with the slit throat, and the bags containing my mother's body. I didn't know exactly how I was going to use these, but I was hoping they'd spark some kind of emotion in Jack to break him out of his angry rampage.

Vic entered the house with a frown stuck on his face. "While you try to negotiate for a fellow task force member and friend's life, you want Katie Copland's murder buddy to help you talk to her pissed-off son whose challenged mental state is a direct result of her repeatedly involving him in her heinous crimes?"

I nodded. "Yes, that's accurate."

"It's insane."

"Did Baxter not communicate my reasoning?"

"Oh, he did. I just think it sucks."

It always amused me to watch my friend's grumpy side take over. And I always goaded him to make it worse. "You got a better idea, Manetti?"

Huffing out a sigh, he griped, "No." He turned on his heel and went back outside.

Baxter came through the door. "Now I know why you sent me to inform Manetti of your half-cocked plan."

I smiled. "Our boy loves to shoot the messenger."

Vic reappeared with Bobby Harper in tow, in handcuffs. He shoved his prisoner unceremoniously toward the couch and barked, "You will do exactly as Ms. Matthews says, without question and without hesitation, or I will personally see to it that you never get to breathe the sweet air of freedom again. You get me, old man?"

I had to bite my lip to keep from laughing at Vic's bad cop bit. Baxter had to turn around.

Vic picked up my phone from the couch and tossed it to me. "It's time. I think you should agree to the suspect's demands with the stipulation that he will first hear you out and talk to Mr. Harper here. If he pushes back, we can pretend to start moving out so he believes we're playing along. FBI SWAT is ready to take the suspect out if things get out of control."

Upon hearing that, Bobby let out a strangled sob. He seemed to genuinely love Jack, infinitely more than Jack's own father ever had. If I didn't despise him so much for the anguish he caused my sister and me over what he likely did to my mother's body, I might have felt sorry for him.

Vic went on. "We have no intention of letting Ms. Carmack move to a second location with the suspect. Basically try to keep him talking as long as you can. The plan is to try first to defuse the situation and allow him to surrender himself. If that doesn't work, we go in with force."

I looked at Bobby. "Mr. Harper, it looks like it's on us to not screw this up."

29

It was decided that Vic and Baxter would stay with us during the call: Vic to help me mediate and Baxter for moral support and to keep Bobby in line in case he got squirrelly.

I took a deep breath, working to center myself and calm my frazzled nerves.

Baxter put a hand on my shoulder. "You good?"

I nodded. "I think so."

He smiled. "I know so. Game face."

Those two words from him were all I ever needed to pull it together. Their meaning to me ran deep—as long as I could put up a good front, he would have my back through anything. With two minutes to spare, I made a FaceTime call to Amanda's phone. Vic readied the equipment he'd brought to record our conversation and pipe it out to the rest of the task force so they could hear everything that was said.

The cobwebby, unfinished wood ceiling of Bobby's basement filled my screen. Jack's voice said, "What's up with the FaceTime? You worried I spent my fifteen minutes doing unspeakable things to your friend?"

He swung the phone toward Amanda, who aside from being duct-taped by the wrists and ankles to a chair and having a dirty handkerchief gagging her mouth seemed none the worse for wear. I hated seeing my friend like this. I knew she was brave enough and smart enough to get through this, but I also knew the toll it was going to take on her long into the coming weeks.

I took a deep breath. "No, Jack. I trusted you to keep your word. Thank you for showing us Amanda's okay. I'm going to keep trusting you to keep your word so we can get everyone the outcome they want today. The brass has agreed to back off and start getting out of here . . . but it'll take a little time for the deputies to get your nosy neighbors to disperse so they can move their barricades and other shit and roll out. That's not something we can negotiate—it's simple logistics. Okay?"

Jack turned the camera back to himself. "It feels like you're stalling."

I frowned at him. "Can you not see out to the street from the basement? It's like a freaking block party out there. Besides, we have some stuff to hash out before you leave."

"Nah, I'm done talking, and your 'logistics' are not my problem. You have two minutes."

I snapped, "No, Jack. That's not how this is going to work. You lay a finger on Amanda, and you'll pay for it. You make one stupid mistake, and you'll never see daylight again."

He scoffed. "They give you yard time in prison."

"I meant you'll be dead."

Vic waved his hands at me to get my attention, then shook his head and made a "settle down" gesture with his hands. I knew I was pushing it, but I also knew nineteen-year-olds. Legal adults still saddled with teenage brains and hormones, it was always a tossup as to whether they'd make good or bad choices. They also folded pretty easily when the consequences of their actions threatened to bite them hard in the ass.

Jack's cocky expression faltered. "But I'd take her with me."

"And that would make you less dead, how?"

Bobby had been sitting quietly on the couch, listening to our exchange, until I started threatening Jack. Out of the corner of my eye, I'd seen him grow more and more agitated, hoping if I pushed it he'd finally blow his top. He didn't disappoint.

"Jack, they ain't joking around. You got to stop this," Bobby begged as I slowly turned my phone so Jack could see him. "I can't bear to lose you, too."

Jack griped, "Maybe you should have thought of that before you tied me up in your basement and left me there, motherf—"

Bobby evidently didn't like being called names, because he cut him off, bellowing, "Son, I done it for your own good. Everything I ever done has been for your own good."

Jack fired back, "Enabling my mother to murder people was for my own good? Making me help you bury Jihyo after I watched my mother slit her throat was for my own good? She was the only one of Dad's bitches I actually liked."

Bobby grumbled, "You liked Patty enough to screw her."

My jaw dropped, as did Vic's and Baxter's. I felt like I'd been sucker punched. Then I worked out the math . . . if Jack had slept with my mother even at the very end of her life, that would have made him *at most* fifteen years old. I felt a wave of nausea. I would have been so much more okay with my mother committing murder than statutory rape.

I let out a shaky breath and turned the phone back to myself. "Why in the hell would you want to have sex with my mother?"

Jack let out a mirthless laugh. "I didn't. I hated my dad and wanted to piss him off, so I closed my eyes and powered through. Almost had to ask her to put a bag over her head. She was gross."

Bobby snapped, "Don't disrespect this lady's mama like that."

Rolling his eyes, Jack spat, "Eat a bag of dicks, you old—"

I cut in. "You know he's literally the one person you have left in this world who's on your side, right? He knew you killed your dad and made it a point to cover for you to us while he was being interrogated as a person of interest for that very homicide. We brought him in here to help you get through this. Jack, you're unstable. And it's your mother's fault, straight up. We know you watched her try to kill Shanice Simpkins when you were only eleven." I got out his drawing of the woman being strangled and held it up to my phone for him to see. "I'm sure it was hard to get the image out of your head. And even harder for you to wrap your mind around what you watched your mother do."

His words were sharp, but I noticed his eyes were strained. "Again with the psychoanalyzing, Ellie? You got no room to do that to me."

"Okay, that's fair. What I do have room to do is demand to know what the hell you were thinking when you shot our sheriff last night. That was stupid and so unnecessary."

Jack seemed surprised. "I didn't shoot anybody. I was in Muncie last night."

Vic, Baxter, and I all turned to Bobby. He hung his head.

I griped at him, "You're still committing felonies for these people?" I shook my head and muttered, "Sick bastard."

Jack heard me and snickered. "With role models like that, I had no chance."

I turned my attention back to Jack. "Still not an excuse to murder your mom, you douche."

"Whatever. I had plenty of excuses to murder that crazy bitch."

Bobby looked up and bellowed, "Yeah, to steal everything she'd worked herself to the bone for so you could keep living a lie."

"Living a lie . . . about your health?" I asked Jack. "You seem fine for someone who supposedly couldn't even drive himself to the doctor today."

He shrugged, pulling a sad face with puppy dog eyes. "Our sister is more than happy to take care of me, so I let her." He let out a couple of pathetic coughs and smiled devilishly at me.

This kid was a full sociopath. He had no intention of surrendering. I sighed and flicked my eyes at Vic, hoping he'd understand how done I was with this bullshit negotiation. He nodded and started typing on his phone. I was thinking of a way to wrap this up when Vic turned his screen toward me. *Sniper can't get a clear shot. We need more time.*

Damn it.

I said to Jack, "I think they've got the street almost cleared out. You cool with Amanda's van as your getaway vehicle?"

He huffed. "I was hoping for something a little cooler."

"Killers can't be choosers." I knew there was no way Jack was making it out of that house alive. Might as well speed things along. He'd been sitting for most of the time we'd been negotiating. If I could get him to stand up and move around, maybe the sniper could get his shot. "You should start untying Amanda and be ready to move."

The FaceTime image jostled as Jack got up from where he was sitting and walked across the room. I braced myself that I might witness Jack's death at any moment. Good luck getting that image out of my head anytime in the foreseeable future. Jack gave Amanda his phone to hold while he worked on the duct tape restraining her other hand.

Amanda turned the phone toward herself. She looked terrified. It dawned on me that she had no idea what we'd been planning to get her away from her captor. For all she knew, she was about to get in a vehicle with a murderer and drive out of town.

Hoping I could somehow convey to her that she was not going to be in further danger, I said, "Hey Amanda, in case you didn't hear, they're *readying your van* so you guys can get on the road. And once Jack drops you off in a *secure* location, we will have someone there ASAP to pick you up." From the still-frightened look on her face, I'd biffed getting any of my point across.

I was about to take another stab at a cryptic message when she ripped the gag from her mouth with her now free hand and cried frantically, "Ellie, the three of them kept your mom down here! The wood shavings in her hair were from Bobby Harper's whittling, not—"

The call abruptly ended.

Vic flew out the door without a word.

My hands started shaking so badly I dropped my phone. Rage ripping through me, I turned on Bobby Harper. "I'm going to ask you one question, and I hope for your sake you give me the answer I want. Was Patty Copland alive or dead when you and your crew of psychos started chopping her up?"

He closed his eyes. "Katie . . . I thought she was done with the killing. She'd married Marcus again, and things was going good, or so she thought." He shook his head. "You have to understand . . . Katie found them two, you know, *together*, and had an episode."

Tears pooled in my eyes. "So Marcus watched her kill my mother and what, did nothing?" Baxter moved over to place a protective arm around my shoulders.

"Marcus? No. I'm talking about Jack. His plan was to screw your mom and have Marcus walk in and catch them. Jack didn't tell Katie what he was doing, and she walked in instead. Poor woman saw her worst enemy with her baby boy and lost her mind. She picked up the nearest thing—Jack's baseball bat—and clobbered your mother right in Jack's bed."

My hands flew to my mouth. I'd seen it. My mother's murder weapon was still in Jack's room. Baxter tightened his grip on my shoulder.

Bobby went on. "Jack . . . that kid hadn't been right since . . ." He put his head in his hands.

Baxter supplied, "Since watching his mother try to kill Shanice Simpkins?"

"Yeah," he rasped, a tear rolling down his cheek. "The only one I managed to stop with no bloodshed." He wiped his face on his sleeve. "Jack didn't bat an eye at what Katie did to your mother. Turns out he hated her every bit as much as Katie did for breaking up their family. In fact—" He stopped to choke back a sob. "He's who brought your mother over to my basement. I was at work. I got home and found them . . . torturing her."

I couldn't hold back my tears any longer. I buried my face in Baxter's chest.

I heard Bobby say, "I'm so sorry. I had no idea what they done. I told them they had to stop, and I made them leave. I was going to cut your mother loose, but she was too far gone. She'd taken too many hits to the head to survive, so . . . I'm the one who killed her. I couldn't stand watching the poor woman suffer, so . . . I put her out of her misery. I done it right quick. I don't think she felt it. That's how I knew your face. It haunts my nightmares."

Raising my head to look at him, I said, "So you just looked past all the awful things Katie and Jack did and happily helped them chop my mother to pieces?"

"I wasn't happy about it, but . . . I loved them. And they needed my help, so I helped them . . . like I always did." He flicked his eyes toward Baxter and then back at me. "I reckon you might be able to understand loving someone so much that you'd do anything for them without hesitation."

I looked up at Baxter. I remember telling him once I'd help him bury a body if he needed me to, and I hadn't been joking. But he loved me enough that he'd never ask me to do anything that would compromise my morals.

Katie and Bobby had been a broken pair, their version of love only serving to enable each other to be their worst selves.

I stepped toward Bobby on my own. "Love is no excuse to behave like a monster. And if you'd truly loved Katie, you would have gotten her the help she needed, not given her the help she wanted. I hope you think about that every day while you're rotting in prison for the rest of your miserable—"

A quick succession of four gunshots rang out.

"No!" Bobby cried, sliding off the couch onto his knees.

Baxter stuck his head out the front door and hailed one of the deputies to come in and take custody of Bobby. He then took my hand and led me out the back door so we could watch the scene next door unfold from a safe distance.

FBI SWAT had descended on the place, and every law enforcement official who'd been out front earlier was now in Bobby Harper's backyard. When one of the SWAT team members emerged from the basement steps with his arm around a very relieved-looking Amanda, we all broke out in applause. Sterling took off like a shot from where he was standing with the rest of the task force and nearly tackled Amanda in a hug. She didn't seem to mind, melting into him and holding on as if for dear life. He suddenly let go and took a step back from her, which confused me until I realized what he was doing. My hand flew to my pocket for my phone, but I'd forgotten about dropping it inside. Baxter was already on it and had his phone trained on the two of them.

Jason Sterling got down on one knee in front of Amanda. And at a crime scene with three dozen law enforcement officials watching, he said to her, "I'm not going to wait another minute to lock you down. Amanda Carmack, will you marry me?"

I'd never seen her so happy and glowing, despite what I was pretty sure was high-velocity blood spatter on her shirt and neck from where SWAT had shot Jack Copland in her close proximity. She said, "Yes, of course I'll marry you!"

The crowd again erupted in cheers and applause.

Baxter turned to me. "That was something I didn't expect to see today."

I laughed wearily. "I've lost count of the things I didn't expect to see today."

~

SINCE IT WAS FBI SWAT who ran the op to take down Jack Copland, the FBI's crime scene unit was assigned to process the scene. Amanda was a victim, so she couldn't go anywhere near the scene. Beck, of course, was fired. So it would have been left up to me, and probably Baxter, who undoubtedly would have taken pity on me and offered to help. We were more than happy to hand over the job to someone else.

With the exception of Amanda, who was getting checked out at the hospital, and Sterling, who Jayne insisted accompany her, the task force met for a quick debriefing. It was mostly so Vic, Baxter, and I could relay to the rest of them what had been said during my phone conversations with Jack Copland and my furious interrogation of Bobby Harper. It wasn't easy to share the news that my mother had committed statutory rape, even though she was the one who'd been duped and had paid the ultimate price for it.

After the meeting, we all trooped down to the interrogation rooms to watch Vic and the chief absolutely demolish Bobby Harper. They managed to get everything we wanted to know out of him.

Katie Copland had had a rough go of it the first time Marcus left her, but managed with Bobby's support to get her life back in order. She'd done fine until Jack came home one day and announced that his dad was having another baby with his girlfriend, Amy. The news sent Katie into a spiral culminating in her stalking Amy, seeing a chance to put the pregnancy at risk, and pushing her down a flight of stairs. She instantly realized she'd gone too far and went to Bobby for help. He fixed everything, starting with whisking her quickly to the high school football game and making sure people saw them there. Then he spun a tale to Marcus about how Amy had been stalking Katie and accusing her of all kinds of crazy things, warning his friend to steer clear of her. For added insurance, he began threatening Amy to leave town, finally degrading to gaslighting her into thinking Marcus never wanted to see her again and telling her he'd said since she'd killed their baby that maybe she should just kill herself, too. She left the next week for Mexico and did exactly that. Bobby cried throughout the telling of this story, saying he never imagined she'd actually do it.

When Marcus moved on so quickly to Alice, Katie finally began to notice how selfish he could be. She'd followed Alice one day and tried to calmly tell her about Marcus's disappointing tendencies, but Alice had looked down her nose at Katie and laughed in her face. After a month or two of obsessing over Alice's treatment of her, Katie decided to pay her another visit, this time to get an apology out of her. Alice laughed at her even harder and called her pathetic for how she mooned over such a big loser as Marcus. Katie flew at her, and before she knew what she'd done, Alice was missing a chunk of hair and was no longer breathing. Katie realized she didn't even know Alice's last name, so she took out her driver's license. She heard a noise, got spooked, and ran home. She told Bobby everything, but when he got back to where Katie had left Alice, the police were there. It was too late for Bobby to fix her mess this time, but luckily Katie was never linked to Alice's death, so that was a second bullet dodged.

Bobby reiterated what Baxter had told me about Katie's assault of Shanice Simpkins, adding that after the incident Jack had locked himself in his room for days. When he finally came out, he didn't talk for weeks. After that, he became increasingly violent, starting with burning bugs with a magnifying glass. He expanded to dismembering lizards he found in the yard and worked his way up to catching mice and squirrels to stab with the hunting knife Marcus had stupidly given him for his twelfth birthday.

Then there was Jihyo. Katie didn't even seem sorry this time. She drove her car to Bobby's house, tossed him the keys, and told him there was some trash in the trunk for him to dump. He'd been down on his back from a work injury and couldn't move the body by himself. Katie had taken some pills and passed out on her bed, so his only choice was to have Jack help him. They buried Jihyo that night at his friend's farm in Sheridan, picking a spot where he thought his friend never planted anything. A year later when the friend found the body, Bobby realized his mistake, but kept his mouth shut.

Jack had grown even more moody after Jihyo's death, quitting baseball in favor of locking himself in his room for hours, drawing disturbing images in his sketchbooks. He was constantly in trouble in school, and his teachers worried about his artwork. Katie paid less and less attention to him, having finally caught Marcus's eye again and convincing him they should remarry. Having his dad back in his life didn't help Jack's behavior. Once he got into high school, he fell in with the wrong crowd. They were doing drugs, much of which he stole from Marcus when Marcus was too high to notice, which was most of the time. Then he started to notice girls. Bobby had been convinced Jack would father several children before he could even drive, but by some miracle he didn't. Then Jack set his sights on Patty, and it was all downhill from there. After Patty, Bobby had had it with Katie's jealousy killings, and he'd had it with Marcus's selfish actions hurting Jack. He made a few anonymous threats, and Marcus caved, fleeing town like a bat out of hell.

Jack had several bouts of illnesses as a result of his lifestyle, including a couple of gnarly infections that had him in the hospital for several days each. The moment he got sick, he was suddenly interesting to Katie again. She doted on him, and he got used to the attention. After he recovered from the last illness and seemed to be on the mend, his mother began to lose interest. Jack was smart, and he had developed enough sociopathic tendencies that it wasn't difficult for him to dream up a phantom pain and play up the ailment in a near Oscar-worthy performance. Katie went back to pouring all of her attention into her son, and Jack enjoyed the better quality of a prescription painkiller high. Jack also enjoyed his mother and friends chauffeuring him everywhere, neighbors bringing him meals, being "too sick" to hold down a job, and his mother waiting on him hand and foot while she worked two jobs to support them.

Even with the added stress of two jobs and taking care of Jack, Katie had been stable until Marcus showed back up in town. Katie began pulling away from Bobby again like she had the last time Marcus set his sights on her. Bobby wasn't letting the perfect world he'd finally attained be destroyed, so he bought two burner phones and started threatening Marcus again to leave. Then everything started crumbling at once. Marcus figured out Jack's little fake illness scheme and told Katie right in front of Jack. Katie and Bobby had had no idea, and they were devastated Jack would take advantage of them like that. Katie gave her son two weeks to find a job and a new place to live.

Jack didn't want to give up his cushy life. The closer the deadline loomed, the more his mother nagged him. The more his mother nagged him, the angrier he got at both his mother and father. He figured out a way to solve his problems with little to no work. And he found a scapegoat to take the blame for everything, who, to be fair, was already to blame for everything. Jack went to see Marcus, bringing a bottle of his favorite whiskey to toast his mother's memory. He slipped some roofies in Marcus's glass to make sure he was pliable and then shot him up with enough heroin to kill the common man. He'd been disappointed to get the call from the hospital that Marcus was hanging on by a thread, but when he got there and found out he'd been summoned essentially to give his dad's kill order, he was thrilled. Of course he had to play the part of the distraught son in front of his sister, but that was the stuff he lived for.

Jack found out from Rachel that Marcus had visited our home around the time of his mother's death. Worried it was only a matter of time before the cops figured that out and began looking for another suspect, he went to Bobby for help. Bobby again agreed to clean up another Copland mess, so he was the one who leaked the story to the press. That didn't work to put pressure on our team to follow his narrative, so he threatened Jayne. When she didn't seem to take his threat seriously over the phone, he shot at her to get his message across. When that didn't work to stop the task force, he suggested to Jack that it was time for him to disappear for a while. During their conversation, Jack made an offhand comment about Katie that made Bobby realize he'd killed his mother as well.

Bobby nonchalantly invited Jack over for lunch, knocked him out with one punch, and tied him up in his basement. When Jack came to, Bobby interrogated him about Katie's and Marcus's deaths. Jack played the Katie card and begged Bobby to protect him again. He said he was off his depression meds and had acted out in anger, and he was so very sorry. Bobby didn't know what to do, so he left Jack in his basement and took a walk around the block to think. When he got back, law enforcement had Jack's house surrounded. At that point, all he could think to do was turn himself in and hope for mercy.

Upon finishing his tale of woe, Bobby Harper collapsed in a heap on the table, bawling.

Baxter, Shane, Jayne, and I all let out a collective breath.

"Damn," Shane said, shaking his head. "That's some high drama. This guy's life story could be a movie."

Baxter joked, "Wonder who'd play us."

"A-list Oscar winners, of course," I said with a smile. "We're such complex characters."

Jayne chuckled wearily. "Let's wrap this case before you three start putting out casting calls. But not tonight. Go home, hug your loved ones, and get some rest. Your reports can wait, but only until tomorrow."

EPILOGUE

As we were leaving the station, Baxter said, "Since Rachel and Nate were well on their way to the safe house before getting the all clear that the threat to them had been neutralized, it'll be a while before they get home. Let me finally take you on that dinner date I've been promising you."

I wanted nothing more than to go home, sit on my couch in my give-up pants, and eat a whole pizza straight out of the box. Truth be told, I could have used some alone time. Not that I needed or wanted time away from Baxter, but I had some decompressing to do, and I was afraid it wasn't going to be pretty. But he'd been trying to reschedule this dinner all week and seemed so adamant about taking me out, I caved.

Smiling, I said, "That sounds wonderful."

He took me to Prime 47 in Carmel, of all places. The food was out of this world, but it was hella expensive and I always worried I wasn't classy enough to go there. We had a lovely time, and even though I nearly nodded off while we waited for dessert, I was happy we went.

When we got to my house, he asked, "Want to take a walk?"

I absolutely didn't, but after taking one look at his sweet, eager face, I couldn't say no. Besides, a walk around the block would help me better digest all the heavy food I just ate. He took my hand and led me north toward the Noblesville town square. This wasn't our usual route, but I didn't care. Being with him was what mattered, and I was happy I didn't push him away tonight to stew in my own juices. Jayne had had the right idea, as had Sterling. Life was short, and it was useless to squander it on the stuff that didn't matter.

As we neared O'Loughlin's Bar, where Baxter and I had hung out a couple of times when we were first getting to know each other, he stopped walking and faced me.

"Are we turning around?" I asked, unable to stifle a yawn.

He grinned down at me, but his eyes were strained. "Not exactly."

"What's wrong?" I asked, my gut clenching in apprehension.

"Nothing's wrong. Everything is . . . right."

I relaxed, but now felt confused. "Okay."

"Do you remember me walking you home that one night from O'Loughlin's?"

I made a face. "Vaguely. I was super drunk. Not my finest hour."

He shrugged. "I thought it was pretty great. It was the first time you opened up to me and told me some things about yourself."

"Oh, right."

I'd been drunk enough to lower my defenses and tell a stranger all about my mother's death and how it haunted me. I would rather have reminisced about the time we were out walking a couple of months ago, when I got stung by a bee and shouted every curse word I knew in front of a bunch of little kids playing in their yard.

Baxter took my hands. "It was also the day I fell in love with you."

I laughed. "That was the day? Really?"

"Really. Why, what was yours?"

I said, "When you barged into my house after I'd met with Rachel's kidnapper alone so you could yell at me in person for being stupid."

Shaking his head, he said, "Not *my* finest hour."

"It was, because after you got done yelling, you cleaned up and bandaged the wound he gave me, carried me to the couch, kissed me for the first time, apologized for kissing me, and told me your life story. And then you slept next to me on the couch so I'd feel safe."

"Oh, yeah. That was a pretty good hour. I think I can do better, though."

"I don't know. The Nick Baxter who was trying to get in my pants worked a lot harder than—" I stopped short when he dropped down to one knee and held up a stunning diamond ring.

I'd never seen him smile so sweetly as he said, "Ellie, I love you. We've been through so much together, and I couldn't have gotten through any of it without you. I want to keep going through the tough times with you. I want to sit and do nothing with you. I want to get old and crochety with you. Forever. Will you marry me?"

Tears of pure joy spilling onto my cheeks, I replied, "Yes, Nick. Nothing would make me happier."

Damaging Secrets
Book #1 of the Rachel Ryder Series

Bestselling author Carolyn Ridder Aspenson is back—this time with a scrappy heroine whose bold detective work and well-timed one-liners will leave you riveted—and entertained—at every turn.

"Detective Rachel Ryder is smart, tough, and fearless—readers will gladly follow her through every twist of Aspenson's knockout first installment in this riveting new series." —LynDee Walker, Amazon Charts bestselling author of *Fear No Truth*

New to town and a little rough around the edges, Detective Rachel Ryder finds herself on the receiving end of a suspicious person's call in Hamby, Georgia. When the call turns out to be a dead body, the medical examiner is quick to rule the death a suicide. But was it something more sinister?

Everyone in the small department believes the case is closed—except for Rachel. The sudden passing of a local politician during the mayor's run for Congress strikes her as a little too coincidental, and Rachel is eager to follow her instincts. Her partner, Rob, a 30-year veteran, isn't the type to disobey his boss or ruffle any feathers, but he can't convince strong-willed Rachel to let it go.

Obsessed with finding out the truth, Rachel begins to examine the evidence and drags her reluctant partner along for the ride. But the clues are confusing. Nothing is adding up.

Puzzled and running out of time, Rachel and Rob rush to work every angle and bring the elusive killer to justice before someone else ends up dead.

Get your copy today at
severnriverbooks.com

ACKNOWLEDGMENTS

Huge thanks to my family for cheering me on throughout the process of my writing. I appreciate your understanding and willingness to help out more than you know (and that no one—except me—complained about all the takeout food)! Thank you to my friends for their encouragement and support as well. And thank you to Megan Copenhaver, Cassie Gitkin, and the Severn River Publishing team for their guidance and advice!

ABOUT THE AUTHOR

Caroline Fardig is the *USA Today* bestselling author of over a dozen mystery novels. She worked as a schoolteacher, church organist, insurance agent, banking trust specialist, funeral parlor associate, stay-at-home mom, and coffeehouse owner before she realized that she wanted to be a writer when she grew up. When she's not writing, she likes to travel, lift weights, play pickleball, and join in on vocals, piano, or guitar with any band who'll have her. She's also the host of a lively podcast for Gen Xers called *Wrong Side of 40*. Born and raised in a small town in Indiana, Fardig still lives in that same town with an understanding husband, two sweet kids, and three exhaustingly energetic dogs.

Sign up for Caroline Fardig's reader list at
severnriverbooks.com

Printed in the United States
by Baker & Taylor Publisher Services